HIGHLAND EMBRACE

"Look at me, Gisele," Nigel commanded softly, brushing a tender kiss across her mouth.

"I am not sure I wish to."

"Come, look at me. See with your own eyes who is about to love you. If ye keep your bonny eyes shut, I fear memory may overcome fact."

Slowly, she opened her eyes, pushing her shyness aside as she recognized the wisdom of his reasoning. "There. I am looking at you," she said, hearing the sulkiness in her voice despite the huskiness that still deepened it.

Nigel ignored her touch of ill humor, for he could still hear the passion in her voice, feel it in the faint trembling of her lithe body, and see it in the flush upon her smooth, high-boned cheeks. "Ye need not fear the manhood, lassie, only the mon who wields it."

"I know that. In my mind, I truly do know that most of the time."

"Then keep your eyes open, so that your mind and heart can remember it. Keep them wide open so that that bastard's memory cannae rise up to destroy what we can share."

Gisele nodded and curled her arms around his neck, keeping her gaze firmly fixed upon his face even as he covered her face with slow, gentle kisses. Suddenly, a rich feeling began to blossom within her . . . a wondrous feeling. She clung to Nigel, wrapping herself around him as he whispered husky words of encouragement before a blinding wave of intense feeling swept over her and she cried out his name. . . .

Books by Hannah Howell

ONLY FOR YOU
MY VALIANT KNIGHT
UNCONQUERED
WILD ROSES
A TASTE OF FIRE
HIGHLAND DESTINY
A JOYOUS SEASON
(with Fern Michaels, Jennifer Blake, and Olga Bicos)

Published by Zebra Books

HIGHLAND HONOR

Hannah Howell

Zebra Books
Kensington Publishing Corp.
http://www.zebrabooks.com

ZEBRA BOOKS are published by

Kensington Publishing Corp.
850 Third Avenue
New York, NY 10022

First Printing: January, 1999
10 9 8 7 6 5 4 3 2 1

Printed in the United States of America

One

A deep groan escaped Nigel Murray as he awkwardly sat up. He clutched his head, wincing at the thick coat of filth caking his brown hair, and squinted painfully in the faint light of dawn as he looked around. It took him a moment to recognize where he was. Then he grimaced in self-disgust. He had not even made it inside his small tent, having fallen asleep in the mud just in front of it.

"I am fortunate I didnae drown in the muck," he grumbled as he staggered to his feet, the pounding in his head adding to his unsteadiness.

Slowly, he became aware of a rancid smell. His disgust with himself increased tenfold when he realized that the unpleasant smell was emanating from him. Nigel cursed and started toward the small river the army had camped near. He needed to scrub the stench away and clear his head. The cold water would do both adequately.

Matters had gotten completely out of hand, he decided as he wended his way through the trees. When a man woke up sprawled in the mud, not sure where he was or how he had gotten there, that man needed to take a long, hard look at himself. Nigel had thought that of several of his compatriots during the seven long years he had been fighting for the French. Now he had to apply his own advice to himself. He knew he had reached the point where he either changed or he died.

Once at the river he located a shallow spot, yanked off his boots, unbuckled his sword and scabbard, and stepped into the water. After briefly immersing his head in the almost too cold water he lay down in it, resting his head on the softly grassed, gently sloping bank. He sprawled there, eyes closed, letting the chill of the water push aside the wine-induced clouds in his mind and the current take away the stench clinging to his clothes and his body.

Since he had come to France he had increasingly immersed himself in drinking and a multitude of faceless, nameless women. The occasional battles with the English or the French enemies of whichever French lordling was paying for his sword at the time were the only things that caused any break in his continuous round of dissipation. Nigel knew he was lucky that he was still alive after seven years of such stupidity. He could have fallen face down in the mud last night, too drunk to keep himself from drowning in the mire. He could have staggered into the enemy's camp and been cut down before he even recognized his error. He could have had his throat cut and been robbed by one of the many shadowy figures that lurked close to the army, or even one of his fellow soldiers. He had slipped into a strange madness that could easily cost him his life in any one of a hundred ways.

And why? That was the question he had to ask himself. At first he had turned to wine and women to ease the ache in his heart, to try to end the pain that had driven him from his home, from Scotland and Donncoill. Now he suspected it had become a habit. The wine offered a tempting numbness, a welcome inability to think, and the women gave his body a temporary relief. That, he decided firmly, was not enough to put his life at risk. When he had left Scotland he had assured his brothers that he was not coming to France to try to die in battle. He certainly did not want to die in a drunken stupor.

Voices reached his ears, pulling him free of his dark thoughts and uncomfortable self-examination. Nigel dragged himself into a sitting position and listened carefully. Once sure of the direction the voices came from, he grabbed his boots and sword and stealthily approached. Curiosity drove him. So did the temptation of some diversion from looking at how low he had sunk in the last seven years.

Nigel barely stopped himself from walking right up to the pair he was tracking. They were nearer than he had realized, and were standing in a clearing that was not easily seen until one stepped right into it. He quickly ducked behind a clump of low-growing berry bushes. It was a poor hiding place, but the two people standing in the clearing were so intent upon what they were saying and doing that Nigel was sure they would never see him as long as he made no noise.

The young man was someone Nigel recognized, but it took him a moment to recall the man's name. It was the smaller one of the pair that caught and held Nigel's interest. Why was Guy Lucette talking so intently to a tiny, black-haired woman dressed in ill-fitting boy's clothing? A quick glance at the pile of thick, raven locks on the ground told Nigel that the woman's cap of curls was a very recent change. He felt an odd pang of regret when he looked at the discarded hair, and wondered why. Nigel decided that any man would regret seeing such long, beautiful hair shorn and cast away. Such hair was a woman's glory. That made him wonder why the little lady would do such a drastic thing. He forced himself to stop thinking and listen to what was being said, struggling to follow the fast pace of their French.

"This is madness, Gisele," Guy muttered as he helped her lace up her stained, deerhide leggings and worn, padded *jupon*. "We are soon to face the English in battle. That is no place for a woman."

"DeVeau's lands are no place for a woman, either. Especially this woman," snapped the young lady as she touched her new, very short curls with long, unsteady fingers. "I could kill the man for this alone."

"The man is already dead."

"That does not stop me from wanting to kill him."

"Why? He did not slash off your hair, nor did he ask you to do so."

"The bastard pushed me to it, rather, his cursed family did. I had no idea that the DeVeaux were such prolific breeders. It seems that there is one at every corner I turn, under every bush I walk past."

"And there are probably some DeVeaux within the army that is gathered here," Guy said quietly. "Did you not consider that when you devised this mad plan?"

"I did," she replied as she tugged at her jupon and then smoothed her small hands down the front to assure herself that her breasts were not shaping the front of her garment. "I also considered the fact that many of the DeVeaux know, or could easily discover, that you are my cousin. It all matters not. No man will think to look for me amongst the many pages scurrying about this camp."

"That may be true, but I still want you to stay close to me. Better, stay within my tent as much as you can without drawing any suspicion to yourself." Guy carefully studied their handiwork, then nodded in silent satisfaction. "Being seen by your enemy, being discovered here by them, could easily mean your death. The DeVeaux have put a hefty bounty on your pretty little head, and many men will hunger to fill their pockets with it."

Nigel idly wondered how much the DeVeaux would be willing to pay for the lady, then shrugged. It did not matter. He was intrigued, curiosity putting the spark of life back into his veins. He was interested in something besides his own misery and battle for the first time since he had fled Scotland, and he reveled in it. Questions crowded his mind, and he really did not care what the answers were. He just wanted to hear them.

Guy and the slender, young woman he had called Gisele buried her clothes and shorn hair in a shallow grave and then left. Nigel paused in following them only long enough to collect what they had tried to hide. He made a small sack out of her shawl, wrapped the hair and other clothes inside it, and hurriedly took it to his tent before making his way to Guy's small tent.

It was very easy to get near to Guy's tent without being seen. The young knight had lost his two compatriots in the last skirmish with the English and had yet to replace them. Guy and

Gisele were clearly doing a very poor job of watching their backs. Any man who hunted the girl and discovered where she was would not even work up a sweat in the capture of her.

Staring at the opening of Guy's tent, Nigel wondered what to do next. He also wondered why he should care if the fools were cut down, then decided that anything which diverted him from the destructive path he had been walking was a good thing. And, he did not yet know if the pair had done anything that deserved a death sentence. It could all be a simple misunderstanding. His family knew well the cost of such errors. They had fought a long, bloody feud over a mistake. A lot of good men had died before the whole truth had come out. Nigel realized that it might be more than curiosity that drove him when he was chilled by the thought of any harm coming to Gisele. Telling himself that any man with blood in his veins would hate to see a lass as pretty as Gisele harmed, especially over some misunderstanding, did not fully explain away the intensity of his distaste.

"Cease your dawdling, Nigel," he scolded himself as he slowly paced back and forth in front of Guy's tent.

No clever way to approach the pair came to mind, and Nigel cursed. Either there was no simple way to do it or his mind was still too clouded with wine to form even the most meager of plans. The direct approach was the best way, he decided, and, yelling out a greeting, he strode into Guy's tent. The wide-eyed, agape looks the cousins gave him were so amusing Nigel had to smile. Guy's reaction was far too slow to have saved them if an enemy had just entered, but the youth finally acted, anyway. Nigel just smiled more widely when Guy drew his sword, even as he pushed Gisele behind him. The young man clearly did not realize that his actions toward Gisele gave away her identity as a woman far more quickly than any good, hard look would.

"There is no need of that," Nigel said in English, praying that they understood his language, for his French was so heavily accented that few could figure out what he was saying when he tried to use it. He held his hands out to the side slightly to show that he had no intention of drawing his weapon.

"No? Why have you thrust yourself into our presence if you mean no harm?" Guy demanded.

Pushing aside a brief pang of envy over the proof that Guy could speak English far better than he could speak French, Nigel looked at Gisele, who watched him closely from behind Guy's broad back. She had wide, beautiful eyes of a green so true that he had only seen it once before.

" 'Tis most odd that your page doesnae draw a sword and stand at your side," Nigel drawled, laughing softly when Guy's dark eyes widened briefly and the youth softly cursed. "Ye can make a lass look like a laddie, at least to those who but glance quickly, but 'tis verra hard to remember to treat her as one."

Gisele felt the chill of fear, then grew confused. Her first thought had been that this handsome Scot had been hired by the DeVeaux, but there was no threat to see in his beguiling smile or relaxed stance. Although it took her a moment to see beyond the beauty of his dark, amber eyes, she could see only amusement and curiosity there. That look began to annoy her, for she could see no cause for amusement in her dire situation, nor was it something that some bored knight should be interfering in just to ease a sense of ennui. Her very life hung in the balance.

Despite her growing anger and the Scot's untidy appearance, she was unable to ignore his fine looks. He was tall, and built with a lean, graceful strength, something revealed very clearly by the way his wet clothes clung to his powerful body. His hair was also wet, hanging in curling tendrils past his broad shoulders, but enough of it had dried to show that the golden color in his eyes was carried through into his hair. His face held her gaze for a long time. He looked exhausted and had not scraped the beard from his face for several days, but he was still one of the most handsome men she had ever set eyes on. He had high cheekbones, a long, straight nose that had somehow escaped the battering most knights suffered from, a strong chin, and a temptingly shaped mouth that Gisele was certain had lured many a woman to taste its soft warmth. She was surprised at how saddened she was to see the beginning signs of dissipation, the lines drawn by too much wine and quite probably an overindulgence in the pleasures of the flesh. She had seen such lines on her husband's face. What troubles could this strong, handsome Scot have which caused him to wallow in wine and women?

His gaze met hers, and Gisele flushed. She had been staring at him too hard and too long, and he had finally noticed. Gisele quickly looked away, embarrassed. It took her a moment to compose herself and revive her anger over his ill-placed amusement. When she looked back at him he was smiling crookedly, and Gisele had to fight to hold onto her annoyance.

"Since I have only now assumed this guise, might you tell me how you know about it?" she demanded.

"I was also down at the river."

"Merde," she muttered, and glared at him when he laughed. "So, you are a spy."

"Nay. I am but a mon who occasionally likes to be clean."

She decided to ignore that piece of levity and stepped out from behind Guy. "If you are not hunting me, then of what interest is it to you how I dress or what I might try to be?"

"Curiosity is a strong force."

"And you are a big, strong knight. Fight it."

"Gisele," Guy hissed, elbowing his cousin in the side. "We should find out what he wants before you hone your tongue on his hide," he said in French.

"I can speak French," Nigel murmured in French, and grinned when both the cousins glared at him.

"Appallingly," Gisele said, then cursed when Guy nudged her again.

"I know you, do I not?" Guy asked, frowning at Nigel.

"Only by sight." Nigel bowed slightly. "Sir Nigel Murray."

"Sir Guy Lucette. My cousin, Gisele DeVeau. Do you mean to expose our deception? Or do you seek some recompense to hold fast to our secret?"

"How ye wound me." Nigel was not insulted, understanding that his actions invited suspicion. "I swear upon my clan's honor 'tis only curiosity which prompts me to intrude."

"Such blind obedience to curiosity could easily get you

killed," Guy said even as he sheathed his sword. "I fear it must go unsated this time."

"Must it?"

"Yes," snapped Gisele. "This is not your concern. Not your business at all."

"And ye feel no need for help? For another sword protecting your backs?" Nigel noticed that Guy frowned, obviously considering his words, but Gisele showed no such hesitation.

"This is a family matter, sir," she said. "We need no help."

"Nay? Your deception has only just begun, yet I have discovered it."

"Only because you were spying on us."

"Mayhap I was not the only one," he said softly, trying to make her understand the import of his discovery and his presence.

Guy paled and Nigel nodded, glad that the young man understood. Gisele looked an intriguing mixture of nervous and angry. Good sense should tell them that they were sorely in need of some help, but Nigel knew a lot of things could stand in the way of doing what good sense dictated. They did not know him except by sight, and thus had no reason to trust in him. There was also the problem of pride, something he suspected the cousins had a hefty dose of. Pride would stop them from admitting that they needed any help. Nigel could only hope that neither caution nor pride held them captive for too long.

"I believe we would have noticed if the wood around us teemed with spies," muttered Gisele, and she grimaced when Guy yet again gently nudged her in a punitive manner.

"Sir Murray, I understand what you are trying to tell us," Guy said, hastily glaring Gisele into silence when she started to speak. "We shall certainly be much more careful, watch our backs more closely"

"But ye refuse my help."

"I must. This is not your trouble. It would be discourteous to pull you into the midst of our difficulties."

"Even if I am willing to be pulled into the midst of them?"

"Just so."

Nigel shrugged. "As ye wish."

"We do thank you most heartily for your kind concern."

"We?" said Gisele, but Nigel just smiled and Guy ignored her interruption.

"Despite your courteous refusal of my aid," Nigel said, "be assured that it still stands. Ye ken where to find me if you change your mind."

Nigel bowed slightly and left. Only feet from Guy's tent he stopped and looked back. He briefly considered sneaking back and lurking around the tent to listen to what was said, then shook his head. They would be more cautious now, would whisper and guard their words, making eavesdropping impossible. He could only wait and pray that they sought his aid before whatever threat they feared caught up with them.

"That may have been a mistake," Guy said softly as he secured the flaps of his tent.

"We do not need the Scotsman's help," Gisele said as she sat down on a small, blanket-covered chest.

"Such confidence you have in my ability to keep you safe." Guy sat down by the small, rock encircled pit in the middle of the dirt floor and began to make a fire.

"You are most skilled and highly honored as a knight."

"Thank you for that accolade, but my reputation, meager as it is, has been earned in battle, in honorable combat. This is different. I am all that stands between you and a veritable horde of vengeful DeVeaux and their hirelings, none of whom are known for acting honorably. Another sword could be helpful."

"We do not know if he means to use that sword to help us or to prod us into the hands of our enemies. The Scotsman could well be one of those DeVeau hirelings."

Guy shook his head. "I cannot believe that."

"You do not know the man."

"True, but neither have I heard ill of him. We should not discard him completely."

Gisele inwardly cursed and rubbed her hands over her newly

shorn hair. She could not believe Sir Murray meant them any harm, but feared her opinion was formed by the man's fine face and beautiful eyes. Guy admitting to feeling the same trust in the man only lessened her unease a little. She had been running and hiding for too long to trust easily, even in her own opinions. Some of her own kinsmen believed the accusations against her, had turned their backs on her, so why should some stranger from a strange land offer to help? And would he still offer once he learned why the DeVeaux hunted her, or how much they were offering for her capture?

"Then we will not discard him completely," she finally said, "but neither will we blindly accept him as our friend."

"Sometimes one can be too cautious, cousin."

"True, but do not forget why I am in hiding. Sir Murray may not be so friendly or so ready to aid us when he learns the reason for our caution and this deception." She smiled faintly. "Many a man finds it difficult to forgive a woman who kills her husband."

"But you did not kill him."

"The DeVeaux believe I did, as do some of our own kinsmen. Why should a stranger believe me over all of them?" She nodded when Guy grimaced and softly cursed. "We will watch and make our decision about the Scotsman with care."

"Agreed. I but pray that the DeVeaux do not find us first."

Two

"Most pages dinnae wear such bonny amulets."

Gisele cursed, shoved her garnet-encrusted locket back inside her jupon, and glared at the grinning Scotsman as she hefted her sack of wood over her shoulder. She did her best to ignore his beautiful smile as she started to walk through the wood, back toward Guy's tent. It had been one full week since Sir Murray had intruded upon her secret. The man had shadowed her every move. She was constantly bumping into him, seeing that alluring grin at every turn. Gisele was not sure what annoyed her more, his persistence or her unshakable attraction to the rogue.

"Do ye want some help with that kindling?" Nigel asked as he fell into step by her side.

"Non," she snapped, irritated that she was unable to walk faster than he could. "Have you not considered the chance that all of your attention to me could rouse some suspicion?"

"Aye, but I dinnae think that the suspicion will be that ye are really a lass and nay a lad."

"What could they think if not that?"

"That I have grown weary of women."

She frowned, then gasped and blushed as she understood what he meant. "That is disgusting."

Nigel shrugged. " 'Tis France."

"Be wary, my fine knight. I am French."

"Aye, and ye are the bonniest sight I have set eyes upon in the long seven years that I have roamed this land."

That effusive flattery made her heart beat a little faster, and Gisele silently cursed the man. "Have you nothing else to occupy your time and thoughts beside my paltry problems?"

"Not at this time."

At the edge of the wood, while they were still sheltered by the trees and the shadows they cast, Gisele turned to look at him. Why did he have to be so handsome? Why did she feel anything for him at all? She had been so sure that her brutal husband had killed all interest in men for her, but she recognized the signs of a dangerous attraction even though it had been well over a year since she had felt any such thing. Where had this fine knight been when she could have enjoyed a flirtation, savored the warming of her blood and the clouding of her thoughts without fear? *He was out wallowing in wine and women,* she suddenly thought, and scowled.

"This is not a trouble you need to concern yourself with," she said.

"I ken it, but I have chosen to intrude." He briefly grinned as he leaned against a tree and crossed his arms over his broad chest. "Why are the DeVeaux hunting you?"

"Merde, you are like a hungry dog who has sunk his teeth into a bone."

"My brothers always said that I could be a stubborn bastard. Lass, I ken ye are being hunted, and I ken by whom. Your disguise has been no secret to me since the moment ye donned it. I also ken that ye have a bounty upon your sweet head. The only thing I dinnae ken is the why of it all." He met her gaze and held it. "Why do the DeVeaux want ye dead? I think 'tis because they believe ye killed one of their kinsmen. If that is the truth of it, then which kinsman, and why should they ever think that a wee, bonny lass like yourself would kill anyone?"

He was close to the truth, she thought, captivated by the warmth of his amber eyes. Too close. A large part of her desperately wanted to confide in him. More alarmingly, a large part of her desperately wanted him to believe in her innocence.

She forced herself to look away, afraid that his gaze would pull the truth from her. To trust him with the truth would be to gamble with her life and, quite possibly, with Guy's. She simply could not take that chance. To her disgust, she was also afraid that he would not believe her, would turn against her like so many others, and she knew that would deeply hurt her.

"As I have tried to tell you—" she began, then realized that he was no longer listening to her, had instead straightened up and was staring intently toward the camp. "Is something wrong?"

"The Sassanachs," he hissed.

"The who?"

"The English." He pushed her ahead of him as he began to hurry back to the camp. "Ye must get to Guy's quarters and stay there."

"But, I see nothing. No alarm has been sounded. How can you know that the English are close at hand?" She stumbled, only to be roughly straightened up by him and pushed forward. *"Merde,* do you smell them or something, or are you just mad?"

"Oh, aye, I can smell the bastards."

Before Gisele could question that a cry rippled through the camp. Men scrambled to arm themselves. She looked at Nigel in amazement even as he shoved her inside Guy's tent and disappeared. The first sound of swords clashing reached her ears and yanked her free of her bemusement. She tossed her sack of kindling aside and grabbed one of Guy's daggers, then sat down on the dirt floor facing the tent opening. If the battle came to her she was ready to meet it.

As she sat there, tense and alert, she found herself wondering about the Scotsman, something that happened far too often now for her liking. This was not a good time to be concerned about anyone, especially a man. Such distraction could easily cost her her life. All of her attention had to be on one thing and one thing only—eluding the DeVeaux. Her heart and mind, however, did not seem to want to heed that truth. No matter how hard she tried to get the amber-eyed Scotsman out of her head, thoughts of him continually crept back in.

Nigel Murray was an exceptionally handsome man, and many a woman would be unable to resist thinking about him. That knowledge did little to soothe Gisele's concern and irritation. She should be better than that. She had seen the dark side of men, seen the black heart a beautiful face could hide. The Scotsman did not seem to carry that taint, but Gisele knew she could no longer trust herself to make that judgment. Although she had adamantly if futilely refused to wed DeVeau, having believed all the dark tales about the man, even she had not realized the depths of his amoral and brutal nature.

Gisele cursed as thoughts of her dead husband brought the dark memories of her time with him rushing to the fore of her mind. It had been almost a year since she had found his mutilated body and, knowing that she would be blamed, had run for her life. They had only been married for six months, but she knew the things DeVeau had done to her would scar her for life. So, too, would what she saw as her betrayal by her family. They had done nothing to help her before or after her marriage to DeVeau, and many of them had believed the DeVeaux claim that she had murdered her husband. That was beginning to change, but she knew she would be slow to forgive and forget.

A scream brought her attention back to her precarious position. It was the chilling sound of a man dying, but what alarmed her more was how near it was. The battle had drawn dangerously close to the tent. Gisele slowly stood up as the clash of swords continued at what sounded like only a few paces away. Hiding within the tent no longer felt safe. It began to feel very much like a trap.

The dagger held tightly in her hand, she inched through the tent opening and then halted. Horror and fear held her rooted to the spot. Guy was in a fierce battle for his life with two men whose shields held the heraldic colors of the house of DeVeau. They had found her, and they were about to cut down one of the few members of her large family who had believed in her, just as they had cut down Guy's friend Charles. Gisele shuddered as she quickly looked away from the amiable young knight's body.

"Get away!" bellowed Guy as he nimbly evaded a lethal thrust of a sword.

Just as Gisele realized that if Guy knew she was there so did the DeVeaux, a third DeVeau man appeared and slowly approached her sword in hand. She held out her dagger and knew that the huge knight had every right to grin so arrogantly. She and her tiny weapon were no threat to him.

"Drop the dagger, you murderous whore," he said, his deep voice little more than a rough growl.

"And make this injustice easier for you to commit? *Non,* I think not," she replied.

"Injustice? *Non,* this is justice. You killed your husband, cut off his manhood, and rammed it down his throat. You deserve all the DeVeaux wish to inflict upon you."

It suddenly occurred to Gisele that the manner of her husband's mutilation promised that she would never find an ally amongst the men hunting her. The way the knight had spoken of it told her he found it of far more consequence than the murder itself. She found herself wondering if Sir Nigel would be equally appalled and withdraw his support, perhaps even join the DeVeaux, then forced herself to pay heed to something of far greater importance—staying alive.

"I will not go back to the DeVeau lair," she said, careful to keep just out of reach of the knight as she tried to get around him, to find a clear route of escape.

"Oh, *oui,* you will. Alive or dead."

"Dead? I believe the DeVeau pack of dogs wish me alive so that they might show me more of their brutality."

"This chase has lasted for so long that I think they no longer care."

"Ah, but I care. I would prefer the wee lass alive," drawled a thickly accented voice in English.

Gisele's eyes widened when she saw Sir Nigel standing behind the knight who confronted her, but she did not think she looked as surprised as the knight himself. She certainly did not share the DeVeau man's obvious fear. She quickly stepped back as the knight whirled around to face Sir Nigel. He was much too slow to save himself. Although his death was far more merciful than the one he had planned to deliver her to, she still felt sickened as Nigel cut him down. Silently, she pointed to Guy, who was hard pressed to simply hold back the two men trying to kill him.

Even though she was afraid to look and did not want to see any more death, especially not Guy's or Nigel's, she turned to watch the battle. Its outcome would decide her next step, and that could be a decision she had to make immediately. She also prayed, vehemently, that Sir Nigel and Guy would not pay too dearly for protecting her.

When Nigel cut down his opponent Gisele felt relieved, almost cheered, for one brief moment. Then Guy's opponent made a skilled thrust that Guy was too slow to deflect. She cried out along with Guy when the sword cut into his left shoulder. Only his quick shift to the right kept the blade from piercing his heart. Even as she moved to help her cousin, Nigel stopped the DeVeau man from delivering the death stroke, swiftly turning the man's attention from taking a life to desperately trying to save his own. It was a short battle, and Sir Nigel quickly ended the man's life. Gisele was just kneeling beside Guy when Sir Nigel wiped his sword on the dead man's *jupon,* sheathed his weapon, and moved to help her.

"Sorry, cousin," muttered Guy, clenching his teeth in pain as Gisele struggled to open his bloodsoaked *jupon.*

"For what?" she asked, fighting to ignore the blood and the pain she had to cause him.

"My first attempt to protect you was a miserable one."

"Non, fool, it was most gallant."

"Charles is dead?"

"I fear so."

"Curse the DeVeaux and all their progeny. Charles was a good man, the best of companions."

"I will see that his body is tended with care and honor," Nigel said.

"Thank you most kindly." Guy looked at Nigel and smiled faintly. "Where did you come from?"

"When I listened to ye speaking by the river I heard the name DeVeau. I took it upon myself to find out what I might about the family. Then in the heat of the battle, I saw ye and your friend turn and run this way. Then I spied the DeVeau men, and felt ye may need some help."

"And he needs more help now," Gisele said. "All I need to tend to his wound is within our tent."

Nigel lifted Guy up and carried him into the tent. Gisele followed, pointed to a bed of sheepskins covered by a blanket, and he gently set the younger man down on it. As Gisele worked to clean, stitch, and bind her cousin's wound, Nigel found a wineskin, sat on a chest, and helped himself to a hearty drink.

When he had realized that Gisele was in danger he had been seized by an urgency he had not felt in a long time. Seeing her facing a large, sword-wielding knight with only a strong spirit and a small dagger had stirred his admiration, and also made him eager to cut down the man threatening her. He found that both curious and unsettling. It had been a very long time since he had felt any such emotion.

As she stitched Guy's wound, her face pale with concern, Nigel studied her. She was tiny in height and stature. In the clothes she wore there was little indication that she was a woman, yet his body had no difficulty in reacting to her as one, swiftly and regularly. Gisele was unquestionably pretty with her small face, faintly pointed chin, straight nose, and wide, vividly green eyes. Her dark brows were delicately arched, enhancing the wideness of her eyes, and her lashes were long and thick. She had the most beautiful eyes he had seen in years. None of it, however, explained the feelings she stirred within him. Adorable though she was, she was no blinding beauty who could inspire men to risk all for no more than a kind word from her full lips. And yet she drew him to her as if she were.

Entangling himself in her troubles was unwise. From all he had learned of the DeVeaux they were a huge family, rich, powerful, and brutal. A man with his wits about him would do all he could to distance himself from such a family's enemies, would be very careful never to let a DeVeau mark him as an enemy, too. Instead, he had rushed in, sword raised, and killed three DeVeau knights. He could still save himself, for all witnesses to his rescue were dead or would never tell the DeVeaux, but he

knew he would not back away now. He felt compelled to help
Gisele whether she wished him to or not.

"You have decided not to return to the battle?" Gisele asked
as she finished washing up and moved to start a fire.

"That fight was near o'er when I decided to come and save
your bonny skin."

She scowled at him, watching very closely as he had a long,
hearty drink of her wine. "Guy and I were doing well enough,
although I thank you for your kind aid." She cursed softly when
he grinned, revealing that he did not believe her claim any more
than she did herself. She and Guy had desperately needed his
help, and she somewhat resented that.

"Ye find it verra hard to admit that ye are neck deep in the
mire and sinking fast, dinnae ye?" he asked, still grinning.

"A vivid turn of phrase," she murmured. "I have cared for
myself for nearly a year with no more than an occasional assist
from my family. I believe I can continue to survive."

"Whate'er ye are running from, lass, is beginning to catch up
with you. Aye, 'tis so close that it has taken the life of a friend
and nearly taken that of your kinsmon. Has that happened ere
now?"

Gisele sat down before the growing fire, snatched the wineskin
from his hand, and took a large drink. *"Non,* that has not happened before. I am sorry for Charles, very sorry, for he was
young and honorable, a boyhood friend of Guy's. Guy's wound
has weakened him, but it will not kill him if properly cared for."

"True, but I think ye will find that a difficult task."

"I have some skill at healing."

"I am sure ye do, as much skill as ye have at running away
from and hiding from your enemies. But, how much skill do ye
think ye have for doing both at the same time?" He smiled in
sympathy when she paled and began to twist her delicate, long-
fingered hands together in her lap. "Ye can no longer stay here,
lass."

"You killed the men who found me."

"But were they the only ones DeVeau sent here? They may
have sent word back to the ones hunting you, word that they had

found their prey. More will come. And, I dinnae think ye need me to tell you that ye cannae run and hide verra weel if ye are dragging a wounded mon about with you. 'Twould endanger you, and may weel make the lad's wound a fatal one."

Gisele closed her eyes and fought to calm herself. When she had first sought out Guy it had seemed such a clever plan. Who would think to look for a delicate, well-bred lady in the midst of an army, or think that she would risk dishonor by dressing as a boy? She could not believe that the DeVeaux had guessed her plans. They had simply searched out Guy hoping to find her or, at least, learn where she might have gone.

Sir Nigel was right. Soon the DeVeaux would know where she was and, worse, that Guy had helped her. She could no longer stay where she was, but she could not leave Guy behind, either. He needed her help, and now he also needed to hide from the revenge the DeVeau family was so avidly seeking. Slowly, she opened her eyes and looked at the man who had thrust himself into the midst of her troubles as if he had some right to be there.

"And what do you think I should do?" she asked.

Nigel leaned forward and looked directly into her eyes. "Run."

"I cannot leave Guy behind at the mercy of his wounds and my enemies."

"I ken it. Ye must get him to a safe place first. There must be someone who will shelter him even if they willnae shelter ye as weel."

"Our cousin Maigrat. She lives but a short day's ride from here."

"Then we shall take him there."

"We?"

"Aye—we. I am offering ye my protection, wee Gisele."

"Why?" She frowned when he laughed and shrugged his broad shoulders.

"I dinnae have a good answer for that," he replied. "I can offer ye the protection ye need and mayhap a safe haven, as weel. Ere I stumbled upon your troubles, I had thoughts of returning home. Ye can come with me."

"To Scotland?" she whispered, shocked at his suggestion yet seeing that it could be a very good plan.

"To Scotland, to my home. Even if the DeVeaux discover ye are with me and where ye have gone, ye will still be safer than ye are now and in this land. In Scotland the DeVeaux will be the strangers, unable to hide."

Gisele wanted to accept his offer, but hesitated. She would be placing her life in the hands of a man she did not really know. It was madness, yet she was not sure she had much choice.

"Ye need to consider my offer," he said, as he stood up. "I understand. I will tend to young Charles's body as I promised your cousin, and we can talk when I return."

"Any of the French knights can tell you where he must go. I believe his family would prefer to bury him on their own lands."

Nigel paused in the opening of the tent to look back at her. "There is one thing I ask of ye for my help, lass, and one thing only."

"And what is that?"

"The truth."

She cursed as he left and briefly buried her face in her hands. The truth, he said. That was his price for his much needed aid. Unfortunately, the truth could make him swiftly take back his offer. He might not believe her claim of innocence any more than so many others did.

And there was still the question of why he offered to risk his life for hers. He had no real answer for her, and many of the reasons she thought of were not kind. If he was just bored, how long would she hold his interest? Might she not soon find herself deserted in the midst of some strange land? He claimed he only wanted the truth in payment for his aid, but they would be alone together for weeks, perhaps months. He could be hoping to extract a higher payment. And what if he worked for the DeVeaux? Perhaps he was just a more subtle trap, one who would lure her to her enemies by making her trust him. That could even be a plan of his own devising, one thought up after he heard of the bounty offered for her. He had not killed her enemies to save her, but to keep all of the bounty for himself.

Gisele found that she detested even thinking such things about the handsome Scot. They had to be considered, however. He could be just what he seemed, a good, honorable man offering to help her for reasons even he could not articulate. But, just as she had no proof that he was her enemy, she had no proof that he was the friend and ally he claimed to be.

"I simply do not know what to do," she said aloud, her voice weighted with despair.

"You must go with him," came a weak, unsteady voice from behind her.

"Guy." She hurried to his side and helped him take a drink of the wine. "I thought you were asleep."

"Non. I suffered but a brief swoon from the pain."

"I am sorry. I tried to be gentle."

"That was no rebuke of your admirable skill, cousin. You do have a gentle touch, but even your clever hands cannot tend to a wound without causing some pain. That is the nature of a wound."

"It is not a mortal wound, bless God. I am so sorry about Charles."

"No need to be. You did not kill him."

"I led his murderers here."

"Cease this chastisement of yourself, cousin. None of this is your fault. If your family had heeded you from the beginning you would not have even married that bastard. You are innocent in all of this. Any knight worthy of his accolades would feel honorbound to help you."

"Do you think that is what Sir Nigel Murray is doing?" She dampened a cloth and bathed the sweat from his face.

"I believe so. I told you, I have never heard any ill of the man. He is a mercenary, sells his sword to French lords, and has done so for many years, but most Scots within our ranks do the same. It is said that he chooses more carefully than most. He is said to have a taste for women and wine, yet I have watched him closely this last week and seen none of that. If that is true, then he knows when to cast such frivolity aside and stand firm to his duty, with a clear head and a steady hand."

Gisele sighed, still uncertain yet beginning to see that she had little choice. "So, you believe I should do as he says—take you to Maigrat and go with him?"

"I do. All he asks is the truth."

"That could easily cause him to change his mind."

"Perhaps, but I think he will believe you. I am sorry, cousin, but now I think you have no choice but to play that game out. If he is not what he says, if he plays some treacherous trick, I trust that you will have the wit to smell it out before it costs you too dearly."

Before Gisele could express her doubt about that, Sir Nigel returned. He looked strong, a good man to have at one's side, but she simply could not be sure. It angered her that the DeVeaux had pushed her so tightly into a corner that she had no choice but to gamble on the honor of a man she did not know.

"Charles will be taken to his family," Nigel announced, watching the cousins closely.

"Thank you, Sir Murray," Guy said. "I pray that you are the godsend you appear to be, for now my cousin and I will accept your offer of protection and help."

"I had not agreed yet," Gisele muttered, but then softly cursed as she met Guy's stern gaze. "But I do now."

Nigel bit back a smile. "And do I get the boon I requested? The truth? I feel I deserve that much since 'tis clear that I will be placing my verra life at risk."

"*Oui,* you do deserve that," Gisele agreed. "And you will have it as soon as we get Guy safely to Maigrat's."

"Gisele—" Guy began to protest.

"*Non,* that is how it must be." She looked at Nigel. "It is an ugly tale I must tell you, Sir Murray. You may yet change your mind about helping me. I must see that Guy is safe before I risk that."

"Fair enough. I will collect all of my belongings and tell all who need to ken it that we now leave this army. We will leave here at first light," he added as he left.

"I feel certain that this is the right thing to do," Guy said after a moment of weighted silence. "I wish you would look more confident."

"And I dearly wish I could feel more confident," Gisele said, then sighed and forced a smile for Guy. "All will be well."

"You do not actually mean those words."

"*Non,* yet I feel I should have more faith in them."

"You confuse me."

"I confuse myself. I have no reason to mistrust Sir Nigel, none at all, yet I am afraid. From the moment I fled my husband's lands I have, more or less, fended for myself. Even here, even seeking your protection, I still felt as if I led the way, as if I had some control over the path I walked. The moment I agreed with you and accepted Sir Murray's protection, I suddenly felt as if I had given that control away."

Guy frowned and patted her hand in a weak attempt to soothe her. "I think you grow fanciful. I truly believe he is a good man."

"I think that deep in my battered heart I feel the same, yet even that does not ease my fear."

"Then perhaps we . . ."

"*Non,* there can be no *we* now. You must heal, and I must run again. The two are not compatible. I should set aside my worries, ones that seem born of no more than my own timid heart, and thank God that there is someone willing to help me." She grimaced. "That is what I will set my mind to doing, and mayhap this feeling that I have just stepped off a very high cliff will pass."

Three

Gisele slowly paced her cousin Maigrat's kitchen. They had made good time in their journey to her small *demanse*, but Guy had suffered. He had been pale and bathed in sweat by the time they had reached Maigrat's gates. His dire appearance had been all that had gotten them within the walls, Gisele was sure of it, and she found that a painful truth to face. There was no ignoring how they had been swiftly brought around to the rear, tersely ordered to hide their faces as they went, and left to stand in the kitchens only after Maigrat had cleared them of servants. Nor could she ignore the lack of any offer of refreshment. Maigrat had always prided herself on her courtesy. Gisele suspected that her cousin hoped they would be gone by the time she had put Guy abed, but Gisele stubbornly stayed where she was. She would not leave until she was sure Guy would be cared for.

She glanced at Nigel, who was sprawled in a chair at the well-scrubbed table, idly tapping his long fingers on the smooth surface. She felt ashamed for her cousin Maigrat. Although she knew nothing of the customs of Scotland she felt sure that he could see how poorly they were being treated. At least now he would believe her when she told him that they could not count on much help from her family. Gisele just prayed that he would believe everything else she said. She was not looking forward to telling him the whole sordid story, but that time was drawing near.

"I believe she will care for Guy," Nigel said, watching Gisele closely and feeling sorry for the pain her family was so obviously causing her.

"I believe she will, too," Gisele replied softly.

"But nay you."

"*Non,* she will have none of me." Gisele smiled crookedly, wishing she could hide her pain but knowing his sharp gaze had already seen it. "I think Maigrat hopes I will slip away ere she returns, but she will be forced to look upon me one more time. I must hear her swear that she will care for Guy."

"Agreed. If ye can do so without choking on your pride, ye may also ask her for a few supplies."

"Must I?"

"Does she have any reason to refuse ye even that meager aid?"

"None."

"Then ask, and shame her into giving it. We need all we can gather, for there may not be many opportunities to gather supplies, either by our own hands or with coin."

"Do you think we will be that hard pressed?"

He shrugged. "I cannae say, but 'tis wise to be prepared for a hard ride."

She nodded and then tensed as Maigrat strode into the kitchen. The tight-lipped look on the older woman's round face conveyed her displeasure at finding Gisele still there better than any words could. Gisele did not want to ask the woman for anything, but forced herself to do as Nigel asked, and swallowed her pride.

"You will care for Guy and keep him safe?" she asked. "Do you swear to that, Maigrat?"

"Of course," Maigrat snapped. "We fostered the boy for many years. He is as a son to me. You should never have pulled him into your troubles."

"He is out of them now."

"As is poor young Charles." Maigrat nodded when Gisele paled. "You have developed a true skill at leaving dead men in your wake. And now you sink even deeper into shame. Look at you. No woman with honor in her soul would dress herself in such a scandalous manner."

Out of the corner of her eye, Gisele saw Nigel rise to his feet, his handsome face taut with anger, and she quickly signaled him to remain silent. He could not protect her from everything, and should not be asked to. This was a family matter, and painful as it was it was not worth entangling him in it.

"Perhaps, cousin, I have decided that life is of more value to me than honor," she said quietly. "I need a few supplies, and then I will leave you."

"I have put myself at risk taking Guy in and allowing you to even step upon my lands, and yet you ask more of me?"

"I do. What matter if you give me a few scraps of food and a little wine? If the DeVeaux discover I was here they will think you did as much, anyway."

Gisele stood silently as a softly cursing Maigrat stuffed a flour sack full of food, thrust it at her, and then gave Nigel two full wineskins. She had to fight back the urge to toss everything at the woman and walk out. What she had told Maigrat was true. She did think life was more important than honor. Certainly it had to be more important than pride.

"Is this a new fool you have ensnared to help you flee justice?" Maigrat asked.

"Let it lie, Nigel," Gisele murmured when he took a step toward Maigrat. "It is not worth your trouble." She looked at her cousin. "Some people actually pause to listen to my tale, and do not judge me solely on what the DeVeaux said. It is most sad that few of those can be found within my own family. Tell Guy I will let him know when I am safely away," she added as she walked out of the kitchen.

Gisele said nothing as she and Nigel returned to their horses, sheltered their faces with the hoods of their cloaks, and rode away from her cousin's *demanse.* She was too choked with hurt and her own stung pride to say a word. It was almost dark by the time she pulled herself free of that emotional quagmire to look around. A moment later, Nigel signaled her to halt.

"We will camp here for the night," he said, as he dismounted. " 'Tis sheltered enough to hide us but not so enclosed that it could become a trap, and there is water near at hand."

She nodded and dismounted. Silence reigned as they tended to their horses and built a fire. It was not until they had filled their bellies with Maigrat's bread and cheese that Gisele sensed Nigel had had enough of silence. She looked up from the fire she had been staring into to catch him moving closer to her. He smiled faintly and held out the wineskin.

"I think 'tis time ye told me the truth," he said quietly as she drank.

"Which truth? Mine, or the one so many others choose to believe?" She grimaced and took another drink of wine as she heard the bitterness in her voice.

"Just tell me what ye see as the truth. I believe I have the wit to judge for myself."

"I wed Lord DeVeau nearly a year and a half ago. Oh, I protested the marriage in every way I could, but none would heed me or help me. He was of good family, a powerful family with a heavy purse. Such an honored knight could not be as evil as the rumors said he was."

"But ye believed the rumors."

"There were too many rumors, too many stories of his evil, for them all to be lies."

"So, ye were forced to the altar."

She had barely begun her tale and yet he could already see the pain it caused her. Nigel was tempted to tell her it did not matter, that she did not have to continue, but he bit back the words. He had to know what he was involved in. It would be hard enough to keep her safe until they reached Scotland. It would only be more difficult if he did not know why she was running, and from whom.

"I was. On my wedding night I realized that the rumors were true." She expelled a short, unsteady laugh. "The rumors had not even begun to reveal the beast that was my husband. I again turned to my family, but they shrugged aside my pleas and sto-

ries as the fancies of a new bride. My only salvation came in
the fact that my husband soon grew bored with me. Oh, he still
insisted on bedding his wife, on making me the kind of wife
he thought he needed, but the times he sought me out grew less
and less very quickly. I was to be the breeder of his heirs. Aside
from that, if I kept quiet and out of his sight he paid little heed
to me. There were other women to pursue."

Nigel found himself wishing that DeVeau was still alive so
that he might kill him. She made no clear accusations, talked
of how she was treated in subtleties, but he knew all too well
the brutality she must have endured. The lingering horror of it
could still be heard in her soft, trembling voice. He put his arm
around her shoulders and felt her tense, but when she did not
pull away he continued to hold her.

"My marriage fell into a pattern. He would beat me, bed me,
and then leave me be for a while so long as I did not intrude.
Becoming a shadow was difficult for me."

"Aye, I can imagine. Ye arenae the sort of woman who wishes
to be so meek."

"He made me want it. I continued to try to gain the help of
my family and to believe I was starting to get them to listen to
me. I fear I did not help my cause by occasionally wishing the
man dead, even saying that if someone did not free me of this
torment soon I would free myself."

Gisele felt Nigel's arm tighten around her shoulders and
fought the fear rising up within her, the fear she had learned in
DeVeau's hands. Nigel was merely offering an innocent comfort. Lurking right beside the fear was a sense of safety, of
comfort, and she struggled to grasp that and push the blind fear
away. It did feel good to be held gently by such a strong, handsome man, and she refused to let DeVeau steal her ability to
enjoy that.

"Did no one seek proof of what ye said? Look at your
bruises?"

"I was too ashamed to show them much proof."

"Ye had naught to be ashamed of."

"Mayhap. I was not a sweet child, and had grown into a woman cursed with a quick and often sharp tongue. I believe they thought I was finally getting the discipline no one had given me before. There were insults and injuries I could not bring myself to speak of. Private injuries," she added in a whisper. "As the sixth month of my marriage began I was girding myself to bear all to my family. I realize now that one thing which had kept me silent was a fear that even those insults and brutalities would not turn them to my side. Then someone took the decision out of my hands."

"Your husband was killed."

"Oui, murdered. My husband felt all women were his for the taking. He took a young maid, a local farmer's daughter. He brutalized her and left her near to death. The farmer could get no one to exact justice for this crime, so he and his family took justice into their own hands. They found my husband sprawled in a drunken stupor upon his bed and cut his throat, then mutilated him."

"Mutilated him?"

Gisele blushed and stared into the fire. "They cut off his manhood and choked him with it. In truth, I think they did that first, then cut his throat. I found the body and there was a look upon his face that told me he did not die easily. For his crime, I think that is the punishment they would have exacted."

"Aye, a horrible way to die but ye are right, it fits the crime. And the DeVeaux and your own family think ye did that?"

"Well, I fear I did threaten such gruesome things from time to time. They had already begun to watch me closely. I knew the moment I saw DeVeau lying there, I just knew, they would blame me. It may not have been wise but I ran, as swiftly as I could. I am certain some of the servants suffered for my escape, as the DeVeaux would have felt they had to have seen me leave. They did, and they did nothing to stop me. I ran straight to my family."

"Only to find that they wouldnae help you."

Gisele struggled to swallow her tears. That had been the

greatest hurt of all, and she still felt the power of it even after so many months "They would not. They feared the scandal, questioned me, even spoke of holding me for the DeVeaux. I did not wait to see if they would hand me over yet again. I fled, and that has been the way I have lived for nearly a year."

Although she wished she could compose herself enough to clear the tears from her eyes, Gisele looked up at Nigel. "I swear on all I hold dear, on Guy's life if you will, that I did not kill the man. I am innocent of the crime, but since so few of my own family believe me it is taking a long time to prove that."

Nigel stared down into her upturned face, its delicate lines highlighted beautifully by the soft light of the fire. He knew it was possible that he was being influenced by her beauty, by how strongly she affected him, but he could not believe she had killed the man. And, he mused as he gently brushed a tear from her cheek, even if she had it had been justified. He was certain that Gisele had not told him the true depths of the injuries De-Veau had inflicted upon her, and might never do so.

"No mon has the right to treat a woman as he treated you," Nigel said quietly.

"So, you believe that I am innocent."

"I believe that DeVeau got exactly what he deserved."

Gisele stared at him, captivated by the warmth in his dark, amber eyes. It felt dangerously good to be held so close to his warmth. He would help her. Some of her fears eased. When he softly kissed the mark the tear had left upon her cheek, she trembled. She knew she should move away, but could not bring herself to leave the haven of his arms. Then she frowned, wondering if she had been right, if Nigel thought to gain more than the truth as payment for his help.

"I have told you the truth as you asked," she said.

"Aye, ye have." He idly traced her small face with kisses, enjoying the feel of her soft skin beneath his lips but watchful for any sign of fear or rejection.

"And that was the only price you asked for helping me."

"It was."

"Then why do I begin to suspect that you seek more of me?"

"Because ye are a clever lass?"

She tensed slightly as he touched his lips to hers. They were soft, warm, and very inviting. Fear stirred within her, but so did curiosity. Since she had first set eyes upon him she had wondered what it would feel like to kiss him, had wondered if she could do so without being afraid. It was not wise, for he clearly sought to seduce her, might even think she was agreeing to share his bed in return for his protection, yet she could not bring herself to immediately and forcefully push him away.

"I need help and a strong sword arm, but I will not play the whore to gain those things."

"I wasnae asking ye to."

"You are trying to kiss me."

"Oh, aye, that I am. I have made no secret of the fact that I think ye are a bonny lass. I but seek a wee taste of the lips I have coveted for a week."

"And maybe a lot more?"

"Your suspicions are unwarranted, bonny Gisele. Aye, I willnae lie and say I will treat ye as a nun, but ye may rest assured that I will ne'er take what ye dinnae want to give. Weel, except for this one kiss."

"I am not sure you will be stealing that," she whispered.

Nigel lightly tightened his grip on her, deeply aroused by her soft words but suspecting that it would be wise to hide that. He brushed his lips over hers, savoring the sweetness of her trembling mouth. It was undoubtedly dishonorable to even think of seducing a woman who had turned to him for protection, especially one who had been as mistreated as Gisele, but Nigel knew he was going to try to do just that. As he slowly deepened the kiss, he swore that he would do nothing to add to her pain. Instead, he would do all in his power to show her that not all men were like her brutal husband.

Gisele clung to Nigel, timidly opening her mouth when he nudged her lips with his tongue. A war waged inside of her. Passion battled for dominance over fear. Each stroke of his tongue, the feel of his strong body pressed close to hers, called to her passion. It felt good. He felt good. Gisele desperately wanted to cling to that, to begin to learn what the minstrels sang about. But her fear continued to grow.

Suddenly, so swiftly that it nearly blinded her, her fear rose up and killed her passion. She went cold, her body stiffening with panic. Just as she grasped the sense to pull away, Nigel ended the kiss. She closed her eyes as he gently grasped her by the shoulders and held her away from him. After several slow, deep breaths she began to gain control, and cautiously opened her eyes to look at him. Her eyes widened when she still saw the warmth of passion in his eyes, a warmth tinged with a look of sadness instead of the anger she had been taught to expect.

"Ye need not fear me, Gisele," he said quietly.

"I do not believe I do." She smiled slightly as he released her and handed her the wineskin. "I do know that that fear was not caused by you."

"I suspected that. Ye have told me the truth, as much as I really need to ken, but I think ye havenae told me everything. Howbeit, that kiss did tell me more than the fact that I wish to kiss ye again. It told me that DeVeau bred a terror in you, a terror so deep and strong that it could kill the passion I felt, sadly brief though it was. For that alone the mon deserved to die."

She grew still and stared at him as she watched him spread out their blankets. "You think I killed him."

"Weel, nay and aye."

"You cannot believe in both my innocence and my guilt. I am either one or the other."

"Ye are innocent, and dinnae deserve to die. I just havenae decided if ye killed the mon or nay. He deserved to die, Gisele. If it is any comfort, I dinnae see ye as some vicious monkiller. If ye did do it, ye were driven to it by crimes I am nay sure I want to hear about." He sprawled on his blanket and patted the one spread out beside him. "Come to bed, lass. Ye need to rest.

There is a long, hard ride ahead of us, and time to rest may
soon be verra hard to find."

Gisele was stunned and moved to her bed, unable to speak.
She had wanted Nigel to believe in her innocence, but he only
accepted that she was justified in killing the man. As she curled
up in her blanket she wondered why she was not furious and
insulted. She supposed it was because he gave her tale more
weight than many of her family did. Despite that, she found
that she desperately wanted him to believe that she had not
killed the man. Although it was good to know that he felt confident she would have been justified, that she would have simply
been defending herself, she realized she wanted him to know
that she was stronger than that.

"You show me more kindness and understanding than my
family does," she said, turning to look at him. "I should be
satisfied with that."

"But ye are not."

"I fear not. I am stronger than you think. I would have found
another way to get free. By the time we get to Scotland I promise
that I will have you believing in my complete innocence."

"Fair enough. I, too, make a promise."

"Do I really wish to hear this?" She saw him grin, and silently
cursed.

"Nay, probably not, but I feel it only fair that I tell you. Call
it a warning if ye will. By the time we get to Scotland I mean
to prove to you that not all men are like your husband. I mean
to resurrect the passion he killed within you."

Gisele quickly turned away from him. She felt an odd mix
of excitement and terror. Part of her desperately wanted him to
be able to fulfill that promise, and part of her was desperately
afraid of the same thing. As she closed her eyes, she prayed she
would have the strength to allow him to fulfill his promise.

Four

The cold water of the small river felt good against her skin and Gisele ached to immerse herself in it. There was no time, however. Nigel was watering the horses but a few feet away, and he had made it very clear that this would be a brief respite from their travel. For two long days they had ridden from sunrise to sunset with only a few stops. Her whole body ached. Fortunately, she was so exhausted by nightfall that even her extreme discomfort was not enough to rob her of sleep. She could not recall ever having worked so hard to elude her enemies.

She glanced at Nigel. He stood by the horses looking as limber and rested as if he had just risen from a soft, comfortable bed after a long, peaceful night's sleep. It annoyed Gisele, yet she knew it should not. Nigel was a knight, one of a breed who was probably set in a saddle before he could walk. He should look hale, not at all troubled by a few long days of riding. She knew she was jealous of his strength even as she was unsettled by her lack thereof.

As she straightened up from where she knelt by the riverbank, Gisele winced and rubbed at the ache in her lower back. She thanked God that she still wore a page's attire, sure that it had protected her soft skin far better than any gown would have. Gisele just wished she could find something that could protect her aching bones and stiff muscles.

"If ye are quick about it, ye can bathe," Nigel said as he stepped up beside her.

Gisele started, surprised by his sudden appearance so close at hand. She scowled at his feet, wondering if the soft, deerhide boots he wore aided him in moving around so silently. It was a skill she had envied from the first moment he had revealed it. No matter how hard she tried, however, she could not imitate it.

"I think I need to hang a bell on you," she muttered as she looked up at him.

Nigel just grinned. "Do ye want a wee bath or nay, lass?"

"You wished to keep riding."

"Aye, I did. I still do. 'Tis why I say ye must be quick about it."

As she lightly bit her bottom lip, she glanced around. "There is no place to be private."

"I will turn my back." He shrugged when she scowled at him again. " 'Tis all I can give you, lass. Ye must choose atween your privacy and your safety." He placed his hand on his heart and added, "I swear I shall only set my gaze upon the horizon, shall look only for our enemies."

Since she had entrusted her safety, her very life, into his care, Gisele decided she was being foolish in hesitating to entrust him with her modesty. "Agreed."

"I mean what I say. Ye must be quick. Heed me on that," he said even as he turned and walked back to the horses.

After glancing his way to assure herself that he still had his back to her, Gisele began to unlace her *jupon,* then cursed her own stupidity. She could not put these filthy clothes back on once she had bathed. "Sir Nigel," she called. "I need my saddlepack."

He tossed it to her with an ease and an accuracy that startled her. The man was proving to have a vast array of skills, she mused as she hastily unpacked her only other set of page's clothes and a drying cloth. Shedding her clothes and tightly clenching the thin sliver of soap she had so carefully preserved throughout her travels, Gisele stepped into the water. She gasped in reaction to the biting chill of the water, then steeled herself to endure it. This could well be her only chance to bathe for quite awhile.

Nigel heard her gasp and almost turned around, then smiled. He realized that it was no cry of alarm, only the sound that most people made when their warm skin hit cold water. There was a part of him that was strongly tempted to use that soft noise as an excuse to turn and look at her, but he forcefully quelled that urge. He had promised her that he would not look, and instinct told him that he would gain far more from holding fast to that promise than from trying to sneak a quick peek like some errant, fevered youth.

Trust was important to Gisele, he was certain of it, and she had had hers betrayed too often. It would take a lot of hard work to make her trust him, but he was determined to try. Bluntly telling her that he intended to be her lover was, perhaps, not the best start, but at least he had been completely honest. There had been, as yet, very little time to begin his seduction, but she had been fairly warned. Nigel also knew that, as he attempted to pull her passion free of the fears that still held it captive, he would have to convince her that not all men were brutish swine who felt it was their godgiven right to treat a woman cruelly.

He sighed and rubbed the back of his neck. Some would say that seducing a woman when he was not sure if he wished to claim her as his wife was cruel. He tried not to look at it that way. Gisele was a widow, so he would not be stealing her innocence. And if she *had* murdered her husband, then she was certainly strong enough and willful enough to accept or deny a lover. No matter how long or hard he thought on the matter, however, he could not shake the uneasy feeling that he might be allowing his strong desire for her to lead him astray. He could find himself adding to her pain instead of healing it.

And how much of his passion was born of the challenge she presented, of a chance to turn a frightened woman made cold by betrayal and brutality into a passionate lover? He quickly shook that thought away. Nigel was sure that his vanity had little to do with his desire for Gisele, although it was probably the only thing he *was* sure of. Gisele was a puzzle, and the way she drew him to her was an even bigger one.

"You may turn around now," Gisele called, yanking him free of his unwelcome thoughts.

Even as he looked at her she stopped rubbing her hair with

the drying cloth, and Nigel had to bite back a grin. Her short hair was a mass of wild curls, several tumbling alluringly onto her forehead. No man could look at her now and think that she was a boy, despite her clothing. He reached into his bag and pulled out a cap.

"I think ye had best put this on," he advised.

Gisele frowned as she took the dull, brown cap made of a rough, homespun cloth. "It is not cold."

"Nay, but I think that will now aid your disguise. Trust me, lass. Your hair now makes ye look verra much like a woman."

"Oh." She reached up to touch her damp hair, felt all the thick, wild curls, and grimaced as she tugged on the cap. "I should have recalled how it grows after it has been cut. I had to have it all shaved off once when I was but a child, because of a wretched fever I was suffering with, and it grew just like this. It was most unmanageable until it gained some length and weight. Then these foolish curls became waves. Mayhap I should cut it again."

"Nay. Soon it willnae matter if all who see ye ken that ye are a lass. The cap isnae verra bonny, but it will do what is needed for now. Next I shall ask ye to allow me a wee moment or two of privacy." He removed some clean clothing from his saddlepack.

"Oh. You wish to bathe?"

"We Scots do so from time to time."

"And from all I have heard of your land you should be well accustomed to cold water."

"Aye, it can be colder in Scotland. The weather doesnae pamper us there as it does ye French. Now, I best be about my bath. Turn your back, lass," he said, as he started to walk away. Then he looked over his shoulder at her before she had completely turned around. "Of course, if ye wish to take a wee peek, I willnae fault ye for it," he added, and winked.

Gisele decided not to grace that impertinence with a reply, and completely turned her back on him. Despite her best efforts, however, a small grin crossed her face. It quickly disappeared when she realized that she was tempted to look at him, strongly tempted. It was that which made her hesitate to take 'a wee peek'.

That could be all that was needed to dangerously enhance an already growing attraction. His face was certainly pleasing to her eye. She knew it could be perilous indeed to discover that his body was, as well.

It could, however, be a good test of how deep and pervasive her fears were, she mused as she idly stroked her horse's nose. Her husband had used his manhood like a weapon, hurting her and debasing her. Gisele knew that the cruel things he had done to her had made her afraid of a man's embrace. If that fear could also be stirred by simply viewing a naked man, it could prove that she was far more deeply scarred than she had guessed. When she realized that she could not recall a time since her husband's death that she had seen a man unclothed despite her rough travels, Gisele wondered if she had been purposely avoiding such a sight. The fact that she had not glimpsed even one in the time she had been with the army—not even Guy, despite sharing a tent with him—seemed to confirm that. She did not like the thought that DeVeau had made her that much a coward.

Although a small voice told her that she was just making excuses so that she could look at a man who intrigued her, Gisele moved to stand in front of her horse. With her side toward Nigel instead of her back, it would be easier to steal a look or two and not be caught. Curiosity also drove her to take the risk, she decided, and grimaced, for it had always been a fault of hers. Gisele just wanted to know what she would feel if she caught a look of his partly or fully unclothed form.

She moved so that her horse's nose was between her and Nigel, praying that that would be enough to hide her indiscretion. A deep breath steadied her, and she raised her gaze toward the river. She had dawdled for so long in deciding that he was already finished with his bath. He stood on the riverbank rubbing himself down with a large drying cloth. His tall, lean body shone gold in the sun. His broad back was toward her, and Gisele found herself wondering what his smooth skin would feel like beneath her hands. She quickly looked down his body, admiring his trim waist, his slim, well-shaped backside, and his long, perfectly formed, muscular legs. When she caught herself hoping he would turn around, she sucked in her breath so sharply she choked and began to cough.

"Are ye all right?" Nigel asked, frowning toward a badly coughing Gisele as he hastily pulled on his clothes.

"Oui," she gasped, stumbling to the river's edge and drinking some water from her cupped hands.

Since she had ceased to cough, Nigel took the time to lace up his shirt, don his jupon, and tug on his boots. "Ye arenae ailing with something, are ye?"

"Non." She lightly splashed some of the cool water on her face, praying she did not look as warm or as agitated as she felt. "I but gagged on a bug, I am thinking."

He grinned at her as he laced on his boots. "If ye are that greedy for some meat, lass, I will go ahunting when we stop to camp for the night."

"What an amusing fellow you are, Sir Murray." She hastily rinsed her travel-stained clothes in the water and wrung them out. "I assume you kept your drinking companions crippled with laughter." She tied a strip of rawhide around her clothes and hung them from her saddlepack, hoping they would dry and not simply get filthy again.

Nigel did the same with his clothes, then watched her closely as they mounted. "So ye heard a few tales about me, did ye?" he asked as he led her away from the small river.

Gisele wondered if she should make a polite denial, then decided that it would be best if she were honest. "Guy said you favored wine and women. He also told me that he had seen none of that in the days that he watched you."

"He watched me, did he?"

"You knew our secrets. He would have been a fool not to."

"Aye, true enough." Nigel fidgeted with his reins. She had not asked for any explanation, but he felt compelled to say something. "I didnae leave Scotland simply because I had a hunger to kill the English." He winked at her. "Although most of my kind would say that was reason enough."

"Most of my kind would, as well. In truth, at times I wonder how there can be so many men still left, for the killing has continued for many years."

"Oh, aye, and I believe 'twill continue long after we have turned to dust. But, e'en though 'tis much the same in my land, 'tis still not what brought me here."

"You owe me no explanations, Sir Murray," she said quietly, for she could sense his discomfort and reluctance.

"Weel, something must be said. Ye have placed your life in my hands, as has Guy. 'Tis only fair that ye ken it was a wise decision. Aye, I drank a lot when there was no battle to fight. And, aye, I sought out the company of women more often than was wise and, at times, with a greed that was a sort of madness. The fighting, the drinking, and, I am ashamed to admit, the women, were all used for but one purpose."

"To forget?" That was something Gisele found very easy to understand.

Nigel sighed and nodded. "Aye, 'tis the sad truth of it. I have spent seven long years of my life, nay, wasted it, trying to forget. My only salvation is that I never dishonored my clan in battle. I may not have been fighting for the right reasons, but I always fought weel, fought fairly, and chose my battles wisely."

"That is no small thing, Sir Murray." Gisele desperately wanted to ask what he had been trying so hard to forget, but she did not feel she had the right to press for a truth he could not offer freely. "And have you forgotten?" was as much as she dared to ask. "If you would find it painful or dangerous to return home, we could find safety elsewhere."

"Nay, there is no safety for you in this land, and I ken only this place and Scotland. Ere I first discovered ye and Guy by the river I had decided that it was time to return. I woke up in the mud unable to recall how I got there and, shall we say, saw the folly of my life. 'Tis time to leave this embattled land and return to my kin." He met her gaze and smiled faintly. "Ye need not fear. I am nay a hunted mon. I willnae be leading ye away from your enemies just to face down some of my own."

Gisele smiled back, then inwardly sighed with disappointment when he returned his attention to the faint, little used trail they followed. At least for now he was not going to tell her why he had fled his home, nor why he had buried his heart and mind in battle, drink, and women. For a brief moment, she was angry. He had insisted that she tell him all of her secrets, yet he was unwilling to reciprocate. Gisele then told herself not to be so foolish. Nigel needed to know everything about her troubles so that he would know what dangers they would face. There was no need for her to know his secrets. They did not affect their safety at all.

Despite that, Gisele could not stop herself from wondering. What could make a man leave the home he loved? She knew he loved both his home and his family. She could hear it in his deep voice whenever he spoke of them. Gisele also believed his claim that he was not a hunted man, had not fled any enemies, and that he was not helping her run from one danger only to thrust her into the middle of another. That did not leave her many choices, and the one that came to mind made her uneasy. There was one thing that could make even the strongest and bravest of knights flee a place like the basest of cowards. One thing that could turn a man to wine and women, that could change a sober, righteous man into a drunken lecher. A woman. Nigel was in France to try to forget a woman.

After several moments of silently cursing, Gisele wondered why that should trouble her so much. There was no question that Nigel was one of the most handsome men she had ever seen and that she did feel some attraction for him, but she should not be concerned about whether or not his heart was taken or broken. In truth, Gisele thought angrily, the only thing she should be wondering about was whether men had any hearts at all.

It did not matter, she told herself firmly. If he had fled Scotland because of a woman it was obviously because he could not have her. If he still loved the woman that was his concern, and not Gisele's. She had neither the time nor the inclination to chase after the man's heart. Gisele knew her one and only concern should be to stay alive until she could prove her innocence.

She sighed and tried to fix her attention on following Nigel. Gisele hoped that she could make herself believe all that, but a

small part of her told her it was hopeless. Nigel had shown her
that passion still lurked inside her although fear held it captive.
He had also shown her that he might be the one who could free
it again. She had thought a lot about the kiss they had shared,
about the feelings it had stirred within her before the terror De-
Veau had bred in her had killed them all. Gisele wanted to know
what passion, what fierce and fearless desire, could feel like, and
instinct told her that Sir Nigel Murray could show her. What she
feared was that, she would want more once he showed her. She
would not only want to be his lover, but his love. If she were
right about his reasons for leaving home, his love was not free
for the taking. His heart was held by some other woman. If, she
gave her heart when she gave her body, she could well be handing
it to someone who had no use for it, nor the capability of ever
returning her feelings. It might be wondrous to discover the joy
that could be passion, but Gisele was not sure she wanted to also
discover what true heartbreak was.

"I ken that the journey is hard, lass," Nigel said, catching a
glimpse of the dark frown on her face.

A little concerned that her thoughts were so clear to read,
Gisele forced a brief smile in response. "I but mourn my
wretched lot in life, Sir Murray. Do not fear that I will allow my
occasional descents into maudlin self-pity to interfere with our
journey."

Nigel laughed softly, then shook his head. "Ye have earned a
few moments of melancholy. More so than many another."

Gisele shrugged. "I may have earned the right to indulge myself, but it is useless. It does not ease the pain of the past, or help
me solve my difficulties now. In truth, I find it more pleasurable
to get angry."

"Especially at men."

"Oh, *oui,* especially at men. Worry not, my fine knight, I shall
not be cutting your throat in the dead of night simply because
you are a man and I have stirred myself into a fury."

He started to laugh, then eyed her closely, enjoying the faint,
impish grin that curved her full mouth but also made a little
uneasy by the way she could jest about the manner in which her

husband died. "And just what might make ye creep about and cut my throat whilst I sleep?" he asked.

"You will know when the time has come."

"Oh, aye, when I am strangling in my own blood."

Even as she opened her mouth to make a humorous reply, Gisele suddenly realized what she was saying. In her mind she saw her husband's bloodsoaked body. She could not believe she had been so heartless or so stupid as to make jest of a brutal murder, especially one she had been accused of. The memory of what she had found that day was slow to recede, and she gagged, certain she could still smell the blood.

"Are ye unwell?" Nigel asked, reaching out to touch her arm and struggling not to be offended by the way she yanked it out of his reach.

"I am fine. I but swallowed a bug."

"Another one? Ye had best be more wary, lass, or ye shall be too full to eat when we make camp."

He rode a few paces in front of her, then smiled with relief when he heard her softly curse him. She had looked so pale and stricken for a moment that he had ached to pull her into his arms and shelter her from her dark memories. Gisele had obviously realized that she was making jest of the manner in which her husband had been murdered. Nigel was sure she had then become horrified, but he knew that his desire for her was so strong that it could easily cloud his judgement. There was, after all, the chance that the look he had seen had not been horror or self-disgust but fear, fear that she had just revealed her own guilt. He decided that he was going to have to try harder to convince her that he simply did not care if she had killed the man whether he believed in her innocence or not. Until he could make her understand that she would always feel constrained, unable to be completely honest or to trust him. He needed both from her if they were going to get to Scotland alive.

Five

It was a soft, distant howl, but it made Gisele's blood run cold, and she huddled closer to the fire. Nigel had chosen a lovely clearing in the forest for their camp. At least, it had been lovely until he had left her alone to go hunting, something that was taking far longer than she thought was necessary. No matter how often she told herself it had not really been that long, she began to worry about him. The sound of wolves howling, distant though it was, only added to her growing concern. There was a much greater chance that Nigel had stumbled upon some of her enemies than that he had been eaten by wolves. Yet, foolish though it was, she feared the wolves more.

The horses shifted, blowing softly, and Gisele tensed. Someone or something was out there. She slipped her hand inside of her jupon and began to withdraw her dagger from the sheath sewn inside. A moment later Nigel emerged from the wood proudly holding up two rabbits readied for the spit. Gisele felt both weak with relief and tempted to strike him. Then she looked at the rabbits again, realized how hungry she was, and decided to forgive the man his long absence and continuously alarming stealth.

"Did I nay say earlier this fine day that I would find us some meat?" he said, grinning as he sat down on the opposite side of the fire and quickly set the rabbits on the spit.

"You did," she replied, deciding not to remark upon the vanity of preparing the spits before he had set out on his hunt. "I did not realize how I hungered for some meat until you crept out of the wood holding your catch."

"Ye are troubled by my silence, are ye?" He had a sip of wine and handed her the wineskin.

Gisele shrugged and helped herself. "It can be frightening, especially in the dark."

"I shall teach you the trick of it. If ye acquire the skill ye willnae find it so unsettling."

"I would like that," she said, not able to hide all of her excitement. "When we walk together I feel as if I make more noise than the horses. And with the danger I cannot seem to free myself of, it could prove to be a most useful skill."

"Aye, it is, but ye will soon be free of the threat that has hounded you for so long."

"God willing," she murmured, and then smiled faintly. "You should be more careful in your boasting, Sir Murray. Some say God frowns upon such vanities, and I think we could use His favor right now, do you not agree?"

Nigel smiled. "Oh, aye, but I dinnae consider it a boast or e'en vanity. 'Tis a vow, upon my honor. Your running will soon end. Ye have suffered enough injustice at the hands of the De-Veaux. 'Tis past time it ceased."

She really wanted to believe him, wanted to accept his vow and feel at peace, but she had been afraid for too long. Nigel might mean every word he spoke, but she needed far more than brave words. Over the last year a few friends and kinsmen had vowed to put an end to her travails, including Guy, and yet she was still running, still hiding. She could not even feel certain that Scotland would be the haven Nigel thought it would be, only that it had to be better than France. What puzzled her was how he could make such a vow when he was not convinced of her innocence in the murder of her husband.

"Ye dinnae believe me. I can see the doubt in your bonny eyes," he said, as he turned the rabbits so that they would cook more evenly. "I am a mon of my word."

"I am sure that you are, Sir Murray. That was not why I

frowned. I but wondered how you could vow so adamantly that you would keep me safe when you are as yet uncertain of my innocence."

"I have told ye, lass, whether I think ye wielded that knife or nay doesnae matter. That bastard deserved to die, and ye dinnae deserve to suffer for what was a righteous killing. The men of your clan should have been the ones to do it, should have made DeVeau pay dearly the first time he raised a hand against you. If ye were forced to do their duty for them, 'tis no fault of yours. Aye, and those kinsmen of yours should be here now," he added in a hard, angry voice. "They should be all about you, swords raised, to shield you from the carrion the DeVeaux have yapping at your heels. But, since they are too cowardly, then I am more than willing to take up the cause."

Gisele stared at the fire, struggling to quell a sudden urge to weep—Nigel's defense deeply touched her—but she was not sure she wanted him to know that. As she fought to compose herself, she prayed she was not about to suffer another disappointment or, worse, betrayal. She prayed that Nigel Murray was all he appeared to be, an honorable knight who believed she was worthy of his protection. The reminder that he did not completely believe in her innocence helped calm her. As deeply grateful as she was for his help, that irritated her.

"My family believed that DeVeau was an excellent match, gaining our family both power and wealth," she said quietly. "I must believe that such things are also of importance in a marriage arrangement in Scotland."

"Aye," he admitted reluctantly.

"It is often difficult to make people believe that something is terribly wrong with what they all thought was so perfect. And, to be fair to my family, they are not strange in their belief that a man has the right to discipline his wife. I suspect that not all men, or women, in Scotland believe as you do."

"Nay, but what DeVeau did to you wasnae discipline, 'twas torture."

"But my family only had my word on that. Is the rabbit cooked now?"

Nigel grinned. "Ye end a discussion with little subtlety, lass."

She returned his smile and shrugged. "I find talk of my family's betrayal and lack of trust very uncomfortable."

"Weel, fill your belly with this fine meat. They say a full stomach can cure many an ill."

"And they sound most wise." She laughed softly as he lifted one spitted rabbit from the fire and gently waved it back and forth to cool it. "If you drop that in the dirt one of us is going to go hungry."

He laughed and handed her the rabbit, taking the second one for himself. Gisele did not think she had ever tasted anything so good, or eaten with such a complete lack of delicacy before. She found it both sad and amusing that sitting in the wood with a man she barely knew, tearing at a cooked rabbit like a savage, could make her feel so alive. Gisele began to wonder if she had been alone and running for her life for too long. It had finally given her a fever of the brain.

Too full to eat any more, Gisele went to where their saddlepacks were, carefully wrapped what was left of her meat, and tucked it in the pack with the rest of their food. She washed her hands and face with a small amount of water, then returned to sit by the fire. Suddenly, she was very tired, and she hastily raised her hand to hide a huge yawn.

"I feel the same, lass," Nigel said as he wiped his face and hands with a dampened scrap of cloth. " 'Tis best if we seek our beds now. I will stand watch if ye wish to slip into the shadows for a moment."

Gisele hoped that the darkness hid her blushes as she nodded and slipped away. She was finding the lack of privacy hard to endure, although she was not sure why. Privacy had become a rare privilege since she had fled her husband's lands. She had thought that she had become accustomed to the loss. Somehow, being with Nigel had made her painfully aware of it again.

When she returned to the fire Nigel slipped away, and Gisele lectured herself yet again on her foolishness. He had no privacy, either, and it had to be difficult for him as well, although she suspected that men were less troubled by such a thing. It was time, she decided, to stop thinking about herself so much and try to consider Nigel a little more. He had freely offered his protection, but she doubted he had fully considered all of the complications that could arise while racing across France with a woman. She swore that she would try to stop thinking of how hard it was for her, and try to make it easier for him.

The moment Nigel returned he collected their bedding. Gisele quickly took hers from him and laid it out herself. She ignored his smile when he saw that she had made her bed across the fire from him. If he chose to think she was simply enforcing a distance between them, that was fine with her. Soon he would see that she intended to do her share of the work now, not to just sit around and wait to be cared for.

Nigel banked the fire, yanked off his boots, and unbuckled his sword. He set his weapons close to his rough bed in case they were needed in the night. He sprawled on top of the quilted mat, wrapped the thin blanket around himself, and turned on his side to watch Gisele across the fire. She could not fully hide a wince as she eased her body down onto her bed. Nigel started to reach out to her in sympathy, but quickly restrained himself. There was nothing he could do for her. She would just have to endure until she grew harder.

"Ye havenae done much long, hard riding, have ye, lass?"

"Non." She turned on her side to look at him across the dwindling fire. "If I grew weary of riding, I rested. There was no place for me to run to, so my concern was simply to remain hidden."

"A good strategy."

"Was it? I am still being hunted."

"Aye, but ye are also still alive."

She smiled faintly at that simple truth, then sighed. "It is no longer enough."

"Nay," Nigel agreed. "There are too many hounds on your

trail now. Mayhap your enemies thought ye would be easy to catch, that a wee lass couldnae escape them for long. They now ken that ye arenae easy prey, and the hunt is truly on. That is why I press ye so hard, lass. Now ye must run, run hard, run fast, and run far."

"So you have said. Do you truly believe the pursuit is that strong, that unrelenting, now?"

"Aye, I do. 'Tis nay only your husband's kin ye must elude, but as the bounty offered for ye grows near every mon with a greed for some coin will be searching for you."

"A chilling thought."

Nigel nodded. "It is, and, although I dinnae like to add to your fears, 'tis one ye must hold fast to. 'Twill keep ye wary of all ye might meet, and that will keep ye alive."

Gisele murmured in agreement. It was advice well worth heeding. She had lived with fear for the last year, yet as time had passed and she was neither harmed nor captured, she knew it had lost its sharpness. Having a tall, battle-hardened Scot at her side had also made her feel safer. Nigel could not be expected to protect her from everything. He was but one man with one sword. He also did not deserve to face a danger just because she was blissfully ignoring the threat to both their lives.

Until the DeVeaux accepted her claim of innocence her life was in danger, and she was a fool if she ever let that knowledge slip from the fore of her thoughts. Despite the hard ride to reach Scotland as soon as possible, Gisele knew she had done so from time to time. That had to stop. The only thing she should be thinking of at all times was how swiftly and how elusively she and Nigel could reach Scotland.

As she closed her eyes Gisele took one last look at Nigel and decided she could be forgiven her moments of distraction. He was a man who could easily distract even the most strong-minded of women. It was nice to once again think of a man without fear or loathing, but Gisele knew she would need to wait to indulge in that frivolity. She might not be certain of her feelings for Nigel, of how true or deep or well deserved they were, but she was sure that she did not want to be the cause of any harm coming to him.

Nigel watched her fall asleep and inwardly laughed at himself. He meant everything he had told her about why he had made himself her protector, but there were other reasons he had no intention of revealing to her. There was whatever had him lying there staring at her small face like some lovesick youth. It was whatever made him so hungry for her that he found it difficult to sleep. It was also whatever had him aching to heal all of her heart's wounds. If her husband were still alive, Nigel knew he would hunt the man down and kill him with his bare hands.

For the first time in seven years he was alive with emotion. Gisele had yanked him free of his black melancholy with one look from her deep, green eyes. He just wished he were sure of what she had pulled him into, of which emotion he should trust. She looked a lot like the woman he had run away from and, although he wanted to believe he had more sense, he had to wonder if that was why he was so drawn to Gisele. If nothing else, it was only fair to her to try to decide if he truly cared for her or if he were just reaching out to the ghost of Maldie, his brother's wife.

That was something he had to know by the time they reached Scotland, he thought with a grimace as he turned on his back and stared up at the stars. Gisele would see her resemblance to Maldie the minute she set eyes on the woman. If he and Gisele had become lovers by then, he needed to know his own heart and mind, for he would certainly have to explain himself. And he knew that Gisele would not be easy to convince after having suffered so many bitter betrayals.

He closed his eyes and readied himself to go to sleep. He prayed that when the time came that Gisele accepted him as her lover he would at least be certain that he truly wanted Gisele DeVeau, was not simply using her and fooling himself. Using Gisele to sate a hunger for another woman was an insult he could not inflict upon her. The cause of his lust should be easier to discern than the cause of the feelings twisting his insides into knots. For the latter, he mused as he felt sleep weight his body, he was going to need time, a lot of time. Scotland suddenly did not seem that far away.

Gisele awoke in a cold sweat. Tense, her hand curled tightly around the handle of her dagger, she listened intently to the sounds of the wood. A soft howling was carried on the wind, and she knew why she was suddenly awake and terrified.

"I hate wolves," she whispered, a little comforted by the faint agitation of the horses. It was good to know that she was not the only one made uneasy by the wolves.

For several long moments she lay, eyes tightly closed, and tried to ignore the sound. One glance at the peacefully sleeping Nigel told her that he was not worried, so she should not be, either. Her determination to be brave wavered almost immediately as more howls disturbed the peace of the night. It would take a lot more than bold talk and strong will to cure her of her terror of wolves. It was an old and hardened fear. She knew she would not get to sleep lying there trying to ignore them, just as she knew she desperately needed to get some rest. If she became too exhausted she could slow everything down.

She cautiously sat up and looked at Nigel. Not only did he look safe and strong, but close at his side was his sword. Gisele gently nibbled at her bottom lip as she tried to make up her mind. She did not want to appear a complete coward. She also did not wish to make Nigel think that she sought any more than a respite from her own fears. A shiver tore through her body as the wolves continued their eerie music, and she gathered up her bedding. If Nigel woke, she would worry about explaining herself then.

As silently as she could she held tightly to her bedding and crept to his side. She was embarrassed by her cowardice, but that shame was not enough to stop her. If the knowledge that the wolves were far away and that the fire would keep them at

bay could not stop her, self-disgust certainly would not. Taut
with worry that she would wake Nigel and have to confess her
fear, she carefully spread out her bedding right by his side.

She was just settling down and wrapping herself in her blanket when she knew he was awake. It did not surprise her when
she turned and found him looking at her, but she inwardly
cursed her ill luck.

"Cold?" Nigel asked, wondering why she looked so guilty.
He hastily subdued a surge of hope that she had sought him out
for reasons of passion. It was too soon.

"Oui," she agreed hastily, then jumped and edged a little
closer to him when the wolves howled.

"Afraid of the wolves, are ye?"

"Oui, afraid of the wolves," she grumbled.

"They arenae near enough to trouble you," he said.

"I know."

"The fire, small as it is, will keep them at bay."

"I know that, too," she snapped, and glared at him when he
laughed. "It is not funny."

"Nay, your fear isnae to be laughed at," he agreed. "Howbeit,
your anger at it is amusing."

Gisele grimaced and dragged her fingers through her tight
curls. "It is a weakness."

"Not a troublesome one, lass, and many people fear wolves.
I dinnae find the sound of them verra comforting."

She smiled briefly. "The fear of them angers me because it
will not be swayed by reason. Those wolves are no threat to
me. I know that. And yet, I still feel afraid each time they call
out. It is senseless, and I hate that."

"Those fears are indeed the hardest to tolerate. Everyone has
one he must deal with."

"You need not lie to comfort me. I find it hard to believe
that you suffer from such a weakness."

"I will confess that I havenae faced it yet." He moved his
sword to his other side so that there was no chance that she
would roll onto it in the middle of the night. "It could be hidden

by pride or vanity, or I simply havenae done or seen what is needed to bring it forward. Howbeit, I truly believe that we each have a fear like that, a fear that willnae heed reason and fact."

"If it will not heed reason or fact, then how can one ever conquer it?"

"One doesnae." He grinned when she cursed, then grew serious. "Ye shouldnae let it plague ye so. If one must be blindly afraid of something, then wolves are a wise choice. Lass, it isnae the fear that is the weakness, but how ye act when ye must truly face it."

"Then I have failed that test, for I am here, cowering behind you."

"Nay, beside me." He laughed when she swatted him on the arm. "Ye havenae truly faced it, lass. Ye can but hear the wolves in the distance, so 'tis no real crime to let your fear have its reign. The true test of courage comes when ye must confront them, and what ye do then decides whether or not ye or someone else dies."

"I pray that day never comes," she whispered, shivering at the mere thought of it.

"Sleep, lass. The beasts willnae trouble us this night."

Gisele nodded and closed her eyes. The wolves did not grow silent, but she knew she would have no trouble sleeping. She was not sure if Nigel's assurances or his presence at her side calmed her fears the most, but either reason still left her feeling very disappointed in herself. After being alone and caring for herself for nearly a year, she had thought she was strong enough and capable enough to endure alone, to survive anything with no one's help. It troubled her to discover that she might have been wrong or just vain, for she could still have a long fight ahead of her and might not always have Nigel at her side. As sleep weighted her body, she decided that she would worry about it later.

Nigel heard her breathing grow slow and quiet, and softly cursed. It could prove to be a very long night. He could understand her fear. He did not like to hear the wolves, either. That sound meant that he might be wrong to think the forest was safer than the open road. Then he shook his head, abruptly dismissing that concern. There was only a small chance of confronting an animal that could hurt him or Gisele, but a very good chance of meeting with a DeVeau or someone who hungered after the bounty if he and Gisele did not stay hidden as long as possible. It was still a good plan to keep their forays into the more settled areas to as few as possible.

When she murmured in her sleep and moved closer, her lithe body touching his side, Nigel closed his eyes and struggled to rein in his errant desires. She was not inviting him to take her into his arms, just blindly seeking his warmth. He was a little alarmed and somewhat surprised at how quickly and strongly his passion soared in response to such an innocent touch. It also made him all the more eager to make love to her. If she could stir him so when she was asleep and unwilling, he could only imagine how she could make him feel if she were awake and eager. He silently laughed. If he kept thinking like that, it was indeed going to be a very long night.

Six

Warmth surrounded Gisele, and she huddled closer to it. She felt comforted and safe, just as she used to when, as a small child, she crawled into her grandmother's bed. Her grandmother had always been ready to listen to her, to soothe her fears, and to believe in her. It was so nice to have her grandmother back.

As Gisele became more awake, more alert to her surroundings, she realized that something was wrong with her pleasant dream. The body she was curled up to was hard, not soft. The arms wrapped around her were big and strong, not those of an aging woman. There was no scent of roses, long her favorite flower. And her grandmother had never moved her small, frail hands over her back in such a way.

The moment she became aware of the fact that she was in Nigel's arms, Gisele was reluctant to open her eyes. It felt good. The warmth of his lips as he lightly brushed kisses over her face and neck stirred her blood. His strong hands moved slowly, gently, over her body in a way that tempted her to press closer to him. If she opened her eyes she would have to acknowledge that she was awake, that she was willingly letting him move against her in a way that left no doubt about what he wanted from her. It was nicer to pretend that she still lingered within a dream. When he covered her mouth with his she welcomed his kiss even as she wondered how long she could savor it this time before the fear returned.

Nigel fought for the strength to proceed slowly. Gisele was

warm, willing, and—he was certain—wide awake. He did not want to do anything that would stir up the terror he had glimpsed in her eyes the last time they had kissed. That fear had been bred in her by brutality. Nigel prayed that gentleness would keep it chained, and let passion rule.

When he first heard the sound, he ignored it. Gisele tasted so sweet and felt so good in his arms that he did not want to allow anything to distract him. His instincts, however, sharpened by years of battle, refused to allow him to be so foolish. Their lives depended on him being alert and prepared to act. It took every scrap of his willpower to do so, but he pulled away from Gisele and sat up.

Gisele found herself cast aside so abruptly that she felt cold, bereft. She had not yet felt any fear, so she knew the sudden ending of the embrace was not caused because she had somehow, pushed him away or resisted him. It was very confusing to be kissed passionately by a man one moment and then watch him buckle on his sword the next. If this was how Nigel intended to seduce her, Gisele doubted they would ever become lovers.

"Get up, lass," Nigel ordered even as he swiftly rolled up his bedding.

Without hesitation, Gisele did as he said. The tone of his voice demanded obedience. Instinct also told her that this was not the time to take offense at that tone. She just wished she knew what had spurred him into this sudden decamping.

As she finished securing her saddlepack on her horse, Gisele got the answer to why they were hurrying so. There was no mistaking the sound of horsemen approaching through the wood. Even as she mounted her horse, she stared at Nigel with a mixture of awe and astonishment. How had he heard the men and realized that they were a threat so much sooner than she had? In truth, she was still not sure the approaching horsemen *were* a threat. She opened her mouth to ask a few questions, but Nigel just grinned and slapped the rump of her horse, sending the animal out of the clearing at a fast trot.

Gisele risked one quick look behind her as they rode away. The riders she had heard were just coming into sight, and there was no mistaking the DeVeau colors. She could not believe they had found her, and began to fear that there was no escaping pursuit—perhaps no escaping death, either.

The sun was high in the sky before Nigel allowed them to stop by a small brook. As he watered the horses, Gisele stole a moment of privacy and performed a hasty *toilette*. She could not recall escape ever being so exhausting, and began to think that Nigel was right. The DeVeaux had not really thought she could elude them for very long, and so had not tried very hard to hunt her down. Now the chase had truly begun. Gisele was not sure she could survive it all the way to Scotland.

"Dinnae fret yourself, lass," Nigel said as Gisele knelt by the brook and refilled their waterskins. "We will shake these dogs off our tail ere the day is o'er."

"You sound very certain of that," she said, as she hung her waterskin over her saddlehorn. "These dogs could easily run me to death."

"Nay, lass, ye are stronger than that."

"Am I? And, before we begin to ride again, could you tell me how you knew they were near at hand?"

Nigel shrugged. "Smelled them?"

"I begin to think you have a nose stronger than the best hunting dog in my father's pack."

He laughed softly as he mounted and waited for her to do the same. "I dinnae ken how I knew. At times, I just ken that danger approaches. When challenged, I fear I have no sensible explanation."

"Do you have visions?" she asked as she nudged her horse to follow his.

"Nay, I am nay gifted with the sight. 'Tis as if some unseen hand gives me a wee shake, as if some wee voice whispers to me to take heed. This morning I wasnae listening or watching anything but you," he said, glancing at her as he spoke and smiling at her blushes, "yet I was suddenly alert to the danger coming our way. I would say that I heard a sound, for I truly thought I did, yet the riders were too far away for anyone to hear. I ken that now."

"Someone watches over you."

"It would seem so, although I am awed by the loyalty of that unseen ally. I havenae been much worth saving for many a year."

Gisele felt a twinge of sympathy for him, then told herself not to be such a fool. He was a grown man. He had chosen his path. She did concede that he deserved some praise for finally seeing how deep he had sunk into the mire. And, although she might not agree with all he had done, she had no trouble in sympathizing with a broken heart.

"It might be that unseen ally who finally pulled you out of the quagmire you had sunk into," she suggested.

"Aye, it might have been. And, who is to say that, mayhap, saving your bonny head wasnae why he saved mine."

She laughed softly and shook her head. "I cannot believe your angel works to save your life just so that you may save my unworthy hide from my enemies."

"Ah, weel, since we are both so unworthy perhaps 'tis an angel who works his wonders out of pity."

"How very sad," Gisele murmured. Then she laughed. "Whatever causes you to be so quick to sense danger, I pray it does not desert you. You are right. The DeVeaux are now most ardent in their pursuit. If something had not warned you of those men approaching we would have been an easy kill."

Nigel simply nodded in agreement with that grim truth. She had not reproached him for not keeping a closer watch, but she did not need to. He was doing it himself, thoroughly and passionately. It had been foolish and dangerous to become so completely distracted. He wondered if he already depended too much upon his strange gift, a gift that could desert him as quickly as it had come to him on the day he had been knighted. It had weakened, even failed him, from time to time, as if to scold him for his carelessness and arrogance. Using his own wits and skill he had escaped danger then, but now it was not just his own life at risk. He had sworn upon his honor to protect Gisele, and he needed to do a better job.

"Do you think we have lost them?" she asked, interrupting his self-castigation.

"Nay, we have just put some distance between us and them," he replied. "If we can hold that distance for a while longer, then I will steal some of that precious time to try to hide our trail."

"Let us pray that one of them does not share your gift for sniffing out the enemy," she said quietly, chancing one look behind her before she followed Nigel in nudging her horse to a faster pace.

Gisele grew silent, all her thoughts and strength used for one thing only—eluding the DeVeaux. When Nigel took the time to disguise their trail she nervously stood watch. Although she had been successful in her escape for nearly a year, the chase was growing so fierce she began to feel helpless. The fact that she really needed Nigel to keep her free and alive also made her feel helpless, for she had now lost what few choices she had had. With each step they took, each time he saved her life and kept her out of her enemy's hands, she became more dependent upon the man, and Gisele found that somewhat alarming. What would happen to her if she lost Nigel, either through death or injury or in finding some proof of her occasional fear that he would betray her as so many others had?

The only way to soothe those fears, she decided, was to learn all she could for as long as she was with Nigel. Instead of simply allowing him to lead, she would closely watch everything he did. She had no hope of being suddenly blessed with his strange gift of sensing danger long before anyone else could, but she could learn all of his skills. If fate were unkind enough to leave her alone again, she needed to know how to follow a trail, to best choose a hiding place, and hide her own trail from those who pursued her. That would at least give her a fighting chance against her enemies.

Throughout the afternoon they played a tense game of hide-and-seek with the DeVeaux. They spent so much time hiding their trail that Gisele was surprised the DeVeaux were not now in front of them instead of still dogging their heels. Just once did they draw near enough for her to see them, yet Nigel acted as if at any moment the DeVeaux would burst through the surrounding trees and cut them dead.

At only one time during the afternoon did they take what might be called a rest. They paused so that Nigel might hide their trail yet again and try to lay a false one. Gisele tried very hard to pay close attention, thinking the trick a good one to know, but slumped against her mount, surrendering to her weariness. Nigel suddenly appeared and, without a word, dragged her into a cluster of boulders at the base of a hill. There he secured their horses, then pushed and pulled her up the hill until they reached a smaller grouping of rocks.

"Are they here?" she asked when he pushed her inside and tugged her down with him as he crouched behind one of the larger rocks.

"Nay, not yet," he replied in a tense whisper, not taking his gaze from the trail they had just deserted.

"Then why are we hiding?" she asked in an equally soft voice. "Why do we not just ride away?"

"I need to see how easily they can be fooled."

She thought that was a useful thing to know, and started to rise up enough to peer over the rock, then gave up. As she rested against the rock and closed her eyes she decided Nigel would be a better judge of such things, anyway. There were still several hours of daylight left, several more long, exhausting hours of running and hiding. If she were going to survive it, she felt that a little rest was far more important than seeing for herself if the DeVeaux could be fooled into heading the wrong way.

It seemed as if she had only just closed her eyes when she felt Nigel shaking her awake. "Cease, I am awake now," she grumbled as she rubbed her eyes. "Are they gone?"

"Aye," he replied as he pulled her to her feet and led her down the hill. "For a moment I feared one sharp-eyed mon had seen our horses, but he hadnae. They just rode along the trail I laid for them."

"Then we are safe." She could not fully hide a grimace as she pulled her stiff body into her saddle and nudged her horse into following Nigel.

"Aye, for the moment. 'Twill take them a wee while to see that that trail goes nowhere. I hope to regain the time and the distance we lost in making it."

"I thought you were trying to shake them free."

"I was. I am. But one shouldnae rely on such a trick working that weel. They have held fast to our trail for this long. That means that at least one of them has some skill."

Gisele did not find that news very comforting. She wanted reassurances. She wanted to be told that their enemies were gone, well and truly lost in the wilderness, never to haunt them again. As she struggled to quietly follow Nigel, Gisele wondered if he grew as weary of this game as she did.

When Nigel finally chose a campsite for the night, Gisele nearly cheered aloud. She was weary to the bone and not at all sure where they were after all the twists and turns Nigel had indulged in to elude the DeVeaux. After they had spent from dawn to dusk running for their lives, she also wondered how and when Nigel had decided they were safe enough to stop for the night.

She tended to her horse and slipped into the shelter of the surrounding wood for a moment of privacy. As she spread her bed out she glanced at the fire Nigel had built, and frowned. It was a small fire, well sheltered by encircling stones, but such a light could still be easily seen from a distance in the night. When he returned from stealing a moment of privacy for himself, Gisele sat down on her bedding and looked at him. She blithely ignored his brief but telling glance at her bed, which she had spread out on the same side of the fire as his.

"Are you certain we should have a fire?" she asked. "Welcome though it is, is it not a beacon for our enemies to follow?"

"They are too far away to see this wee light," he replied.

Gisele blinked slowly, and stared at him hard for a long moment. "And just when did you decide they were a safe distance away?"

"Not many moments after they hied off down my false trail." He watched her closely as he set out the remainder of the rabbit, the last of their bread, and a small chunk of cheese. He suspected she was angry, but he was not sure why she should be.

"Then why have you made us ride so hard and fast for hours?" Gisele grabbed a share of the food and struggled against the urge to strike him.

"I felt it best that we put as many miles as we could between us and them."

As she chewed on the stale bread, she fought to control her anger. He was right. It *was* wise to put as much distance as possible between themselves and the people who were so eager to kill her. She was achingly tired, and she dearly wanted to blame someone for that. Nigel was not the one, however. The one who deserved her fury was far beyond her reach. She was going to have to try to accept her lot with more grace and patience.

"I ask your pardon, Sir Murray," she said quietly as she accepted the wineskin he held out to her and took a small drink, a little dismayed at how nearly empty it was. "I am tired, and am in an ill temper."

"That is easy to understand, lass."

"It may be, but you do not deserve the sharp edge of my tongue. It is not your fault that I ache and am enduring a miserable ride across France. I but search for someone to pay for this unjust discomfort I am suffering, and there is no one. The man who set me on this much cursed path is dead, and beyond the reach of my curses."

He patted her shoulder in a brief gesture of sympathy. "If justice has been served, lass, your husband is suffering dearly, enduring far more torment and torture than ye could e'er mete out."

"Do not be so certain. I can mete out a great deal." She weakly returned his grin.

" 'Twill soon be over."

"Will it, or will I simply be further away than I have been before now?" She sighed and held up her hand when he started to speak. "Do not trouble yourself to try to soothe my ill humor. That is all it is, an ill humor brought on because I am tired and cannot have what I want."

"And what do ye want, Gisele?" Nigel asked softly.

"I want to go home." She grimaced. *"Merde,* I sound like a small child, but there is the truth of it. I want to go home. I want to sleep in my own warm, soft bed, bathe whenever the mood overcomes me, and eat whatever and whenever I want. I want to have no more reason to feel sorry for myself. And, for all of my complaining, I do recall that you suffer the same as I. I want that to stop, too. You deserve this no more than I do."

"But I am hardened to these discomforts, and ye arenae. I should try harder to remember that."

"Non, do not change what you are doing and must continue to do to keep us alive," she said firmly. "For it *is* us now, not just me. The DeVeaux are hunting me, but they would kill you without hesitation, either because you stood in their way or because you have helped me. I cannot swear that I will not again whimper over my pains or feel sorry for myself, but you must pay it no heed. Running for one's life is much exhausting, and I do not often behave well or with any wit when I am so tired."

"Few of us do, lass. Ye can rest this night, for we have lost that pack of dogs."

"How can you be so certain? They found us, and I would never have believed they would."

Nigel shrugged. "I dinnae have a good answer for how they found us. They were lucky, and we were unlucky. It may be no more than that. I didnae hide our trail weel. I sought distance o'er secrecy. Now I will pay more heed to secrecy." He smiled gently when she hastily raised a hand to cover a wide yawn. "Rest, wee Gisele. It has been a long day."

She sprawled on her bedding and weakly wrapped herself up in her thin blanket. "And there are many more long days ahead, are there not, Sir Murray?"

"Some, aye," he replied as he settled down on his bed. " 'Tis getting into and out of a port that will prove the hardest."

Gisele cursed softly. "Of course. The DeVeaux will have them all watched much closely."

"Verra closely."

"Pardon?"

"Not much closely, verra closely."

"This English is not an easy language."

"Ye speak it verra weel, far better than I can speak your language. Who taught it to you?"

"My *grandmère*. She was from Wales." Gisele lightly touched the amulet she wore.

"That explains the odd lilt to your words. Ye have the hint of the French to your words, but I did puzzle o'er that other note I could hear." He looked at the ornate medallion she idly stroked. "She gave you that?"

"*Oui.* She said the entwined circles of silver were formed by her father's father, or even the father before that. She was not completely sure. The seven garnets mark the seven sons he was blessed with. *Grandmère* said it would bring me good fortune."

"I think it has. Ye have survived a year despite being hunted down by a verra powerful and verra rich clan. There is good fortune many would envy."

"Then I pray it continues to bless us," she murmured and closed her eyes, unable to keep them open a moment longer. "If you have any more questions to ask of me, Sir Murray, I fear they must wait until the morrow."

Nigel laughed softly when she almost immediately fell asleep, then grew solemn as he lightly brushed a dusting of dirt from her soft cheek. She was a strong little woman, enduring a lot, but he was not sure how much more she could tolerate. There was little choice, however. He hated to see her so weary and sore, but he did not wish to see her die, either, and that was the fate awaiting her if the DeVeaux caught up with them. As he closed his eyes and welcomed a much needed sleep, he swore that he would gift her with every comfort as soon as they reached Scotland. He also swore that he would do what her own family seemed incapable of or unwilling to do—free her from the DeVeaux's blind and unending thirst for revenge.

Seven

"Are you certain this is wise?" Gisele asked as she and Nigel paused on a hillside and looked down on the village below.

She was still sore from their daylong flight from the DeVeaux, one night of rest not enough to fully replenish her strength. Fear also held her back. Her enemies had drawn very close to her and Nigel yesterday. She did not wish to give them another chance to catch her, and entering a busy village seemed to promise to do just that. Gisele was not sure they had any choice, however.

"We need supplies, lass," Nigel said. " 'Tis the wrong time of the year to glean all we need from the land."

"I know, and in the last few years there has not been much left to glean, anyway. The soldiers take it all."

Nigel sighed and nodded as he led them down the hill. "The army can be verra greedy. I have seen the men take all a land has to offer, leaving nothing for the poor souls who live there. It is one of the sadder consequences of war."

"And this country has been scarred by war time and time and time again. It is unending." She shook her head. "I do not understand why it continues, although men always have a ready answer, speaking boldly of honor, bravery, rightful kings, and on and on. My grandmother once said that men are more easily offended than some withered, old, too pious nun with the bile."

For one long moment Nigel struggled to look at her sternly. The woman should not speak so insultingly about men. It could cause her a great deal of trouble. Men did not take kindly to such

Hannah Howell

ridicule. Then he laughed, almost able to hear the old woman's sharp voice.

"Aye, lass," he said, as he shared a smile with her, "sometimes it does seem exactly like that." He grew serious as he reined to a halt before the stables at the edge of the village. " 'Tis a shame that men tend to kill people when they are in the midst of a dark pout. In my land it becomes a feud that is passed from son to son and becomes a bloody heritage."

"Did your family suffer from such a tragedy?"

"Almost, but the truth was revealed and the bloodletting ceased."

Before she could ask him any more he dismounted and moved to speak to the stabler. Gisele felt uneasy, but when Nigel signaled her to dismount she did so without question. She had to trust someone at some time. Nigel seemed to be a good choice to start with. It did make her nervous to leave their horses in the hands of a stranger, however. That could make a swift escape a little difficult.

"Dinnae look so fearful, lass," Nigel said quietly as he took her by the arm and led her into town. "I cannae promise that we are completely safe, but I dinnae have any feeling that danger lurks around the next corner."

"You do not smell any enemies?" She tried to walk like a boy but some of the sharp looks she got told her that she might not be succeeding.

"Nay, I dinnae smell anything. Lass, the horses need to be reshod. They may last a day or all the way to Donncoille, my family's keep in Scotland, but we could also have one of our mounts begin limping but a mile outside of the village."

"They are that worn?"

"Aye, they are."

"Then they must be tended to. Lingering here may be dangerous, but trying to flee the DeVeaux on a lame horse would be more so." She looked around. "It appears to be a prosperous village, as yet unscarred by this newest war, so we should be able to find all we need." She frowned as he moved toward a tiny bakery. "Do you want me to talk to the merchants?"

"I can speak the language."

"I know, but you have confessed that you find it difficult to speak it in a way all can understand and that you often find it difficult to catch every word when we speak quickly."

"All of that is true, but I would feel better if I did it. Ye may look like a lad if one but peeks quickly, but I dinnae think ye will pass a verra close study." He smiled faintly. "We rough-speaking Scots arenae such a strange sight any longer. Wait here, lass, and dinnae speak to anyone."

Gisele muttered a curse, but she did as she was ordered to. Even with her cap on she had begun to realize that her disguise was not as good as she had thought it was. Lurking silently in the shadows was probably the safest thing for her to do. She was beginning to think there was no way she could truly hide. As a woman she had been easily seen and easily remembered. She was not really having any better luck as a boy. There did not seem to be any other choices, however, except hiding deep in a cave until someone proved her innocence or the DeVeaux forgot about her and found someone else to torment. Gisele did not believe either would happen. She could not survive in a cave without some help, and the DeVeaux were well known to have very long memories.

A young man stepped out of the inn across the badly rutted road and abruptly captured all of Gisele's wandering attention. She tensed, torn between hope and fear. There was no mistaking her slender, almost beautiful, cousin David. What she was not sure of was whether or not she should approach him. He had not rushed to her defense when her troubles had begun, but she could not believe that he would hand her over to the DeVeaux, either. When he started to walk away, she impulsively hurried over to him, catching up to him just outside of a small, dark alley.

"Here, boy, what game do you play?" David demanded when Gisele shoved him into the alley.

"David, it is your cousin, Gisele." She yanked off her cap and ruffled her curls. "Do you not remember me, cousin?"

She waited, standing stiffly before him as he stared at her. Suddenly, he gaped and grabbed her by the shoulders. After a long moment of silence, Gisele shifted on her feet and tugged free of his hold.

"Are you completely mad?" he said, his voice hoarse and softened by shock.

"I was beginning to fear that you were. You were staring at me as if I were some vision you were ill-pleased to see," she grumbled as she tugged her cap back on.

"What have you done to your hair, and why are you dressed like that?"

"I never thought you lacking in wit, cousin. I am trying to look like a boy." She glared at him when a look of pure derision settled on his beautiful face. "These clothes belonged to Guy's page."

"I am not surprised that fool Guy is behind this madness." He paced back and forth for a moment before facing her again. "You nearly got Guy killed."

"Ah, so you have spoken to our sweet-tongued cousin, Maigrat."

David grinned briefly, then frowned, dragging his long fingers through his thick black hair. "She has no great love for you, that is true enough. She does not like people who speak their minds as sharply as she does, especially if what they say disputes her truths."

"I may have disagreed with her a time or two," she said, ignoring the mocking sound he made, "but that is not reason enough to decry me as a murderer, or believe that I would do anything that would hurt Guy."

David put his arm around her shoulders and gave her a brief hug. "I found it hard to believe that you would hurt Guy, and he was most adamant in his support of you."

"He is well?"

"Almost healed enough to walk out of Maigrat's *demanse,* just as he threatens to every day."

Gisele laughed and then watched David closely as she said, "Guy was one of the few people who believed in my innocence."

He blushed and took a step back. "I wish I could deny that, but I fear you speak the ugly truth. The only defense we all have, and it is a very weak one, is that you had made your loathing of the man evident to anyone who would listen to you, and you often threatened him with some heinous punishments. There is no pardon for us. You should never have been given to him. We were blinded by power and wealth, I think. No one of such a high standing had ever joined our family before, and we hungered for it."

"You keep saying we and us. Do you speak for the others?"

"Most of them. A few, like Maigrat, have their own reasons to refuse to change their minds, and I fear that refusal has more to do with their dislike of you than the truth." David watched her a little warily as he said, "You can be curt, Gisele, and are cursed with a sharp, bitter tongue that can stir some people's anger and dislike."

"They are but humorless, and I have no need of them. Is my family going to help me now?" She waited tensely for his reply, knowing she had let her hopes spring to life and afraid that they were about to be crushed again.

"We have already begun to try to find the truth," he replied then returned her impulsive hug. "We have also been trying to find you. You must come with me now. You can no longer be allowed to run about France alone and unprotected."

"Alone?" Gisele frowned as she moved away from him. "Did Guy tell you that I was alone?"

"He said something about a Scotsman, a knight who survived by selling his sword. He has obviously deserted you. One can expect little else from a man of his ilk."

"No, Nigel would not desert me." Gisele felt as surprised by her sharp defense of Nigel as David looked. "He is gathering some fresh supplies and having our horses tended to."

"You are still with the man? That will not do, cousin. You cannot travel alone with a man, especially one no one knows. I will pay this man his fee and send him on his way."

Gisele stared at her cousin, eager to tell him that he was a complete idiot, but knowing that this was not the time for an argument. Here was a trouble she had not foreseen, and she cursed her blindness. Men were always eager to defend their women against the sinful thoughts and inclinations of other men, and since he had done nothing to protect her from her brutal husband guilt could easily make David very hard to turn aside. Nigel would soon be looking for her, and Gisele was sure her cousin would not be greeting Nigel cordially when he met him. Gisele lightly chewed on her bottom lip and wondered how she could pull Nigel out of the confrontation she had unthinkingly thrust him into.

Nigel stepped out of the baker's too warm shop, took a deep breath of the cool outside air, and immediately knew that something was wrong. He felt the first stirrings of panic when he could not see Gisele where he had left her. His hand on his sword, he began to search the small village. He stopped and stared when he found her just inside a narrow, shadowed alley not far from the inn.

The young man she stood with presented no clear threat, yet Nigel disliked him immediately. He inwardly grimaced, ruefully admitting, that some of that dislike was born of jealousy. The youth was tall, lean, dark-haired, and dark-eyed, and even Nigel could recognize his beauty. None of that diminished the danger Gisele could be putting herself in, however. Her safety depended heavily on her remaining hidden. When Nigel heard the youth say he would pay him and send him on his way, dismissing him like the basest of mercenaries, he stepped forward.

"Keep your wee purse tied to your belt, laddie," Nigel said as he stood next to Gisele. "I ask no coin for protecting the lass."

Gisele looked from Nigel to David and inwardly cursed. Both men were tense, their expressions ones of cold anger, and their hands resting on their swords. One wrong word or step, and she would have to watch her protector and her cousin try to cut each other down. Men, she decided, were very odd creatures, and even these two had to know that no one would gain from such a confrontation, least of all her, the one they both claimed they wanted to protect.

"Nigel," she placed a hand on his arm, "this is my cousin,

Sir David Lucette. David, this is Sir Nigel Murray, the man who has gallantly offered to protect me from my enemies."

"Aye, doing what her kinsmen dared not," Nigel said, then grunted softly when Gisele nudged him hard in the side.

"Her family can care for her now," David said in halting English, easing his taut stance only slightly when he saw how Gisele was glaring at him.

"Ye have ignored her peril for nearly a year," Nigel responded in a cold voice. "Ye left her alone to fight her enemies and try to prove her innocence. And now ye want me to cast aside my pledge and just leave her in your inept care? Nay, I think not."

"This is a woman of good birth and honorable name. She cannot ride over the land alone, with a man not related to her by blood."

Before Nigel could respond to that, Gisele cursed and placed herself directly between David and Nigel. "Must you behave like ill-weaned children fighting over a toy?"

"Ah, lass," Nigel said, placing his hand over his heart, "ye wound me. Ye should have more care for a mon's pride."

Gisele ignored his foolishness. It had not taken her long to see that Nigel could be almost nonsensical at the oddest of times. The look on her cousin's face, however, told her that he was completely confused. Gisele idly wondered if that was why Nigel did it. A confused foe was probably easier to defeat.

"Cousin," she said in what she hoped was a calm but firm voice, "Sir Murray has sworn upon his honor to be my protector."

"Gisele, I understand that we have failed you," David said in French as he took Gisele's hands between his. "We have insulted you with our suspicions and disbelief. It is all different now. Let us care for you."

Nigel tensed. He found it hard to closely follow the youth's rapid French, but understood enough to know that David was trying a gentle persuasion to take Gisele away. There was not much he could do if she decided to return to her family, to accept their belated offer of help. He could not even be sure if his protests would be born of an honest belief that she was safer with him, or out of a fear of losing her.

It was hard but Gisele stared into her cousin's beautiful, be-seeching eyes and knew she would say no. She just wished she knew all the reasons why she was about to turn her back on the chance to reunite with her family. They had hurt her with their betrayal, but here was a chance to heal those wounds and she was going to refuse it. Gisele had the unsettling feeling that, muddled up with all of the very good reasons to stay with Nigel, was simply a strong reluctance to leave him. She prayed she was not about to make a serious misstep just for the sake of a hand-some face and sweet kisses.

"Non, David. I will stay with Sir Murray," she replied, speak-ing in English so as not to exclude Nigel from the discussion, knowing that was what her cousin had been trying to do. "I chose this path and I will stay on it."

"I swear you will not be treated in the same shameful manner you have been," David replied in English, his reluctance to use the language clear in his deep voice.

"I believe you. That does not matter."

"Are you certain you are not allowing hurt feelings to guide your steps?"

She smiled briefly and shrugged. "I will not deny that those feelings are there, but they do not lead me. This is for the best, believe me." Gisele could tell by the dark look on David's face that he thought she and Nigel were already lovers, but was prob-ably not sure who to blame for that. After all, she was no longer some naive virgin. "We have a good plan. You need not worry about me."

"Not worry? How many times must I say it? You are traveling all over the land dressed as a boy with a man none of us know. Do you have no thought to how you are blackening your name?"

Gisele laughed—a short, bitter sound. "Blackening my name? For a year now even some of my own family has decried me as a murderer, a woman who not only killed her husband but mu-tilated him. I doubt what I do now could stain my precious name any deeper than that." She took a deep breath to steady herself. "Sir Nigel is taking me to a safe place. That is what is needed now."

"We could find you a safe place, cousin," David said, but his deep voice carried a hint of uncertainty.

"Non, you cannot, and we both know it. The DeVeaux watch every member of our family very closely. What happened to poor Guy is hard proof of that. There is nowhere amongst you that I can truly hide. Whomever I abide with I will put in danger. Do you truly wish to pull our whole family into a war with the De-Veaux? A war that could easily set you against the king himself? I did not think so," she murmured when he frowned.

"But, now that we have come to our senses we can do nothing else except help you, or we risk our honor."

"Then do help me. Find out who truly killed my husband. Now is the perfect time to do that. All DeVeau eyes are turned upon me, and all of their strength and interest is aimed at me. That should give someone a very good chance of discovering exactly what happened to my husband."

"It will not be an easy task," David muttered as he rubbed his chin.

"Non, it will not be. If it were easy I would have found out the truth myself by now. I have had little chance to ferret out the real murderer myself, and now that the DeVeaux offer a hefty purse for my miserable head I will have no time at all. I have no time for anything except running and hiding."

"That is no life for a woman."

"Non, it is not, so find out who really cut up my loathsome worm of a husband and free me from it."

She waited with some apprehension as David considered her words. He could cause her a great deal of trouble if he refused to accept her decision, and she felt she had more than enough to deal with already. Although a part of her was still not completely sure she could trust Nigel, she knew she could not leave him. Every instinct told her to hold firmly to the path she was on, but she did not want to push away the family that had finally come to her aid.

"I do not like this," David muttered, sending Nigel a brief, hard glare before tightly hugging Gisele. "I will honor your wishes. Stay with the man, and your family shall set its mind and heart to getting you exonerated."

"Ye made the wise choice," Nigel said as he tugged Gisele to his side.

"I do not believe I was given much of a choice at all," David replied, fixing his gaze on Gisele after one brief glare toward Nigel. "I hope you do not regret this, cousin." He bowed and strode away.

Gisele sighed, suddenly unsure of herself, but she repressed the urge to call her cousin back. She could not let herself waver simply because she missed her family. Although she was ready to forgive them, she could not really ignore the fact that Nigel had been more steadfast than they had. David had assured her that they had joined her cause now, but a lingering hurt and an all too clear memory of their betrayal kept her from fully believing him. She was fighting for her life. She could not afford to gamble on anyone or anything.

She looked up at Nigel, who was watching her closely, and decided that she had indulged in all the gambling she dared to for now, and that was putting her trust in him. David's complaint that she was hurting her reputation by traveling with Nigel was foolish, but he had been right about one thing. No one really knew Nigel Murray. He was a Scot who sold his sword to the French and, amongst his fellow soldiers there were few who spoke ill of him. It really was not much to bet one's life on.

"Are ye regretting your decision, lass?" Nigel asked, fighting to hide the unease he felt. Her gaze was intent, considering, and he feared she was about to change her mind. "We could easily call your cousin back," he said, hoping she would never know how hard it was for him to choke out those words.

"Non." She frowned, then shook her head. "This is best. I but faltered for a moment."

"It is nay an easy choice to make."

"Non, it is not. I have missed my family. As I told you, I dearly want to go home. Not yet. And not with him."

"Ye dinnae think he spoke the truth?"

"Oh, he spoke the truth as he sees it. It is not him I doubt. In truth, I do not wish to doubt the others, but I cannot stop myself."

He gently tucked a stray curl back up under her cap. "They turned their backs on ye when ye most needed them. 'Tis a hard betrayal, one not easily set aside just because they say they are sorry for it."

She smiled at him, touched by his understanding. "*Non,* it is not. I was torn. wanted to believe in him, to trust in my family again, and then felt like the basest of traitors because I could not, not with a whole heart."

"Ye dinnae need to don the hair shirt o'er it, Gisele. They may be kinsmen, but they betrayed you, and they must earn your trust again."

"And now, in the midst of fleeing for my life, is not the time to play out that game."

She stared in the direction David had gone and fought a sudden urge to cry. She could see her home, the mossy stone walls and high towers. She could almost smell the roses her grandmother had taken such care of, of which she had taken charge when the old woman had died. The urge to return home and curl up in her soft bed was so strong she ached with it, but she had to fight it. At home there was no safety for her, and she could easily bring danger to those she loved.

Gisele smoothed her hand over Nigel's sleeve, then crossed her arms over her chest to stop herself from clinging to him for the strength she lacked. She had refused David's offer—in part, because it would put her family in peril—yet she chose to put Nigel there. It made no sense, and she was suddenly ashamed of herself. He had willingly offered to be her protector and take her to safety in Scotland, but he had not truly known how much trouble that would bring down on his head. Since she had just been given a choice it was past time she gave him one, she decided, and she took a deep breath and looked at him.

"I was just thinking," she began.

"Ah, and why do I get the feeling that I willnae like it?"

She just frowned at him and doggedly continued, "I speak of not wishing to endanger my family, that I think of their safety, too, when I refuse to rejoin them. I also think of your safety, Sir Nigel."

"Now I am *sure* I willnae like this."

"May I be allowed to finish?" When he feigned a bow she said, "I was just blessed with a choice, and I believe it is past time I offered you one. When you first offered to help me you may not have realized how large and deep a quagmire you were stepping into. You now have a better idea of the trouble I bring. I will understand if you wish to leave."

"Ye might, but I wouldnae think many others would," he murmured, smiling faintly, for her taut stance told him she was finding it hard to offer him this chance to step down as her protector. "I gave my word of honor, lass."

"To me, so you can lose none if I say I release you."

"Many might think so, but nay I. I will stay. I said I would get ye to Scotland where ye can safely work to clear your name, and that is what I mean to do."

She was weak with relief, but struggled not to show it. "You are a very stubborn man, Sir Murray."

"That I am." He took her by the arm and led her out of the alley. "I am also most thoughtful, kind, and generous."

"And vain."

"I prefer to think of it as having a simple knowledge of my strengths."

Gisele giggled and shook her head. "A blithe and interesting explanation, but what prompts you to boast so?"

"I have planned a wee surprise for you, lass, and I may be vain but I do think ye will like it."

Eight

Gisele almost moaned aloud with pleasure as she eased her body into the hot water. Nigel had led her into the inn, talked to the innkeeper, and presented her with a room containing a soft bed and a tub that was soon brimming with hot, rose-scented water. She knew his surprise had been conceived even as they had walked out of the alley, but she was not inclined to argue that.

As the innkeeper's wife and daughters had filled the tub with hot water, Gisele had been so eager to climb in that she had barely waited for the door to close behind Nigel before she had begun to shed her clothes. Only briefly did she worry that by revealing she was not a page she was revealing some deep secret. The lack of surprise on the women's faces told her they had already guessed her sex.

"I really need to find out what I am doing wrong," she murmured as she began to wash her hair. "It would be most disappointing to think I cut all of my hair off for no real gain."

She poured water over her hair to rinse away the soap, then groped for the drying cloth the women had left on a stool next to the tub. After she wiped her face she rubbed her hair dry and looked around the room. This had to be costing Nigel a goodly number of his hard-earned coin. It cost to have a room all to one's self, most inns having only one or two. A tub filled with hot water and rose scent was not a luxury many could afford, either. *Or rose-scented soap,* she mused as she sniffed the bar of soap and then began to wash.

The more she considered the matter, the more it troubled her. She realized she had not once given any thought to how they would pay for anything. Since he had been wounded and nearly senseless when they had left him, Gisele doubted that Guy had given Nigel any money, and she had not given him any, either. She did not have any to give. That meant that Nigel was not only risking his life to protect her, but was paying for the privilege.

She looked at her amulet, which she had carefully laid on the stool. She could probably get some money for that. Then she shook her head. She could not bring herself to sell it. Even the thought of it made her shiver. It was all she had left of her grandmother, of the woman who had been more of a mother to her than her own. She would have to find some other way to make recompense to Nigel. Now that her family appeared to have accepted her back into the fold, it should not be too hard to get some money.

Sinking into the water to savor the last of its warmth, she smiled at her own foolishness. It was not just that the amulet was an heirloom that made her so reluctant to part with it. Her grandmother had said that it brought good luck, and Gisele ruefully admitted to herself that she had begun to believe that. She had a feeling that her grandmother was having a fine chuckle over that.

Closing her eyes, she idly wondered what her grandmother would have thought of Nigel, then laughed softly. She felt sure that her grandmother and Nigel would have become fast friends. Her Nana would probably have delighted in the man's odd sense of humor.

A trickle of concern disturbed Gisele's comfort. They had only just escaped capture, spent the whole previous day working to elude the DeVeaux. It did not seem wise to stop so soon for such luxuries as a soft bed and a hot bath. She cursed and forced the thought from her mind. Nigel had done his job well so far.

She would trust him to know what was safe and what was not. She just wished she did not have to keep reminding herself to do that. It seemed disloyal to question his every move. Until she cured herself of the distrust learned over the past year she would just have to make sure that Nigel never saw her doubts. Gisele returned to thoroughly enjoying her bath, telling herself firmly not to worry, that Nigel was keeping a close watch for any trouble.

Nigel cursed and hastily rubbed himself dry. Only briefly did he resent the fact that he was bathing in a cold stream while Gisele was sprawled in a tub of hot water. She deserved the treat he had arranged for her, and needed it more than he did. It had been a hasty decision to stop over at the inn, and an expensive one, but he did not really regret it. There had been such sadness in her eyes after her cousin had walked away that he had felt compelled to do something to lift her spirits.

He shook his head as he put on clean clothes. Uncertainty still plagued him. At one moment he felt that he was right to keep her with him, that it was better for everyone, and then he questioned his reasons. Nigel suspected that would puzzle him for a very long time.

He knelt by the stream and scrubbed out his dirty clothes, praying they would dry overnight. Just as he finished wringing them out, he tensed. Too late he heard the soft footfall behind him. As he slowly rose to his feet he wondered if his gift had finally deserted him, or was trying to teach him another lesson. When he turned around and saw David standing there, he cursed even as he felt relieved. He had not felt any sense of danger because there was none. David might not trust or like him, but he felt sure the man would not hurt him.

"I had thought ye had hied away home," he said as he sat down to lace up his boots.

"I do not leave until the morrow. My horse is being reshod," David replied.

"Ah, so ye are the reason Gisele and I have to wait for the same to be done to our mounts. And so ye thought to take a wee stroll along the water?"

David glared at him. "You leave one thinking that you do not take him seriously as a threat."

"Do I?" Nigel watched him closely as he stood up again. "And are ye a threat, Sir Lucette?"

"I should be—a deadly one, too. I do not believe that you are as safe a haven as my cousin does. She can be most naive from time to time."

"She is a widow, nay a virgin who has no knowledge of men."

"And so you feel she is ripe for the plucking?"

"When ye finally decide to concern yourself about the lass's weel-being, ye get verra heated, dinnae ye?"

David cursed, and paced back and forth on the soft grass for a moment before facing Nigel again. "I only accept such insults because I have the wit to know I deserve them, but 'ware, Sir Nigel, I have never been known to be a patient man. I may deserve the bite of shame, but I will not endure it long. *Oui,* I have failed that girl, as has most of the rest of our family. That is something that must be settled between us and her, not you. It also does not mean that my concern about you is not heart-felt."

"There is no need to be concerned over me."

"Non? Are you about to tell me that you do not lust for the girl?"

Nigel smiled. "Nay. I am nay that big a liar."

He almost laughed when David cursed again. The younger man was easy to torment, and Nigel knew he ought to stop. There might come a time when he needed the good favor of Gisele's kinsmen. On the other hand, he felt David and the others who had turned their backs on Gisele did not deserve much consideration. He did not think he would be as quick to forgive them as Gisele would be, even though he was not sure why it should anger him so.

"Honesty must be praised, I suppose. If you are such a truthful man, then mayhap you will tell me exactly what you plan for my little cousin."

"I dinnae believe it is any of your business, but I plan to get her safely to my keep in Scotland. There she can abide until the injustice she suffers from here has been ended." He pointedly looked David over, then asked, "Do ye think ye can clear her name, and get these DeVeaux carrion off her trail?"

"I have said I would."

"I heard ye. I just wonder why ye think ye can do it now when no one has accomplished the task in nearly a year." He frowned when David blushed. "No one has really tried, have they? They decided on her guilt or innocence, and went no further. What is it about that wee lass that makes ye think she would do that to a mon with no cause?"

David's eyes widened. "You think she did it."

"I am nay sure what I believe about that. I ken only what I have been told and, since I first heard the tale I havenae had the time to seek out the whole truth for myself."

"But why would you work so hard to protect a woman you think killed her husband?"

"Because the bastard deserved all he got and more," Nigel answered coldly.

"Well, he was unkind. We have learned that much."

Nigel laughed harshly. "Unkind? Ye have learned nothing at all."

As succinctly as he could he told the youth all Gisele had told him. He also told David what he had guessed at simply by watching the way Gisele acted at times. It pleased him to see the youth grow pale with horror and fury. David sank down onto the grass and covered his face with his hands. Nigel quietly sat down facing him, patiently waiting for the man to control himself.

"We should have seen it," David finally whispered.

"Someone should have kenned what was going on," Nigel agreed. "Gisele might not have been too clear in her explanations or too exact in her complaints, but the scars are there if one but bothers to look. I saw them, and I dinnae e'en ken the lass, not as her family should have."

"*Non,* not as her family should have. She did not speak to me." David grimaced. "And now I but reach for a way to excuse my own blindness. I cannot be sure I would have heeded her or seen things more clearly than the ones she did turn to. I cannot even be sure that how she was treated would have made much difference, even if we all knew it. *Oui,* some would have cried out, and she and her husband might have been more closely watched, but I do not feel certain that anyone would have tried to take her home again. Bastard though he was, he was her husband. Those are bonds that are not easy to break. In truth, killing him was one of the few ways to do that, and you see what trouble that has wrought."

"Better this than what she was enduring."

"Mayhap. If all of his cruelty had been known, it certainly would not have made us believe in her innocence any more than we did, mayhap even less."

"I fear I will probably ne'er understand how so many of ye could believe it at all. Aye, the lass has a sharp tongue and speaks her mind more than some would find comfortable in a woman, but a killer? Nay, I would ne'er have thought her one. I only doubt now because I ken what she went through. Weel, some of it. I am nay sure she will e'er tell anyone all of it. When a mon treats a woman like that she will either grow weak and terrified and be lost to it all or she will o'ercome that fear and run. And, if there is nowhere to run to I believe she will kill, and I cannae fault her for that."

"*Non,* I do not think I can, either. It will be easier to stop the DeVeaux from trying to kill her if she is truly innocent, however," David drawled, and he smiled briefly, then grew solemn again. "These are not men who will see her killing of that beast as justified, will not see what he did to her as wrong. They are all of the same ilk. We just had not listened, or not believed how evil that ilk was. It will be best if we can find another who did the killing."

"I am nay sure they should suffer, either, but better them than Gisele, if she truly is innocent. She wouldnae stomach ye setting someone on the scaffold in her place unless they deserved to be there." He smiled faintly, rose to his feet, and gave David a hand up. "So ye had better put that thought from your mind. Dinnae rush into some foolish solution. The lass is safe with me."

"Is she? Even if I ignore the fact that you will probably try to seduce the girl."

"Probably?" Nigel murmured.

David ignored him and went on. "There are few places she can hide from the DeVeaux or the ones seeking the huge bounty they have set on her head. I think even some of your countrymen may be tempted by it. And do not think that your plan to take her to Scotland will not be guessed at. It is already known that she rides with a Scotsman."

"It is?" That was not good news. Nigel had hoped that secret would not get out for a little while yet.

"It is. So, if they cannot find her in France they will look elsewhere. They will follow you, or send others after you. The coin offered for her head will only make this hunt grow fiercer each day."

"The bounty is that tempting?"

"Oui, and it may continue to grow. The DeVeaux have more coin than the king."

"Then ye had best get to work, laddie, and prove her innocence. I am returning to the inn. It is nay a good idea to leave her alone for verra long."

"You intend to share that room with her?"

Nigel just smiled at David's outrage. "Aye."

"A gentleman would sleep elsewhere."

"Nay, he wouldnae, unless he had no choice. And, Sir Lucette, 'twill be verra hard to protect her as I must if me and my sword arenae e'en close at hand." He patted the younger man on the shoulder, then started back toward the village. "And I dinnae think I need to tell ye that Gisele has the wit and the strength to cry me a nay if she chooses to. Sleep weel, lad."

Gisele barely had the strength to open one eye when Nigel entered the room. She had waited for him, but soon after her bath she had swiftly grown too tired and had crawled into bed. A light meal had been delivered just before she had fallen completely asleep, and she had roused herself enough to have some food but then hurried back into the soft, warm bed.

"You were gone a very long time," she murmured, watching him as he spread his damp clothing out to dry then sat on the edge of the bed and helped himself to some food.

"Weel, I felt a need to bathe and then met with your cousin again."

"You did not fight, did you?"

"Nay, lass, although I think the lad wished to strike at me a time or two."

"You taunted him."

"A wee bit. He confesses that it is deserved. They should have been there at your side from the start, lass."

She sighed. "I know, and their desertion cut deeply, but I can also understand why they were not. The DeVeaux are nearly as powerful as the king, at least in this province. They are feared by everyone. To stand with me was to stand against them, and few have the stomach or the strength to do that. And one must not forget that the DeVeaux are very close to the king, so if one stands against them one also runs the chance of being seen as standing against the king, too. That is a dangerous place to be."

Nigel nodded, set the tray of food aside, and began to take off his boots. He had not discussed the sleeping arrangements with Gisele, and watched her closely as he prepared for bed. When she did not immediately question him, just closed her eyes, he decided he was safe. In deference to her sense of modesty, he kept his braies on. When he slid into bed beside her he

felt her tense slightly, and inwardly grimaced. He was not going
to win on every count.

"I willnae hurt ye, lass," he whispered, fighting the urge to
pull her into his arms.

"I know. It is not you who make me stiffen with fear. There
has only been one other man who has shared my bed, and he was
not welcome. It has been a long time since he touched me, but
I begin to think the fear he bred in me will live longer than I do."

"Nay. 'Tis just that ye havenae done anything to banish it yet."

She looked at him and frowned. He was right, but she could
not help but wonder why he should concern himself so much
with her fears, their cause, or their strength. Gisele hoped he was
not going to try to seduce her by saying he could cure her. Instinct
told her that he just might be able to, but she realized she wanted
him to desire her for herself, not because it would stroke his
vanity to repair what another man had tried so hard to destroy.

"Lass, ye really must cease to think ill of me so quickly," he
murmured. "Ye are sorely bruising my vanity."

Although she smiled at his nonsense, it made her a little
uncomfortable that he could so easily guess her thoughts. "I
was just hoping that you were not going to claim you could
cure me."

"Ah, it would disappoint you if I tried to seduce ye with that
tale, would it?"

"I think it might. You would show yourself to be not as clever
as I think you are."

Nigel grinned. "Oh, aye, I am clever. Have I nay got ye alone
in a room and in a soft bed?"

"And now you try to make me suspicious. It may be odd, but
I assumed from the start that you meant to share this bed. It
cost you dearly, of that I am sure, and I felt it only fair and
reasonable that you would wish to share in its comfort. And
that recalls me to a matter I wish to discuss with you."

"Ye are about to say something that will annoy me."

"You are a big, strong knight. I suspect you can bear that
burden." She met his narrow-eyed glance with a brief, too sweet

smile. "You are paying for my rescue out of your own purse, are you not?"

"I am not a poor mon," he said.

"It would matter naught to me if you were. I simply do not think it right that you risk your life and empty your purse. I am not poor, either. Sadly, I cannot get my hands on any of my fortune. I will pay you back, however, as soon as I can."

"That is not necessary."

"It is," she said firmly. "Mayhap it is just pride. In truth, I believe that is exactly what it is. It pains me a little that I am unable to settle this matter by myself, that I must depend upon the strength of others to keep myself alive."

He tentatively reached out and smoothed his hand over her shoulder. "Ye are just a wee lass. There is only so much ye can do on your own. Ye have done weel so far. There is no shame in recognizing that the time has come to get some help."

She nodded. "I understand that, but pride can sometimes refuse to heed reason. Allow me this weak salve. I will pay you back all you have needed to spend to get me to Scotland."

"As ye wish."

Nigel decided that now was not the time to argue about that. He also understood how she felt. It had to be difficult to be so completely at the mercy of someone else's good favor, especially when one had survived so long on one's own. It carried the same bitter taste as defeat.

"Why do I have the feeling that you have not really agreed?" Gisele murmured as she closed her eyes.

"Ye worry on things too much, sweeting." He lightly brushed a few stray curls from her forehead. "Rest. That is what ye need. Savor this moment of peace and comfort, and cease looking for troubles and conflicts."

"I do not need to look very hard, or too far."

"If ye keep thinking such dark thoughts ye will ne'er get the sleep ye need."

"And you wish me to cease talking so that you can go to sleep."

"Aye, there is that." He grinned when she laughed softly.

"Sleep safe, Sir Murray."

He decided that was a very good wish, and softly returned it. It would be nice to sleep safe for a change, to not have to keep one eye open. Nigel realized he had grown deeply weary of war, of fighting to stay alive. It was going to be good to be back at Donncoille, back where there were many who were willing to watch his back so that he could rest secure.

It would be good for Gisele, too, he mused as he gently slipped one arm around her. Guy was right. She would not be as safe as he had hoped for. But she would at least be able to sleep secure. He wondered only briefly if it were wrong to bring such trouble to his clan. They would be more than willing to help a woman in such desperate trouble.

Yet again he had evaded another chance to speak of home, to warn Gisele in some small way about what he had left behind. He was courting trouble there, knew that he ought to give Gisele some small hint of why he had left home, but he was a coward. Pride also stopped him. It was embarrassing to know he had fled the land and the people he loved because he wanted his brother's wife and was not sure he could trust himself to behave with honor as long as he was close to her. It was certainly not a confession that would win Gisele to his side, either.

Another reason he held silent was that if he told her the whole truth she was sure to ask questions, and he did not have any answers—none that would soothe the suspicions she was sure to have. When she did find out that he had left Scotland because he was in love with his brother's wife, and that the woman looked a lot like her, Nigel wanted to be able to look Gisele square in the eyes and truthfully swear that it was not why he wanted her. He could not do that yet. What worried him was that he might not be able to do that until he stood at the gates of Donncoille and could look from one woman to the other. And he still dreaded that moment of truth, still feared that he might never be able to say those things to Gisele.

She murmured softly in her sleep and turned toward him,

huddling closer to his warmth. Nigel sighed and wrapped his arms around her. She allowed him these small embraces when she was asleep. It could be a good sign.

The way his body tautened with hunger as he held her close seemed real and honest enough—it was Gisele he saw and Gisele's name upon his lips—but the poison of uncertainty still lingered in his heart. He had never loved a woman as he had loved Maldie, and he could not be sure a man could recover from that.

Until he knew the answer to that he should leave Gisele alone, but Nigel knew he would not do that, either. He liked the feel of her in his arms, liked the taste of her, the smell of her. He wanted to be her lover, wanted to savor her passion, and he knew he would not have the strength to turn her away just because he could not understand his own heart.

There was one other solution to his problem and he inwardly grimaced, feeling the bite of shame that he would even consider it but unable to cast it aside. If he still had not explained everything to Gisele by the time they reached Donncoille, if he still had no honest idea of who held his heart in her small hands, when she saw Maldie and turned to him for an explanation he would lie. He would look her straight in the eyes and tell her whatever she needed to hear. It made him uneasy, and it was far from honorable, but it would be the kindest thing to do. In the end it could come to a choice between maintaining his sense of honor or cruelly hurting Gisele. Faced with that choice, Nigel knew which way he would go. Gisele deserved a little kindness. And if he had taken Gisele as his lover without even knowing if he could truly love her, then he deserved to pay for that.

Nine

Her dream was so nice, so sweet yet exciting, that Gisele did not want to wake up. Nigel was touching her, slowly moving his big, strong hands over her body, and there was no fear, only passion. She knew this was how it was supposed to be, and did not want dark memory to spoil it. Soft lips touched hers, and she clung tightly to the man who held her in his arms. Just once she wanted to taste what the minstrels all sang about.

"Gisele," Nigel whispered against the soft skin of her neck, "look at me."

"Non." She shuddered beneath his touch as he lightly stroked her breast.

"Come, lass, look at me. I want ye to ken who is touching you."

She closed her eyes even tighter and shook her head. "Can you not leave me in the dream?"

"Nay, for that is a lie."

"It is a nice lie." The warmth of his breath caressed her as he laughed against her shoulder.

She slowly opened her eyes. It made her a little uncomfortable to look at the man while he was touching her so intimately, and she wondered why he insisted that she do so. She had been letting him have his way. It seemed to her that it would have been wiser to just let it happen, to not disturb the moment in any way.

"I knew it was you," she said, surprised at how soft and husky her voice was.

"For the moment. Before, with your eyes closed, your thoughts went their own way, slipping into the past and resurrecting all your fears."

"Opening my eyes could resurrect my sense of modesty."

"At least that would be a refusal of me, and not of your ghosts."

Gisele gasped softly as he slid his hands down her back and then pressed her closer. She did not really feel inclined to refuse him, even though she knew honor and modesty demanded it of her. What he said made an odd kind of sense, but she knew it was going to be a struggle to keep her eyes open. With each new feeling that sped through her body she felt compelled to close her eyes, as if by doing so she could savor those feelings more fully.

It surprised her when she moved her body against his, silently asking for something she had thought she would never wish to endure again. She shyly moved her hands over his back, enjoying the feel of hard muscle and smooth skin. Nigel did not remove his braies, however. He made no move at all to try to complete their feverish lovemaking.

Nigel slid his hand up between her thighs, and Gisele cried out in a mixture of shock and delight. He took swift advantage of her parted lips and kissed her. A small voice told her she should be outraged that this man would touch her so intimately, but she ignored it, opening to his touch even as she greedily returned his kiss. She did not understand what he was doing to her, but she liked it too much to turn away from it.

He kissed the hardened tip of her breast, then gently sucked through the thin linen of the shirt she still wore. All the while he continued to stroke her. Gisele kept trying to wrap her body around his, but he still made no attempt to join their bodies. He just kept kissing her and stroking her. She was almost ready to speak, to risk ruining the moment by breaking the silence, when she was suddenly robbed of the wit and the ability to say anything.

Fierce, blinding feelings tore through her body, and she cried out Nigel's name. He replied with a hungry kiss, holding her tightly as her body shuddered. It was a long time before Gisele regained her senses, and then she swiftly began to feel both confused and embarrassed. Nigel still lightly caressed her. She briefly considered breaking free of his hold, then realized that his touch calmed her, soothed away her beginning sense of humiliation.

"What did you just do?" she whispered, hiding her face against his shoulder as she spoke. "In truth, you did not just do anything. *Non,* I mean you have not—"

Nigel smiled faintly. "This was for you."

Gisele did not understand, and she hated that more than she hated being embarrassed. She had been told that she had an unbecoming greed for knowledge for a woman, wanting to know all about things men felt she had no right or need to know. Her refusal to remain ignorant had only been hardened by her marriage. She truly believed that if she had known more about what could happen between a man and a woman, what was right and what was wrong, she might have been able to save herself some pain. She would have at least been able to better articulate her problems with the man her family had given her to.

She slowly looked at Nigel, lightly biting her bottom lip as she struggled with her words. Her hesitation to ask him the questions pounding in her mind surprised her. She realized that she dreaded hearing Nigel's disapproval of her intense curiosity, and she grew annoyed with herself.

His face was taut, a light flush accentuating the lines of his high cheekbones. Gisele recognized the signs of a man infected with a strong passion. It was something she had learned to watch for in her husband so that she could slip away and hide before he turned to her. She was rather pleased that the look on Nigel's face did not frighten her. She realized that his expression lacked that hint of viciousness that had always tainted her husband's look. It also made her all the more curious about why Nigel had done nothing to sate that desire.

"I do not understand," she said.

"And that troubles ye, doesnae it?" He could not help but smile at the look of irritation that flickered over her still flushed face.

"*Oui.* You told me you would seduce me and you just did, yet you did not complete the act. I believe there was no confusion about my willingness, yet you held yourself back. That confuses me. Is this some game?"

"Such a suspicious mind." He kissed the tip of her nose. "No game. Did ye e'er once lie with a mon who didnae hurt ye when he took what he needed?"

"I have only bedded down with one man in my life, my husband, and the answer is no. You guessed that. You saw my fear. It is plain that I am free of those fears now."

He shrugged. "Mayhap. Lass, I just thought it might help if, just once before we truly became lovers, ye learned what ye can feel. Aye, ye were willing, but how swiftly would that have faded once I settled my body on yours? Is that nay when the worst of the pain was inflicted?"

She blushed, but before she could respond a loud banging sounded at the door. Nigel cursed and rapidly got to his feet. He grabbed his sword and strode to the door. Gisele moved quickly to don her clothes.

"Who goes there?" Nigel demanded.

"It is David," called the man on the other side of the thick door. "Let me in."

"Ye pick an ill time to come aknocking. Come back later."

"If I come back later it may be just to bury you."

Nigel hastily opened the door, scowling at David as the young man strode in. "What do ye mean?"

"The DeVeaux will soon be kicking down your door."

"They are here?" Nigel began to dress.

"Just outside of the village. Some fool in the inn must have realized who you are and sought them out. I was afraid of this. The greed of men could become your deadliest enemy." He looked at Gisele as a cursing Nigel finished dressing. "Are you well, cousin?"

Gisele knew what stirred David's concern. The way he kept scowling at Nigel told her who he was ready to blame if she claimed any injury or upset. His concern was too little, too late, she thought crossly. Her innocence had been ripped away a long time ago, and no one had listened to her cries.

"I am fine," she replied a little curtly, unable to hide all of her anger.

"I just wondered—"

"Well, you may cease your wondering. None of this is your concern. I think the fact that my enemies have sniffed me out again is of more importance."

David blushed slightly and nodded. "Your mounts are saddled and ready."

"Good lad," Nigel murmured as he flung their saddlepacks over his shoulder. "I think ye should leave this place, as weel."

"I intend to. My horse is also ready. I do not wish to be found by the DeVeaux." He kissed Gisele on the cheek. "Take care, cousin. I swear on what little honor I have left that I will find the ones who killed your husband and free you of this horror."

She barely had time to thank him before Nigel was hurrying her out of the room. The sun was only beginning to rise, and the dim light it shed made the badly rutted road they rushed along somewhat treacherous. Gisele stumbled several times, but Nigel quickly steadied her and pulled her after him as he nearly ran for the stables.

"David has not followed us," she said even as Nigel tossed her up into her saddle and threw her saddlepack across the saddle in front of her.

"Clever lad." Nigel secured his saddlepack, mounted, and rode out of the stables.

"How is that clever? Should he not be fleeing this village as fast as we are?"

"Aye, but nay at the same time and nay in the same direction."

Nigel spit out a vicious curse and slapped her horse on the rump, startling the animal into a gallop. A heartbeat later she heard a cry go up on her right, and she knew they had been seen. The moment Nigel moved in front of her, Gisele set all of her attention on following him as closely as she could. She did not need to look behind them to know that her enemies were close at hand. She could hear them nipping at her heels.

This time they could have been trapped in the inn if David had not warned them. It was as if her enemies returned more fiercely and got even closer to her each time she escaped. Gisele was deeply afraid, terrified that her luck was rapidly running out. And it was clear that Nigel's ability to sense danger could fail him miserably at times.

It was nearly high noon before they had a chance to stop long enough to dismount and water the horses. Gisele dampened a small rag with water and wiped her face, then held the cloth against her throat as she tried to cool herself. Summer was drawing nigh, and it was growing too warm to do so much hard riding. She hoped the men chasing them were as uncomfortable as she was. It would be a small, welcome justice.

"We will shake them soon, lass," Nigel reassured her.

"Will we? DeVeaux or those seeking to earn their coin seem to be awaiting us at every turn." She sighed. "We shall need an army to get to the port."

"Nay, just cunning."

Gisele looked at him, wondering idly if the heat was beginning to affect his wits. "I know that it is oftimes said that cunning can be sharp, but I do not think it will serve to cut a path through our enemies."

Nigel laughed softly and handed her a large piece of bread. "Gnaw on this, lass. 'Twill take the bite of hunger away, and may soften the bite of your tongue. Now, we both ken that we arenae strong enough to stand and fight. There are too many men thrashing about looking for you. So, we must use all of our wits to elude them." He leaned against a tree on Gisele's right, took a long drink from the wineskin, and then handed it to her.

"I know that our only true choice is to run." She helped

herself to a long, satisfying drink of wine. "It just holds the stink of cowardice at times."

"Ye have heeded too many tales of grand valor, the ones where the knight faces thrice his number and dies rather than turn and hie for the safety of the hills."

She did not need to ask what Nigel thought of those tales The scorn weighting his deep voice made it very clear. "You do not think that such acts reveal great bravery?"

"Only if the mon has no other choice. If he is cornered with no place to turn, then, aye, 'tis brave to stand tall, sword in hand, and make those who would take your life pay dearly for it. Far better than cowering and begging for one's life. But if there is a choice, a way to escape sure death, then he is a fool to nay grab it and live to fight another day." He smiled and shrugged. "What purpose is served? Ye are dead and your enemies may ride away and continue whatever evil they wish to, and your family and friends have one less skilled fighter to protect them. Ye just give the minstrels something new to sing about."

After staring at him for a moment, Gisele laughed. "You have a true skill at cutting to the heart of nonsense."

"Nay always, sweeting. I used to listen to the tales and think it all so glorious. Then I faced such a choice and thought, nay, this is madness. In truth, 'tis much akin to suicide. I took myself to a place where I could face my enemies on a more equal footing and give them a real fight, nay just a moment's sport. And that is what we do now."

"And it is most reasonable. I just grow weary, and feel a need to bemoan my fate."

"That is easy to understand. I am sorry, but we must be on our way again."

"Allow me but a few moments to seek some privacy," she said, pleased that she no longer blushed when she asked for such a privilege.

"Be quick, lass. I dinnae like to linger in one place for too long when our enemies are so close at hand."

Gisele nodded and trotted away into the trees. She did not

need Nigel to tell her to hurry. The fact that they had to flee the village at dawn and had been closely followed all morning made her very aware of the danger they faced. Despite her brave talk of standing and fighting, she did not really want to face the DeVeaux, and she certainly did not want to do so without Nigel at her side. She talked boldly, Gisele mused with a grimace of self-disgust, but she did not have the stomach to honor her own words.

As she straightened her clothes and prepared herself to return to Nigel, Gisele suddenly tensed. She was sure she had heard something, but could see nothing. Her heart pounding so hard and fast it was painful, Gisele spun around and found herself facing a very large, hairy man, his colors proclaiming him a DeVeau. Even as she turned to run she knew it was too late to save herself. She cried out in pain and fear as the man grabbed her and threw her to the ground. She stared up at him, praying he was the only one so that she might still have a chance to save herself.

Nigel tensed, then cursed. Something was wrong. Every instinct told him so. Since there was no sight or sound of their enemy approaching him, he decided that it was Gisele who had roused his sudden concern. He hesitated, not wanting to act rashly. After hours of running he could simply be imagining danger around every corner, and all he would accomplish by hunting her down was robbing her of a moment of privacy. Then he heard a soft cry and hurried into the wood, striving for both silence and speed.

When he saw the man standing over Gisele, sword drawn, Nigel struggled against the urge to charge to her aid. The man could easily kill Gisele before he could be stopped. What puzzled Nigel was where the man had come from. He had seen no other DeVeaux. This man had to be a scout, or the DeVeaux had spread themselves far and wide in the hope of improving their chances of capturing Gisele. There was also the possibility that the man acted alone, simply hoping to gain all of the reward for himself. As he edged closer, Nigel decided that the man deserved to pay dearly for his greed.

"Do you wish to murder me, or take me to others who will commit the deed for you?" Gisele asked, tensed and prepared for any chance to get away.

"You will be easier to handle if you are dead," the man replied, smiling faintly.

"Such a brave man you are to cut dead a small, unarmed woman."

"You are a murdering bitch. Is it not better to die by the sword than to hang, dying slowly and painfully as you have all of your life's breath choked out of you?"

"I would prefer not to die at all." He painted a bone-chilling picture, but Gisele refused to allow him to see her fear. "It astounds me to discover how many people believe the word of the DeVeaux. Rich and powerful they may be, but they have long been known to have little honor. The truth rarely stains their tongues, either."

"What concern is that of mine? This quarrel is between you and them, and they have the coin."

"I have coin," she said, wondering if she could simply buy her way out of danger, but his quick, rough laugh swiftly killed that hope.

"No one has a purse as large as the DeVeaux."

She inched back as he stepped closer, the point of his sword aimed at her heart. "So greed is why you are ready to stain your hands with the blood of an innocent woman."

"Innocent or not, I care not, and my hands are already well stained. A few more drops will make no difference."

He started to move, and Gisele struggled to get to her feet, her heart pounding when she realized how hard it was going to be to elude the thrust of his sword. Then, suddenly, he stopped moving, a look of horrified surprise twisting his homely face. As he slowly fell to his knees, Gisele realized that Nigel stood behind him. She carefully stood up as Nigel wiped the blood from his sword, using the dead man's jupon.

"I was attempting to talk him out of killing me," she said and took several slow, deep breaths to calm herself.

"Was there much chance that ye were going to succeed?" Nigel asked, stepping up beside her and gently rubbing her back, pleased to feel her trembling still beneath his hand.

"No chance at all. Greed had blinded him to all reason."

"Your cousin warned ye." Nigel took her by the hand and started to lead her back to the horses.

"I know. It stirs my gall to admit he was right." She exchanged a brief grin with him. "I fear a part of me believed that my small size and sex would give me some protection. That was folly."

"It was, lass. The men following the DeVeaux lead would probably nay care if ye were but a suckling bairn. Whichever one of your husband's kinsmen is leading this chase, he hasnae asked that ye be captured alive."

"They do not care who metes out their justice, as long as it is done." When they reached the horses, she frowned and looked around even as she mounted. "It would appear that the man was alone."

"Aye, it would," Nigel agreed as he mounted his horse and started to ride. "He didnae wish to share the bounty. That greed led him to his grave. What I cannae be certain of is how far away his companions are."

Gisele shivered, unable to fully suppress her fear. This time she had come chillingly close to paying with her life for a murder she had not committed. Although she tried to be strong by clinging to false hope, she knew she had truly stared death in the face. She needed a respite from the danger in order to regain her strength.

That confrontation had also revealed that she had several faults in her thinking. What she had feared most, what she had really been fighting against, was capture and being dragged before some DeVeau to suffer an unjust trial. Deep in her heart she had never truly believed that anyone other than a DeVeau would kill a small, unarmed woman. She had had faith in the rules a knight was expected to live by, that they would protect, or at least not harm, those who were weaker than they. That had been foolish. The sort of man who would do the bidding of a DeVeau did not abide by any chivalrous code. She had to put such beliefs out of her mind and fully understand that she was not just saving herself from her husband's family, but from every knave in service to the DeVeaux and some simply trying to earn the bounty placed on her head.

Nigel glanced back at her as he led them across a shallow, rock-strewn creek. He had saved her, but it had been a near thing, too near. The thought of how close he had come to losing her still chilled his blood. He hoped it would make them both more cautious, but he also did not want to leave Gisele too afraid.

"Dinnae look so fretful, lass." he said. "We can neither see nor hear a DeVeau, so our enemies cannae be too close."

"We did not see or hear that man, either," she replied.

"Aye, true enough. But now we ken that they may come at us one at a time, and we can watch for that threat."

She smiled sadly. "We need more eyes if we are to do all of this watching and do it well."

"It would be helpful if we had some ally watching our backs, but I am nay sure it would help us in any other way. 'Tis much easier for two people to hide than three or more. And how can we be sure of who we can trust?" He smiled faintly when she cursed. "I would trust my kinsmen, but they arenae here."

"And I do not trust all of my kinsmen," she said. "I trusted Guy, but he can no longer help us. Beyond that?" She shrugged.

"Ye dinnae trust your cousin David?" Nigel recognized that a lingering touch of jealousy prompted his question.

"I want to but I cannot, not completely. He stood with those who condemned me for almost a year. Now, because he claims he has had a change of heart I must believe in him, simply because he is my blood? I think not. When my husband was murdered and I stood accused, my family lost all they had hoped to gain by my marriage to DeVeau. How can I be sure that they are not seeking to recoup some of that loss by gaining the bounty the DeVeaux offer?"

Nigel stared at her for a moment, then grimaced and turned his attention back to the trail they followed. He really wanted to argue in favor of her family, but he could not. He did not know any of them well enough to vouch for them. What Gisele said also made a great deal of sense. His family would never betray him like that, but he had no way to be sure that her family would not.

"Ye cannae be sure," he reluctantly admitted, "but ye should-nae judge your kinsmen that harshly. Aye, they betrayed you—by refusing to believe your claims of innocence and refusing to help you in even the smallest of ways—but there is a long journey from that to actually joining with your pursuers and trying to profit from your death."

"But you do agree that I cannot completely discard the possibility, long journey though it may be?"

"Nay, just dinnae let their first betrayal, their failure to help you, completely poison how, when, and if, ye trust them again. They are your kinsmen. They may not be perfect or ever faithful, but they are blood. One should ne'er completely turn one's back on one's blood. After all, not all of your family deserted you, and many may have just committed the sin of silence."

Gisele nodded and smiled, her spirits lifted slightly by his words. It was sad that she could no longer place her full trust in her family, but Nigel was right. She did not have to completely turn her back on all of them. Many of them might not be dear friends she could trust with her life and her deepest secrets, but she did not have to see them all as her enemies, either. As she nudged her mount into a faster pace in order to keep up with Nigel's increased speed, Gisele realized that she now had some hope. When the threat to her life was finally over, she might well be able to go home again.

Ten

The water was cold, but it was also sweetly clean and refreshing. Gisele sat on the softly grassed bank of the small pond and washed herself off, relieved to bathe away the dirt from a long day of riding. She looked around the spot Nigel had chosen for their campsite, and was moved by its beauty.

Tall, lush trees surrounded the clearing, sheltering them from the heat and from the sight of their enemies. The late spring wildflowers were all abloom, scattered thickly around the glade, adding color and a soft scent. It was so lovely, so peaceful yet filled with the sounds of birds and small animals, that Gisele felt as if her very spirit was being soothed. She could not believe that any harm could come to her in such a tranquil place although she knew it would be foolish to let the place lull her into believing she was safe. Gisele sighed as she bent over the water and, using her cupped hands to scoop up water, rinsed the dust from her hair. If she and Nigel could find this beautiful glade, then so could the DeVeaux.

She hastily rubbed her hair dry, straightened her clothing, and went to build the campfire. If she kept herself busy, she might not do so much thinking. Thinking too much only left her upset, uneasy, and, sometimes, even afraid.

Once the fire was started, Gisele sat down beside it and looked around. The soft, golden light of the setting sun made the glade even more beautiful. This was not a place to allow dark thoughts, worries, and fears intrude upon its peace, she mused. She breathed deeply, savoring the quiet, then cursed when her thoughts turned to Nigel. Why would her mind not obey her wish for peace?

Now that she was not running for her life, now that Nigel had evaded the DeVeaux for a while, it was hard not to think about what had happened between them at the inn. She was still not sure she understood what he had done to her, or why. No one had ever made her feel such things, certainly not her husband. Gisele suspected she should be outraged, perhaps even a little afraid, but found that she was mostly curious.

Was that what all the minstrels sang about? It was a glorious feeling, and instinct told her that it would probably be even better if shared. That a man with a gentle, skilled touch could stir such feeling in a woman also explained why some women took lovers. After enduring her husband's brutal attacks, Gisele had often wondered how any woman could willingly go to any man, and had been struck dumb to realize that some women embraced more than one. Now she began to understand.

Nigel had surprised her this morning, seduced her while she was more asleep than awake. Gisele supposed she ought to be furious, appalled, and offended, but no matter how deep she looked within herself she was none of those things. He had warned her that he planned to seduce her, and she had not firmly told him that she would not allow it. In a way, she had accepted the challenge. Neither had he used any tactics that were cruel or dishonorable. Gisele knew that some of her ease with his attempts to seduce her came from the surety that Nigel Murray would always heed a no.

She had not said no this morning, she thought with a grimace and a flush of embarrassment. She had been most willing, so willing she may well have shouted yes at the top of her voice. *Another weakness,* she mused, and shook her head. She was uncovering a great many of those.

One thing she did know for certain was that she had to make some decision about Nigel. There was passion between them. She could no longer deny or ignore it. And after this morning she could no longer just leave Nigel to play his game, a game she was certain he would now play much more seriously. He knew he could win, now. Before they bedded down for the night she had to decide if she were going to allow him to win or put a firm end to it now, and perhaps, forever.

Gisele gasped in surprise when Nigel suddenly appeared at her side, proudly displaying a quail ready for cooking. She felt unsettled by his abrupt arrival, since she had been thinking about him, and prayed that the shadows of sunset hid her blushes. Hoping he would think her unease was due to his habit of sneaking up on her, Gisele returned his smile.

"So, we will feast tonight," she murmured as he put the bird on a spit and sat down across from her.

"One should enjoy God's bounty when one can," he said. "It makes the leaner times a little easier to bear."

"Does it? I would have thought it would make those times harder to endure because one would more easily recall all one once had."

"Such a dour eye ye set upon the world." He laughed softly and shook his head. "Ye are one of those who prepare for the great deluge the priests speak of when it rains for several days in a row, arenae ye?"

She had to smile at his gentle teasing, and at herself, for there was some truth to his words. From the moment she was old enough to form an opinion on anything, she had always formed a solemn one. If there was a choice of fates, she had always selected the most dire. Marriage to DeVeau had not inspired her to change.

"There is no harm in being prepared for the worst, Sir Murray."

"Nay, there isnae," he agreed. "Howbeit, one doesnae want to see only the worst, expect only disaster and death. It can breed a darkness in the soul."

"My Nana used to tell me that."

"A wise woman."

"Because she agreed with you?"

"Aye," he said, and grinned when she giggled, but a moment later he became serious. "There is truth in what I, and your Nana, say. If one sets one's eyes only on the dark and the evil, soon 'tis all one sees, and all one expects from others. 'Tisnae a good path to be walking on."

"I know. Truly," she reassured him. "If I were going to turn into such a woman, I believe my marriage would have done it."

"And it hasnae?" he asked, watching her closely as he waited for her reply. Nigel was still not sure that Gisele trusted him, and searched for some clue to tell him if she ever would.

"Not completely," she answered, then grimaced. "I have not had much cause or time to see the good in people in these last months, or to have much hope. I have not lost the ability to recognize and enjoy beauty, however. I realized that when I saw this place. Nor have I lost the craving for peace, or the wish to trust in people again. When I am free again I believe I will cease to be such a morbid soul."

Nigel smiled as he turned the bird on the spit so that it could cook more evenly. Gisele moved to get the two metal plates Nigel carried in his saddlepacks, as well as the bread and the wineskin. She hungered for the food he prepared, and as she sat back down she hoped she had the patience to wait for it to be properly cooked.

She had to smile when she realized she was leaning toward the fire, breathing deeply of the delicious aroma of the roasting bird. In the last few days her appetite had grown tenfold. Gisele knew it was because she was working so hard just to stay alive, to avoid capture by her enemies. Her grandmother would be pleased, she thought, and smiled a little wider.

"What has ye looking so happy?" asked Nigel as he unsheathed his dagger, cut the bird into equal parts, and handed Gisele her share.

"I was just thinking how pleased my Nana would be to see me eating like this," Gisele replied. "She was ever putting food in front of me and trying to coax me to eat more."

Nigel chuckled. " 'Tis a common urging of one's elders. And, ye are a wee lass. I can easily see how ye would inspire such coddling and coaxing."

Gisele was barely able to smile in response. She was too busy eating. For the next several moments eating was all she and Nigel did, pausing only to pass the wineskin back and forth. Gisele was not surprised when there was nothing left to set aside for another meal. It had been a small bird, and they had clearly been very hungry. It might not have been wise to indulge in such gluttony, but Gisele decided that it had certainly been very satisfying.

She collected the plates and took them to the small pond. Digging a shallow hole in the soft dirt, she buried the bones so that the scavengers who roamed in the night would not be attracted to their campsite. She washed off the plates, then washed her face and hands. As she put the plates back in Nigel's saddlepacks, she sensed him watching her. As she returned to her seat by the fire she felt a little uncomfortable beneath his steady gaze.

Nigel smiled inwardly when he saw how nervous Gisele was. He excused himself and sought a moment of privacy in the surrounding woods. Nervousness was something he could deal with, could soothe away with words and kisses. Outrage or anger would have shown him that he had made a serious error at the inn, but he had seen none of that. If he judged Gisele right, she was simply uncertain.

He ached to make love to her. She had been so welcoming in the morning, her passion free and hot, but he had forced himself not to take full advantage of that. From what little she had told him of her disastrous marriage, she had never been made love to, only repeatedly raped. She had never known pleasure, only pain and humiliation. He had decided that it was time she learned that a man's touch could bring her pleasure, time that a man gave her body some joy without taking anything from her. Nigel prayed he had accomplished that task as well as he thought he had, and that now her fears would be more controllable. He knew he had to be patient with Gisele, but that was growing more difficult every day as his desire for her grew, yet remained unsatisfied.

When he returned to camp he saw that she had laid out their bedding. Their beds were close, yet not quite side by side. It was not the blatant invitation he would have preferred, but it was promising. If she had decided to put a firm end to his seduction she would have returned to sleeping on the opposite side of the fire. All he had to determine was just how undecided she was.

Gisele found that she could not even look at Nigel as they settled down on their beds. She inwardly cursed her sudden onslaught of timidity. It would make matters very awkward, and that was the last thing she wanted. She kept telling herself that she was a grown woman who should be able to look Nigel in the eye and say exactly what she thought, but it only helped a little.

While Nigel had been gone she had finally come to a decision. He had shown her that passion could be pleasurable, and she wanted to know the whole of it—not just what he could give her, but what they could share. The more she had thought about the matter, the more she believed that he could indeed soothe away at least some of her fears. If just once she were held in a man's arms and knew only gentleness, passion, and pleasure, it had to soften the grip of the dark memories her husband had left her with. Gisele wanted that, wanted desperately to gain some freedom from her fears.

A small voice had tried to tell her to consider her good name, but she had easily silenced it. Even if she were proclaimed innocent of murder, her good name was already irredeemably stained. She had been on her own for a year, and now spent days and nights alone with a man who was not related to her by blood. That was not a secret any longer, and everyone who heard the tale would assume that she and Nigel were lovers, no matter how vehemently or truthfully she tried to deny it. And if that were not enough to thoroughly blacken her name, she had cut her hair and was running all over France dressed as a boy. Since everyone would believe she had committed the sin of taking a lover, she saw no reason to deny herself the pleasure of doing so.

She was not sure how to let Nigel know that she was willing to continue what they had begun that morning. She had never been wooed or seduced, and had little idea of how the game was played. The only thing she had been able to think of was placing their beds close together and hope Nigel would act upon that subtle acceptance.

Taking a deep breath to steady herself, Gisele turned on her side to look at Nigel. It did not really surprise her to find him looking at her. She had sensed it. She silently cursed the blush that stung her cheeks, however. She wished to proceed with a calm forthrightness. If she were going to convince Nigel that she knew exactly what she was doing and that she asked nothing more of him than a shared passion, it would help if she did not look like some red-faced child. She opened her mouth to speak, realized that she could not think of what to say, and sighed.

Nigel smiled, reached out, and gently stroked her cheek. Despite all she had been through, Gisele was still very innocent. She had obviously never learned the ways of flirtation or the art of gentle seduction. Gisele might have had her maidenhead brutally stolen by her husband, but she remained virginal in many other ways.

"The easy way, lass," he said quietly, "would be to just edge your wee bed closer to mine."

The way he could so unerringly guess her thoughts was very unsettling, Gisele thought. He was, however, correct in what he said. Even as she moved her bedding next to his, she had to admit that it was certainly the easiest way to say yes. She was still blushing, but at least she was not babbling like some complete fool.

"Are ye sure?" he asked as he followed the delicate lines of her face with soft kisses.

"I am here now, am I not?" She was not surprised to hear the husky unsteadiness in her voice, for his tender kisses were soothing away all uncertainty and embarrassment, replacing them with growing desire.

"True, but are ye sure why ye are here in my arms?"

"I am not trying to repay a debt or anything so foolish as that, if that is what you are thinking."

He smiled against the smooth skin of her throat. "Calm yourself, my sweet companion." He watched her carefully as he subtly unlaced her jupon. "Aye, I will confess that that thought winged its way through my mind, but its visit was verra brief."

"Was it?" She tensed slightly as he began to remove her clothes, then relaxed when she realized she had reacted out of embarrassment and not fear.

"Ye are too proud, and I dinnae believe the idea would occur to you, anyway."

She frowned, not completely sure that that was a compliment. "I am not without some wit."

"Oh, aye, sweeting, ye have wit, more than some men would find becoming in a lass. I rather like it. Nay, I just dinnae think ye could be that devious and, even if all of your reasons were good and honorable, as I said, ye have far too much pride."

Gisele suddenly realized that, as he had talked, he had removed all of her clothes except for her shirt. She knew she had been paying close heed to his words and had been lulled by his stroking hands, but it still seemed unsettlingly skillful of the man. Then she thought of how and where he had gained such expertise. She was about to take as a lover a man who had, in his own words, used a large number of women, women she doubted he could recall by name or face. Although Gisele was not demanding love and marriage for her favors, she was not sure she wanted them taken too lightly.

"You disrobe a woman with an admirable skill and speed," she murmured.

"Ah, and ye dinnae really find it admirable, do ye?" He began to slowly unlace her shirt.

"Perhaps not."

"My poor bonny Gisele," he murmured as he brushed a kiss

over her lips and slid his hand inside of her shirt. "Aye, I was a heartless, rutting bastard for seven years. I am nay sure I learned this particular skill during that time, however. To my shame, I was also drunk most of that time. I think some of what ye see as my skill comes from the fact that ye are wearing clothes much like I wore for most of my youth."

"Oh." Gisele was not sure if her breathy response was an expression of agreement or delight, for he was moving his big, lightly calloused hands over her breasts, brushing the tips to a tingling hardness with his thumb. "I just did not wish to be another body tossed upon that heap. I ask for no bonds or promises. I just do not wish to be a nothing. I have been that once, and never wish to be such a thing again."

"Ye could never be a nothing, Gisele," he whispered against the silken, soft skin of her breast, savoring the way she trembled beneath his caress.

Gisele thrust her hands into his thick, long hair, holding him close as he covered her breasts with warm kisses. A touch had never felt so good, certainly not a man's. She doubted her fear would rear its ugly head, for her husband had never made her feel this way, and his touch had never been gentle. Gisele could not believe she could be so blind or foolish as to ever compare Nigel to her brute of a husband. One simply did not make her think of the other, unless it was to praise God that she was now with Nigel.

When Nigel began to gently suck on one of her breasts, Gisele cried out and held him even closer. There was a great deal wrong with what she was allowing him to do, but she decided that there was far more that was right. She was finally going to discover what so many reached for and rhapsodized about, and as Nigel turned his passionate attentions to her other breast Gisele decided that discovery was worth whatever price she had to pay.

When Nigel tugged off her shirt she found the need to let go of him almost painful. The moment he tossed it aside she clung to him again and greedily returned his kiss. As long as she could hold him, she did not think, only felt, and that, she realized, was exactly how she wanted it.

He covered her body in kisses and gentle caresses, and she welcomed each one. She moved her hands over his broad back, loving the feel of his smooth, taut skin beneath her fingers. It felt almost as good to touch Nigel as it felt to have him touch her. Gisele wished she knew more, had gained some skill so that she could give Nigel as much pleasure as he was giving her.

A small interruption in her heedless revel in passion came when Nigel removed his braies. He rested his long body full against hers. Gisele felt his engorged manhood pressed against her thigh, and fought against letting even one of her dark memories intrude upon her desire, but it was difficult. Kisses and caresses had been easy to slowly accept without fear, though her husband had given her few of either, and never a gentle one. This, however, was something she recognized, something she had always associated with hurt and shame. It was going to be a little hard to make herself believe that the same part of a man which had always been used as a weapon against her could now be a source of pleasure. She feared that all the sweetness she had just tasted was about to turn very sour.

Nigel felt the faint tension in Gisele's body and fought the urge to just take her before fear could make her change her mind. It was not only wrong, but such an act could easily convince her that all of her fears were justified. There was even a chance that he could add to that fear, for it would be much akin to what her husband had subjected her to. The mere thought of such a consequence gave him the restraint he sought. He cupped her face in his hands, smiling faintly at how tightly she kept her eyes shut.

"Look at me, Gisele," he commanded softly, and brushed a tender kiss across her mouth.

"I am not sure I wish to."

"Come, look at me. See with your own eyes who is about to love you. If ye keep your bonny eyes shut, I fear memory may overcome fact."

Slowly, she opened her eyes, pushing her shyness aside as she recognized the wisdom of his reasoning. Her fears had been slowly coming to life, stirred by the feel of something every man possessed. She did need to put a face to the man who held her.

It angered her that she could grow so senseless with fear over something she could destroy with one quick slash of her dagger, something that was, in a battle situation, considered one of a man's weak points. If she were going to be afraid of some part of a man, it made more sense to be afraid of his hands or of his sword arm, parts that could so easily kill her. To deny that fear was foolish, however, and could easily put an end to something she was enjoying a great deal.

"There. I am looking at you," she said, hearing the sulkiness in her voice despite the huskiness that still deepened it.

Nigel ignored her touch of ill humor, for he could still hear the passion in her voice, feel it in the faint trembling of her lithe body, and see it in the flush upon her smooth, high-boned cheeks. "Ye need not fear the manhood, lassie, only the mon who wields it." As he spoke, he settled himself between her slim thighs.

"I know that. In my mind, I truly do know that most of the time."

"Then keep your eyes open, my sweet French rose, so that your mind and heart can remember it. Keep them wide open, so that bastard's memory cannae rise up to destroy what we can share."

Gisele nodded and curled her arms around his neck, keeping her gaze firmly fixed upon his face even as he covered her face with slow, gentle kisses. She tensed as he eased into her, but realized that it was more with anticipation than with fear. A soft gasp of pleasured surprise escaped her when he began to move within her, and a heartbeat later passion robbed her of all ability to think clearly. She only knew whose body was joined with hers, knew Nigel would never intentionally hurt her, and knew she wanted him to continue.

Suddenly, a rich feeling began to blossom within her, a feeling that was both wondrous and made her somewhat desperate. She clung to Nigel, wrapping her arms and legs around him. She could hear him mumbling husky words of encouragement, and then a blinding wave of intense feeling swept over her and she cried out his name. Gisele was only faintly aware of how the man she held so tightly began to move more fiercely, then tensed, shuddered, and called out to her. It was several long minutes before she realized he had slumped in her arms, resting his full weight on top of her.

"You are a little heavy," she whispered, smiling faintly as he eased the intimacy of their embrace and moved to the side.

"Are ye all right, Gisele?" he asked in a soft voice.

It puzzled Gisele a little that she should feel so tired, so compelled to sleep, but moments after she had felt so alive. "I am much fine, thank you, Sir Nigel."

Nigel laughed. *"Verra* fine, and dinnae ye think ye can call me simply Nigel now?"

"Then I am very fine, simply Nigel."

He laughed again and shook his head when he saw that she was already sound asleep. Carefully, even though he doubted he could wake her, he turned onto his back and tucked her up against his side. He was eager to make love to her again, but knew that it was best if she got some sleep.

Although it felt good to know he had been the man to put her fears to rest and stir her passion, Nigel knew what moved him most was that she had willingly shared that with him. He did not fear that she would have any regrets or recriminations in the morning. Instinct told him that Gisele was not the type to suffer much from either, not when she had chosen to do something.

He would probably be the one who was suffering from doubts and uncertainties. He was already beginning to feel guilty. Nigel could not recall if he had ever found lovemaking so exciting or fulfilling, yet he could not be completely sure why that was. He certainly could not offer Gisele any promises, more than sweet words of passion and flattery, at least not until he knew his own heart better than he did now. She had said that she asked for no vows or words of love, but he felt she deserved far more than he was offering.

As he closed his eyes, Nigel decided they would linger in the glade for a little while, a day or two. He felt sure they had distanced themselves from the DeVeaux hounds enough to allow for a short respite. Perhaps, as they rested and took time to savor the passion they shared, he would be able to sort through the confusion in his mind and heart. Gisele deserved at least that much for the gift she had shared with him.

Eleven

Passion drew Gisele from her sleep and thrust her into pleasure. She returned Nigel's hungry kiss as he slowly joined their bodies. Her greed for him surprised her, but she let it have full reign. It all felt too good to question. She arched her body toward his, eagerly meeting his every thrust. As her desire crested she clutched at his trim hips and pulled him deeper within her, savoring the way his cries of pleasure echoed hers.

It was not until he eased the intimacy of their embrace that she began to feel the touch of embarrassment and uncertainty. This was not the way she had been taught a young woman of good breeding should act. She was breaking so many rules, of society and of the church, that it made her head spin. There had been some excuse, albeit a thin one, for allowing the first lovemaking. She felt she could be forgiven curiosity and the need to cast aside the fears her husband had bred in her heart. Now, however, there was only one reason to continue, and that was because she enjoyed it. That carried the distasteful taint of behaving like a whore.

"Regrets?" Nigel asked, a little concerned about the dark frown growing on Gisele's still flushed face.

She finally looked at him and grimaced. "I was battling with a few."

"And have ye vanquished them?"

"I will. When I was curious and wanted to know passion

without fear, it was easier to excuse my behavior. Now I am just behaving badly."

"I thought ye behaved verra weel," he murmured and gave an exaggerated expression of pain when she swatted him on the arm.

"This is a serious matter for a woman. You need to treat it with more respect." She had to smile at the way the glitter of laughter in his eyes belied his solemn expression, then she grew serious again. "You need not fear that I am about to turn against you and claim all manner of unjust things, trying to blame you for all that has happened."

"I ne'er really feared that. Ye are a sensible lass, and a fair one."

"I am certain most women are."

Nigel said nothing, just smiled faintly and let her believe he agreed with her. That was not an argument he wanted to get into. To support his side of it he would have to tell her about women he had known, and this was a bad time to remind her of his less than illustrious past.

"So, what troubles ye, then?" He smoothed a finger down the faint crease of a frown forming between her eyes.

"I just began to think of all the rules I am breaking."

"No more than many another has, and will."

"That does not make it right or acceptable," she said sternly.

"Nay, of course it doesnae, but this doesnae make ye the greatest of sinners, either." He was a little concerned that she was about to turn righteous on him and demand that he never touch her again. Although he did not think Gisele would behave that way, he could not fully discard the possibility.

"I know that," she said, then sighed and shook her head. "I will overcome this sudden attack of guilt over my own irresponsible behavior. It will just take a little while. Before I said yes I reminded myself that I will be accused of just this sort of thing because of the way I have lived for the last year. No one will believe otherwise no matter what I say or do, so what matter

if I actually do it? I will just remind myself of that from time
to time."

"Such flattery. I am overcome with humility."

She tried to scowl at him, barely repressing the urge to laugh.
"You are a scoundrel."

"Aye, quite possibly."

Gisele suddenly realized that the sun was already climbing
in the sky, and frowned. "We are getting a late start today, are
we not?"

"We are not going to get any start today at all," he said as
he rose from his bed and pulled on his clothes.

"What do you mean?"

"I mean that we are taking a much earned rest."

"Do you think the DeVeaux are resting?"

"Probably not, but they are nowhere about."

She began to tug on her clothes, using the blanket as a shield
for her modesty. "I hate to question you on this, but are you
very certain about that?"

"As certain as I can be without tracking them down and finding out exactly where they are. Lass, we are very near the port
I seek. I believe that the DeVeaux are there, waiting for us. They
are not here. Of that I am sure. I also intend to take myself into
the wood and set up a few traps, something to warn us just in
case they do wander too close to our little sanctuary."

Gisele watched him disappear into the wood and slowly rose
to put their bedding away. It would be nice to spend a quiet day,
a day without riding and looking over her shoulder. She was
just not sure it was wise. The fact that Nigel was going to sur-
round them with traps made her feel only a little more secure.

She shook her head and silently scolded herself. Nigel knew
what he was doing. Perhaps, because she had spent so long
running and hiding, she simply did not know how to stop and
rest anymore. It would do them both good to just rest, to enjoy
a lazy day in the sun.

As she slipped away into the trees for a moment of privacy,
she had to smile. She was sure that Nigel had plans for them

that did not necessarily include rest. Gisele had no doubt about his passion for her, even though she might question its depth and longevity. She would be very surprised if the man did not have plans to further explore the desire they shared.

A brief pang of guilt plucked at her heart and mind, but she forced it away. She had chosen her path, and she would stay with it. There were worse crimes she could have committed. She would pay her penance later. Even if she had to spend months on her knees saying her rosary, the passion she shared with Nigel was worth it.

Once back at the campsite, she went to the pond, removed her boots, and dangled her feet in the cold water. Her thoughts turned to Nigel, and she realized that she was probably not going to be able to just savor the passion and then leave when her name was cleared and she was free. Already questions formed in her mind about the future, and she knew that she had no answers, that, quite possibly, there were none. Not with him. Even now, after only one night in his arms, that realization stung. Doing a long, hard penance might well be the smallest of her worries.

"Idiot," she scolded herself, and kicked at the water.

"Talking to yourself?" asked a deep, familiar voice from right behind her.

Gisele screeched in surprise, barely kept herself from falling into the pond, and spun around to glare at Nigel. "One of these times you are going to frighten me so much my poor heart shall stop dead in my chest."

He laughed and sat down beside her. "Why were ye calling yourself an idiot?"

"Because I cannot seem to just take my ease and enjoy a day with nothing to do." She stared at the water as she answered him, a little afraid that he would read her evasion in her face.

"It is long past time that ye had a rest, loving."

"Mayhap, but I have been running and hiding for so long it just feels wrong."

"Then we must keep ye busy so that ye cannae think on it too much."

"Keep me busy?" She eyed him with a touch of suspicion as he stood up and held out his hand.

"Now, lass, ye must trust me and cease questioning my motives." He pulled her into his arms and gave her a brief, hard kiss. "Did ye not ask me to teach ye how to walk softly?"

Gisele smiled and nodded. "I will confess that I may be envious of how you can do that, and that is why I wish to learn the skill. Howbeit, I am also thinking it is a much—" she hesitated, then corrected herself—*"very* useful skill. There is no knowing how long I will have to remain hidden, is there?"

"It will end soon."

"How can you be so certain of that?"

"Your kinsmen now work to get ye free of this."

"But if, as you believe, I killed my husband, how can they release me from that accusation? DeVeau was a rich, powerful man with connections to the king himself. Few would dismiss my crime simply because they felt the man deserved to die. Few would think my killing him was justice just because he treated me so poorly."

"Put your boots on."

Gisele smiled faintly as she did as he ordered. "You have not answered me."

"Ye try to trick me with questions that are difficult to answer and with clever assumptions."

"Perhaps."

"There is no perhaps about it. If I respond one way, ye hear me admit that I think ye are guilty. If I answer in another way, then ye can say that I think ye are innocent. Since I have yet to decide, 'tis best if I dinnae answer at all."

She cursed softly as she stood up and scowled at him. *"Oui,* I try to get you to proclaim me one or the other, guilty or innocent. We have been together for a week, and knew each other for a week before that, but you still have not decided? Do you truly believe me capable of such bloodthirstiness? *Oui,* simply killing him, that I might have done. There were many times when I ached to do so. But I would never have desecrated his body in such a manner, no matter how much I loathed that part of the man. I certainly would never have tortured him, mutilating him first and then killing him."

Nigel was not sure why he could not just agree that she was innocent, especially since he was beginning to think she was. He decided that he just needed some more proof, no matter how he felt about her. His indecision was aided by the feeling that no woman could or should be faulted for killing such a man. It was, in many ways, self-defense.

"Aye, I do find it hard to believe that ye could disfigure a mon. Why do ye ne'er call your husband by his name, his full name? Ye always call him DeVeau."

Gisele felt as if she were banging her head against a very hard wall, but decided to just give up on the argument. It only made her angry, and now she realized that his doubt also hurt. Badgering the man to proclaim her innocence would also ruin what could be a very nice day, and she needed one.

"His name was Michael," she said, not surprised to hear a hint of anger still lingering in her voice. It would take a few minutes for her to regain her calm. "I called him by that name once, at our wedding. After our wedding night, I called him only DeVeau to his face, and many unkind things when he could not hear me. I did call him some rougher names to his face, but only a few times in the beginning, for the beatings I got quickly taught me some discretion."

He hugged her in a brief expression of sympathy, and inwardly cursed DeVeau. It was such tales, however, that made him hesitant to completely believe her claim of total innocence. Gisele was a proud woman, spirited, and she possessed a temper. At some point in her marriage, the humiliation and brutality DeVeau meted out could have driven her to kill him. There was also the chance that, horrified by what she had done, she had simply cast the memory from her mind. He just wished that his indecision did not upset her as it did.

"You were going to teach me how to walk quietly, how to slip through the wood like a ghost," she reminded him as she stepped out of his hold.

Nigel smiled faintly and carefully explained the way one had to walk to make each step quiet. "Ye must train yourself to walk toe to heel, rolling your wee foot down even as ye start to do the same with the other foot. What ye are trying to do is nay set too much weight on any part of your foot as ye walk."

"Am I to float above the ground like some spirit?"

He just laughed and took her by the hand. "It can be difficult to explain. Watch me closely, and do as I do."

Gisele tried, again and again. She could see how he moved, but found that it was hard to imitate. When she finally stumbled over a half-buried tree root because she was paying more attention to how to walk than to where she was walking, she quit and sat down on the soft grass. Cursing softly over her embarrassing clumsiness, she rubbed her aching legs.

"Ye didnae do too badly, lass," Nigel said as he sat down next to her.

"Empty flattery. I was terrible, and my legs hurt."

"Aye, they will until ye learn the trick of it. Ye were close a time or two."

"Close, but I moved so slowly that a man hobbled in both legs could have run me down." She smiled faintly when he laughed. "This is not a trick one can learn quickly or easily."

"Nay. I was taught when I was just a small lad, and e'en though the young can learn quickly, it was a long, long time ere I could do it right and without thought."

"And just why would you be taught such a skill? You are a mounted knight."

"Aye, but I could lose my mount, or a horse can become a hindrance if I am on a raid where stealth is necessary." He leaned closer to her and began to kiss the side of her neck.

"A raid?" She did nothing to stop him as he gently pushed her down onto the grass. "Thievery."

"Weel, aye, there is a wee bit of that."

Her soft laughter was stopped by his hungry kiss. As he began to tug her clothes off, she was briefly concerned about doing something so intimate in the full light of day, and in the open on the grass. Then he started to kiss her breasts, and she decided she did not care. Tentatively, she began to help Nigel shed his clothes as well, and when he revealed only approval of her aid, she grew bolder.

Once they were both naked, Nigel moved so that she was on top of his clothes, her soft skin protected from the ground. As he kissed and caressed her, Gisele moved her hands over his strong body with increasing daring. Cautiously, she slid her hand down his stomach and, after taking a deep breath to steady herself, touched his erection. When he gasped and jerked beneath her shy touch, she started to pull her hand away, but he quickly put it back.

Although shocked by her own boldness, Gisele stroked him. Nigel had shown her that this part of a man could bring pleasure, and she realized that knowledge had roused her curiosity. The way Nigel's breathing grew fast and unsteady, the faint tremor that began to ripple through his lean body, told her that he liked her touch, and that made her even more curious. Then, suddenly, Nigel tugged her hand away, and Gisele feared that she had grown too bold or had even caused him some pain.

"I am sorry," she whispered, although she was not quite sure what she was apologizing for.

"Nay, lass." Nigel pressed his forehead against hers, lightly kissed the end of her nose, and struggled to regain the control he had almost lost. "Ye did nothing wrong. In truth, ye did everything right." He began to trail kisses down her long, slim neck.

Gisele threaded her fingers into his hair and held him close as he covered her breasts with kisses. "If I did everything right, then why did you stop me? I thought I had hurt you in some manner."

"There is only so much pleasure a mon can endure, lass."

He kissed her taut stomach and teased her soft skin with brief licks of his tongue. "If I had let ye continue your delightful play I would have been finished, and I didnae want that, nay so quickly."

Before she could ask him what he meant by finished, she felt the warmth of his mouth between her legs and cried out in shock. Gisele tried to pull away from the intimate kiss, but Nigel gripped her by her hips and stopped her retreat. A heartbeat later, shock was replaced by intense pleasure. She opened to him, welcoming his caress, giving him free reign over her body. She called out to him as she felt her desire reach its height, but he ignored her, and Gisele arched into his kiss as she cried out with the power of her release.

She barely had time to catch her breath before he was restoking her passion. This time when she called out to him, wanting him to share in her pleasure, he returned to her arms. She groaned with delight as he joined their bodies, then gasped with surprise when Nigel suddenly rolled onto his back. He gently urged her to sit up, then moved her body on his, silently showing her what he wanted her to do. Gisele shuddered and quickly took the reins of their lovemaking into her hands. Even as her release ripped through her body, she felt Nigel grasp her more firmly by the hips and hold her tightly against him. He shuddered and moaned her name. She savored the warmth of his release as she collapsed in his arms.

Nigel gave her no time to catch her breath, to really begin to think about what she was doing. Gisele recognized the game he played, and she decided to just let him play it. It was fun to forget all of her worries, to act as if she were completely carefree, able to do whatever she pleased without fear of any consequences. She laughed and wrapped her arms around his neck when he picked her up and carried her to the pond.

"Can ye swim, lass?" he asked, grinning widely as he stood by the edge of the pond.

"Oui, my Nana insisted that I learn the skill," she replied. Then her eyes widened as she realized why he was asking.

"Non!" was all she managed to scream as he laughed and tossed her into the water.

She was just bobbing to the surface, prepared to call him every crude name she could think of, when he leapt into the water beside her. Gisele laughed and swam away from him. For a little while they feigned a game of "catch me," then Gisele allowed him to win it. The grin on his handsome face told her he knew she had.

They made love in the water, then bathed each other. She and Nigel knelt on the bank of the pond and washed all of their clothing, spreading it out on the grass so that the sun could dry it. Then they sprawled face down on the grass themselves, letting the sun warm them even as it dried the water from their skin.

Gisele began to wonder if she had gone mad. It was difficult to believe that she was lying naked next to a man she had only known for two weeks. She smiled faintly. It was difficult to believe that she was lying naked in front of anyone at all. It was shocking and shamefully brazen, but she felt no great urge to slip away and cover herself.

When Nigel idly ran his hand down her back Gisele knew exactly why she was behaving so immodestly. He had shown her the pleasure to be found in lovemaking, and she hungered for it. That delight pushed aside all of her fears and all of her worries. While she was in his arms, her desire hot and wild, she could think of nothing else but the man and how he made her feel. After a year of being surrounded by dark memories, fears, and suspicions, she craved those moments of blind passion. Her greed for something she had feared for so long amazed her. As Nigel pulled her closer, she was pleased to realize that her greed was fully shared.

Nigel smiled as he spread a blanket over the sleeping Gisele. She had not stirred since he had risen from her arms and spread out their bedding next to the cold campfire, not even when he had picked her up and carried her to the bed. He left her dagger where she could easily reach it, slipped on his clothes, and walked into the forest.

It was past time he looked around to be certain that they were still safe. He had allowed himself to become completely entranced by Gisele, firmly captivated by her passion. Although it had been satisfying and great fun, it had been somewhat foolish. He had not sensed any encroaching danger, but he was no longer sure that his special gift was working properly, or if he would even have been aware enough to notice if it had tried to warn him.

The depth and heat of Gisele's passion had been a surprise to him, albeit a very welcome one. He had never known a woman to be so free and daring in her desire. Gisele was willing to try anything, suffering only the occasional but fortunately brief pinch of modesty. Once her fear had been taken away—at least her fear of any and all men—it was as if she had become curious to know all she had missed.

As soon as he was sure that there were no DeVeaux closing in on them, Nigel went hunting. After having spent most of the day in vigorous lovemaking, he was hungry for something far more filling than bread and cheese. He smiled when he thought that Gisele probably would be, as well. The woman was proving to have a healthy appetite for a great many things.

Gisele awoke to the mouthwatering smell of roasting meat. Her stomach growled loudly, she heard Nigel chuckle, and she cursed. Reaching out from under the blanket she retrieved her shirt and braies from the pile of clothing Nigel had set next to her. She knew she was amusing him as she struggled to dress herself beneath her blanket. She could almost feel his grin. He would probably never understand that, although she had spent most of the day romping naked in the glade, the mood had changed. She was not sure she really understood. There was also the fact that she needed to slip into the forest to attend to her personal needs, and she did not want to be away from the camp wearing nothing but her skin.

Even in amongst the thick trees she could still smell the tempting aroma of food. She did what she needed to do as fast as she could and hurried back to the camp, a little annoyed when her haste seemed to further amuse Nigel. Everything appeared to be amusing the man at the moment.

"Your excessive good humor is rapidly putting mine to death," she said, as she sat down on their bedding, but there was no real anger in her voice.

" 'Tis just your hunger that makes ye less than cheerful," he said even as he divided the rabbit and handed her her share on her plate.

"Such an easy explanation," she murmured, but said no more as she began to greedily devour her meal, relieved to see Nigel do the same.

The speed with which they finished their hearty meal made Gisele a little ashamed of herself. She cleaned up after the meal, then returned to the campfire to share some wine with Nigel. Sitting there surrounded by beauty, replete with food, wine, and lovemaking, she could almost believe that everything would be all right.

"It has been a very nice day," she murmured. Then she blushed a little, afraid he would think she referred to the lovemaking alone.

Nigel smiled, put his arm around her slim shoulders, and kissed her on the cheek. "It has been a verra nice day indeed. We are rested, and the horses are rested. Aye, and all of us have been watered and fed weel."

She sighed. "And so tomorrow we must begin to run again."

"I fear so, loving. We needed this time, but it isnae wise to remain too long in one place when so many people are looking for you."

"Mayhap God will smile upon us and give them a sickness in the belly that keeps them squatting in the woods, allowing us a free ride to the port." She smiled when he laughed.

"That would be a wondrous gift, but I dinnae think we should plan on it."

"Sadly, *non*. At least we have clean clothes."

"Aye, and one doesnae realize how much one appreciates that until ye cannae have it. I also miss a soft bed. It has been far too long since I have slept in one."

"*Oui*, I, too, dearly miss that comfort."

"There are soft beds at Donncoille," he whispered against her cheek.

"I look forward to getting there."

"And verra big beds too."

Gisele giggled as he gently pushed her down onto the bed. "Should we not rest for the journey?" she asked even as she twined her arms around his neck and tilted her head back to welcome his kisses against her throat.

"The night is still verra young."

"And you, Sir Nigel, are very greedy."

"Aye, my sweet French rose, verra greedy indeed."

She knew she did not have to tell him that she shared his greed. She had more than shown that during the day. Gisele also sensed a touch of desperation in the way she held him. It had been a peaceful respite, a sweet retreat from the world and all its ugliness. She was going to be sorry to see it end, especially since she had no idea what lay ahead. This could well be the last night she would spend in Nigel's strong arms, and she intended to savor every moment.

Twelve

Nigel frowned and looked around. He could see nothing, but he still felt uneasy, and he moved so that he rode at Gisele's side instead of in front of her. He briefly wished they could return to the glade and steal another day of rest and enjoyment, for one had certainly not been enough for him, especially not if the chase were to begin again so soon. He just wished he could see how, and from what direction.

"Is something amiss?" Gisele asked, wondering why Nigel was no longer leading her but flanking her, his hand resting on his sword.

"I am nay sure," he replied.

"But you sense some danger, do you not?"

"I do, but I see nothing and hear nothing."

Gisele looked around, even though she doubted she had keener eyes or could ever see something Nigel could not. "Your instincts have not failed us thus far. I believe it would be wise to heed them now."

"Aye, then let us ride for those hills to the west. 'Twill be easier to evade pursuit there."

They had barely kicked their horses into a gallop when half a dozen men rode out of the trees. The cry that went up from their pursuers told Gisele that these were DeVeau men, but she still felt a need to glance back just to be sure. What she saw made her blood run cold. It was the DeVeaux, without any doubt, and this time they had a couple of archers riding with them, men who appeared ready and able to shoot even as they rode. Gisele was about to shout this dire news to Nigel when an arrow whistled by her head. She flattened herself against the neck of her horse and shouted a warning.

Nigel cursed and also bent low in the saddle. This was a new and chilling danger. When it was just swordsmen they faced, being seen and chased had meant little more than the discomfort of a long hard ride, losing them, and hiding. Archers meant it was now deadly to even be seen from a distance, and these men were well within range of their targets.

It was now much more important to reach the hills. There they could seek shelter and—he glanced down at the bow and quiver of arrows hanging from his saddle—have a chance to fight back. There were six of them and Gisele could not fight, but Nigel felt he could hold his own if he could find a position of strength to fight from. If he were fortunate there would be some cowards in the group, men who would readily try to run down two people, but would waver and flee when faced with a hard fight.

He looked at Gisele, pleased to see that she was not only holding steady at his side, but had made herself a very small target. This heated, deadly pursuit told him that they no longer had any secrets from their enemies. The DeVeaux clearly knew that Gisele was not alone, knew who she rode with, knew that she was dressed as a lad, and that they were trying very hard to get to a port. He had guessed some of that bad news, and David had also warned him, but this made it all horrifyingly clear. The De-Veaux were determined not to let Gisele leave France alive. The long miles left to reach a port were going to have to be traveled very cautiously, hiding every step of the way.

Encircling the hills was a thick, dark forest that did not thin out until it nearly touched the rocky base. Nigel felt a hint of relief when they entered it far ahead of their pursuers. The distance he and Gisele had gained had not protected them from the arrows, but it would allow them a few minutes to hide from sight within the trees. He signaled Gisele to ride close behind him. Although he ached to put his body between her and their enemies, he had to lead them, for Gisele had no idea where they were going.

Gisele took several deep breaths in an attempt to calm herself after the hard gallop. The archers had added a new terror. She was not sure how Nigel could protect them from that. Before today, their biggest fear had been that they would be trapped with no place to run to, no way to even reach their horses. Now it appeared that they were safe only if they stayed miles away from her enemies or remained hidden. This was going to make reaching Scotland a great deal more treacherous.

She trembled, unable to fully hide her fear as she heard their enemies' voices echo in the forest surrounding them. It was hard not to be afraid even though she trusted Nigel to keep her safe. These men wanted them dead.

What had she ever done to deserve this, she thought. A moment later she forcefully shook away that attack of self-pity and the encroaching sense of helplessness. Nigel needed her to be alert to his every move, to any signal he might make. Bemoaning the injustice of it all would not keep them alive.

"Dismount, lass," Nigel whispered even as he slipped from his saddle.

Although she immediately did as he ordered, she asked in a hushed voice, "We have not lost them, have we?"

"Nay, but we cannae ride up such a steep slope, nay silently."

Her eyes widened slightly as he led her up a rock strewn hillside. The hills had not looked so rough or steep from a distance. Gisele suddenly wondered where Nigel had led her. This was not the soft, gentle land she had grown up with. When they had a moment to talk, she decided that she would ask the man where they were and where they were going. As long as they found places to be safe, places to hide, she supposed it did not really matter, but she was increasingly curious. It was also somewhat annoying that a Scot knew her land better than she did.

Suddenly Nigel grabbed her reins. She stood quietly as he tethered the horses in a sheltered area. When he took her by the hand and led her higher up into the rocks and wind-contorted trees, she had to bite her lip to keep from asking what his plan was. The fact that he was carrying his bow and arrows told her that he might be thinking of making a stand, and that made her uneasy.

Nigel halted, leaned against a large rock, and then notched an arrow in his bow. When he looked down the hillside, over the rock, Gisele cautiously edged to his side and also looked down. Her eyes widened slightly when she saw the men who were hunting them riding close together amongst the thinning trees at the base of the hill.

"Do you think you can kill all six of them?" she asked softly, not really sympathizing with the men who wished to kill her and Nigel, but a little horrified by the growing toll of lives her quest for freedom was exacting.

"Nay, but I may take one or two down ere the others gather the wit to scatter and hide," he replied, deciding to aim for the two archers who had put them in such danger.

"And the others?"

"I am praying that they are cowards who will run when they realize we arenae easy game to trap."

It was not the best plan she had ever heard, but Gisele decided that there was probably no other. As she huddled behind the rock she knew she would be hard pressed to devise another one. She needed to learn to fight, she decided. Her lack of skill had been no problem when all they had done was run and hide, but, now, as they faced six men eager to kill them, it was a dangerous hindrance. It should be two against six, not one. If nothing else, Nigel had no one to guard his back. The best that she could do was to shout a warning.

A scream sounded from below and she closed her eyes. She heard the soft but deadly sound of Nigel releasing a second arrow, heard a second scream, and felt sickened by the relief that swept over her. Reminding herself that it was a matter of kill or be killed only soothed her dismay a little. Death was chilling to see, and these men were also dying unshriven. They had been given no chance to atone for what she expected were a great many sins. It made their deaths doubly troublesome. Gisele knew, however, that deep in her heart she much preferred it to be them rather than her or Nigel.

"Only one coward turned and fled," Nigel announced even as he let loose another arrow. "Now there are just two," he said coldly as a scream rose up from below, followed by a great deal of shouting and cursing.

"I fear it sounds as if you have just infuriated the last two," she murmured.

He smiled as he set down his bow and arrows and reassured himself that his sword and dagger were at the ready. "I mean to do a great deal more than that."

"What are you planning to do?"

"Hunt them for a change."

"Nigel," she protested.

He gave her a quick, hard kiss. "Stay here, lass, and keep your wee dagger at hand. I dinnae think ye will be needing it, but 'tis always wise to be at the ready."

She cursed as he slipped away before she could offer any argument. Nigel undoubtedly knew what he was doing, but she did not like it. At least when he was by her side she knew exactly how he fared. Now she could only wait and wonder who was going to win. Gisele slipped her dagger from its sheath and prayed that Nigel was as good a fighter as she thought he was.

Nigel crept through the rocks. He had decided that it was best if he took the fight away from Gisele. When he heard his foes noisily advancing, he almost smiled. It could prove to be a lot easier than he had thought it would be. Anger drove the men onward, and anger could make them reckless.

When he found the first man, Nigel almost felt guilty. The man was completely unaware of the danger creeping up behind him while he sat on a rock, wiping the sweat from his face. Nigel had to wonder if his unease over cutting a man down from behind was what made him suddenly clumsy. He slipped ever so slightly on a moss-covered rock, and the faint sound he made was enough to alert the man.

As he drew his sword, Nigel was pleased to see that he still held the advantage of surprise. The man moved awkwardly, fumbling as he drew his own sword. The fight was over quickly, but, unfortunately, not quietly. The clash of swords sounded like thunder in the quiet hills, and the man died screaming. Nigel was not surprised to hear the man's companion calling out for him. Neither man had revealed any appreciation for the value of stealth.

Hoping to turn this event to his advantage, Nigel swiftly moved away from the body. The other man's yelling had told him where the man was, as did his noisy approach. What he wanted to do was try to meet him halfway, to catch the fool as he scrambled blindly over the rocks to try to reach his companion.

This one was not going to be as easy to cut down, Nigel decided when he finally saw the man. He was not moving over the hills with any grace, but he had his sword at the ready and was very watchful. Nigel waited until the man reached a particularly awkward spot, one where a defense would be difficult, and confronted him.

"Ah, the bastard Scot who now runs with that murdering she-wolf," the man snarled in French as, sword held firmly, he tried to sidle along onto a better footing. "Where is the little bitch?"

"Where you shall never find her," Nigel replied in French, carefully trying to judge the shorter, heavier man's strengths.

"So, swine, you try to keep the bounty for yourself."

"You would believe that. After all, what man would not covet such a heavy purse?"

Gisele clapped her hand over her mouth to smother her gasp. She crouched behind a nearby rock and heartily cursed herself for not staying where Nigel had left her. The moment she had heard a man scream she had been unable to just sit and wait to find out Nigel's fate. Now, instead of waiting in fretful igno-

HIGHLAND HONOR 137

rance, she heard him speak of the bounty on her head in a way
that left her wondering all over again if she could really trust
him. She tried to ease her hurt by telling herself that it was
nothing but an empty taunt tossed out by a man preparing to
fight to the death, but that only helped a little. Betrayal after
betrayal had finally taught her to be cautious, and although
Nigel's remark may have been no more than a sardonic reply
to an enemy's accusation, she knew it would be wise to remember it.

She peered over the rock just in time to see the DeVeau man
lunge at Nigel. A part of her wanted desperately to close her
eyes and just pray, but she forced herself to watch. Nigel might
need her help, she thought as she held her dagger tightly in her
small hand. He might have just shaken the trust she had begun
to have in him in one careless statement, but she certainly did
not want to see him hurt.

When Nigel cut the man down she felt little more than relief.
As Nigel wiped his sword on the dead man's jupon, Gisele
wondered if she could sneak away without him hearing or seeing
her. Then she saw movement at Nigel's back and she forgot all
need to hide, standing up and crying out a warning.

Nigel spun around just in time to stop the attacker from stab-
bing him in the back. "So, the coward returns," he said, as he
struggled to stand up and gain a more solid footing.

"No coward, fool, but a wise man."

"It is wise to come back here to die?"

"Not to die, but to gain all of the bounty for myself. I had
hoped that one of those fools would kill you or at least hobble
you, but they were always poor fighters. Clumsy and inept.
Where is the girl?"

"Somewhere where you will never find her," Nigel replied,
pleased that the man had not yet seen her and praying that Gisele
would have the sense to run and hide. He knew she was near,
that she had been the one who had warned him.

"I do not think it will be too hard to find the murdering
whore. I heard her warn you, so she must be close at hand."

Nigel slashed at the man with his sword, hoping to make the man retreat a little and allow him a chance to move into a better fighting position. This DeVeau hound proved much smarter than the others, however, simply avoiding the strike and keeping Nigel firmly trapped on an uneven ground with a dead body in his way. He was cornered, and he knew it. So did his enemy.

Swiftly reviewing all of the actions he could take, Nigel decided he really had only one, to abruptly attack. It might at least give him the advantage of surprise long enough for him to move out of the trap he was in. If he stayed where he was they would just thrust and parry until he finally lost his footing and was vulnerable to a death stroke. Yelling his clan's battle cry he lunged at his foe, hoping to move the man out of the way by the sheer force of his charge.

It failed. Nigel cursed as the man met his charge squarely, holding him in place. For a moment they fought fiercely, the DeVeau man trying to keep him right where he was and Nigel trying to cut him out of his way. Then what Nigel had feared all along finally happened. Nigel stumbled as a hard lunge by the DeVeau man caused him to back up against the body of the man he had killed earlier. His foe took quick advantage, and Nigel swore in pain as the man's sword cut a deep gash in his side. He blocked the man's next strike, but that sharp move caused him to fall, his sword spinning out of his hand. He sprawled on top of the dead body and stared up at the DeVeau man, who grinned widely as he held the point of his sword against Nigel's heart. Nigel's only clear thought was a prayer that Gisele did not pay too dearly for his failure to protect her.

"You picked a poor cause to give your life for," drawled the DeVeau man.

"No, you picked poorly," Nigel replied in his heavily accented French, silently cursing when he realized he could never reach his dagger in time to deflect the death blow. "I may meet my death before you do, but at least I will not go with my soul stained by the crime of hunting down and killing a young, innocent girl simply to fatten my purse."

The man snarled a curse and raised his sword, preparing to plunge it deep into Nigel's heart. Nigel braced for the blow, but it never came. He stared up at his attacker in open-mouthed astonishment, barely shifting out of the way when the man's sword slipped from his hand. Protruding from the man's thick neck was the hilt of a dagger that Nigel easily recognized. The man frantically clawed at the knife in his throat even as he slowly collapsed onto the ground. DeVeau's hound died quickly, his life's blood pouring out of his body with a speed that even Nigel found unsettling. Clutching at the wound in his side, Nigel slowly sat up and stared at a white-faced Gisele standing stiffly by a nearby rock.

"A good throw, lass," he said, and was relieved to see her shudder a little. Then she turned her too wide but clear gaze toward him.

"I was aiming for his sword arm," she said in an unsteady, husky voice as she began to walk toward him.

"Poor lass. I had intended to scold you for nay staying where I had told ye to when I was finished with that rogue." He smiled faintly. "I believe I may find it in my heart to forgive ye for that impertinence"

"Better a little forgiveness in your heart than cold, hard steel. Is it a bad wound?" she asked as she knelt by his side.

Nigel moved his bloodsoaked hand and frowned at the gash in his side. "I am nay sure, but I think it may be a wee bit more severe than I had first thought, and 'tis bleeding most freely."

Gisele forced herself to pay attention to Nigel and only Nigel. She felt chilled by what she had done, her blood still running cold in her veins, but she could not allow herself the time to think about it now. Nigel was wounded, and he was right—his blood was flowing rather freely. Keeping him hale and alive was far more important than any soul-searching she might do to try to decide if she had been right or wrong to kill a man.

"Nay, lass," Nigel said when she moved to tear a strip of cloth from her shirt so that she could bandage his wound. "If ye can stomach it, take what ye need from one of those men.

We cannae be sure how long we will have to hide, and ye may have need of that shirt."

He was right, but she felt the sting of bile in the back of her throat as she moved toward the man he had killed. To her deep dismay she had to look carefully to find a part of his shirt that was clean enough to temporarily bind Nigel's wound. As soon as she had torn off the strip of cloth she needed, she hurried back to Nigel's side.

"This wound needs to be cleaned and stitched closed," she said, as she wound the cloth tightly around the wound to slow the bleeding.

Gisele tried to sound calm, but she suspected that some of her fear had slipped into her voice, for Nigel watched her closely. She decided to let him think that her fear had been stirred by what she had been forced to do. If he guessed that it was because she was terrified that he could sicken and die it could be upsetting for him, and it could tell him far too much about her feelings. Until she could decide how much weight to give his remark about the bounty, the very last thing she wished him to guess was that she was coming to care for him.

"I cannot properly tend your wound here," she said, "but I do not know where to go. We need somewhere safe and hidden away."

"There is no one left to tell the DeVeaux where to find us."

"True," she reluctantly admitted. "That is not our greatest problem, however. You will need rest and shelter for a while until this wound is healed enough for you to ride again. If all goes well, that could be in just a few days, but we both know it could easily be a lot longer."

Nigel cursed. "I have done a poor job today."

"Non. There were six of them and only one of you. There are now six dead men, and you have but one wound. I do not see that as doing a poor job. Do you know of some place where we might seek some shelter? I have begun to think that you know this land better than I do."

"Some parts of it, aye, quite possibly. There is a cave in these hills. I rested there when I first came to France." He sat up, wincing a little. "I will take us there."

She helped him stand, letting him drape his arm over her shoulders and rest some of his weight on her. "What about our horses?"

"I fear ye will have to come back and collect them, and I am going to have to ask ye to do a distasteful chore."

"The dead men?" She fought to maintain a steady footing as she helped him walk yet let him lead.

"Aye, lass. The three bodies on the hillside should be pushed or dragged back down. Let the carrion find them there, far away from us. Ye must strip them all of anything that could be of use to us. If any of their mounts are still about, keep one, strip the rest of what we might use, and then set all the others free. We can use that one as a packhorse. Can ye do all of that?"

Gisele only hesitated a moment before nodding. It would be a grizzly, horrifying chore, but she recognized the wisdom of his instructions. It was impossible for her to bury all six men to keep the scavengers away, so the only other choice was to make sure the bodies were nowhere near them. They also had a need for supplies, since they might well be holed up somewhere for days. She had a strong distaste for taking from the dead, but she knew she would be a fool to let that make her throw away things that could help her and Nigel survive.

"The cave is just behind that rock there, lass," Nigel said.

She frowned as she looked at him. He was pale and bathed in sweat. The walk to the cave had badly sapped his strength. Leaving him slumped against a rock, she cleared a path through the brush in front of the cave opening As carefully as she was able to without a torch, she checked the cave for signs of animals, then helped Nigel to get inside.

"I will see to our horses first," she said, "for they have what I need to tend to your wound and make you more comfortable. I shall be right back."

"Take my dagger with ye, sweeting."

She suddenly recalled that her dagger still rested in the dead man's neck, that it would have to be retrieved. Then she hastily pushed that horrifying thought aside. Nodding, she took Nigel's dagger and hurried away to get their horses. She found one of the DeVeau horses lingering close to hers and Nigel's. Tethering it so that she could deal with it later, she led their horses back to the cave. It took a little coaxing, but she finally managed to pull the reluctant animals through the opening that was almost too narrow. Then she left them in the far corner near the mouth of the cave and hastily took all she needed from the saddlepacks.

After she removed Nigel's shirt and *jupon,* he was barely conscious. Gisele worked on his wound as swiftly as she could. Once the injury was washed, stitched, and bandaged with clean rags, she spread out their bedding. Nigel was so unsteady she almost had to carry him to the bed. It took only a moment of scurrying around outside of the cave to collect enough wood to make a small fire.

When the fire was lit she checked carefully to make sure that the smoke from the fire was leaving the cave. To her relief it appeared that the cave had a great many holes, ones she could not see but would obviously do a very good job of keeping the air within the cave clean. Gisele prayed that those holes were not so numerous or large that she and Nigel would find that they had no more protection than if they had bedded down outside if it rained.

Certain that Nigel was asleep, Gisele took a long drink of wine to steady herself and went to take care of the bodies and gather what supplies she could. It nearly made her ill, but she even managed to extract her dagger from the man she had killed before pushing him off the hill. All of the horses lingered in the area, and after stripping them of their saddles and packs she set free all but the one she had tethered earlier. It took her two trips back to the cave to bring in all she had gathered. She had even taken some blankets, but she left them outside, unsure of their cleanliness. Nigel might need them for some added warmth, but she was certain he would not be helped much if those extra blankets were filthy and infested with vermin.

Exhausted, she washed herself off, forced a little water into Nigel, and then crawled into bed beside him. As she closed her eyes she paused to pray that Nigel would recover from his wound fully and quickly. She hated to admit it, for it made her feel very helpless, but she needed him hale, strong, and by her side. The battle to stay alive had become larger than she could deal with alone. For now, she was all that stood between them and a horde of DeVeaux searching the whole of the country, eager to catch or kill them. Gisele knew she made a very small shield. With Nigel at her side she had begun to feel safer than she had for a long time, but she suspected that she was going to become fully reacquainted with fear until Nigel was well again.

Thirteen

"Why are ye here?"

Gisele woke up so suddenly that she found herself short of breath. She looked at Nigel, and her eyes widened. He was staring at her as if she were a ghost, and his eyes were glazed. She touched his cheek, and felt her heart skip with fear. He was very hot.

"Ye shouldnae be here," he rasped, grabbing her by the shoulders and shaking her. "I fled home and hearth because of you. Have ye naught better to do than continue to torment me?"

Afraid that his agitation would reopen his wound, she scrambled out of his hold. He fell back onto the bed, softly cursing whoever it was that his fevered mind told him was here at his side. As Gisele got some water to bathe his face, she realized that he spoke of a woman.

It took several moments of washing his face and forcing him to drink some water before he grew calm again. Gisele continued to bathe his heated body as he slowly fell into a restless sleep. She felt an urge to weep, and knowing the reason why did not make her feel any better.

Nigel was still tormented by the woman he had left behind, still cared for the woman. Gisele realized that she had begun to nurture some hope, however small, that one day she and Nigel might share more than a sweet passion. It was clear that his heart was still in firm bondage to another. It would be hard enough to fight for him if her rival were real, and near at hand.

Gisele doubted that anyone could fight the cherished but unattainable dream to which he still clung.

For a brief moment she decided that she would put an end to the lovemaking they indulged in so greedily once he was well again. She did not wish to be used just to soften the hard edges of a memory. Then she sighed and softly cursed her own weaknesses. She did not want to give up the passion she enjoyed so much. There was also a chance that she did not want to give up—the obviously very tiny chance that there might be more between them—but she did not dare to consider that possibility for too long. She had more than enough trouble on her plate. The last thing she needed to start thinking about was what she did or did not feel for Nigel Murray. And there was also the fact that she could not completely fault him if he were using her, knowingly or unknowingly. She was using him, too—to protect her, to fight for her, and to show her what passion should be.

She knew she was going to have to firmly confront her feelings at some point, however. If she lost this battle for her life, it did not really matter what she did or did not feel. She planned to survive, was intending to do everything necessary to clear her name, so the moment of truth lurked upon the horizon. Gisele grimaced as she rose to tend to the horses She hoped she would have enough strength to face that truth when the time came.

Gisele frowned, wondering why she was awake. A glance toward the mouth of the cave told her that it was not yet morning. After two days of nursing Nigel through a fever this was the first time she had been able to sleep for more than an hour or two. It annoyed her that, for no apparent reason, she was wide awake.

Her heart skipped painfully as she suddenly feared there had been some dire change in Nigel's condition and that had been what had wakened her. She turned cautiously, almost afraid to look at him. Tentatively, she touched his forehead, and felt weak with relief. He was cool and damp. In fact, he was soaked with sweat. His fever had finally broken.

She quickly rose to get him a clean shirt and some water to wash him down. The cool air hit the back of her shirt and, as she shivered from a sudden chill, Gisele realized that it was damp. That was obviously what had woken her. She quickly changed her shirt before gathering what she needed for Nigel.

When she tugged off Nigel's shirt he roused and looked at her. Gisele was a little surprised at the depth of emotion she felt when she saw that his eyes were clear and bright, all signs of the fever gone. Matters were obviously getting far more complicated than she had realized, she thought with an inward sigh. There might not be as much time as she had hoped before she had to face up to a few hard, cold facts. Her heart was obviously clamoring for her to heed it. For now, however, she could easily avoid any uncomfortable soul searching by keeping all of her attention fixed firmly on getting Nigel well and strong again.

"I have been unweel?" he asked in a hoarse voice, greedily accepting the drink of water she gave him.

"*Oui,* a little," she replied in a slightly shaky voice as she began to wash the sweat from his body. "I am thinking you took a fever because I did not tend to your wound fast enough."

"Ye couldnae have done it any faster, lass." He gritted his teeth against the pain as she changed his bandage.

"Mayhap not. The delay allowed the bad humors to seep into your body, however. But now you will soon be fine again, *oui?*"

"Aye, but we are losing precious days hiding here. How many so far?"

"Two days. This will be the third." She watched him pale as she helped him into his shirt, but he made no sound. "I have seen no one, heard no one approach this place, so I believe that we are quite safe here."

"Weel, we must still leave here as soon as possible," he mumbled, weakened by enduring the pain of his wound, as he closed his eyes.

"Not until I feel that you may ride your horse without endangering yourself by ripping open your stitches or weakening yourself so much that your fever returns."

"That could take days."

"Then we shall take those days. There is no good served if we leave so quickly it makes you weak and ill."

Nigel knew she was right but he did not like it, and softly cursed. "We could easily be trapped here."

She dampened a cloth with cool water and gently bathed his face. He needed to be calm, but she was not sure what she could do or say to accomplish that. There was a great deal that could go wrong the longer they lingered in one place. She could not really argue the facts that caused him such concern. Lingering where they were for so long troubled her, as well.

"This place is not easy to find, and I have left no sign of our presence where anyone can see it," she said in a soft voice meant to soothe him. "I have even taken the horses' leavings far away from here, dragging the muck away in one of the filthy blankets I took from those men." She shivered slightly. "I have been tossing it down on top of the bodies. In truth, each time I go out for wood I toss a few things down onto those bodies. Rocks, wood that is no good for burning, anything I find that can be thrown down. I do not wish to go near them nor see them, yet I feel somewhat compelled to try to cover them."

"Whatever your reasons, 'tis nay a bad idea. It will hide them from view, and throwing manure on them may also work to keep scavengers away."

"I do not believe the horses have produced enough for that, yet. I am but trying to tell you to be at ease. We are truly hidden here. If it troubles you so greatly to remain in one place then rest, regain your strength as quickly as possible. The sooner you are strong enough to ride, the sooner we may leave this place."

He opened his eyes and smiled faintly. "And you will make sure that I hold fast to that plan, willnae ye?"

"I will, Sir Murray. You may be assured of that."

She smiled when he laughed softly and then closed his eyes.

It took only a few moments for him to fall asleep again. Gisele watched him for a long time, saw no sign of any alarming changes in his soft, even breathing or the return of his fever, and she breathed a long sigh of relief. It was too soon to be certain that Nigel was beginning to recover from his wound, but she had hope now, something that had been sorely depleted in the last two days.

Yawning widely, Gisele moved to tend to the horses She took the manure away and collected some wood for the fire on her way back to the cave. After washing her face and hands, she sprawled on the bedding next to Nigel. He would not be patient with the pace of his recovery, be it fast or slow. Gisele knew that, it would become more important that she be well rested, her wits sharp, as he got stronger. For that she needed sleep, and it was time to try and recoup all she had lost while he had been wracked with fever.

Gisele waited patiently for Nigel to go back to sleep. He had been free of any sign of fever for almost two days, and she felt she could relax her close guard over him. Every time he had woken up she had made him drink plenty of water or wine, as much as she could force down his throat, until he swore he would soon wash away down the hillside. She had also made him eat something. At first it had only been a few bites of stale bread, but the amount he ate had slowly increased, even in the course of the first feverless day. It was good that he was eating well, for it would help him regain his strength, but it had also caused a new problem for her to deal with. They were rapidly running out of food.

There was really only one answer to that problem. She had spent several hours trying to think of another, any other, but there was nothing. They needed some supplies. She could not hunt, and there was nothing left to scavenge in the area. All she had was coin to go and buy something. There was a small village to the west. She had seen it one of the times she had been out searching for wood for the fire.

Nigel was going to be furious, she mused as she slipped out of the cave, dragging her reluctant horse with her. She briefly peeked back inside the cave to reassure herself that Nigel still slept, then hurried down the hill toward the village. It was going to be a risky venture, for she had quickly seen that her disguise fooled very few. She had not seen any of DeVeau's men, but knew that did not mean that they were not around. She and Nigel had been caught by surprise before, and this time she did not have the assistance of Nigel's sharp eyes to scout the area. Gisele knew that if Nigel were hale and had his wits about him he would probably tie her up before he would allow her to go anywhere alone. If he woke up before she could safely return, Gisele suspected he would find the strength to scold her soundly and loudly. She just hoped that if she could return safe and successful, her saddlepacks weighted with food, he would forgive her. A full belly was said to be the cure for a man's ill humor.

Despite assuring herself that she could ride in, get all she needed, and quickly ride out again without any difficulty, Gisele felt her heart clench with fear as she entered the village. Suddenly, she wondered if what she was about to do was pure madness. Then she shook her head. Nigel was now as recognizable as she was, so it did not really matter which one of them showed his face. And she could not wait until he was well enough to watch her back. If she did not get them some food, the man might never get well. If she refused to take a risk, hid away in the cave out of fear, she and Nigel could easily starve to death or—she shuddered at the thought—be forced to dine on one of their horses. She stiffened her spine and kept riding, trying to keep a subtle but close eye on everyone and everything.

Gisele walked into the small, dark baker's shop and inwardly sighed as the man closely watched her approach. "I need three loaves," she said in a deep, firm voice.

"What game do you play with me, child?" the burly, sweat-soaked baker demanded.

"No game. I am here to buy some bread."

"Do not play the innocent. You must think me the greatest of fools if you believe a dirty cap and a youth's clothes will make me think that you are a boy. So, why has a girl dressed herself so?"

She inwardly cursed but struggled to look very young and mournful. "I try no trickery, kind sir. I am an orphan. My only family is my cousin, and he rides to join the army. There was nowhere near our home where he could safely leave me behind. I but try to hide as his page until we can find a convent where the good nuns will accept a poor girl into their care." She breathed a silent sigh of relief when he nodded and gave her a sympathetic smile.

"It is a shame that the good sisters cannot afford to take in all who need care and guidance," he said, as he gave her the bread and watched her count out her coin. "Your cousin should not let you wander about alone, however. He does you a great kindness by taking you under his protection, but he risks your life and virtue by sending you out alone and unguarded."

"I will tell him, sir."

"You do so, and return to his side as quickly as you are able."

"I am nearly done here, sir," she said, as she hurried out of the shop.

Although the man she bought the cheese from and the other merchants she fleetingly dealt with did not feel compelled to give her any advice, it was clear to see upon their faces that they knew exactly what she was. Her saddlepacks finally filled with all she needed, Gisele was more than happy to hurry out of the village. It did not really surprise her when she saw a small group of armed men riding toward the village. She did not even bother to look to be sure that they were DeVeau men. Instinct told her that they were, and her luck had been very poor of late. She rode for the shelter of the trees, trying to keep a good, fast pace and not look as if she were trying to flee and thus raise the men's suspicions.

She hissed a vicious curse when a sly glance behind her revealed that the men had slowed their pace and were looking her way. It took all of Gisele's willpower not to kick her horse into a gallop and flee as fast as she could. Her body held so taut it was painful, she rode into the trees, listening intently for any sign of pursuit.

When she felt sure she was hidden from their sight, she reined in, dismounted, and crept back until she could see the men. She was pleased with her stealth although she would need a lot more practice to be as soft of tread as Nigel. It alarmed her a little to see that they had stopped. They kept looking her way and arguing with each other. She tensed when one man started to slowly ride her way, then breathed a hearty sigh of relief when his companions called him back. The men finally continued on into the village, but Gisele maintained her vigil for several long moments to assure herself that they would not change their minds again and come hieing after her. The last thing she wanted to do was lead them back to the cave, trapping her and a helpless Nigel inside.

Still keeping a close watch behind her, she carefully made her way back to the cave. As she drew near to her shelter, she dismounted and led her horse up the steep, rocky slope. A few feet from the mouth of the cave she stopped and gaped toward it, not wanting to believe what she saw.

Nigel was standing outside the cave, his sword in his hand. He saw her and slumped against the rocks. Even as she rushed to his side he began to slide down until he sat on the cold ground.

"Are you completely mad?" she demanded as she helped him back inside, alarmed by the way his body was shaking with weakness.

"I might ask ye the same thing," he rasped as he sank back onto the bedding and heartily cursed his weakness.

He had woken up to find her gone. At first he had not been very concerned, thinking she had gone out for wood or to scavenge for some food. When he had realized that her horse was gone, however, he had become increasingly worried. The longer he waited and she did not return, the more worried he had become. The moment he had stood up he had known that he would not be much help if she were in trouble, but he had doggedly continued. His sword had felt so heavy in his hand he had known he would not have been able to use it. By the time he had dragged his weak and trembling body outside, he had realized that he could do no more than stand there shaking and sweating, and that had infuriated him. Having her find him in such a poor condition and have to help him back to bed had only added to that anger.

"I am not the one trying to recover from a fever and a wound." She hastily checked his wound, relieved to find that he had not opened it. "Where did you think you were going?" she demanded even as she moved to go and get her horse.

"To find you," he called after her.

"I did not need finding," she replied as she tugged her horse back inside the cave and unpacked the animal.

"Where did ye go?"

"We needed food. I cannot hunt, and none was walking up to the mouth of this cave, so I had to go and get some."

"Ye went into a town?"

She brought him some water and made him take a drink. "A little village to the west of here."

"Ye could have been seen by the DeVeaux."

"I was, but only from a distance," she added hastily when he cursed. "They did not recognize me, and did not follow me."

"Are ye certain?"

She nodded. "I watched to be sure that they went to the village and stayed there."

He frowned. "Someone in the village could tell them that you were there."

"They could, but that still will not tell them if the rider they saw was me, or where I went to. And, I was alone. Now they are looking for two of us. It will probably confuse them."

"We must leave here."

He started to get up, but she easily held him in place with one hand planted firmly on his chest. "We cannot. You could barely get yourself outside. Do you try to tell me that you were not weakened by that, so weakened that you could not take another step?" She smiled faintly when he cursed. "We needed food."

"Ye shouldnae have taken the risk," he snapped.

"Ah, I should have cowered in here until we slowly starved to death."

"Gisele—"

"I did what I had to do. It is unfortunate that the DeVeaux were about, but I do not believe they will be storming our little castle. Now I have the food to help you heal and get strong again. Then we can leave here. Nigel, even I can hold you in place with little effort. You cannot fight, and neither can I. Here is where we must stay, at least for a little while longer."

Nigel said nothing for a moment, hating to admit that she was right, then he curtly nodded in agreement. "Your disguise fools no one, ye ken."

"I am aware of that." She told him what happened with the baker, and was pleased to see him smile faintly. "There was no choice, Nigel. You must see that."

"I do, but that doesnae mean that I must like it."

She just laughed and moved to get him some food. After he ate some bread and cheese and washed it down with some wine, he fell asleep. His attempt to come and find her had sapped his strength, but she felt sure he would quickly regain it, that he had not done himself any lasting damage.

As she washed herself with some of the cool water she decided that she would now have to tell Nigel what she was doing and where she was going. He was no longer sleeping the day away, leaving her free to come and go as she pleased. The man might argue her plans, but if he knew what she was doing he would not try to come and find her again, risking his health.

Nigel woke up one more time as the sun set. She washed him

down, changed his bandage, and fed him. His wound was already beginning to close, but he was too disgusted with his weakness to be very pleased by that news. Gisele sighed, realizing that she had been right. Nigel Murray was going to be a difficult patient.

Just as she prepared to get into bed beside him an eerie noise cut through the still night air, and she felt the hairs on the back of her neck stand on end. Wolves. There was a good chance that they had finally found the bodies, and the things she had thrown on top of them were not going to immediately deter them from trying to scavenge some food. For a moment she sat where she was, frozen by her fear. Then she moved to build a fire near the mouth of the cave. If the wolves were near enough to scent the bodies, it might not take them long to smell the horses and come looking for that prey. She suspected that they could easily scent Nigel if they drew near to the cave, for they were skilled at sniffing out the weak and injured.

Using some of the extra wood she had begun to pile in the back of the cave, she made a large fire, then set a good supply of wood close at hand to feed it with. She picked up one of the swords she had taken from the dead men and sat behind the fire watching the opening to the cave. The fire should be enough to keep the wolves at a distance, but she wanted to be ready in case hunger drove one of them to try to cross that barrier. As she prepared to guard her shelter she took one last covetous glance at the bed.

It was almost dawn before the wolves drew near enough for her to see them. All of her encroaching exhaustion fled as she saw the light of the fire reflect off the eyes of at least a half-dozen of the animals. She clutched at her sword, trembling slightly as she heard them growl.

"Gisele," Nigel called softly from the bed.

"Go back to sleep," she replied in an equally soft voice, never taking her gaze from the enemy before her.

"Are they close?"

"Close enough." She saw no point in worrying him, for he

could do nothing to help, might even stir the animals to attack if he moved closer.

"The fire should keep them away."

"I know. It is working well."

Nigel cursed. "Ye shouldnae have to be protecting me."

"Why not? You have been protecting me for a long time now. A few nights of lost sleep is but a small recompense. Now, go back to sleep. There is nothing you can do to help, and I think all this talk is making them more interested in us than they might otherwise be."

He relaxed, forcing himself to accept her protection. Recalling her fear of wolves, he decided they could not be that close, for she had spoken in a fairly calm voice. She was right. Even if the animals did draw near enough to attack, he would be little more than an easy meal. It hurt his pride to admit that, but he had to face the truth. If he did attempt to go and help her he would only distract her from what she had to do, and that would cause more harm than good. He reached out and pulled his sword closer, however. Having it at hand made him feel a little less like a helpless bairn, he mused as his weakness slowly forced him to accept sleep despite his best attempts to stay awake.

Gisele breathed a sigh of relief when Nigel did not speak again. He had clearly not seen the red eyes she was staring into, so did not realize how close at hand danger was. That was exactly how she wanted it. At the moment the wolves stared at her, and she stared at them. Soon the sun would be up, and she hoped they would slip away. If Nigel had stumbled over to her side, he could have startled them into attacking, fire or no fire. He would also have forced her to divide her attention, and that could have been dangerous. It was terrifying to face the beasts alone, but she knew that, this time, there was no other choice.

By the time the wolves crept away the sun was already over the horizon, and every muscle in Gisele's body ached with tiredness. Each time one of the animals had edged closer she had carefully put a little more wood on the fire, keeping bright. Nigel had remained quiet, and the terrified horses had remained as still as she had. Gisele knew she had been lucky in that, but she still felt proud of herself. Although she knew she was still afraid of the animals, she had learned that her fear did not have to make her a coward.

She put out the fire and wearily tended to the horses. After washing her face and hands she crawled into bed beside Nigel, keeping her sword close at hand. After the long night she had just spent, she knew there was yet another thing she had to learn—how to fight. As she gave in to sleep she wondered if Nigel would be willing to teach her, or if it were going to be something she would have to try to learn on her own. No matter what, she swore that she would never spend another moment like that. Nigel could protest all he wanted, but she would never again face down an enemy knowing that she had no skill to fight them off if they attacked.

Fourteen

"What are ye doing?"

Gisele stumbled, startled into clumsiness when that deep voice sounded directly behind her. Thinking that Nigel was still asleep, she had picked up his sword and practiced swinging it, vainly trying to imitate the way she had seen men fight. She had done the same during every private moment she could steal since facing down the wolves two nights ago. By keeping it a secret she had hoped to avoid any confrontation with Nigel. That confrontation was obviously now at hand, and she slowly turned to face him. She knew she was blushing, from embarrassment over her ineptitude and not from shame over playing at a man's game, but she was able to face him calmly. She might not be able to make him understand it or agree, but she would not allow him to stop her.

"I was attempting to learn how to use a sword," she replied.

Nigel snatched the sword from her grasp. "That isnae something any wee lass should want to do."

She snatched the sword back, his raised brows telling her that her action had surprised him. "There is something else this *wee lass* does not want to do—die."

He reached out to take the sword back again but she quickly sheathed it, and he decided not to get into a wrangle over it. "I am here to protect ye from that dire fate."

"Do not take offense, for I mean no criticism, but you have been ill, wounded, and weak. I have just spent many days with no more protection than my prayers that nothing dangerous would creep our way until you were strong again, and you cannot imagine how helpless that makes one feel. There may also be times when I must face a danger and you cannot be at my side. I decided I needed to learn how to protect myself. I know I am neither big enough nor strong enough to fight as well as a man, but that does not mean that I should just sit on my backside and never learn the skill."

"And when did you come to this great decision?"

Her eyes narrowed as she heard the hint of derision in his voice. "When I went to the village and saw the DeVeaux. They did not pursue me, but what if they had? What if one of them had cornered me? What if one of them had followed me here?"

"That didnae happen," he said cautiously, but—although he hated the idea of Gisele wielding a sword in her small, delicate hands—he was beginning to see the benefit of her learning at least some rudimentary skill.

"Non, it did not. God was watching over us. Mayhap He was also watching over us when the wolves sniffed at our door. As I stared at them for what felt like hours. I was painfully aware of the fact that, even though I held a sword, I had no idea of how to successfully use it. That if they had decided to make a lunge at me, I could do no more than pray that I could thrash the weapon around well enough to cut the beasts down or drive them back."

"The wolves were that close? Ye said nothing."

Inwardly cursing herself for forgetting that she had eased his concern that night with a small lie, she just shrugged. "There was nothing you could have done. In truth, if you had joined me in my vigil the wolves might well have scented that you were wounded and been driven to try to reach you."

Nigel cursed and dragged his fingers through his hair. "Aye, wolves have a good nose for the weak and injured. 'Tis their favorite prey. As ye wish, then. When we camp tonight I will begin to teach ye how to fight."

Her brief moment of elation swiftly faded as she thought over his words. "What do you mean, when we camp tonight? We have already camped—here and now. Why must the lessons wait?"

"Because we must ride today, must leave this place and be on our way."

She gaped at him, then hurried after him as he moved to saddle their horses. "You are not well enough yet."

"I may not be as strong as I would like, but my stitches will be taken out soon, and 'tis clear even to my untrained eye that there is little chance of reopening the wound."

"True, but that does not mean that you have the strength to start riding all over the countryside."

"Then we will ride only a little way."

"If you do not mean to go very far, then what harm in waiting another day or so, waiting until you can ride far and maybe ride hard if the need arises?"

He turned to face her, briefly took her into his arms, and gave her a short, hard kiss. "Your concern over me is verra touching, but 'tis misplaced. Aye, I may not be able to ride verra far today. But tomorrow I will be able to ride even farther, farther still the day after that. And, even though we may not travel far or fast each day, we will still be drawing closer to a port and Scotland and safety. What I cannae do any longer is sit here waiting for us to be discovered by our enemies."

"I have seen no sign of them since that day I went into the village."

"And that is good, but it doesnae mean that we are safe here, either. Mayhap those fools didnae realize what they were so near to, but they might tell someone who could easily see the error they made and ride this way. Nay, lass, 'tis time we leave. 'Tis ne'er good to linger too long in one place, especially not when ye have most of France hunting you."

Gisele did not really have an argument good enough to stop him. He was right. There was still the chance that the men she saw or someone they spoke to could come back here and search for them. It would only take a few quiet talks with the merchants she had dealt with for a DeVeau to know she had been in that village. Their plan had been to escape France and hide her in Scotland, and it was still the best plan they had. Sitting in the cave might be comfortable, might even be safe for a while longer, but it could easily become a death trap, and it certainly was not getting them any closer to Scotland. Nigel was also not going to heed her warnings about his wound, his lack of strength, or anything that hinted that he was still too weak to begin their travels again.

"If I think you are beginning to look ill or too weary to continue, will you heed me when I say we should rest?" she asked. When he hesitated she added, "Once we leave this cave we will be out in sight again, able to be seen and chased. You are not yet strong enough to stay in the saddle for a whole day and endure a hard gallop to flee the enemy. Rest is still important."

"Then we shall rest if and when ye think we must," he reluctantly agreed.

Gisele began to help him pack their things and saddle the horses. She hated leaving the cave, hated beginning their journey once again. Although she had also hated to see Nigel ill and wounded, it had been rather nice to stay in one place for a while. In truth, the cave had begun to feel a little like a home, something she had not enjoyed for over a year. That was foolish. A cave could not be a home. At the moment, France itself could not be her home, only her grave. Nigel was right. They had to start their journey again. She would, however, keep a close watch on him every foot of the way.

They kept their pace slow, ambling along as if they did no more than travel to a kinsman for some celebration. Gisele insisted that they take a long respite from riding at noon, ignoring Nigel's muttered curses as he sulkily complied. She graciously refrained from pointing out that he had needed to sleep for over an hour before they could start riding again. Despite their care, however, he was pale and slightly unsteady by the late afternoon. She knew he was feeling poorly when he made no objection to their stopping before the sun had even begun to set.

The first thing she unpacked was their bedding, and she forced him to lie down as she saw to the horses and made a fire. Then she tended to his wound and helped him wash the dust and sweat from his body. He recovered a little after he ate, and she silently breathed a sigh of relief. They might have to move slowly for several more days, but she began to think that he could do so without any serious consequences.

When she crawled into bed beside him he pulled her into his arms and kissed her. She smiled faintly when he cursed and simply held her. He was healed enough to think about making love, but clearly not enough to enact his thoughts. She huddled close to his warmth and closed her eyes Now that he was no longer in danger of dying from his wound, now that he was well on his way to being completely healed, she, too, thought more and more of how nice it would be to taste the passion they could share. The next few nights were going to be very long.

On the third night of their journey Gisele took out the stitches in Nigel's wound. He insisted it was time, but she had hesitated, unsure of the right time to remove such things. The last thing she wished to do was to have to restitch him because they had moved too quickly and misjudged how much he had healed. Now that they were out, however, she looked closely at the wound and decided it had closed well. The skin was still pink and tender, but she could see no sign that the wound could be easily reopened.

Now he was probably healed enough to begin to properly teach her how to use a sword, if not for a long, hard ride, she mused. Thus far, he had done little more than tell her how to hold a sword and carefully instruct her in different ways to move, how to thrust and parry. At first it had been a little embarrassing to prance around by herself while he sprawled on their bed calling out directions, but she had quickly become used to it. He could show her more clearly now, had the strength to survive the day with enough ability to show her more, perhaps even to engage in a few mock battles.

"So, I am healed now," Nigel said, interrupting her silent planning as he slowly moved his hand over the rough skin covering his wound.

"Nearly," she murmured, finding her position astride his body an enticing one, learning how to fight quickly becoming the last thing on her mind. "The wound no longer needs stitches to keep the skin together and your insides where they belong, but that does not mean that it is strong enough to endure any punishment. You must still be very careful in what you do"

Nigel slid his hands down her sides and slowly caressed her hips. "There are a few things I have been thinking of doing since I began to regain my strength."

"And what would those things be?" she asked, able to see exactly what he was thinking of from the warmth darkening his beautiful amber eyes.

"Weel, they may nay be too easy to gain now that I am a poor, weakened, and scarred mon," he murmured as he kissed the gentle curve of her throat.

Gisele smiled against his skin as she bent and kissed the scar on his side and felt him tremble beneath her lips. For the last three nights she had not been able to stop herself from thinking about how it felt to make love with him. It had begun to rob her of much needed sleep. She had tried to cool her blood by remembering that he was obviously still in love with some woman in Scotland, but all she could think of was that that woman was not present. She had also tried to cling to the memory of what he had said just before he had been wounded, that puzzling remark about how any man would covet such a bounty, but her growing ardor made it easy to discard that as a callous remark intended to unsettle his opponent.

Inwardly, she shook her head in disgust over her inability to decide anything about Nigel except that she wanted him. At the moment, she wanted him very much indeed. She sorely missed the pleasure they could share, how it warmed her and made it so easy to forget all of her troubles, doubts, and fears. As she trailed soft, tender kisses over his taut stomach and heard his breathing grow heavier, she felt increasingly bold.

She found herself wondering what it would be like to make love to Nigel, and even though she felt herself blush she could not shake the thought. He had shown her how beautiful passion could be. He had always been the one to begin the seduction, to make love to her, teaching her and leading her. Now that she was no longer ignorant of the many ways one could make love and stir a lover's desire, what harm could there be in employing that new knowledge by returning some of the delight he had gifted her with?

The more she thought about it, the more daring she felt. The more daring she felt, the more her passion rose. Gisele thought of all he had done to her to make her passion run hot, and suddenly wanted to do the same to him. She had no doubt that he desired her, but now she wanted to make him grow feverish and blind with passion, just as he had made her feel so many times. It would be a very sweet and pleasurable revenge, if he allowed it.

And that, she decided, was the only thing that made her hesitate to act upon her wishes. What if, by her boldness, she deeply offended Nigel in some way? What if she made him think poorly of her? She shook aside her sudden concerns. If Nigel showed any sign of shock or distaste, she would stop and claim ignorance. It would be the truth. No one, certainly not her husband, had ever taught her what she should or should not do with a man.

Nigel trembled beneath the touch of her long fingers as she slowly undid his braies. Only his weakness had kept him from making love to her since he had begun to recover from his fever. It would have been frustrating and somewhat embarrassing if he had begun to love her only to open his stitches and bleed all over her or, worse in his mind, find that he lacked the strength to complete the act. He had occasionally thought of trying to get her to do most of the work, but had hesitated, afraid he would shock her. Gisele was a widow, but he had quickly seen that she had learned little of the art of lovemaking from her swine of a husband. Now it seemed as if she were going to answer his wishes all on her own, and he held himself still, terrified he would say or do something that would make her grow shy and reticent.

When she slid off his braies, covering his legs with soft, heated kisses, he decided that lying still was probably going to be one of the hardest things he had done in a long time. He groaned his approval as she curled her long, slender fingers around his erection and began to stroke him.

The first touch of her lips made him cry out with pleasure. Then he softly cursed when she began to pull away, her pale face telling him clearly that she had misread his cry as shock and disapproval. Murmuring his approval, he threaded his fingers in her hair and gently urged her mouth back down. It was hard to think clearly, but he struggled to keep telling her how good she made him feel, urging her to continue. When she obeyed his soft request to take him into her mouth, he shuddered from the intense pleasure that tore through his body, and knew that he would not have the will to enjoy it for long.

Nigel suddenly pulled her away from him, and Gisele frowned, a little uncertain. He had made it clear that he enjoyed what she was doing to him, but perhaps she had finally gone too far. Although she had only done what he had asked of her, her readiness to do so might finally have dismayed him. Her passion was running so high that she did not really have the wit to figure out what he was feeling. He certainly looked as if he were also held tightly in passion's grip, but she feared she might just be seeing a reflection of all she was feeling.

He slowly dragged her up his body. Gisele tried to stop when she straddled him and join their bodies, but he kept tugging at her. She gasped in a mixture of shock and anticipated pleasure when he pulled her all the way up his body. She guessed what he was about to do, but even as she thought about rejecting such a bold intimacy, his lips touched her heated skin and she relented.

A kiss on the inside of each of her thighs was all that was needed to make her open to him, to welcome his most intimate kiss. Gisele lost all sense of where she was, of what she was doing, was only aware of the pleasure coursing through her body. Even as she felt her release draw nigh and called out to him, he dragged her down his body and united them. Trembling, caught up in the force of her desire, she moved upon him with a nearly frenzied greed, finally collapsing in his arms even as he held her tightly against him. He groaned her name as he filled her with the warmth of his release. After a moment, he silently eased the intimacy of their embrace and held her in his arms, brushing light, almost sleepy kisses against her face as their breathing slowed.

It was a long time before Gisele could speak, even longer before she felt she could look at Nigel without blushing. She had behaved very wantonly. Many might even whisper that she acted no better than a whore. Gisele began to wonder if Nigel might also question her morals now that his blood had cooled.

Turning on her side, she ran her hand over his wound to assure herself that their lovemaking had not harmed him in any way. Then she studied him and smiled slightly, her fears easing. His eyes were closed, his features softened by encroaching sleep, and the hint of a smile was on his tempting lips. Nigel Murray certainly looked like a fully satisfied man.

"Nigel?" She lazily smoothed her hand over his broad, smooth chest.

"What, sweeting?" He tugged her a little closer and aimlessly planted a kiss on her forehead.

"I have a strong feeling that the penances we shall have to pay are piling up very high."

He laughed. "Aye, shameless fools that we are."

"Well, I have no need to worry." She watched him closely. "I am sure that those penances shall pale in comparison to what

I shall have to do to wash away the blood upon my poor, small hands."

Nigel opened one eye and looked at her. Ye can be verra devious when ye have a mind to be, Gisele."

She grinned. "Thank you."

It did not surprise her that he had so easily guessed her ploy, the somewhat thin attempt to get him to proclaim her innocence in some gentlemanly attempt to ease her mind. It was odd, but his refusal to openly declare her innocent of murdering her husband was growing less troublesome by the day. She no longer felt that it was some deep insult, simply saw it as a small irritation. Gisele supposed it was hard to get angry that he believed she had killed her husband when he did not fault her or condemn her for it in any way. And, she mused, although she had not committed the murder she had certainly savored the thought of it time and time again. The church said that impure thoughts were sinful. She suspected ones about brutally murdering one's husband were, as well.

She frowned as she suddenly realized that getting the De-Veaux to admit she was innocent might not be enough to fully clear her name. The hunting of her would stop, but would the whispers of her guilt? She doubted that, and felt a little sad. It would be good to be free, to not have to look over her shoulder every waking minute, but she realized that her life would never again be the same. Although she had accepted that all she had to do to stay alive would destroy her good name and place her chastity in question, she now knew in her heart that she would still suffer the blemish of being an accused murderess, as well. There really was no returning to the blissfully ignorant young girl she had been before her marriage.

"I shouldnae worry too much about what the church frowns upon, lass," Nigel said, breaking into her dark thoughts as he closed his eyes again.

"How can you say such a thing?" She gave him a gentle, punitive slap on the chest. "Do you not worry about the state of your soul? Do you wish to go to hell?"

"Nay, I just dinnae think God wishes to crowd the black halls of hell with so many wee sinners when there are so many bigger ones, so many truly evil men who desperately need to go there. Howbeit, if it will make ye feel more at ease, once we are safe in Scotland ye may go and bruise your bonny knees praying at some altar for forgiveness."

"Nigel! Your impertinence could carry a high price. Do you not fear losing your chance at absolution?" she asked, trying to act horrified by his callous attitude toward piety yet finding herself agreeing with it.

"Nay. I do all I can to follow God's commandments. I praise Him, I respect Him, and I follow His laws as closely as my poor weak flesh will allow me to. As I see it, there isnae much else a mon can do."

"*Non,* I suppose not, although I think many a priest would heartily disagree with you."

"Aye, but I dinnae always have much faith in priests. I have met many that are as weak as any mon, and some who should be roasting in hell alongside the men they have condemned to the place."

"You must have met a few good ones, as well."

"A few, aye. Dinnae frown so, loving." He kissed the line between her eyes. "I am nay turning into a heathen. 'Tis just that I cannae help but be wary of any mon who has the power priests do, oftimes more power than the king. Aye, there are good ones who truly feel the call of God and wish to do good, to save souls. There are also those who use their office merely to enrich themselves and indulge in some verra earthly pleasures and the pursuit of power."

She nodded. "I have heard of a few of those myself. Too many men enter the monasteries and priesthood simply because they are younger sons and have no other means to support themselves."

"They can live by their sword, gain power and wealth through honorable service to their laird or their king."

"True." She laughed softly as she rested her cheek against

his chest and closed her eyes. "I pray that you are right in all you believe, for I fear I am of a like mind."

"Weel then, lass, together we shall go to heaven to sing with the angels or roast in the stinking fires of hell. And now, if ye dinnae mind, I shall end this weighty talk and go to sleep."

"A very good idea," she mumbled, already more asleep than awake.

Nigel kissed the top of her head and smiled to himself. He realized that this tiny woman probably knew as much about what he thought and felt as his brothers did. When she asked her odd, sometimes piercing, questions, he felt no reticence in replying completely and honestly. Her passion was unrestrained, and she could set his blood afire. His friends and family would think him mad to be so undecided about her, to still doubt what he felt or wanted. They would undoubtedly urge him to get her before a priest as soon as possible, and a part of him agreed that he should be doing just that. Yet, in a way, he felt that his doubt and hesitation were fair to Gisele. How could he ask her to give him her heart when he was not sure he could ever do the same?

Nigel inwardly shook his head, knowing that the time for some decision was rapidly drawing near, yet shying away from it. If he decided wrongly they could both suffer. All he could do was pray that some enlightenment would come before he hurt Gisele so much there was no mending it.

Fifteen

"Ye need to hold the sword more firmly, loving," Nigel said as he picked up the sword he had just knocked from Gisele's hand and handed it back to her.

"I think you try much too hard to show me the true depths of my weakness and ineptitude," she muttered, but tried to hold the sword more firmly as she faced him again.

"Nay, I but try hard to help ye overcome them."

She cursed as they began their mock battle once again, the sound of their clashing swords echoing loudly in the small clearing they had chosen for their camp. It had been three days since she had removed Nigel's stitches, and each evening since then Nigel had taken time to try to teach her how to use a sword when they had stopped to camp for the night. Gisele was sorely disappointed over how long it was taking her to learn even the simplest thrust or parry. And what purpose was being served by holding a sword when it could so easily be knocked out of her hands? She suspected that Nigel was very good, but his skill seemed to be discouraging her more than it was helping her.

"Curse it to seven kinds of hell," she snapped as he knocked the sword from her grasp yet again, and she stuck her badly stinging fingers into her mouth in a vain effort to soothe them.

"Ye take this all too much to heart," he said, taking her hand out of her mouth and kissing her still damp fingers before tugging her over to the fire he had built earlier.

"Our lessons are done, are they?" she asked as she sat down, breathing deeply of the delicious scent of the roasting rabbit and once again thanking God for Nigel's hunting skill.

"Once your arm grows weary there is no gain in continuing," he answered as he sat down, drew his dagger from its sheath, and cut the rabbit into two equal shares. "Ye just need to hold your weapon more firmly."

"Or learn how to avoid that blow which is sure to strike it from my hand."

"Aye, that too," he agreed with a smile.

As soon as they had finished eating and cleaned up after their meal, Gisele was able to cajole Nigel into one more mock battle. He carefully instructed her for what had to be the hundredth time on how to hold her sword, and even tried to explain to her which blow to try to avoid. She used that knowledge well, if not exactly in the way he had intended. After several successful parrys, she boldly struck, crying out with delight as she knocked the sword from his hands. Even though she suspected he had allowed the blow to be successful just to show her that she had done it correctly, she was pleased with her success. Gisele held her sword out threateningly, pointing it directly at Nigel's heart. Her eyes widened when he suddenly stepped closer, allowing the tip of her sword to touch his chest.

"And now ye must kill the mon," he said quietly, watching her very closely as he spoke.

Gisele's eyes grew so wide he suspected they would begin to sting her in a moment. She also grew very pale and her hand trembled slightly, causing the point of her sword to pluck at the cloth of his *jupon*. Nigel inwardly smiled as he suddenly and finally decided upon her complete innocence. Gisele had never killed a man, might never be able to. Even in anger, perhaps even in fear for her life, she would hesitate to strike a death blow. He could see the truth of that in her eyes. She had probably not been lying when she had said she had aimed her dagger at his attacker's sword arm back at the cave. He reached out and gently took the sword from her hands.

"Mayhap this is not such a good idea," she murmured, wondering how she could have so foolish as to forget what fighting with swords was meant to accomplish—death. She might be learning how to protect herself, but she was also learning how to kill people.

"Nay, ye have the right of it," he said, as he led her toward their bed spread out next to the fire. "Your life is in danger, and 'tis wise for ye to try to learn how to hold the killers back."

"I am not sure I could kill a man," she whispered, "and that is the true purpose of fighting, is it not?"

"Aye, sometimes, especially when someone is trying to kill you. One doesnae always have to kill. At times, a wee poke or a small drawing of blood is more than enough to turn aside the threat. And ye cannae be certain what ye might be able to do when ye are truly faced with the choice of kill or die. No one can be."

She said nothing as they stripped down to their shirts and braies and crawled beneath their blankets. Nigel tugged her into his arms, and she snuggled into his warmth, then frantically tried to smother a large yawn. He chuckled softly, and gently kissed the top of her head. She had not been his lover for very long, but she recognized that tender gesture as his way of saying that it was acceptable if they just went to sleep. Their journey was rapidly coming to an end, and although Gisele hated to lose any chance to savor the passion they could share since she could not be sure how much longer they would be together, she decided that she would get some much needed rest, instead.

As she allowed sleep to slowly tighten its grip on her, she considered the right and wrong of her decision to learn how to fight. There were more people than she cared to count hunting her down all across France. If she were not killed by one of the men after her bounty, then she would be killed when she was handed over to the nearest DeVeau. It seemed foolish to hesitate to kill any one of them. All of her reasons for wanting to learn how to use a sword were still sound. She just needed to gain the spine to learn the skill and use it well. Tomorrow, she decided firmly, she would begin all over again.

* * *

"Are ye sure, lass?" Nigel asked as he drew his sword and faced her.

He fought the urge to smile as he looked at her. She stood facing him squarely, the heavy sword held firmly in her small hands with admirable skill. Her pretty face was set in stubborn, serious lines, but that look of strength was softened by the way she lightly bit her full bottom lip. Nigel knew she would be angered and probably heartily insulted if he told her she was adorable. She certainly did not look like much of a threat, and if she could gain a reasonable skill with the weapon that could prove to be a very desirable advantage.

"I am sure," she replied as she began to stalk him.

"Ye werenae verra sure last eve," he reminded her as they cautiously circled each other, preparing for their mock battle.

"I but had a moment of weakness. Some clear thinking has cured me of that."

"So, 'tis now kill or be killed?"

"That is the corner the DeVeaux push me into."

"I was hoping that ye would recognize that hard truth. 'Tis most admirable for a wee lass to possess the quality of mercy, but when she is facing men who want her dead mercy becomes a weakness they will certainly take swift advantage of."

"I know, so I have stiffened my spine and hardened my heart."

"Wise lass. Just remember that ye arenae fighting them now," he added with a smile, and then he struck.

Gisele easily blocked the swing of his sword, and he nodded in approval. For a while he restrained himself, not using his full strength as they fought. He was a little surprised at how rapidly her skill with the weapon had improved. Nigel realized that Gisele had not only decided to keep at her lessons, but had come to understand that fighting was merely another means to insure her continued survival, that a sword could indeed be used to kill but it could also be used to stay alive. Gisele would probably never have the strength to be a truly lethal fighter, certainly not in a battle that required excessive endurance, but she had gained the spirit and determination to be a good one.

Slowly he increased the force of his attack. Each time he blocked her sword he told her how he had done it, and how she could possibly evade that. She was already growing tired, and he knew that she needed to learn more subtleties in her fighting style. It would be skill, a keen eye, and cleverness that won the battle for Gisele. She had more strength than many women, but she could never endure a long, hard battle with a fully grown man, not without a few clever tricks up her sleeve.

She cursed when he knocked the sword from her hand. "Mayhap I am wrong, and there truly are just some things that a woman cannot do."

"Nay, lass, ye are doing verra weel, better than I had thought ye would."

"Oh. Good. I do hate to be wrong." She smiled when he laughed, then accepted her sword back and sheathed it. "It is kind of you to flatter me, but I still lose my sword each time we play this game."

"Ye lose it because ye grow weary. Ye need to gain some strength in your sword arm. Ye also need to learn more guile, more subtleties. I think it is wit and speed that will win the battle for you."

"So I must be careful to chose only stupid and slow men to fight with," she drawled.

"It wouldnae hurt."

Gisele shook her head, unable to fully repress a smile when he laughed. It stung a little to be told that she was not strong enough to hold her own against a man, but she knew it was true. She was tiny even in comparison to other women. If she ever had to face a man sword to sword, she suspected the battle would be delayed while he had himself a hearty laugh. There was certainly very little chance that she could win a battle on strength alone. She trailed after Nigel as he moved to build a fire, wondering exactly what he meant by wit and speed. Were there some tricks to it all that he had yet to show her?

"Wit and speed can win a battle?" she asked as she took the food from their saddlepacks.

"Of course. Not every knight is a truly skilled fighter, one who battles with grace and thought behind every move he makes. Some knights just hack away at their foe, back him into a corner through sheer brutish strength, and then cut him down."

She frowned as she spread out their bedding and sat down. "That does not sound very glorious or honorable."

"Mayhap not, but it can work, and the knight survives the battle." He handed her some bread and cheese as he sat down beside her. "That knight might weel recognize that he doesnae have verra much skill and ne'er will, so he uses his only true advantages over others, his size, and his strength. Now, *ye* can ne'er depend upon size and strength, so ye must learn to think carefully, to watch your opponent's every move with keen eyes, and to move with a speed and grace that keep ye out of reach of his sword until ye can find a chance to strike cleanly and quickly. And how ye strike is also important. Ye cannae just keep poking at a mon. Ye must learn how to strike him so that he cannae keep fighting you. That is how ye will survive."

"What you are telling me is that I must learn how to survive until I can kill my enemy," she murmured as she accepted the wineskin from him and took a long drink.

"Aye, lass, cold as it sounds, that is exactly what ye must do. Recognize your weaknesses and find a way to spite them." He leaned back on his elbows and smiled at her. "I think ye could learn to skip about so swiftly ye could make your enemy fair dizzy from trying to watch you. Ye are already verra good at seeing a blow coming and blocking it. Ye just need to gain the strength in your sword arm so that a blow doesnae knock your sword aside and leave ye helpless."

She grimaced and rubbed her arm. It was aching from all the swordplay she had indulged in the last few days. Gisele was not sure she could gain much more strength in it without damaging the poor thing, but she was determined to try. She was willing to concede that she could not win a battle on strength alone, that she needed skill and speed, but she refused to believe that she might always remain too weak to fight at all.

"Then I believe you had best begin to teach me such things," she said, smiling faintly when he tugged her down into his arms. "I pray I shall ne'er have to put all of these skills to the test, for I have no wish to kill or maim a man, but I do not wish to feel helpless again."

"Ye dinnae have to fight all who confront you," he said, as he began to tug off her clothes, starting with her swordbelt. "Ye can still just run and hide." He began to fear that by teaching her some skill with a sword he was imbuing her with a dangerous bravado.

"I know that, and it will always be my first choice. Do not fear that I will now decide to challenge all who chase me down. I may feel less helpless as I gain some skill with a sword, but having a weapon in my hands will not steal away my wits."

Gisele smiled when he began to kiss her throat as he unlaced her shirt. His slightest caress always made her feel so wanton. The soft flatteries he whispered against her skin as he honored her breasts with heated kisses were pleasing, but completely unnecessary. She suspected he could stir her with silence as long as he kept touching her. It struck her as a little odd that hands which had been trained to a sword, hands that could so easily kill a man, could be so gentle and enticing.

He removed the last of her clothing and crouched over her for a moment, studying her in the soft light of the fire. Gisele found his warm, appreciative gaze exciting and, smiling invitingly, she stretched languorously beneath him. She laughed softly when he hastily returned to her arms. His hungry kiss stifled her amusement but stirred her passion. No longer shocked by the way he made love to her, she readily gave him free access to her body as he kissed and stroked her from head to toe and back again. She even eagerly accepted his intimate kiss, gently arching her body in greedy welcome, threading her fingers in his hair as he took her to passion's heights with just a kiss.

She barely had time to catch her breath when he began to restir her passion. Cold air swept over her heated skin when he sat up to strip off his clothes, and she shivered. Just as he tossed aside the last piece of his clothing she sat up and began to give him the same pleasure he had given her. Now that she knew what he liked, she felt no shyness or hesitation. She savored the way he groaned out his appreciation as she loved him with her mouth.

A soft laugh escaped her when Nigel abruptly stopped her play. It changed to a sigh of delight when he slowly joined her body with his, while still seated on their bedding easing her down until she straddled him. With only the slightest prompting from him, she began to move, struggling to control her soaring passion so that they could linger in that exquisite moment of intense desire that came just before release. Then he leaned her back over his arm and slowly drew the hardened tip of her breast deep into his mouth. A heartbeat later Gisele lost all control. She was vaguely aware that Nigel also became somewhat frenzied as they drove themselves blindly toward release.

"If we get any better at this, lass," Nigel said as they finally collapsed onto their bedding, "I am nay sure we will survive."

"We do become quite wild," she agreed, sleepily tugging the blanket over their rapidly chilling bodies.

Nigel smiled against her skin as he kissed her shoulder. He sprawled on his stomach, draped his arm around her slim waist, and tugged her close against his side. He felt totally spent and he loved it, yet he knew he would only need a little encouragement to want her again.

"Aye, wild is a good word for it." He glanced around their campsite. "I sometimes think that the king's whole army could creep up on us and we wouldnae hear them."

"Are you about to tell me that we must begin to behave ourselves for the sake of our own safety?" She grinned as she glanced at him, not surprised to see him grimace at the thought. She might not know how deeply she had touched his heart, if at all, but she had no doubt at all that he thoroughly enjoyed the passion they shared.

"That might be wise," he murmured. "Aye, especially since your screams of delight can probably be heard in Italy."

She blithely ignored his laughter-filled glance and replied calmly, *"Non,* for they are undoubtedly lost in the uproar you make." Giggling, she slapped his hand away when he started to tickle her in gentle retribution.

"Rest, lass," he said quietly when they calmed down, and he kissed her on the cheek. "As my strength increases, I feel a need to try to recoup some of the time and distance we lost whilst I was fevered."

"Which means that you intend to ride from dawn to dusk again."

"Aye, I fear so."

"As you wish. To where?"

"Pardon?"

"Where are we riding to?"

"I told you—to a port, so that we might sail to Scotland."

Gisele muttered a curse under her breath. "I know that. But to which port? France has more than one, I believe."

"Actually, I am nay verra sure of which one. I head now to Cherbourg. 'Tis the port I sailed into seven years ago. There are many towns and villages near there where we might find someone to take us to Scotland, if there is no one to do so at Cherbourg."

"Or if my enemies are there in too great a number." She frowned, trying desperately to recall exactly where Cherbourg was and where it sat in comparison to the nearest DeVeau holdings. It was impossible, however, especially since she did not really know where she was at the moment.

"Do ye think there will be a great many of them? Do they hold any lands near Cherbourg?"

"I do not know. I was just thinking that I am not even sure

where I am now, let alone where Cherbourg is. What suddenly
troubled me was that the name sounded like one I heard often
whilst in my husband's keep. *Non,* I think I am wrong. Now I
think it may have been Caen."

Nigel cursed. "We have but recently slipped past Caen. 'Tis
a miracle that we didnae just ride into our enemies' hands. And,
aye, this certainly means that Cherbourg will be awash in the
bastards and the leeches who feed upon them."

"What a pleasing thought that is," she muttered, then sighed.
"I am sorry. I have become so lost since we left Guy that I truly
do not know where I am from day to day, or where we ride to.
In truth, I was never very clever about such things. And, until
now, I never felt there was much to gain from knowing where
a DeVeau might be roosting."

"Nay, lass, dinnae apologize for what isnae your fault. I complained so sharply because I saw yet another complication and
we have enough to deal with." He gave her a brief, tender kiss.
"Go to sleep, dearling. We shall ride on to Cherbourg in the
morning. We are close, but 'twill take a day or two more of
steady riding."

"Only a day or two?"

"If we meet with no trouble, aye," he said quietly, then
yawned.

She nodded and idly smoothed her hand over his arm. Nigel's
body slowly grew heavy, his breathing measured and soft.
Gisele knew she ought to be joining him in a much needed
sleep, getting the rest she required for what lay ahead, but she
felt no urge to do so. Instead, she stared up at the stars feeling
increasingly uneasy, almost afraid.

At first she thought she grew afraid because she now knew
that they were riding close to DeVeau lands. In a day or two
they would be at the port where there would surely be DeVeau
men searching for her and Nigel. Yet, as she continued to think
about the dangers they would soon be facing, she realized that
was not the cause of her growing fear. It worried her, but it was

not what was slowly tying knots in her belly or causing her to break out in a cold sweat.

Nigel shifted against her side and moved his hand until it rested on her breast. She looked down at him, started to smile, and then froze. No matter how hard she tried, she could not shake the conviction that suddenly flooded her mind. It was Nigel who stirred her agitation. More exactly, it was what she now knew she felt for the man.

Gisele knew, immediately and with no doubt at all, that she loved the man sleeping in her arms. It was a poor time for such a revelation, but she could not ignore the truth. Despite all of her efforts to just savor the passion they could share and keep her heart safely locked away, during the time she and Nigel had been together, she had somehow lost control of her emotions. There had been numerous hints, strong clues to what she was feeling, including occasional foolish thoughts of the future, but she had chosen to ignore them. She had even thought that she could just set them aside, like simple chores, to be seen to when it was convenient. She could no longer play that game.

It was a complete disaster, she thought as she began to edge out of his hold. Nigel loved some woman in Scotland. She had blindly given her heart to a man who had nothing more than passion to give in return. She had told him herself that she asked for no more than that, and he had shown no sign that he wanted any change in the rules they had agreed to. There was also the fact that she had already tasted marriage and found it a very bitter potion. Although she knew that Nigel was nothing like her husband, she did not think she wanted to be bound to any man by law and God again.

Suddenly all of her brief dreams about winning Nigel's heart seemed no more than the mad fancies of an enamored child. She had been a fool, reaching for something that was already firmly held by another. Gisele felt intensely vulnerable and helpless, and she could not abide it for a moment longer. Neither could she bear to face Nigel again, terrified that her newly recognized emotions would be easy to read upon her face or in her eyes. It would now be impossible to be at ease with the man. She would spend every waking moment fearing that she had given herself away by word or deed.

The only clear thought Gisele had was that she needed to distance herself from Nigel. She was not so foolish as to think that distance would take his image from her heart and mind or cure her of needing him, but it would keep her from making an utter fool of herself. The thought of following him to Scotland, of being trapped in a strange land with a man she loved but who could not love her, was an appalling one.

Gisele yanked her clothes on and moved to saddle her horse, keeping a very close eye on Nigel all the while she prepared to leave. A part of her told her that it was pure madness to leave, especially in the middle of the night, but another part told her it would be madness to stay. Now it was all too easy to remember the way he had spoken of the woman he loved while caught in the grip of a fever, and, worse, the way he had spoken of coveting the bounty on her head. It appeared that she had but two choices—to suffer the heartbreak of loving a man who could not or would not ever love her, or to love a man who would betray her, take her to the DeVeaux, and sell her. Both promised a depth of heartbreak that would make all her past ones look weak and sickly in comparison. Gisele decided that she had had more than enough heartbreak and betrayal in her life. Leaving Nigel would also break her heart, but at least she would be able to suffer out of his sight.

Cautiously, she led her horse far away from the campsite before she mounted the animal. She had no idea of where she was going, only that she had to get away. Before she had met Nigel she had eluded the grasp of the DeVeaux for almost a year. She could do it again. At least, now, while she tried to stay out of sight, she could cling to the hope that soon her family would free her from her ordeal.

Wending her way through the dark, thinning forest, she touched the hilt of her sword and sighed. She had just left behind probably the only man in the civilized, Christian world

willing to teach her a skill taught only to men. It was possible
that she had also left behind the only man who could stir her
passion. Gisele felt an overwhelming urge to hurry back to the
shelter of Nigel's arms, but she gritted her teeth and continued
on. With each step she took away from Nigel her pain and longing grew more powerful, and she knew that resisting its pull
would be a long, hard battle. Gisele plodded onward, praying
that soon the pain and longing would ease, that Nigel would
become no more than a sweet memory. If not, leaving him could
easily prove to be the most agonizing choice she had ever made,
one that would torment her for the rest of her life.

Sixteen

Nigel frowned when he woke and saw no sign of Gisele. His concern grew tenfold when, after slipping into the shelter of the trees to see to his personal needs, he returned to the camp and she was still nowhere to be found. Then he saw that her horse was gone, and he felt his heart clench with fear for her.

Even as he rushed to clear the camp and ready the horses, he looked for some sign of what had happened while he had slept. He could not believe that he had slept through an attack or abduction by their enemies, or that the DeVeaux would have left him alive to come after them. Gisele certainly would not have allowed herself to be taken away quietly or easily, yet he found no blood, no sign of a struggle, and no sign that anyone else had been near their camp.

Slowly he came to the chilling realization that Gisele had left willingly and alone. He stood next to the horses, staring blindly around the camp, and tried to understand what his eyes told him. All his instincts told him that she had run away, but when he asked himself why, he found no answers.

How could she love him so passionately one moment and slip away the next? When they were so close to their goal, so near to getting to Scotland and the first taste of safety she had had in a year or more, how could she ride out alone and risk discovery and capture? She had confessed to having little sense of direction, so it seemed pure madness to just ride off unguided. He tried to think of something he might have done or said to hurt or offend her, to make her so upset that she would leave him without a word of farewell, but there was nothing. It was true that he greedily made love to her whenever he could yet never spoke of love, but she had said she did not ask for that. He had certainly seen no sign of unhappiness or dissatisfaction.

The more he tried to understand the reason for her leaving, the less sense it made. Alongside his fear for her safety grew a slow, burning anger. He had pledged to fight for her and keep her safe, had done his best to keep that pledge since Guy had given her into his care. She owed him some explanation for running away.

He mounted and began the slow work of trailing her. Gisele could not simply walk away from him, from what they shared, and she had no right to put her life in danger after all he had done to keep her alive. He refused to believe that the fierce lovemaking they had indulged in last night was her way of saying good-bye, or that she would put herself in danger of being captured by the ever-increasing hordes of people looking for her without a sound reason. Nigel swore that he would hunt her down and get the answers he sought, right after he shook some sense into her.

Gisele reined in on top of the small hillock and stared down at the fields spread out below her. It was going to be difficult to cross such a wide, open area without being seen or without being stopped and questioned if seen. As she dampened a small scrap of cloth with some water from her waterskin and then idly wiped the sweat and dust from her face and neck, she wondered how Nigel had always found such sheltered areas to travel in. A little shade would be most welcome right now, as would something to hide behind. Then she sighed. Unlike her, Nigel always knew where they were going. She was, she reluctantly confessed to herself, just riding blindly, praying God or some good angel would steer her in the right direction.

She already missed Nigel, had begun to do so even as she

had left the campsite just hours ago. Just knowing she was leaving him had been enough to make her start to miss him and want him. It took all of her willpower to stop herself from turning around and going back to him. Far too many times she had to repeat her reasons for leaving him, had to reaffirm their worth in her confused mind. The further she rode, the less weight they carried.

Was not experiencing the sweet passion they shared worth a little heartbreak? Then there was how they talked and laughed together, even how they were quiet together. Was not enjoying that rich companionship also worth a little heartbreak?

"Sweet Mary and Jesu," she muttered. "I am pitifully undecided."

After she took a deep breath to steady the fast pace of her heart and clear her mind, she found she could briefly smile at her own confusion. One moment she was convincing herself that she had to leave Nigel, that there was no other choice. The next, she was convincing herself that there was no harm in going back to him. Unfortunately, the latter was many times easier to accomplish than the former. It kept making her hesitate, and she knew that was dangerous. She was leaving herself vulnerable to being tracked down by Nigel, if he chose to come after her at all, and of being found by her enemies.

It occurred to Gisele that she had lost some of the skills that had kept her alive for nearly a year before she had even met Nigel. She had come to rely on him, had given him a great deal of power over her life and freedom. That should alarm her more than it did, especially since she still had no real proof that he could be trusted. The fact that the man was an exciting lover was not exactly a tribute to or affirmation of his trustworthiness.

Glancing around one last time, she started down the hillock. She was reasonably sure that she was headed in the right direction to reach her cousin Marie, although she knew trusting in her own miserable sense of direction could be a mistake. The woman had helped her once and might be willing to do so again, at least in some small way. Crossing the fields was the most

direct route and, although it was dangerously open, so were all
of the routes that would take her around the fields. If she crossed
the fields she would be exposed to view for the shortest amount
of time.

Halfway across the fields she realized that she had made a
serious error. Nearly a dozen men suddenly appeared just ahead,
and she did not need their triumphant cry to tell her that they
were DeVeau men and that they had recognized her. She turned
her horse and kicked him into a gallop, desperate to get to some
place where she could hide until the danger passed.

One man caught up to her, riding close by her side and reaching out for her reins. She drew her sword and struck out at him.
Although she did not hurt him, slapping him with the flat of
the sword instead of sticking him with the point, she startled
him so with her attack that he veered away and had trouble
staying in the saddle. Leaning low over the neck of her horse,
she pressed the animal for more speed and tore up the small
hillock she had just ridden down. She could see the trees to the
west, back where she had come from, but was not sure she
could reach them in time to lose the men racing after her.

A cry went up from her pursuers as she entered the small
forest, and she knew they were dangerously close. Although it
was treacherous to ride so swiftly in such close quarters, she
slowed down only a little as she wound her way through the
trees. The sounds of the men hunting her grew a little fainter,
and she looked for a place to hide.

To her right she caught sight of a low mound, and she turned
toward it. She had barely reined her horse to a full stop before
she was out of the saddle and pulling him behind it. It was a
poor hiding place, barely enough to hide her mount behind, but
there was little else to choose from. As she leaned against a
knotted tree trunk and struggled to catch her breath, she tried
to listen to the men tracking her down, hoping to learn where
they were simply from the sounds they made.

Slowly, she began to calm down, her heartbeat and breathing
becoming less swift and painful. She could still hear the men,

but none of them seemed to be moving her way. If she remained still and quiet they might miss her, might continue on, thinking she had just kept running straight through the wood.

Just as she began to think she had escaped them, a soft footfall sounded behind her. Her sword in her hands, Gisele whirled around and cursed when she saw the tall, lean man standing there. It was her ill luck that at least one of the DeVeaux dogs had some skill in hunting down his prey. He looked at her and then at her sword and grinned widely. Gisele did not appreciate finding out that she had been right in thinking most men would find a small woman with a sword a source of great amusement. She prayed she would acquit herself well enough to make him see that this was no joke.

"Have you been playing the boy for so long that you now think you are one?" he asked as he drew his sword and began to circle her.

"I may be small, but this sword is not too heavy for my hands, and it has a very sharp edge."

"I am all atremble."

"Soon you will be all *dead.*"

"You have gained a taste for killing men, have you?" He struck out at her, and his dark eyes widened slightly when she neatly blocked his swing.

"I have gained a taste for staying alive," she said, keeping her voice low and calm and hiding the very real fear she felt.

"I approached you unarmed, my sword sheathed. I was not planning to kill you," he said in a quiet voice, obviously trying to cajole her into surrendering.

"Mayhap you have no intention of killing me yourself, but you mean to take me to those who will." She swiftly knocked aside another of his thrusts.

"You murdered a DeVeau, the one with the highest standing, and the king's ear. I but mean to take you to face justice."

"A DeVeau would not know justice if it grew legs, walked up to him, and spit in his eye."

The man smiled, then attacked her with a vengeance. Gisele

fought hard, struggling to remember every little thing Nigel had told her about what to watch for and how to strike back. She was just beginning to think she might have a chance, albeit a small one, of winning, when she felt a sharp, blinding pain in the back of her head. Gisele cried out and staggered from the force of the blow. Her sword fell from her hands as she reached up to clutch her head and stumbled to her knees. She cried out in pain as the man who had struck her from behind grabbed her roughly by the arm and yanked her to her feet.

"I was rather enjoying my little battle," said her opponent as he picked up her sword.

"I could not believe my eyes when I came around the side of the hill and saw you fighting this bitch," said the short, hulking man who held her captive.

"She was revealing some interesting skill. Someone has taught her well, Louis."

"Probably that fool Scot she has been whoring for. You should have just killed her and been done with it, George."

"I was told to find her, not execute her," George said in a hard, cold voice. "If DeVeau wants her dead, let him get her blood on his own hands."

"He will not be as soft of heart as you. She butchered his cousin."

"Vachel hated his cousin Michael. His grief is born of the fact that, as long as she lives, he cannot claim his full inheritance as the next in line. And now they have to try to find someone else who can cuddle up to the king."

"You should speak with more care, George. Vachel DeVeau deals harshly with those he believes are against him."

"I shall be sweet of tongue and nature when I face him. Then I shall gather the bounty owed me and leave this cursed place." He frowned at Gisele. "Where is the Scotsman?"

He no longer rides with me," Gisele answered, praying that Nigel would now be left alone.

"Did you kill him, too?" grumbled Louis as he started to walk away from the hill, roughly dragging her along with him.

"I have never killed anyone," she snapped, knowing that was not really the truth. The man she had killed to save Nigel's life could well be a friend or kinsman of one of these men, though, and she decided it was a secret well kept.

"That is not the tale the DeVeaux tell."

"And every word from their cold lips is the truth, is it? You are a greater fool than you look if you believe that." She cursed in pain as he gave her arm a vicious yank.

Out of the corner of her eye she caught sight of George frowning, his dark expression revealing all of his doubts. She wondered if she could find an ally there, then told herself not to foolishly raise her hopes. The man wanted the bounty offered for her, and although it might be simple avarice that drove him, he might also have a deep need for the coin—a need so desperate that he would be willing to sacrifice a life to get it. There was also the fact that anyone who helped her would be putting his own life at risk. There were not many people who would put their lives at risk for a woman they did not know, one who could be a murderer.

She studied the other men who waited by Louis's and George's horses. They were a hard-faced, rough looking group. Each one of them watched her with no hint of sympathy or discomfort upon their faces. Nigel had told her that she was pretty, but it was clear that she was not pretty enough to stir a softness in any of these men. There would be no help for her from that quarter.

"Do not try and plead your innocence with me," snarled Louis as he grabbed a length of rope from his saddle and tied her hands securely behind her back. "I do not care whether you killed the bastard or not. Sir Vachel wants you, and I mean to give you to him," he said, as he tossed her up into his saddle and mounted behind her.

"Sir Vachel obviously surrounds himself with witlessly obedient little serfs," she murmured, then cried out in pain when he cuffed her on the side of the head, leaving her ears ringing.

"If you wish to plead, save the begging for his ears."

"I would never give a DeVeau the pleasure of hearing me beg."

"I begin to think you killed your husband by cutting him into little bloody pieces with your sharp tongue," Louis muttered. "Best you keep silent now, woman. Vachel may want you alive, but he did not say you had to be hale and unhurt."

Gisele opened her mouth to say something, caught sight of George shaking his head, and decided to shut up. Speaking her mind might ease the fear and anger churning inside of her, but it would do her no good to arrive at Sir Vachel's manse beaten senseless. Not only would it mean that she would be unable to try to talk her way out of trouble, but she could miss some small chance to escape or be too weak to take advantage of one. She knew she could also be riding to her death, but she decided that, too, would be better met with a clear head. Dragged before her enemy beaten and mute, too weak to even mutter some last words as he cut her down, would not be a dignified way to die.

They crossed the fields, rode past a thick clump of trees, and there before them was a grand keep, its walls thick and tall and very imposing. Gisele inwardly cursed. It looked as if she had just about ridden up to Sir Vachel's gates. If she survived this catastrophe she was going to have to learn how to find her way, at least learn enough to know where not to go. She now saw that she had been a fool to let her raw emotions drive her away from Nigel and his protection, and it had been pure insanity to go off on her own when she had such a true skill for getting lost.

"When we first saw you riding so brazenly across Sir Vachel's fields, we had thought that you had come to surrender yourself," said George.

"And steal away your chance to gather some blood-money?" she replied, her fury at her own stupidity roughening her voice.

George just lifted one eyebrow and stared at her for a moment before saying, "It seemed the only explanation for you to come so close after having stayed free and hidden for a year."

There was a hint of admiration in his deep voice, but Gisele was too heartsick to be flattered by it. "Well, I have another explanation. It would be nice if it stole away some of the glory you may think you have gained by capturing this desperate killer, but it will probably just make me look witless. I got lost." She shrugged when his eyes widened in surprise.

"You got lost?"

"I got lost." She stared up at the huge, iron-studded gates they were about to ride through. "Very, very lost," she whispered.

She prayed that Nigel was not hunting her, that he had found her gone and decided to just go home. He had pledged to protect her and he was a man who took such things very seriously, but she was sure she had deeply offended him by slipping away in the dead of night without a word. She prayed that his sense of outrage would force him to give up on her. This keep was sturdy and well-manned. If he tried to pull her out of the trap she had ridden into, he could easily get himself killed. Gisele felt certain that she would soon be dead, and the last thing she wanted to face as she died was the knowledge that her stupidity had also gotten Nigel killed.

Nigel stared out over the fields and scowled. Such open ground made him uneasy, but he had clearly not made Gisele aware of its dangers. He looked back down at the churned up earth and cursed. Something had taken place here, and he had the sick feeling that some disaster had befallen Gisele.

He had followed her trail to this spot, easily seeing her horse's distinctive hoofmarks upon the ground. At some time, he mused, he ought to go and give the blacksmith who had shod the animal with a scarred shoe a little gift. The fact that one of Gisele's horse's hooves left a mark distinguished by a little slash resembling a lightning bolt had made tracking her almost embarrassingly simple. If he got her out of whatever trouble she was in, he might have to fix that, however. If he recognized it as hers and could follow it so easily, so could someone else.

Dismounting, he studied the signs upon the ground more carefully. Tugging his horse after him he walked into the wood, following her trail straight to the little mound Gisele had tried to shelter behind. There he saw the clear signs of a battle. His brief alarm eased when he saw no blood, but he knew she was not safe. Two men had been with her. She had been taken, but she had been taken alive. He just wished he knew when, and if she were still alive. Where they had taken her would be easy to find out, for they had taken her horse, as well. All he had to do was follow the trail.

Just thinking that Gisele might be dead, that the DeVeaux might have won, sent shivers down Nigel's spine. He felt the chill of that thought deep in his heart. He could not believe God would allow such an injustice, and he clung to that thought. God and luck had kept that girl alive for a year despite so many people searching for her. It had to keep her alive a little longer, just long enough for him to pull her out of the danger she was in. Any other possibility was simply unthinkable.

After taking a deep breath to calm himself, Nigel returned to reading the signs. By the time he found himself back at the top of the little hillock overlooking the fields, he was sure of what had happened. His unease with open ground had been justified, for as Gisele had sat here, clear for all to see, the DeVeaux had spotted her. She had then been chased and finally captured in the wood where she had tried to seek shelter. The DeVeaux had next ridden out over the fields, someone pulling her horse after theirs.

The fields below him were even more dangerously open than the little hillock. It would be quicker and easier if he directly followed their trail, but it would also expose him to the same fate that had befallen Gisele. The DeVeaux knew she had a companion, a Scot riding at her side. They might still be looking for him. Even standing there in full view upon the mossy hillock while he pondered what to do was putting him at risk.

He hurriedly moved toward the high hedgerows that encircled the fields. They would provide some cover. Nigel decided he would follow them around until he picked up his quarry's trail again. It was hard, but he moved slowly, ambling along and leading his horse as if he were in no hurry, were just some traveler courteous enough not to take the straightest route and damage a newly planted crop.

As he had begun his search for Gisele he had been torn two ways. She had left him, willingly and stealthily in the middle of the night. A sensible man would see that as the clear rejection it probably was, but Nigel had come to realize that he was not very sensible when it came to Gisele. He had tried to tell himself that it was his pledge to protect her that had him hunting her down, that it was all a matter of honor, but he knew that was not the whole of it. She had, after all, dismissed him from her service by walking away. No one would ever fault him if he simply walked away, gave up, and went home.

Nigel had to accept the truth. He had come hieing after Gisele because he wanted her back. He also wanted to be certain she was safe, but that had not been a grave concern at the start. She had managed to keep herself safe and alive for a year before he had joined her. It was not until he had seen the signs of trouble that he had added concern for her safety to what drove him.

He was so confused, in his heart and in his mind, that it made his head ache. Nigel placed the blame for that discomfort squarely on Gisele's pretty shoulders. She had gifted him with the sweetest, wildest passion he had ever known and then walked away without a word. He did not know what he felt for her—or even if he could trust his own feelings, anyway—yet the moment she was not at his side he panicked. His heart felt as if it had just had a piece torn away, and that, he knew, should tell him something.

A smile touched his face, and he shook his head. He and Gisele needed someone a lot wiser than they were to untangle them. Instinct told him that she, too, suffered some confusion and doubt. A little vindictively, he hoped it was as much, if not

more, than he did. If he were going to be tormented, then so
should she.

As he reached the side of the field opposite the hillock, he
found the trail he sought. Cautiously, an ominous feeling growing in his belly, he followed it to a thick clump of trees. The
trail went around the trees, but Nigel went inside them, welcoming the shadows. The moment he saw what stood on the
other side, he froze.

"Ye rode right into their hands, didnae ye, loving?" he muttered.

He cursed and, tethering his horses to a branch, he sat down
on the leaf-strewn ground and stared at the fortified *demanse*
in front of him. Nigel knew she was in there, and knew that it
was a DeVeau stronghold. Every instinct he had told him so.
Gisele had ridden away from him straight into the deadly grasp
of her enemy.

For a brief moment, he wondered if that had been her intention. She had become increasingly fretful about the danger she
was pulling him into, had suffered a deep guilt when he had
been wounded. He had thought that he had cured her of all that,
but he may have been wrong. Perhaps, in some mad gesture of
gallantry, she had realized that the only way to make the De-
Veaux stop chasing him was to surrender herself.

"Nay," he whispered, "Gisele isnae that big a fool."

Even as he spoke the words he knew they were true. Gisele
might do such a thing if it were her only choice, if some DeVeau
held a sword to his throat and told her it was his life or her
surrender. There was no such threat, however. She still had had
some choices. Her cousin David had told her that most of her
family now believed in her innocence, and so she could go to
one of them for help. Gisele had too much spirit to simply give
up, had too strong a will to live to just hand herself over to
people who ached to kill her.

What he had to do now was come up with a plan to get her
out of there. The longer he stared at the keep, the more sure he
was that he was mad to think he could get her free. The moment

he tried to reach her in there he would be found and killed, or set beside her on the scaffold. It was a strong, well-manned keep. It looked impenetrable.

He hastily shook his head. Every keep had a weakness, just as every person did. They were built by people, after all. They also had to have some bolthole, some way for people trapped inside to get out. If someone can get out unseen, then someone can get in unseen. At times, a keep's defenses themselves were the weakness. If the men at the gates and on the walls felt too secure, if it had been a long time since they had had to fight in defense of the keep, then they could grow lax in their watch. Nigel knew that all he needed was a moment of inattention, and he could get inside.

It was hard to fully muffle the groan of frustration that slowly escaped him, and he put his head in his hands. And just what was he going to do once he did get inside? His attire would not give him away, but if he had to speak to anyone his heavily accented French would quickly let everyone know he was not one of DeVeau's men. There was also the problem of finding Gisele, releasing her from whatever hole she had been thrown into, and then getting her out of the keep.

Nigel returned to staring at the keep. It was madness. There was nothing he could do, no plan that was not fraught with danger for himself and for Gisele. A wise man would accept defeat, grieve for the loss of the woman, and creep home with his tail between his legs. He sighed with resignation and shook his head, for he knew he would sit there until he rotted or some idea came to him. Nigel prayed that he would be shown the way to free her before Gisele was forced to pay with her life for a murder she did not commit.

Seventeen

Louis dragged Gisele into the great hall, George quietly following behind. She cursed when he shoved her toward the tall, slender man seated in a huge chair at the head table. So hard did Louis shove her that she stumbled and was barely able to right herself before falling into the tall man's lap. Gisele took a deep breath to steady herself, brushed off her clothes, and looked at the man.

Her heart briefly skipped to a stop, and her blood ran cold. For a moment she thought she was looking at her husband, then shook away that mad idea. There was absolutely no doubt in her mind that her husband was dead. She had seen his body. This had to be Vachel, but the resemblance between him and his cousin was so strong it terrified her. Vachel was tall, almost delicate in his slenderness, and nearly beautiful. He had the same perfect features as her late husband, the same perfect skin, even the same thick, long, raven black hair. When she found the strength to look into his eyes, she felt ill. He also had the same beautiful but cold, dark eyes, eyes that held the same look of sly viciousness that Michael's had.

"At last we meet, cousin," he drawled, his voice deep and soft, almost musical. "May I be so bold as to say that you are not looking your best?"

"I am wounded to the heart," she drawled, and ducked just in time to avoid another knock on the head from Louis.

"Do not touch her," commanded Vachel

Even Gisele felt inclined to step back when she heard the ice in Vachel's voice. A quick glance at Louis revealed that the man had grown a little pale. He had taken at least two steps back and clasped his thick fingered hands behind his back in a show of obedience.

There was at least one difference between Vachel and her husband, she mused, as she looked back at the lord of the manor. Michael would have just leapt on the man and beaten him senseless. She knew in her heart that Vachel had that same streak of violence in him but had learned how to refine it, how to imbue his voice with it without shouting or raising his fist. She knew that that made Vachel much more dangerous than Michael ever was. It also made him much more evil and frightening. Michael's cruelty had come forth through anger or a very evident sort of madness, blindly enacted without thought or planning. Vachel could remain calm, would act with complete knowledge of the cruelty he was inflicting and how to make it as horrifying as possible.

"Afraid he may kill me before you can?" she asked, determined not to quail before this DeVeau. She had done it once and found it not only bitter, but useless.

"And what makes you believe I am going to kill you?" Vachel asked, watching her over the edge of his ornately carved silver goblet as he sipped at his drink.

"I have been condemned to death since I fled your cousin's manse. Has my sentence been altered while I was hiding?"

"Your sentence, your punishment for ending Michael's poor, miserable life, is whatever I choose it to be."

Gisele inwardly trembled, praying her fear was not clear to read on her face. She suspected that Vachel could make the slow, choking death of a hanging seem merciful. It was going to be very hard to maintain her act of bravado. Vachel terrified her, far more than her brutal husband ever had.

"Sir," George said as he stepped up beside Gisele. "I was told that there was a bounty on this woman's head?"

"Of course, business should always be done before one indulges in one's little pleasures," Vachel murmured, and he signaled to the cold-faced man seated on his right, who quickly and silently left the room.

Pleasures? Gisele thought, silently repeating the word in her head. That sounded chillingly ominous. She found it a little unsettling when she tried to calm herself by thinking that Vachel was just one of those sick men who would enjoy watching a woman hang. If that were the least of the horrors she thought he would inflict on her, she decided to try to not think of the worst. Such musings could easily cost her her slim grip on courage.

Vachel's man returned with a small sack of coins and handed it to George. She noticed that George had the wisdom not to look inside and chance insulting Vachel with that show of mistrust. As George turned to leave, he met Gisele's gaze. She saw that look of doubt there again, but he quickly looked away and hurried out of the great hall. It did not matter, for even if she could have made use of that doubt she could not do so now, and George would soon be gone. Louis looked after him, obviously wondering if waiting to be dismissed by Vachel would cost him his share of the bounty.

"You had best hurry away, Louis," Vachel drawled. "George may forget to give you the coin you earned." He smiled coldly as Louis hurried out of the room, and then glanced at his man, who had reseated himself on his right. "How many do you think will survive the quarrel over that bounty, Ansel?"

"Half," Ansel replied, his voice little more than a hoarse whisper.

Vachel turned his full attention back to Gisele, caught her looking curiously at the muscular Ansel, and said, "His voice was forever softened by my father's hands about his neck. Ansel's loyalty to me is absolute. He objected to my father trying to beat me to death for sleeping with his third wife."

The curse of her overwhelming curiosity almost made Gisele ask what had happened to the father that had made him stop before Ansel died, but she quickly came to her senses. "If you try to shock me with tales of depravity, do not waste your breath. You may recall that I was married to one of your kinsmen."

"Michael was but a pale shadow of myself."

"Especially now," she murmured. His soft laughter startled her.

"*Oui,* Michael is not the man he used to be. You must have bound him to the bed whilst he was in one of his drunken stupors. Even Michael could have fought off a tiny woman like you."

She rolled her eyes in a gesture of weary frustration. "I did not kill Michael."

"From all I have heard you made no secret of how much you loathed him."

"Loathing him is a long step away from strapping him down, then cutting his member off and choking him with it as I slash his throat."

"Truly? I have always found that loathing and murder are very compatible. And it sounds like a most suitable way for a wife to kill her husband."

"You may think so." She knew there was no talking sense to the man, that he thought in dark, evil ways, that she could not even imagine.

"I do. So much more interesting than poison or hiring someone to slip a knife into his back." He looked at Ansel. "Show her to a room to bathe, and get her a gown."

"You wish me to be clean and properly attired before you hang me?" she asked as Ansel rose, stepped over to her, and took her by the arm.

"You do appear very improper, Gisele. One would not wish to shock the poor people attending your execution, would one?"

"Oh, indeed, one might," she muttered as Ansel dragged her out of the great hall.

Gisele did not understand what was happening, and that frightened her. If Vachel were just going to execute her, what did her cleanliness and attire matter? She disregarded his cold words of explanation. That was just a sick jest. There was really only one reason for him to want to clean her up and dress her as a woman, as far as she could see. Vachel quite possibly shared his cousin's taste for rape.

Ansel shoved her into a large room, where he grabbed a timid maid by the arm and whispered some instructions to her before he shut the door. Gisele ignored the muscular, silent Ansel standing guard and looked around the room. Her fear grew. This was a man's room and, although she dearly wished to be proven wrong, she knew it was Vachel's.

For a brief moment, she wondered if he were going to offer her freedom in return for her favors. Then she recalled with whom she was dealing. She wrapped her arms around herself as she shivered, but nothing would keep the chill of fear away. If she judged Vachel right, he had looked at her, decided he wanted her, and intended to use her until he tired of her. Then he would have her executed for the murder of his cousin. It was a very tidy way to have a mistress and then be rid of her when he got bored, and she suspected Vachel would savor the simplicity of it all.

She looked around the room again, but saw no way to escape. One glance at Ansel told her she would never get any help there. Vachel had warned her that Ansel's loyalty was absolute, and she believed it. Her only hope was escape, for she knew Vachel would show no mercy, but unless some miracle happened she was trapped. Gisele fought the urge to weep with helplessness, not wanting Ansel to see it. He would tell Vachel, and Gisele was sure that man would find some pleasure in her sorrow and fear.

When the tub was brought and filled with hot water she watched the maids closely. The women were all silent, heads bowed and spirits broken. None of them would offer her any aid. As soon as the tub was filled and the maids had slunk away, she turned and looked at Ansel.

"You could at least turn your back," she snapped, fear making her temper short. Was he supposed to have a taste of her, too?

"Non," he rasped.

"I will not disrobe before you."

"You will, or I will do it for you."

Gisele hesitated for a moment and then Ansel took a step toward her. Trembling with embarrassment, she turned her back on him and shed her clothes. Just as she got ready to step into the bath, he grabbed her by the arm and turned her around. Gisele stood stiffly as he looked her over as if she were a slab of meat about to be set upon the Lord's table. The fury she felt over being subjected to such an indignity briefly burned away her fear. When he released her, she spit a curse at him and climbed into the tub. She easily ignored him after that, taking her bath as if she were alone in the room.

Once she was out of the water and rubbing herself dry with a soft drying cloth, Ansel pointed to the clothes one of the maids had spread out on the bed. She really did not want to put them on, for it seemed as if she were accepting her fate by doing so. Unfortunately, the maids had taken away her boy's clothing, and her only other choice was to remain naked. As soon as she was dressed Ansel looked her over again, nodded, then left her alone. She winced as she heard a heavy bar being slid across the door.

Choked with fear and despair, Gisele flung herself onto the bed and indulged in a brief, hearty cry. It did not make her feel all that much better, but she hoped it would relieve her of the urge to do so again. The very last thing she wished to do was show any sign of weakness in front of Vachel or one of his minions.

She was facing rape. Nothing she told herself could change her conviction that that was the fate Vachel had in store for her. Someone who did not know the DeVeaux might think she was about to be forgiven, perhaps even set free, but she knew these men. Ansel had not looked her over to be sure she was not injured. He had done so to be sure she was clean and would not sully his master when the man forced himself upon her.

Nigel had so carefully eased her fears, so gently shown her that passion could be a beautiful thing. She had not forgotten all the cruel, ugly things her husband had done to her and probably never would, but Nigel had helped to soften the hard edges of the memory. Now yet another DeVeau was about to ruin it all. She would have to endure new horrors, new humiliations. Everything she had shared with Nigel was going to be spoiled, even the pleasant memories drowned by new ones bred of cruelty and pain. Gisele found that to be the saddest thing of all.

The bolt was slid back on the door and it slowly opened. Gisele resisted the urge to try to hide somewhere in the large room like a terrified child. She stood tall and straight as Vachel entered. A little maid scurried in silently behind him and set a tray of food and wine on a table near the bed, then scurried back out. As the door shut behind her, Gisele caught sight of the hulking Ansel just outside of the door.

She tensed as Vachel drew near, plucking at her growing curls with his long, pale fingers. It was hard to look at such a beautiful face and believe that it belonged to such a cruel, evil man, but Gisele had no doubt about his true nature. Michael had also been beautiful. It would be a sort of justice, she mused, if such men had faces as twisted as their souls so that they could be more easily recognized.

"You even cut your hair," Vachel murmured. "Was it vanity that made you then curl it as it grew?"

"I did not curl it." The way he studied her as if she were some unusual creature he had found in the forest made her nervous. Gisele did not think it was safe to have a man like Vachel find her interesting. "It grows like this."

"Intriguing. Have you guessed what I plan for you?" He placed his hands over her breasts, his gaze fixed upon hers. "You did not have to bind yourself."

It was hard, but Gisele made herself act as if his touch meant nothing to her, as if she felt absolutely nothing, not even the disgust that was churning her stomach. "It rapidly becomes clear that you do not mean to flatter me to death," she drawled.

"I may yet utter a few flatteries. I am sure my late, unlamented cousin taught you nothing, but I am curious as to what that rough Scot may have shown you."

"He showed me how to escape your family and how to fight. Give me a sword and I will show you."

Vachel stepped back and then slowly circled her before coldly smiling at her. *"Non,* but I will keep your boast in mind. If you speak the truth about your skill, I may be able to make interesting game of it."

Gisele did not even want to think about that. "It will be hard to show you when I am dead, and the hanging will be soon, will it not?"

"It will not," he murmured. "I have other plans. My family hungers for their revenge upon you, but they can hunger for a while longer. They do not need to know that you have been found. You may take your ease here, with me, in this room. We will pleasure each other for a while."

"Do you think I will play the whore for you just to save my neck?"

"I did not say that it would save your pretty neck." He lightly encircled her throat with the long, cold fingers of one hand.

"If it will not save me from the hangman, then why would I even consider letting you touch me?"

She struggled against gasping for air as he tightened his grip on her throat. For a brief moment she thought he was going to kill her right then and there. Gisele suspected that she should welcome a quick death when none of the other choices offered to her were ones she could accept, but she realized that she wanted life more than she wanted anything else. She clutched at his hands, but he just silently continued to tighten his grip, seemingly oblivious to the pain of her fingernails digging into the flesh of his hand. Then, just as suddenly and calmly as he had grabbed her, he let her go. She rubbed at her bruised throat as she gulped air back into her body.

"You will do as I wish because you do not wish to die," he said.

"But you just told me that what I do or do not do will make no difference. You still mean to hang me. It just becomes a matter of when."

"It becomes a matter of how much pain you wish to endure before you give me what I want. And there is always that sweet, useless thing people try to cling to when all seems lost—hope. I think you are very good at clinging to hope. You will want to stay alive as long as you can because you will hope that you can escape me." He smiled faintly. "Or kill me."

She watched silently as he walked to the door. "I begin to think I will do more than hope I can kill you," she rasped as he started to leave the room. "I believe I may pray for it, may come to crave it."

"Good. Such passion puts the color in your cheeks, and you do not look quite so frail. Rest. I shall return to your sweet arms after my meal."

The door shut behind him and she sank down on the edge of the bed. She did not know which she wanted to do more, vomit or cry. One moment the man nearly choked the life from her, the next he was telling her to rest so that she could properly pleasure him when he returned. Madness obviously ran rampant in the DeVeau family. She had been right to think that Vachel was far more dangerous and evil than his cousin.

She looked at the food, briefly considered the possibility of starving herself to death, and then took some bread and began to eat. Vachel was right. As long as she remained alive, she would continue to hope. She would suffer the humiliations and the pains and try to keep herself strong with hope. She would hope that she could escape and that her family would finally prove her innocence and help set her free, and she would also hope that Vachel DeVeau would die a gruesome, agonizing death.

As she ate, Gisele drank a lot of the wine. She idly wondered if she could get drunk enough to be numb to what Vachel did to her or, even better, be so drunk that he lost interest, if only for one night. Even as she contemplated the possibility she poured another goblet of wine, and the black leather jug was suddenly empty. She shook it over her half-filled goblet, then cursed and threw it across the room.

The man had even thought of that, she mused, and then felt an almost overwhelming urge to scream and weep. How could she fight a man who was not only cruel, but clever? If he thought of everything she might do before even she thought of it, there was no chance to outwit him.

To stop herself from sinking too deep into her own misery, she got up and began to meticulously search the room. It did little to improve her mood when she found nothing she could use as a weapon. That struck her as odd, for she was sure this was Vachel's room, and a man like that had to have so many enemies that he would never dare to go to bed without some weapon within reach.

She carefully studied the room again, and cursed. It was not his room. Rather it was made to look like his room. Gisele was astonished at the man's slyness, his secretive nature. She suspected that everyone who came to visit Vachel and probably everyone who lived and worked here thought this was the master's bedchamber, but she sincerely doubted that Vachel ever slept here. Probably not even after he had stolen his pleasure from some poor woman. Vachel's true sleeping quarters were secreted somewhere where no one could find him. The only other person who would know where the lord of the manor slept would be Ansel, and that man would go to his grave before he would betray Vachel.

His little hideaway could even be inside the walls, she mused as she idly inched her way around the room, running her hand over the wall. Gisele was not quite sure what she looked for, just some subtle thing that would be pulled or pushed to reveal a doorway. If his true bedchamber were not in the walls, then the hall leading to it was, for he could not be seen coming and going from this room.

"What are you doing?" asked a cold voice from right behind her.

Gisele gasped softly in surprise and turned to look at Vachel. She had not even heard the door open, yet a quick glance over his shoulder revealed Ansel taking one last look inside before shutting the door. Vachel DeVeau had obviously learned the same little trick that Nigel had. She supposed she should not be surprised. A man like him would find it very useful to be able to move around silently.

"I was looking for your escape door," she answered truthfully.

"What do you mean?"

"Just what I said."

"Why should I wish to escape from my own room?"

She could tell by the way his voice grew colder and softer that he was becoming angry. It was not wise to tell him that she knew one of his greatest secrets. Then she decided that it did not matter. She might even get lucky and say or do something that finally broke his tight control over himself and make him kill her—quickly.

"Because you are hated so much that your enemies number in the thousands. The last thing you would wish them to know is where you sleep. The bedchamber can be the one place where a man is most vulnerable."

"Cleverness is not always appreciated in a woman."

"So your cousin was fond of telling me, either before or after he beat me."

"My cousin obviously did not beat you often enough or hard enough."

"He did his best," she said, moving away from him and picking up the wine decanter she had hurled against the wall.

"Michael did not have a best."

She had just set the decanter down on the table by the bed when she felt his body close to her back. He had neatly pinned her between himself, the table, and the bed. Gisele cursed her own stupidity. She should have watched him more closely.

"You did not send up enough wine," she complained, but her voice wavered ever so slightly as she turned around to face him, their bodies only a deep breath apart.

"I sent up all you would need," he said as he reached out to stroke her hair.

His touch was almost gentle, but she knew that could change at any moment. He had already shown her that his touch could turn hard and brutal in the blink of an eye. And, gentle or not, skilled or not, he was still intending to take from her something she would never give him willingly. She pressed herself up hard against the table in the vain hope of evading his touch.

Although she usually liked to be right, she did not find it comforting that she had been so about the wine. Vachel had sent up a carefully measured amount. He had suspected that she might consider getting senseless with drink. As he trailed his almost soft fingers over her cheek, she heartily wished he had not been so clever. It would have been almost pleasant to be able to pass out from an overindulgence in wine right about now.

A soft cry of alarm escaped her when he suddenly grabbed her and threw her onto the bed. Her whole body tried to press itself deep down into the soft, feather mattress when he sprawled on top of her. There was an unsettling look of consideration in his dark eyes as he looked down at her.

"So, you were caressing my walls in an attempt to find some hidden door," he murmured as he slowly began to unlace her gown.

"You know exactly what I was doing."

Gisele struggled to hold herself very still. Her husband's brutal attentions had taught her that fighting only added to her pain. She had no weapon to kill or maim Vachel, and he was bigger and stronger. Honor might demand that she fight him, but honor did not have to suffer the pain of the beating resistance brought.

"If I had a small hiding place, you must know that I would want it to remain a secret. If you tell me you know my secrets, then you cannot be surprised if I decide it would be wise to silence you."

"Is it not pointless to threaten me with death? You have already made it clear that there is nothing I can do or say that will save my life."

"A person can be silenced in many ways." He slid his hand

inside of her bodice and fondled her breasts. "You do not fight me."

"One thing your cousin taught me was that all I gain from that is more pain."

"So you mean to lie beneath me like a corpse."

"If that troubles you then I suggest you go and find your pleasure elsewhere."

He just smiled. "I did not say that it troubled me. I but thought that you had more spirit than that."

"Spirit does not make one witless. I have no weapon and I cannot match your strength. This crime you commit will bring me pain and humiliation. Trying to stop you will only bring more of the same. I will save my spirit for the time that I can cut your throat."

"As you did my cousin's?"

"I have said that I did not kill Michael. You should be honored. You will be my first kill."

"And mayhap you believe your Scotsman will come riding to your aid," he said.

"Non, I left him. He will not follow."

"Then he will survive. We watch for him, you know."

"If Nigel wanted to get into your keep, you would never see him do so. He is like the thin smoke of a dying fire. He could slip in here and cut your throat before you even realized the door had opened."

"The empty boasts of a besotted lover."

"I will remind you that you said that while you lie drowning in your own blood."

"Enough talk. I have not come here for conversation or idle pleasantries."

"Non, you have come here to steal what would never be given to you willingly."

"I have. After all, who is there to stop me?"

"Weel, I might be willing to give it a wee try," drawled a deep voice, enriched with a thick Scottish accent.

Eighteen

Dusk was rapidly increasing the shadows all around him, and Nigel stood up to stretch. Although he had sat there for several hours, no one had seen him or confronted him. He decided he was right about an arrogant sense of power and safety making the men at arms careless. Nigel felt sure that he could slip into the keep without being seen, but despite long hours of plotting he was still not sure of what he would do once he was in there. Soon they would close the heavy gates, and that left him with just two choices—getting inside the keep before they did and hope for the best, or sitting where he was for the rest of the night praying they did not kill Gisele before he could devise a good plan of rescue, one that had some small chance of success.

Just as he decided that he would slip inside and do the rest of his plotting within the walls of the keep, he watched a lone man ride out through the gates. The man rode straight for the trees, and Nigel moved quickly to intercept him. There was a dark, brooding look on the man's narrow face, and Nigel knew he was troubled about something. Better yet, the man was sunk deep in his own problem, oblivious to all around him. That distraction would allow Nigel to slip up on his prey unnoticed, catch him alive, and pull some important information from him.

Barely a sound escaped the man as Nigel leapt from the shadows, pulled him from his saddle, and threw him to the ground He pulled his dagger, sat on the man, and held his knife to his throat. Nigel frowned as he looked closely at his prisoner's face.

His captive should at least look surprised, preferably afraid, but the man just looked a little amused.

"I am George," the man said. "You must be the Scotsman."

"The Scotsman?" Nigel asked in English, praying that the man not only understood his language but spoke it.

"Oui." George spoke in a thickly accented English as he explained, "You are the man who rides with the Lady Gisele DeVeau. All know about you. I was surprised when we found her alone."

"Ye mean when ye captured her and turned her over to the bastards who want to kill her," he said coldly, pressing his knife just a little closer to the life-giving vein in George's throat.

"I was told that she was a murderess, that she had killed her husband in a particularly brutal way."

"And ye believe without question everything ye are told? Or was your haste to believe that tiny lass capable of such a crime aided by the coin that now weights your purse?"

"I am a poor man, sir, with six whining children and a whining wife. *Oui,* I hungered for the bounty, and I thought it would be fairly earned. As I have said, I believed I joined the hunt for a murderess. There is no crime in that."

Slowly, Nigel got off the man, but he kept his dagger at the ready and watched George carefully as he sat up. George was right There was no crime in trying to get a share of the bounty offered for a murderess. It had taken him a while to believe Gisele had never killed her husband, and *he* knew the whole sordid truth of her brutal marriage. George did not. He had been told by men of title and wealth that one of their number had been murdered by a woman. Why should he doubt it? Yet, Nigel began to get the feeling that George had had a change of heart.

"Did ye hurt her?" he asked coldly, not willing to trust the man too quickly.

"Non. I went to her with my sword sheathed. I agreed to capture her. It was not my place to mete out her punishment. We did have a small battle, however. I think I might have won that, but one of the other men came along and put a stop to it."

"Ye didnae laugh at her, did ye?" he asked, able to smile briefly at the image of Gisele facing this man, sword in hand and ready to fight.

"I admit that I was amused, but I did not laugh. My amusement was short-lived. You taught her well."

"And she will get better. She has a gift for it, if not the strength. So, ye didnae hurt her, but did someone else?"

"One of the men knocked her on the head a couple of times."

"A couple of times?"

"One was to put a stop to the fight, a light blow that knocked her to her knees, but no more. He also was driven to hit her once or twice because she goaded him."

Nigel cursed softly. "She should learn when to guard her tongue."

"It is a little sharp."

"A little?" Nigel murmured. Then he looked at George carefully. "Ye have had a change of heart."

George nodded and sighed, grimacing as he looked down at the purse tied to his scabbard. "I have. I looked at that tiny woman and could not believe she did what they said she did, not even when she tried to skewer me. But what changed my mind the most was the way Sir Vachel looked at her and spoke to her."

"Who is this Sir Vachel?"

"The lord that squats in that keep. He is the cousin of her husband."

"Ye dinnae think he believes she is guilty?"

"I do not believe he cares if she is or not. He certainly does not care that someone killed his cousin. Sir Vachel is a frightening man. I am glad to be free of him and this place. He will hang her, but not any time soon. He means to have his fill of her first." George hastily edged away from Nigel when the man cursed.

"Are you certain of this?"

It was hard for Nigel to control his rage, but he knew that scaring George with it would not get him anywhere. It was not George he was furious with, either, but the DeVeaux. First Michael had tried to crush Gisele, raping and beating her repeatedly. Now his cousin wished to follow in his footsteps. Nigel had finally awakened the passion in Gisele, freed it from the chains of the fear and loathing her husband had instilled in her. Now another DeVeau intended to undo all of his work, to leave poor Gisele with more scars. Nigel was not sure she could survive more brutality and humiliation. This time that glorious passion he had tasted too briefly could be killed, damaged beyond redemption.

"Ye must help me get her away from there," Nigel said.

"Now, sir—" George's protest ended on a squeak as Nigel grabbed him by the front of his padded jupon and glared into his face.

"Ye will help me get the lass out of there. Heed me, hanging would be a blessing to the lass if this Vachel means to abuse her. That is what her husband did to her throughout their thankfully short marriage. Gisele didnae kill Michael DeVeau, but he deserved to die ten times over for each rape and each beating he inflicted on that wee lass. She has only just begun to recover from the scars that mon left on her heart and mind. She willnae survive more of the same. Aye, she might breathe, walk, talk, eat, and piss, but inside she will be dead."

"You said Michael was her husband. A husband cannot—"

"Rape his wife? Of course he can. Ye cannae be that big a fool. If a lass doesnae want the bedding, she doesnae want it, and it makes no difference who is doing the asking. Aye, and even if the lass accepts the bedding as her wifely duty, the mon can be a bastard in the taking of her, cannae he?"

George frowned. "This was to be a simple way to gain the coin I need to survive, but it grows more complicated by the hour."

"Ye felt it was just to capture a murderess and take her to the ones she had wronged. Even if ye dinnae believe that she is innocent, and she is, ye cannae condone what ye say Vachel means to do to her."

"*Non,* I cannot. I felt troubled leaving her behind when I learned what the man planned to do. He seems to think he can keep her a secret from the rest of his family, play with her as he pleases until he grows weary of her, and then hang her as was planned. That is an evil I want no part of. I am just not sure how

I can help you. I occasionally ride with Vachel's men, but I am not his vassal and I rarely enter that keep."

Nigel cursed and dragged his fingers through his hair. "I need to ken where she has been placed within that pile of stone."

"In Vachel's bedchambers. He ordered her bathed and dressed in a gown." He leaned back a little when Nigel paled with fury. "It would have been better if she had been locked in the dungeons. I cannae see how I can get within the keep and slip up into the master's bedchamber without being seen."

"Actually, I think you can get into the lord's bedchambers unseen, at least into the room he lets everyone *think* is his bedchamber." George smiled faintly at Nigel's cross look of confusion. "Vachel thinks that no one knows, but he acts with the arrogance so many of wealth and power do. Those who scurry about doing their lord's bidding are neither blind nor stupid. They see and hear, and they learn all of the secrets."

Nigel nodded as he picked up his wineskin and silently offered George a drink. "My family learned the hard truth of that years ago. We also learned that such hidden folk can also be a source of betrayal."

"*Oui,* and I suspect that Vachel will die in his secret little bed at the hands of one of them, or by someone who was shown the way by them."

"I am little concerned about the mon's fate if he lives out this day. Those gates will soon close, and I need to get the lass out of there."

George took a long drink of the wine, then wiped his mouth with his sleeve. "Come with me, then, and I will show you how to get into the man's bedchamber, in and out without being seen."

"If it is to be so easy why did ye nay do it yourself?"

"Because I am one of those men whose courage is not as strong as it should be," George replied as he stood up and brushed himself off. "Sometimes I need the prick of a knife at my throat to get me to do what I know is right."

Nigel hesitated as they moved to their horses and George mounted. This seemed all too easy. He had not only found a man to work with him but a way to slip in and out without being seen. It could be that he had been given an answer to the prayers he had been muttering for hours, but it could also be a trap. This Sir Vachel had to know that Gisele had a companion, a man who had joined her in the fight to stay alive. He could have sent George out to try and find him and ensnare him.

George looked at Nigel and smiled. "You really have little choice. I am the only hope you have. No one else will be leaving that place, not alone. And I do not believe you will find anyone else amongst them who has even my reluctant sense of what is right and just."

"It just seems suspiciously easy," Nigel said as he mounted. "Do we just ride in?"

"We do. I am even now devising an explanation for returning and bringing you inside. Has anyone seen you up close?"

"None that have survived."

"I shall have to leave this place after this," George sighed, "for someone will recall that I brought a man in."

"Then ye ride in, and I shall sneak in."

"You can sneak in there?"

"Aye, and your return will help me." Nigel dismounted and pulled a small bag of coins from his purse. "Tell them ye wish to buy the lass's horse." He gave George some money. "Then say ye must do something, anything, that will get ye back inside the keep. I will follow ye in there. Then ye can take me to this hiding place."

"We must still get out with the girl."

"I can slip her out as easily as I slip in. Ye just bring the horse to this place."

"If you can slip in and slip away so easily, what need have you of me?"

"I dinnae ken where the lass is, do I? And,"—he spoke in French to make his point more clear—"I can speak the language, but it is clear to all who hear me that I am not French."

George made an exaggerated face of disgust. "I have rarely heard our tongue so completely butchered."

"Go. I will meet up with you inside," Nigel ordered.

He watched George ride away. The man seemed amiable and trustworthy. He seemed to be just what he said he was, a man of reluctant courage who had thought he was doing nothing wrong and needed to be nudged to now do what was right. It was better that they enter the keep separately, however. If Nigel discovered that he was wrong to trust George, the man would not be able to just hand him over to the enemy. He would have to find him first. It was a small advantage, but it was better than nothing.

It was pitifully easy to slip into the keep. Nigel wondered how the lord and his people had managed to survive for so long. He used the cover of the crowd in the baily, neatly blending himself into the muddle of people trying to finish their work before the light of day was completely gone, to get into the keep itself.

Once inside, he hid himself in a small, shadowed alcove near the stairs and waited for George. By the time George sauntered in Nigel was so tense from waiting, to either act or be discovered, that he nearly shouted at the man. The way George was acting made the chance of discovery even greater. The man was trying not to appear as if he were looking for someone, trying so hard that anyone with eyes in his head would think he was acting suspiciously. He hissed to get George's attention, then yanked the man into the tiny dark alcove beside him.

"Ye need practice, George," he whispered. "Ye are about as stealthy as a cow."

"And you are unsettlingly stealthy, like a ghost."

"Where to now?"

"You must just follow me. It is one of those very convoluted things—in this door, out another, down the hall, up the stairs, around the corner." His eyes widened when Nigel briefly clamped a hand over his mouth.

"Just go. I will be right behind you." They slipped out of the shadows, and after George had taken only a few steps the man looked back over his shoulder. Nigel cursed. "Stop looking at me. Ye will just draw other eyes this way."

As they slipped through the halls of the keep, Nigel decided that George had not exaggerated. Sir Vachel might be wrong to think no one knew about his secret room, but he was probably not in any great danger. Anyone trying to get to it risked getting thoroughly lost or eventually seen by someone. Several times he had to use the shadows to hide himself, but he knew he had a true gift for such a thing. It was not boastful to think that few people were as good at it as he was.

When they slipped into what George assured him was the last little hallway, it was completely dark. "How did ye come to learn of this?" he whispered as they inched their way along, hands on the damp wall to guide them.

"I told you that I am not blessed with any great courage," George whispered in reply. "I have a need to find all the places to hide or to escape when I come to these keeps. Once, when I was little more than a beardless youth, I was caught in the storming of a keep. I saved myself by hiding under the dead. I now carefully search every keep I go to. These are not my lords, or my lands. I see no gain in dying for the fools."

Nigel did not have any reply to that. It made too much sense. George was a freedman. In the end, his greatest loyalty was to himself and his large family. He grunted softly when he walked into George's back, then grew very still as he heard the soft murmur of voices.

"We are there?" he asked.

"I but try to find the latch to the door."

"Allow me."

Inching past George, Nigel ran his hands over the heavy door until he found the latch. Holding his breath, tense with the need to be completely silent, he eased the door open. Stealth became a little easier as light from the bedchamber filled the cramped space. George began to inch along behind him as Nigel eased into the room, but he briefly placed a hand on George's chest to hold him where he was. George had shown himself to be less than skilled at creeping around, but the man might yet get through this rescue without any suspicion falling on him if he just stayed out of sight.

The moment he slipped into the room, Nigel saw the couple on the bed. It took all of his willpower not to scream out his rage and immediately attack the man touching Gisele. As he crept up to the bedside, he almost felt Gisele's pain and fear. She sounded brave but her hands were clenched so tightly at her side that the knuckles were shining white in the candlelight. Nigel saw the smallest hint of blood and realized that she had pierced her palms with her nails. He inched up to the side of the bed and silently drew his sword.

"Who is there to stop me?" said Sir Vachel.

Nigel pressed the point of his sword squarely between Sir Vachel's slender shoulder blades. "Weel, I might be willing to give it a wee try."

The man on top of Gisele tensed. Nigel saw him glance to the main door to the room, and his lips started to part. In less than a heartbeat he grabbed him by the hair, lifted him up enough to get a clear view of his face, and punched him on the jaw. He then dragged the man's limp body off the gaping Gisele and quietly set it on the floor. When he saw that Gisele's gown was open, her breasts bared, Nigel grew so furious that he sheathed his sword, drew his dagger, and reached for the unconscious Sir Vachel.

Gisele broke free of her shock as she realized that Nigel was about to cut Vachel's throat. She scrambled to sit up, then grabbed his arm. She shivered when he looked at her, for she had never seen him that furious.

"You cannot kill him," she whispered.

"I cannae believe ye have a drop of mercy in your soul for this bastard."

"None, but I have a great deal of concern for you. Think, Nigel. Clear the anger from your mind and think. I have just lost over a year of my life running from the fury and vengeance of the DeVeaux, hiding from a punishment for a murder, a murder I did not even commit. I now see some chance of getting free of all of that. You have always had the chance to walk away, to turn your back on it all. The moment your knife cuts this man's throat you will lose that freedom, and suffer as I have. We will both suffer being hunted down again, bounties placed on our heads. If you kill him I, too, will carry the weight of it, and this time there will be no way to deny it."

"She is right," whispered George as he tiptoed past them and latched the door to the outer hall.

"George?" Gisele stared after the man in surprise, then blushed and hastily redid her gown.

"I had a change of heart," George muttered as he moved to the bedside, watching closely as Nigel took several deep breaths to calm his fury while he bound and gagged Vachel and finally moved away from the man.

"I see," Gisele murmured as she got off the bed. "You will let me hang for murder, but not allow this." She almost smiled when George just shrugged, then she turned to look at Nigel. "I am most interested in how you got in here, but at the moment I am even more interested in how we can get out."

Nigel gave her one brief, hard hug, pleased to feel no rejection of his touch, then took her by the hand and led her toward the passageway. "I have a few things I am curious about, too. One being why a usually clever lass would flee safety and hand herself o'er to the enemy."

Clinging tightly to Nigel's hand as the three of them inched their way along the dark passage, she whispered in protest, "I did not hand myself over to them."

"Ye practically rode up to their gates and knocked on them."

"I got lost."

Even though it was too dark to see anything, Gisele knew that Nigel had just looked at her. She also knew that that look had not been a flattering one. It struck her as odd, even a little funny, that after her first shock at seeing Nigel at the bedside she just accepted his rescue as nothing so unusual. She had not wanted him to risk himself by trying to save her, or even thought that he would after she had deserted him, yet it did not completely surprise her that he was there, dragging her along a dark hallway toward freedom. Her thoughts were cut short when Nigel stopped, and a moment later George bumped into them.

"We are there?" asked George.

"We are where?" she asked.

"At the end of Sir Vachel's little hiding place," Nigel replied as he inched open the door and peered out to make sure that no one was there to see them leave a place they should not even know about.

"He sleeps in this dark, dank hall?"

"Nay, there is a passage or two off this one. His wee bed is probably down one of them." Nigel looked at Gisele and grimaced. "It would have been easier to get ye out of here if they hadnae taken your laddie's clothes away."

"Wait here," George said as he slipped past them and out the door.

"Are you certain you can trust that man?" Gisele asked as Nigel pulled the door shut enough to hide them, leaving a bit of room for the light to shine in.

"Now I am. I had my doubts at first. No longer. He may not be the bravest and most honorable of men, but he didnae like what was going to be done to you. I think he even had a few doubts about your guilt after ye met him sword to sword."

She was glad the light was too dim to see well, for she could feel herself blush. "I do not know how well I did, for I was stopped before any true test of my skill occurred."

"He seemed to think ye were verra good. Ah, George," he greeted the man when he returned and handed them a cape. "Not only clever, but a good thief, I am thinking."

Gisele saw George frown, and patted him on the arm. "He means that as a great compliment."

The moment she was wrapped in the cape they all slipped out of the passage. Until Nigel signaled him that they could go on alone, George led them through all the confusing twists and turns. Gisele said nothing as Nigel led her the rest of the way through the keep, flattening herself against the walls and ducking into corners each time he did. Her heart began to pound so hard and fast when they entered the baily that she was afraid the people around them would hear it.

Suddenly they were outside the gates. Gisele felt a little dizzy that it had happened so fast. She could tell from the tension in Nigel's lean body that he shared her urge to run, but they ambled along toward the small wood as if they had nothing to fear. The moment they were in the shelter of the trees, she sat down on the ground, her legs too weak to hold her upright any longer. Her whole body shook, and she realized that a lot of her calm had been hard wrung, a facade even to her.

George arrived a few moments later and greedily accepted the drink of wine Nigel offered him. "I believe that will be the last honorable deed I do for a great while," George said, wiping the sweat from his brow with his sleeve.

"Ye did weel, George," Nigel said as he took hold of the reins of Gisele's horse. "I am glad ye were able to get this fool beast back."

"His lordship was not yet aware that he had gained a mount," George explained as he handed Nigel what was left of the money he had given him. "His stablemaster was more than pleased to let it go and pocket the coin."

"If, somehow, they guess that ye had aught to do with this and ye feel a need to leave this land, ye are welcome on mine. The Murrays of Donncoill. Ye will find how to reach us in Perth. In most any port, in truth, for we deal in some trading."

George nodded his gratitude, then sent Gisele a small smile before quickly riding away. Still weak, Gisele allowed Nigel to help her on her horse. She ached to rest, to lie down and close her eyes and pretend the horror of the last few hours had never happened, but she knew it was important for them to get away. Vachel was not dead, and when the man woke he would not be in a good temper. As she followed Nigel out of the little wood, she suspected that all she had accomplished with her bid for freedom was to make sure that the hunt for them would grow even more determined.

Nineteen

"We will camp here for the night, lass."

Those soft words were enough to pull Gisele from her stupor. She looked around, but noticed very little until she saw the small brook. Without a word she slipped off her horse, unpacked her drying cloth and sliver of soap, and walked to the edge of the brook. Still silent, she shed her clothes, stepped into the shallow cold water, slowly sat down, and began to wash.

She could hear Nigel tending to the horses and setting up their camp, but she kept her back to him. Once they had started on their way, fleeing the wood and Vachel's lands as fast as they could, she had failed to stop herself from thinking about what had happened to her. From time to time Nigel had spoken to her and she had struggled to answer, his frowns telling her that she was doing a poor job of it. Nothing, not Nigel's concern or her own strong will, had stopped her from slipping into a dangerously dark mood.

From the moment Sir Vachel had touched her, she had ached to have a bath. It was the same sick, unclean feeling her husband had always left her with. During her brief marriage she had sometimes scrubbed her skin raw, stopped from doing herself real harm only by the watchful eyes of the maids. They had lived with Michael long enough to understand what she was suffering. Just as she had after Michael had used her, she now felt as if she needed to peel away every piece of skin Vachel had touched. Only once did she pause in her continuous wash-

ing, and that was to stare in surprise at the cuts on the palms
of her hands. As she briefly soaked them in the cold water, she
wondered how she could have buried her fingernails so deeply
into her own flesh and not been aware of it. Then, almost blindly,
she returned to scrubbing her skin.

Nigel leaned against a slender tree, took a slow drink from
his wineskin, and watched Gisele carefully. She had said nothing since they had left the DeVeau keep. He had kept looking
back at her, afraid she had fallen asleep and was at risk of
slipping out of her saddle. Each time he had been made uneasy
by the almost lifeless look upon her face, the strange distance
in her eyes. The few times he had spoken to her, tried to pull
her from her intense silence, her response had been spoken in
a voice nearly as dead as her eyes.

When he had first rescued her she had seemed fine, no more
than a little shaken. Now he was not so sure. He was also not
so sure that he had been in time to save her from all Vachel had
planned to do to her. Perhaps that was not the first time the
man had been on that bed with her. She had been alone at the
keep for several hours before he had found a way to reach her.
More than enough time for the man to have already raped her
once, mayhap more.

He cursed softly and ran a hand over his chin. It did not take
a very clever man to see that something deeply troubled Gisele.
What did require a great deal of cleverness was knowing exactly
how to help her. This was the sort of thing a woman often did
not wish to talk about, yet, how could he know how to help her
if she did refuse to talk about it? There was also a reluctance
lurking inside of him, a wish to not know anything about what
had happened to her while she was trapped inside of Vachel's
keep. If he did not wish to hear anything and she did not wish
to say anything, they would certainly not get very far in solving
her problem, he thought sourly.

There was one thing he *could* do, he decided as he tossed
his wineskin aside and moved toward the brook. He could stop
her incessant scrubbing. If she continued with it for very much

longer she would be nothing more than a tiny lump of raw flesh.
Nigel had the unsettling feeling that that was her intention, that
she wanted to remove the flesh that had been defiled by Vachel.
He was surprised that she could sit in the water for so long.
Her shapely backside had to be nearly frozen to the rocky bottom of the brook. She was also frightening him a little, for she
seemed to be caught up in some repetitive dream, so that she
was not completely aware of what she was doing to herself. It
was almost as if the insanity of the DeVeaux had finally infected
her.

"Gisele," he called, but she paid him no heed, so he reached
out to gently touch her shoulder. "Gisele!"

"I heard you the first time," she said quietly, staring at her
empty hand as she slowly realized that she had no soap left.
"My soap is all gone."

"Ye are clean enough."

"Am I?"

Even though she still felt an urge to keep washing herself,
she allowed Nigel to pull her out of the water. She stood silently
as he briskly rubbed her down with the drying cloth, obviously
trying to warm her as much as he was drying her skin. When
he reached for her clothes and saw the gown he hesitated, then
frowned at her. Gisele finally roused herself enough to speak.

"I have no ill feeling about the clothes," she said.

"I mean no offense, nor do I wish to stir up any ill memory,
but I am surprised he found something to fit ye so quickly."

She gave him the sad ghost of a smile. "The cut of the clothes
tells me they probably belonged to a young maid. The chemise
will be good enough for now."

Nigel gently tugged the chemise over her head and laced it
up, then led her over to their bed by the fire. For one brief
moment he had thought about separating their beds, then decided that would not really help. It might even make her think
that he was setting her aside because of what Vachel had done.

He quickly gathered up the things she had left by the brook
and put them in her saddlepack. As he got some wine and food

for their meal, he kept a close but subtle watch on her. The way she just sat there staring into the fire made him uneasy. He felt an urge to slap some life back into her. Nigel shook his head as he sat down beside her and gave her some food. Brutality had caused her troubles. He would be no better than DeVeau if he used brutality to try to pull her free of her dark mood.

"Did he rape ye, lass?" he asked, deciding the best way to try to solve her problem was to be direct.

"Non," she replied as she slowly began to eat, her hunger beginning to revive as she tasted the food.

"Praise God," he muttered, and briefly squeezed one of her hands. "I feared that ye had suffered while I sat in that wood trying to plan your rescue. That because I wasnae quick or clever enough, ye had endured some pain."

"Nigel, you were in time. Vachel but touched me a little. I let that trouble me far more than I should have. Even if you had not succeeded in saving me from that bastard's unwanted attentions, you would have still saved me from a hanging. That is no small thing. In truth, I was not expecting your help at all."

"Why? Because ye had crept away from me like a thief in the night?" He watched her closely, and felt relieved when she cast him a look that was an amusing mixture of embarrassment and irritation. She was beginning to recover.

"I had my reasons for leaving." She hoped that would end the discussion, but a quick peek at Nigel's face told her that she was not going to be allowed to just dismiss the matter.

"And I should like to hear what those reasons were."

"It was suddenly clear to me that this hunt had grown much fiercer than it had ever been, and much more dangerous. I no longer felt able to put your life at risk, to use you to shelter me from my enemies."

"So, ye would have me believe that after we have spent weeks hacking our way through DeVeau's men ye suddenly woke up in the middle of the night and decided it was now becoming too dangerous? And that riding off alone, nay kenning where ye were going, leaving me alone in my weakened condition, was safer for both of us?"

It did sound remarkably witless the way he told it, but Gisele had no intention of letting him know that. She was also not going to let him try to stir her guilt by speaking of his 'weakened condition'. Nigel had tossed Vachel DeVeau around as if he were no more than an empty sack. That was hardly the act of a sickly man. Gisele thought it a little harsh of Nigel to be questioning her and expecting sensible answers after all she had just endured.

"As you had just explained to me last eve, we were either near or even on DeVeau lands, and that ensured that the port you were taking us to would be swarming with the fools. I just felt that it had all become too complicated. There had always been a chance that we could get to a port, onto a ship, and sail far away from my troubles. Suddenly, it did not look as if that were possible any longer." Gisele softly cursed and glared at Nigel when he greeted her explanation with a mocking sound of disbelief. She thought that it was rather clever, and deserved better than his blatant derision.

"Ye may have thought that, lass, but I fear I dinnae believe that is the whole truth of it." It took only one quick glance at the stubborn, cross look on her face for Nigel to realize that she was not going to tell him any more. "Ye stumbled right into your enemy's arms, loving," he added quietly as he put his arm around her shoulders and tugged her close to his side, pleased when she revealed no fear or resistance.

"I know that," she grumbled, then sighed and leaned against him. "I was traveling to my cousin Marie's. At least I thought I was. It is clear to me now that I really did not know the way to get there. Marie does not live anywhere near a DeVeau. I know that because I sought her aid once before."

He idly picked up her medallion from where it rested against her chest and studied it for a moment. "Ye are fortunate none of the men took this from you," he said, as he released his hold on it. " 'Tis a fine piece that could have brought them a few coins."

"I am not sure any of them really saw it, praise God. It was hidden beneath my jupon, as it has been most times since you reminded me that lads do not wear such fine baubles. The ones who did see it, Vachel and his man Ansel, saw it as nothing remarkable. It is obviously still bringing me good fortune."

"Aye, it is. Gisele, I am nay calling ye a liar, but something does puzzle me."

"And what is that?"

"Ye said that Sir Vachel didnae rape ye, only touched ye a wee bit."

"That is correct."

"Then why would ye try to flay the flesh from your wee bones with unending scrubbing? It makes no sense to me."

Gisele smiled sadly and allowed him to gently push her down onto the bed. The weight of his body as he lightly sprawled on top of her felt comforting as well as exciting, and she was glad. The very last thing she wanted was for her stupidity and Vachel's unwavering, cruel arrogance to destroy what she felt for Nigel. It would have been easy for Vachel to make her the frightened woman she had been when she had first met Nigel. That would have been too high a price to pay for her cowardice.

And it was cowardice, she mused. She had run from what she felt for Nigel, tried to run as fast and as far away as she could. It was also foolish. There was no running away from it. The love she had for Nigel stayed with her. All she did was deprive herself of seeing him, of touching him, and of savoring his touch upon her skin. Gisele doubted she could completely flee all that, either, for the memory would stay with her always.

She met his gaze and sighed. He was waiting patiently for her to answer his question. Nigel could be annoyingly stubborn. Gisele suspected he could calmly wait for her answer far longer than she could calmly tolerate it.

"I am not sure what I was doing makes very much sense to me, either," she finally replied. "Vachel looks very much like my husband Michael. So much so that, briefly, I feared I was seeing a ghost."

Nigel frowned. He found that news a little unsettling. Although he had only seen Vachel briefly through a fog of rage, he had recognized the man's beauty. Then he cursed himself for an idiot, and pushed aside his bout of jealousy. The DeVeau men might be beautiful to look upon, but they were black-hearted bastards who had caused Gisele only pain and humiliation. No one knew that better than she did. He doubted the beauty of the men affected her in any way.

"That must have made it all the more troublesome for you," he said, slowly running his hand up and down her side.

"It did," she whispered, then took a deep breath to steady herself. "It was worse than even I could have guessed it would be. *Oui,* Vachel looked like Michael, but, whereas Michael's cruelty revealed itself in rages and bouts of clear madness, Vachel's is the cold sort. Vachel does not blindly strike out. He is calm. He thinks carefully about what he is doing and, I think, enjoys it. He planned to keep me and use me until he wearied of me, and then he would hang me."

After cursing viciously for a moment, Nigel wished yet again that he had killed the man. "That is what George said, but I didnae really want to believe it. 'Tis done, my bonny French rose. Ye must put it from your mind. That bastard isnae worth even one bad memory."

"I would like to forget it all, but Vachel DeVeau is not a man you forget easily. He is truly evil, Nigel. I think he may be mad, but it is a frightening madness, one that twists the soul yet leaves him appearing sane, and he is a very clever man."

"So, ye dinnae think that ye washed him away."

Gisele smiled in response to his insight and also in silent acquiescence, for he began to tentatively unlace her chemise. *"Oui.* I was trying to wash his touch away. I used to do the same when my husband touched me. In my poor, confused mind it was the same. A madness seizes me, and I have a wish to remove the skin from all the places I was touched. When I was in my husband's *demanse,* the maids would stop me before I did myself harm. This time, I fear I imposed that sad chore upon you. I humbly beg your pardon."

"There is naught ye have to apologize for."

"Oui, there is. What troubles me at such times is none of your doing. You should not have to contend with the results of other men's crimes against me."

Nigel knew there was nothing more he could say to assure her that he did not mind, so he kissed her, trying to imbue his kiss with all of the tenderness he felt toward her. He knew she did not need his strength. She had her own. Nor could he mend all of her hurts, only understand them. It was that willingness to understand that he tried to convey in his touch.

What he ached to do now was make love to her. Part of him desperately wanted to caress away all memory of Vachel's touch, to stroke away the man's mark upon her. It was an act of possession, and he knew it. Like some beast of the wood he wanted to put his scent back on her skin. What softened that feral attitude was that he also wished to remind her, through a sweet, gentle sharing of passion, that not all men were like the De-Veaux. She needed to know that if she were ever going to conquer her bad memories. Nigel was just not sure that she was in any mood to be reminded, however.

Cautiously, he slid his hand inside her chemise. When she did nothing to stop him, did not even tense beneath his caress, he breathed a silent sigh of relief. Vachel had not harmed her enough to kill her passion or make her want to shy away from any touch. It was mostly a selfish relief, he admitted to himself. He had feared losing all chance to savor Gisele's passion again. Hand in hand with that selfishness, however, was a deep gratitude that very few scars had been added to the ones Gisele already carried. She did not deserve such cruelty.

"I cannae understand how your parents could give ye to such a family," he murmured as he slowly tugged off her chemise. " 'Tis hard to believe that no one kenned that the DeVeaux are all mad."

"That it is," she agreed, smiling at him as he shed his own clothes. "My parents are long dead, God rest their souls. It was my guardians, an aging uncle and a distant cousin, who made the marriage agreement." She readily accepted him back into her arms. "My *grandmére* had much of the raising of me, but she, too, died ere this catastrophe befell me. I like to believe that my parents or Nana would have never made such a betrothal if they had survived. They would have at least helped me when Michael's true nature revealed itself.

"In truth, I begin to think this path I have been forced down was my fate from the day I came screaming out of my mother's womb." She shrugged when Nigel looked at her doubtfully. "The youth I was first betrothed to died at a very young age, and my parents arranged nothing new before they, too, died. One other betrothal was made by my guardians, but that man got himself killed by a jealous husband. My guardians were having some difficulty in arranging yet another marriage for me when Michael saw me at the king's court and approached them. My guardians, indeed my whole family, could not believe their good fortune. I was seen, bid upon, and sold before I barely realized what had happened."

" 'Tis a wrong that can ne'er be righted, but now that your kinsmen see the error of their ways and intend to help you, mayhap the sting of it will ease some."

"I pray that it will." She curled her body around his. "Now, my gallant Scottish knight, do you really wish to keep talking about my family and my troubles?"

Gisele was surprised at how eager she was to make love to Nigel. After all she had endured she ought to shy away from a man's touch, if only for a little while, just long enough for the fear Vachel had instilled in her to fade. As she rubbed her body against Nigel's, though, silently encouraging him, she realized that this time her passion was born of purely selfish reasons. Gisele felt confident that Nigel's touch could wipe away the memory of Vachel's cool, soft hands against her skin. Surrounding herself with Nigel's scent would take away the last vestiges of Vachel's perfume, and in a way both she and Nigel could enjoy. It would also strongly remind her that not all men were the heartless, soulless beasts the DeVeaux were, that passion did not have to be about power and pain.

Nigel made love to her slowly and thoroughly. Gisele eagerly returned his every kiss, his every touch, aching to soak herself in the feel of him. With a soft cry of greed and desperation, she accepted him into her body. She savored the way her body shook with the strength of her release, the way Nigel tensed and groaned her name as he shared in that deep pleasure. When he collapsed in her arms, she held him tightly against her, wrapping her body snugly around his. She mumbled a protest when he finally ended the intimacy of their embrace.

"Did that help?" he asked as he tugged the blanket around their chilling bodies.

She laughed slightly as he pulled her back into his arms and she snuggled against his warmth. It should probably alarm her that this man knew her so well, could seem to guess her every thought and mood with ease, but it did not. Gisele just felt closer to him, more comfortable in his presence. She knew she could tell him anything, and that he would still understand even if she could not find the words to correctly express what she felt. The only thing that troubled her about such a rich companionship was the fear that he could look deeper into her heart than she wanted him to, that somehow he could guess how much she loved him. She prayed that he would be kind enough to conceal his knowledge if he did discover that he held her heart in his big hands, especially if he could not return her feelings.

"*Oui,* it helped. I did not mean to make you feel used," she added quietly, suddenly feeling a little guilty.

"If that is the only way ye use me, then feel free to use me all ye wish." He smiled briefly when she giggled and then grew serious as he combed his fingers through her thick curls. "I shall now confess that, in a small way, I was using you for the same reasons ye were using me. I wanted that bastard to be completely gone. I wanted to take away all thought of him, all feel of him upon your bonny skin, and, aye, even all smell of him. To be painfully truthful, lass, I wanted to take his mark off of your sweet body and put mine back on there." Nigel waited a little tensely for her response to his confession, feeling both relieved and surprised when she just grinned and kissed his cheek.

He sounded jealous, and Gisele took great pleasure in that. She knew she should not get her hopes up, but that strong hint of jealousy meant that he was not without some strong feeling for her. It was a far cry from the love she needed from him, but she would gladly accept this small salve to her vanity and bruised heart.

"We stumble down the same path, *mon cher*," she murmured. "What you reluctantly admit to is exactly what I wished you to do. I, too, wanted Vachel's touch rubbed away, wanted the smell of that man gone from my skin. And I have discovered something since we became lovers."

"Oh, aye? What?"

She winked at him. "That rolling about on the ground with you is a very good way to clear my head and heart of all troubles and fears."

"I am glad that I can be of some service to you, m'lady."

"Well, since you insist upon staying around, I suppose I must put you to some use."

Gisele squealed with laughter and mock fear when he sought retribution by tickling her. She was breathless by the time he ceased playfully tormenting her, and suddenly very tired, as well. As she curled up in his arms she fought against a yawn, and loudly lost the battle.

"Go to sleep, loving," Nigel urged, stroking her hair as she rested her head on his shoulder. "Ye have had a long and eventful day. And, ye had verra little sleep last eve, for ye spent it running away from me and straight into your enemy's grasp. It can be exhausting to make such a large mistake." He grunted in feigned pain when she punched him lightly on the chest.

"You do not intend to allow me to forget that, do you?"

"Nay. It may be needed from time to time to keep ye humble."

He kissed the top of her head. "Rest. We have a long road to travel yet ahead of us."

And I have just made it even longer, she mused as she closed her eyes. Although Nigel clearly loved to tease her, he did not say that, at least not aloud, and she was heartily relieved. Her stupidity could easily have gotten them both killed, and although she still did not know where they were she was sure she had added at least a day to their journey toward a port they could sail from. She had been headed in the opposite direction that Nigel had chosen for a whole night and part of the next day. She prayed they could easily recover all of that lost time.

Nigel cursed as a small, hard fist connected soundly with his jaw. He caught Gisele by the wrist before she could complete her second swing at his face. Her eyes were still closed, and he realized that she was caught in the tight grip of some dream. It was not hard to guess what she dreamed about, and the dream was certainly not a pleasant one, not if he correctly understood some of the rapid French she was spitting out.

When he caught the full force of her knee against the inside of his thigh, only a swift move to the right saving him great pain, he cursed and decided he could no longer wait for her to pull herself free of her nightmare. He turned so that she was neatly pinned beneath his body. The moment he ended the flailing of her arms and legs she began to grow calmer.

"Gisele," he snapped. "Wake up, lass. Heed me," he said more calmly, softening his tone as well as easing his hold on her. " 'Tis Nigel ye are trying to bloody. Wake up, sweeting, so ye can see who is truly here and cast the shadows from your mind. Come now, look at me and nay at the ghosts in your head."

Gisele felt her terror ease as she slowly woke up. Then she cursed. She had thought herself strong enough to cast aside the memory of what Vachel had done and of all he had threatened to do, but it was clear that she had not done so. Her mind did not care that he had not succeeded in raping her, that Nigel had saved her from that horror. The fear was still there, the chilling memory still near at hand, and ready to darken her dreams. Worse, the memory of Vachel brought forth all the memories of Michael. All the fear and shame she had endured under his cruel fists was new and sharp again. She cautiously opened her eyes and recalled that in her dream she had delivered a sound punch to Vachel's jaw, just as she had ached to do when he had held her captive. Tentatively, she reached out to touch Nigel's jaw.

"I am sorry," she whispered. "I struck you, did I not?"

"Aye, ye did, and it was a good, sound blow. And," he added, kissing the tip of her small nose, "there isnae any cause to beg my pardon. 'Twas just a dream. Ye werenae truly hitting me. I just got in the way of your ghosts."

"*Oui,*" I guess that bastard Vachel is not gone yet. Neither of them are," she whispered, fighting the urge to cry as she wondered if she would ever be free of the fear and bad memories.

Nigel held her close and kissed her cheek. "Weel, I am still insisting on staying around."

It took Gisele a moment to recall the conversation she and Nigel had had just before she had gone to sleep. She laughed and curled her body around his in silent welcome. "It is obvious that your job is not yet done. You shall have to work harder to push all these demons from my poor tormented head."

As he turned, settling her beneath him, Nigel drawled, "I am nay sure I can work much harder and still be alive come the dawn."

She just giggled in response, then heartily returned his kiss. It might not be right to use the passion she and Nigel shared to push back the dark memories she struggled with, but there was no ignoring how well it worked. Gisele prayed that this time it would work well enough and for long enough that she could fall into a deep, dreamless sleep until dawn, when it would be time to mount her horse and flee her demons in a more practical way.

Twenty

"Where did all of these people come from?" Gisele asked as she peeked around the corner of the building.

Nigel yanked her back into the shelter of the shadows. "I believe it may be market day. Sadly, I also believe Sir Vachel awoke from that blow I gave him in an evil temper and vengeful humor. Many of those men weaving in and out of the market day crowd are weel armed. 'Tis verra clear that they are searching for something, and I dinnae believe it is cloth or ale."

"It is me," she whispered.

Despite her brief attempt to leave Nigel and all the trouble it caused them, they had reached the port in only two days. She had been feeling pleased with their success, almost hopeful. They had even accomplished it without seeing or needing to flee from any DeVeaux. Now she knew why they had not seen any of her enemies. The Deveaux and their many new allies were all here, waiting for her and Nigel to try to leave France.

"How can they be so certain that we will be trying to leave, that we will attempt to sail away and out of their reach?" she asked as she slumped against the cool stone wall of the little building. "We only told our plans to Guy and David, and I do not wish to think that either of them would betray us and tell the DeVeaux."

"Rest easy, lass. They didnae tell anyone. They didnae have to." Nigel leaned against the wall by her side. "Once the De-Veaux learned that ye were with me it didnae take much wit to ken where I would try to take you. And ye did say that ye thought Vachel was a clever mon. If he has been the one leading this hunt, this shouldnae surprise us at all. In truth, I should have planned for this. I did in a way, but I ne'er thought the numbers guarding the ports would be this great," he muttered as he dragged his hands through his hair.

"You do not think we can get through or around them?"

He sighed and shook his head. "Nay, and it doesnae do us much good to linger here if we cannae find out who might be setting sail for Scotland. That information is to be found at the docks themselves, or in the alehouses near them."

"And the DeVeau men would know that too, would they not?"

"Aye, and they would watch those places much more carefully than they do anywhere else."

"So, must we now go and find another port to sail from?" she asked, sensing his anger and wishing she could do something to ease it.

"We can, but I dinnae think any of the ones near here will be any safer than this one. We may have to take a verra long journey to reach a place the DeVeaux havenae thought to guard, or, at least, guard as well as this one. And I fear not every port has the chance of offering us someone who is sailing to Scotland. Again, not as good a chance as this one does."

When he fell silent, scowling down at the muddy ground of the narrow, dark alley they had sheltered in, Gisele forced herself to be quiet. He did not need any more questions. He needed to think and plan what they should do next. Gisele prayed that he could solve their grave problem, for she did not really want to do any more riding over the countryside. She wanted to be done with running and hiding, and she had allowed herself to hope that reaching this port finally meant an end to it all. It did not really lighten her mood any to know that Nigel had to be at least as disappointed as she was. He not only wished to flee the DeVeaux, but to return to the home and family he had not seen in seven long years.

She idly brushed the dirt from her padded *jupon* and was surprised to find that she missed the gown she had been wearing when Nigel had rescued her. It was strange to want anything Vachel had touched, but she did. Gisele realized that she was weary of being a boy, that at least once she would like Nigel to see her dressed in a woman's finery. It was all vanity and she knew it, but she could not discard the urge so easily. Not even when she reminded herself that Nigel clearly had no trouble thinking of her as a woman, and a desirable one. She even found herself wondering if the woman who had claimed Nigel's heart had worn elegant gowns for him.

Hoping that she could push such nonsense from her mind, she turned to look at Nigel again and gasped in fear. Two men had entered the narrow alley from the other end, and were creeping toward her and the yet unaware Nigel. Both men already had their swords drawn, so there could be little doubt that they meant trouble. She sharply nudged Nigel as she unsheathed her dagger.

Nigel cursed and drew his sword just as the first man charged him. The battle was a quick one, his foe proving to have very little skill with a sword. The man had been hoping surprise would win the day, but had not even been very skilled at surprising a man, either.

His gaze fixed firmly on the second man, Nigel wiped his sword clean on the dead man's ragged jupon, then slowly straightened up. That the tall, red-haired man had stood back, making no effort to give his companion any aid, puzzled Nigel until he looked the man over more carefully. The man held firm, sword in hand, but what caught most of Nigel's attention was the clan badge on the man's padded *jupon*. Nigel felt a stirring of hope, but tried to suppress it and remain calm and wary. The man might be a Scot, but he was still armed, still confronting him, and still ominously silent. If he only had himself to consider, Nigel knew he would take a chance on his fellow countryman, but he did not need the feel of Gisele gently trembling at his back to remind him that he had a great deal more than himself to consider.

"Ye are a Scot," he said.

"Aye," replied the man.

"I am nay sure of the clan though I recognize the badge ye wear."

"MacGregor."

"Ah, of course. I am Sir Nigel Murray of Donncoill."

"I ken it," the man drawled, smiling briefly. "Ye are well kenned by many in this land. I am Duncan. I am nay kenned well at all."

Nigel slowly began to relax, although he was not sure why. Just because the man seemed amiable enough, even showed a little bit of humor, did not mean that he and Gisele were now safe. Neither did it mean that this man would help them in any way. It was not only the French who could be tempted by the vast bounty on Gisele's head.

"Have ye come here to try to take the lass to her enemies?" he demanded.

"Weel, now, I did think on it. 'Twas why I was here with this wee fool." Duncan moved close enough to nudge the dead Frenchman with the toe of his boot. " 'Tis a great deal of money, and we MacGregors have e'er had a yearning for coin."

"So I have heard. I willnae let ye take her."

"Nay, I dinnae think ye will. What did she do to her hair?"

Gisele gaped as she peered around Nigel to look at the man. She felt she would not be blamed if she began to think that all Scotsmen were mad fools. The two men faced each other with swords drawn, the port swarmed with her enemies, a dead man sprawled at their feet, and yet they just kept talking. Now the man named MacGregor wanted to know why she had cut her hair. Even stranger to her was that Nigel did not appear to be surprised, insulted, or even amused by the odd question.

"Well, she is trying to look like a wee lad," replied Nigel.

"She doesnae. Dinnae think she would e'en if she had scraped every last curl away."

"Nay, neither do I. Are ye going to try to collect the bounty?" he asked again.

The man hesitated a moment, then sighed and sheathed his sword. "Nay. I have gained a full purse from fighting here for three years. I dinnae need to add any blood money to coin gained in honest battle. Especially not when that money is being offered for such a wee lass and one of my fellow countrymen. Are those your horses round the corner?" he asked, nodding his head toward the way he had come from.

"Aye," Nigel slowly sheathed his sword.

"That wee grey mare is a fine beast."

Nigel almost laughed. The man was not going to collect what he called blood money, but he obviously did not wish to go away empty-handed. Since he had every intention of trying to get the man to help them get onto a ship, he decided it was good to know that Duncan MacGregor coveted something he had. Payment would not be asked for, but he risked offense if he did not offer some.

"Aye, she is. Do ye think she is fine enough to pay for slipping two people on board a ship headed for Scotland?"

"She may be."

"I need to get the lass out of this country. I also wish to smell the heather again. It has been seven long years for me."

"Too long, lad. Much too long."

"I agree."

Duncan frowned for a moment, then nodded. "There is a ship leaving in but a few hours. There are near to a dozen of us. I think they will be willing to help a clansmon and a wee lass."

"Even though she is worth a great deal of coin?"

Nigel was not sure he wanted too many people knowing he and Gisele were here. That increased the chances that someone would let greed lead them, and instead of sailing for Scotland he and Gisele would find themselves captured by Sir Vachel. This time the man would not be so easily defeated, and Gisele would undoubtedly pay dearly for not staying in his bed.

"Dinnae worry so, laddie. These are good men and they willnae want blood money, either. Nay, especially when they see that the ones these French fools are hunting are a Scot and a tiny, thin lass with no hair."

"I have hair," Gisele muttered, but neither man paid her any heed.

"Wait here," ordered Duncan.

"I am nay sure this place is safe for us now," Nigel said.

"Safe enough, and far safer than many another place. Me and that fool only saw ye because I was hungering after the horses. He felt a need to see who the beasts belonged to, saw ye hiding here, and got verra excited. As I said, for a wee moment I was tempted by the coin, and he convinced me to give him a hand." Duncan shrugged. "Fear I had already begun to change my mind when we entered the alley, but I didnae get a chance to tell him."

"Then we will wait here until I feel the danger grows too great."

The moment Duncan slipped away, Nigel turned to Gisele and was not surprised to see her looking at him as if he had lost his mind. He was not sure that she was entirely wrong to worry. If she had heard some of the tales he had about the MacGregors, she would be even more concerned. There was no reason to trust in Duncan, but he did. Nigel just prayed that he was not being ruled solely by the fact that the man was a Scotsman.

"You do not know this man, do you?" she asked.

"Nay. This is the first time I have e'er seen him," Nigel replied.

"I see. Was there something about the way he held his sword at your throat that told you he was just the man you wished to trust with our lives?"

Gisele knew she sounded snide, even mildly insulting, but she could not help herself. From what little she had seen Duncan MacGregor had given no one reason to trust him about anything, let alone a matter of life and death. He simply shared a language and birthplace with Nigel.

Nigel half-smiled over the sharpness of her tongue. When Gisele decided to put a bite in her words, she put in an enviable one. He was almost tempted to look himself over carefully to be sure she had not drawn blood with her words.

"I wish I could tell ye why I think we can trust him, loving, but I cannae. I have no reason that can be put into words. I just do." He shrugged. "Mayhap it is because he really did not attack us, revealed his reluctance to do so from the beginning."

"Let us say that I allow you that weak reasoning to trust in Duncan. Can you safely use the same to trust in all he may tell? He admitted that he was tempted by the bounty offered for me. There may even be one for you now. May there not be more men who will be tempted? Men amongst those he is, even now, telling about us?"

"There could be." He pulled her into his arms and gave her a brief kiss. "We are trapped, lass. Aye, we may be able to slip away from here unseen, but each port we go to will be the same. We are here. A ship is soon to sail for Scotland. I may have found someone who will help us get to that ship. Can we really give into fear and mistrust and flee from what might be our only chance to escape this land?"

Gisele cursed, and briefly paced the ground in front of him. *"Non,* we cannot. Is there any way we can protect ourselves just in case he is about to return with some greedy friends?"

"We can run." He tried to soothe her glare with a quick grin, then grew serious. "Nay, there is no way to protect ourselves and trust him at the same time."

She stared at him for one long minute before slumping against the wall again and softly cursing to herself in French. It would be wonderful to believe they had found someone to help them, but they could not trust anyone. Nigel was also right to say that they really did not have many choices left to them. There was a ship there ready to sail to Scotland. There was a man who said he would get them on it. All they had to do was wait and pray to God that he was not trying to get them to stay in one place until he could bring enough men to capture them. Gisele did not like the odds.

When Nigel leaned against the wall at her side, she sent him a crooked smile. He shared her concerns. She could read that in his amber eyes. There was no gain to be had in badgering him with them. She reached out and took his hand in hers. In truth, she was more afraid for him, but she did not want to tell him that, either. If they were about to be betrayed, they would die together. If they were taken to Vachel that death would be most unpleasant, especially for Nigel, who had struck the man. She wished she could think of some way that Nigel could better protect himself while they gambled on Duncan MacGregor, but nothing came to mind. In her heart, she knew that Nigel would not take it even if she did think of a way.

"I keep having to face the fact that I and all of my troubles could get you killed," she murmured.

"Nay, the DeVeaux in all their madness could get me killed," he said, gently squeezing her hand in a gesture of comfort. "Ye must cease blaming yourself for all of our difficulties. Ye are not at fault in all of this."

"That may be true, but simply saying so does not make me feel any less at fault."

"That is because ye are a stubborn lass who willnae heed the truth, not if it means ye must change your mind."

"I am stubborn? This condemnation from the king of all stubbornness leaves me humbled."

"Such a sharp tongue."

"If the two of ye are done with your wooing, we can go now," drawled a deep voice from right beside Nigel.

Right beside the fear that gripped Gisele at Duncan's sudden appearance was absolute astonishment, even a hint of glee, that someone had finally snuck up on Nigel the same way he was always sneaking up on her. Nigel had already spun around, his hand on his sword, before he had realized it was Duncan. Although he did not draw his sword, and Duncan and the thin man with him showed no sign of drawing theirs, he remained tense.

Gisele realized that Nigel did not really believe all he had told her in an effort to calm her. He did not completely trust Duncan, and did not like the situation they were in any better than she did.

"Ye should be wary about creeping up on people," Nigel said quietly.

"Old habit," Duncan replied, then he nodded toward the too thin man at his side. "This shadow of a mon is Colin, my cousin. I thought I might need a hand getting the two of ye through the crowd of carrion gleaning the area for you."

"I thought a lot of them looked like DeVeau men."

"Near half, if I guess right. Can the lass make herself look more like a lass?"

"Aye," Nigel answered cautiously. "Ye need her to do so?"

"Well, if we can make ourselves look like a few drunken men and a whore as we weave through the crowd, we may get to the ship without having to hack our way through Frenchmen."

"It might work." Nigel's appreciation of the plan was clear in his voice, but then he looked at Gisele and frowned. There is no place for her to safely change into the gown and cloak we have in our saddlepacks."

"There is no one at the back of these buildings. Everyone is in the streets where the market is. I didnae want anyone to see me steal three horses any more than ye want someone seeing ye and the lass."

"You will be there," Gisele said quietly, knowing his idea was a good one but uneasy about changing her clothes with two strange men near at hand.

"Well, now, lassie, it seems to me that ye have to make a choice. Do ye fret o'er your modesty or your life?"

Gisele stared at Duncan for a moment and then at his silent cousin, a little annoyed at the amusement in their eyes. She then looked at Nigel, who was frowning at her in apparent indecision. He obviously did not like the idea of her changing clothes in front of the men any more than she did, but clearly saw the merit of Duncan's plan.

"Well, if one of you can hold up a blanket, I believe I am small enough to shelter behind it."

Duncan guffawed, then quickly swallowed his laughter when she glared at him. Without another word, they all moved to the rear of the buildings where Nigel had tethered the horses. She reached for the pack that held the gown Vachel had given her but Nigel stayed her hand. Gisele frowned in confusion as he pulled a gown from his saddlepack, pausing to put away something wrapped inside of it. It was not until he handed it to her that she recognized it as the gown she and Guy had tried to bury by the river.

"What are you doing with this?"

"I didnae see any reason for ye to throw away a perfectly good gown," he replied.

She shook it out, a little surprised that it was in such good condition after being stuffed in his saddlepack for so long. "It is somewhat wrinkled," she murmured.

"It is better than marching through a town filled with DeVeau men wearing a gown their lord gave you. I wouldnae doubt that he gave his men a verra good description of it."

"Aye, and it looks fine enough for a whore to be wearing," said Duncan. The man shrugged when both Nigel and Gisele glared at him. "In truth, it looks a wee bit too fine," he muttered.

"If that was an attempt to take back any insult you might have inflicted, it was a poor one," Gisele said.

"Do ye ken, I thought it a wee bit odd when they added that ye had a sharp tongue in the description of ye. Doesnae matter to how ye look. I begin to see why they did, though."

"They said I had a sharp tongue?"

"Aye. Ye are being described as a wee lass, black curls, thin, and with a sharp tongue. Oh, aye, and dressed in ill-fitting lad's clothes." He glanced at Nigel, ignoring Gisele's gasp of outrage. "Ye are described as a fine, braw Scot with red hair. 'Tisnae that red."

"It only has some red in it," muttered Gisele. "It is more of a golden brown."

"This is all most interesting," Nigel snapped as he held up the blanket. "But, I think we had best get out of here, dinnae ye?"

Standing between the blanket and the horse, Gisele struggled out of her clothes and then hurriedly donned the gown. The way Nigel was intensely watching the other two men to be sure they did not peek at her insured her almost complete privacy. Once she had dressed, Nigel did not give her much time to think. He threw her cloak over her shoulders and took her by the arm. Duncan stopped him from walking toward the ship that way, however. Gisele briefly feared that now they would suffer the man's betrayal, then felt deeply guilty when Duncan revealed that he was simply thinking of the best way to protect them on their dangerous walk to the ship.

"She must needs go along on my arm, or Colin's, if ye prefer," Duncan said.

"And why is that?" demanded Nigel.

"Because it be the two of ye together that they are all sniffing the ground for. 'Tis wise to separate the two of ye until we can get to the ship."

"It makes sense," Nigel replied cautiously, then nudged Gisele toward Colin. "Your cousin is the better choice, for he has dark hair. A woman and a red-haired Scot would still raise an eyebrow or two, and we dinnae want those dogs to come anywhere near us."

"What about the horses?" Gisele asked, as Colin took her by the arm and they started out of the alley.

"I will send two other men back here to get them," answered Duncan. "Two more faces they arenae looking for. They will just think the men lead their own mounts back home." He glanced back at Colin and Gisele. "Try to recall that ye are soaked in wine, drunk, and amorous, and pull the lass's hood up to shield her face."

Colin did as his cousin ordered. Gisele tried to relax when the man draped one thin arm around her shoulders and held her close. Nigel glared at them once before Duncan put an arm around his shoulders, leaning against him as if he were unsteady on his feet, and led them out into the street.

As they entered the crowded streets Gisele tensed, terrified of discovery and eager to run. Colin tightened his hold on her, and she was a little surprised by the strength in that thin arm. He pressed his cheek against the top of her head and began to speak in a language she did not understand. She glanced up at him, forcing herself to grin, and caught his dark eyes fixed firmly upon her face.

"English? French?" she asked in whisper.

"Nay. Gaelic. Smile. Ye are a happy whore who is about to make some coin."

Although she was not sure how that would make a woman act, Gisele began to pretend that she was more drunk than sober and eager to please the man who stumbled down the street with her. She risked the occasional and very brief glance at Nigel and Duncan, who were acting very drunk indeed, even bursting into raucous song once or twice. The way Duncan tended to bump into people may have been the correct way for a drunk man to behave, but it made her so nervous she had to stop looking at him.

Only once did someone try to stop them. Duncan callously and slyly knocked Nigel face down on the ground when he held his arms wide to greet the curious Frenchman, playing as if his unsteady support was all that had kept Nigel on his feet. Colin held her even closer and played at nuzzling her neck. She could feel his long lashes move against her skin, and knew he was watching the whole confrontation closely. When the Frenchman cursed Duncan as a fool and marched away, Duncan helped Nigel to his feet.

All they had to deal with for the rest of the walk to the ship were a few curses and crude jests. Once on board, Gisele pulled away from Colin. Duncan released Nigel and called to two men to go and get their horses. As the men brushed by her on their way off the boat, she wrapped her arms around herself as she began to tremble slightly. When Nigel suddenly put a hand on her shoulder, she jumped.

"Are ye all right, loving?" he asked softly.

She nodded. "I will sit over there for a moment until I can still the fear that long walk stirred in me."

"I was nay discourteous to her," Colin said, "or, I tried not to be. But she was to appear to be a whore."

Seeing that Gisele had sat down on a thick coil of heavy rope and wrapped herself in her cape, Nigel looked back at an uneasy Colin. "That isnae your doing. She wasnae treated well by her husband or his cousin. She shies from a strange mon's touch, is all. This may also be because we were so closed in by those who wish to give her back to those bastards. If the DeVeaux get ahold of her, she is a dead woman."

"Aye," murmured Duncan as he began to closely watch one young man. "And so are you dead. The men searching that wee village werenae just after the lass. A certain Lord Vachel has been screaming for your head on a pike."

Before Nigel could say anything Duncan cursed, pulled out his dagger, and threw it. A soft squeal from behind him made Nigel turn around to see where Duncan's knife had landed. A pockmarked youth was pinned neatly to the railing by Duncan's knife. It looked to Nigel as if the blade had come very close to the youth's flesh. He followed Duncan as the man walked over to the youth.

"And where did ye think ye were going, laddie?" Duncan asked the pale, trembling youth as he retrieved his dagger.

"To help Ian and Thomas with the horses?" the young man replied in a quavering voice.

"Nay, I think not. We agreed that we willnae sell one of our own to the French, didnae we? But mayhap ye thought that just meant that ye could gain all of the bounty for yourself."

"Nay!"

"Ye are a poor liar, William. Robert," Duncan called to another one of the Scots on board. "Take this greedy child below deck and make sure he doesnae leave your sight until we are far out to sea. Then I will decide if I want to toss him over the side or nay."

"Many men have been tempted by that bounty," Nigel said.

"Aye, I ken it. Including me. Dinnae fret, I willnae hurt the boy. But 'twill do him good to sweat with fear for a while."

Nigel smiled his understanding and moved to Gisele's side. He sat down and took her hand in his. "Have ye calmed yourself, sweeting?"

She nodded slowly. "Do you think we will actually slip out of this village safely?"

"Aye, I begin to." He watched the men working around the ship for a moment. "We will be setting sail verra soon. Then we can have about three days of rest, nay looking o'er our shoulders every minute." Gisele thought that sounded lovely and waited eagerly for that brief taste of freedom from pursuit.

Her delight faded very quickly when the ship finally got under sail. They could still see the coast of France behind them when Gisele discovered that she would never be a sailor.

Shaking after violently emptying her stomach over the rail of the ship, Gisele accepted the dampened cloth Nigel held out to her and washed her face. She clutched it tightly in her hand as, with a shudder, she felt the urge to hang her head over the rail again. She had heard of *mal de mer,* and knew that was what ailed her. She just wished she had an idea of how long it might last.

"Pity, lass. Ye are no sailor, are ye?" Nigel patted her on the back. "Weel, not to worry yourself. It will pass once ye have your feet back on steady ground."

Gisele clung to the rail and decided that she must love Nigel very much, for she was not even trying to push him into the sea.

Twenty-one

Gisele groaned and sat down on a large, damp rock. She knew she was probably ruining her dress, but she did not care. It was undoubtedly in a sad state, anyway, after all it had been through with her in the last few days. Her legs were as unsteady as her stomach, and she did not have the strength to search for a cleaner place to sit down. She thought that they had sailed for three days, but she could not be sure, for she had spent most of that time sicker than she had ever been in her whole life. Not long after they had left France the whole journey had become little more than a wretched nightmare to her. Since the only way to return to France was by ship, she decided that Scotland would make a very good new home.

Lass, ye will get filthy and wet if ye continue to sit there," Nigel said.

She looked up at Nigel and his two new friends, Duncan and the taciturn Colin. As far as she was concerned, none of them had shown the appropriate amount of concern for her. They had just kept telling her that she would feel better soon, that the journey was not that long, and other such banalities. She also felt that it was nearly beyond forgiving that they had not immediately produced some miraculous cure for her misery. If she had not been so sick she would have made them all very sorry, indeed.

"I need to be still for a little while," she said even as she accepted Nigel's help in standing up.

"Ye will get your land legs back soon, lass," Duncan said.

"How nice. And when do I get my stomach back? As far as I can see it will have been washed up with the tide, for I believe I lost it but a few hours sail from France." Gisele glared at Duncan and Colin when the two men laughed. She glanced up at Nigel and noticed that he had the good sense to just be quietly amused.

While Nigel thanked the men for their help and gave Duncan the grey mare he had coveted, Gisele tried to just stand in one place without swaying. She looked at the saddled horses and inwardly groaned. She knew it was wise to leave the port as swiftly as possible. If the DeVeaux were after them, or already had allies in Scotland, this would be the first place they would search. Gisele just prayed that Nigel would not make her ride very far. She had not been joking when she had said she needed to be still for a while. It was not simply a wish to be on solid, unmoving ground, either. After being ill for several long days she was thoroughly exhausted.

Honest gratitude and well taught courtesy gave her the strength to move, however, when Duncan and his cousin started to leave. She walked over to the men, murmured her heartfelt thanks, and hugged each man in turn, smiling to herself when they blushed vividly as she kissed their cheeks. On the ship she had had little time or inclination to come to know them very well, but they had tried, however ineptly, to help her. Nigel liked them, and she accepted that as sound accolade of their worth. They had also gotten her and Nigel safely through a harbor town full of DeVeaux and out of France. They deserved far more than a kiss and a horse, but both men seemed heartily pleased with what they had.

The moment the two MacGregors left, Nigel lifted Gisele up into her saddle. "We willnae ride for long, dearling."

"There is no need to be so apologetic," she said, as she watched him gracefully swing his long body into the saddle. "I understand that it is not wise to linger here. If the DeVeaux guessed we would go to a port in France, then they have guessed that we would sail here."

"And they might be watching these ports even now," he said as he led them through the crowded streets and out of town. "Here and in other towns such as this a few Frenchmen wandering about wouldnae be noticed much." He glanced back at her and frowned at how pale she was. "If ye cannae abide it any longer, let me ken it, and I will find us a place to make camp."

"Now that I am off that ship, I believe I will begin to recover."

Nigel kept their pace slow, and she was grateful for that consideration. The fresh air, cool and damp though it was, and the steady gait of her horse began to revive her. The movement of the horse was one she was accustomed to, unlike the roll of the ship's deck. Gisele was astounded that anyone would willingly step on board one of those conveyances from hell, let alone choose to make a living off them, sailing off on the cursed things day after day. If it were not for Lent and many another rule of the church that dictated what she ate and when, Gisele doubted that she would even want to dine upon fish again.

The land around them drew her interest for a while. The village and its people had been a stark mixture of wealth and deep poverty, but she had seen many such disparities in France, too. The land itself, however, was different. France, too, had hills and rocks and trees and all the rest, but here it all looked so much more wild, even harsh. She knew the grey, misty weather added to that, but it was not the only reason it all looked so strange to her. And yet, she mused, it was also beautiful. She took a deep breath and could almost smell the wildness, the challenge the land offered anyone who wanted to try to survive in it. Gisele decided that she could easily come to love the place nearly as much as she loved one of its sons.

She fixed her gaze on Nigel's broad back as they rode. Now that he was actually on Scottish soil she could almost feel his eagerness to get back to his family and his lands. Gisele wished she could share in his happy anticipation. She was accused of killing her husband, and she was not even sure Nigel believed in her innocence. It was hard to believe that his family would accept her as their honored guest. Even if they did allow her into their keep, graciously offering her shelter there, a great deal of trouble could follow right behind her. To bring that to the gates of a family who offered her their hospitality seemed, at the very least, extremely rude. Gisele decided that she was going to have to thoroughly discuss the matter with Nigel when they stopped to camp for the night.

"Rude?" Nigel briefly halted in unsaddling their horses to stare at Gisele in amazement. "Ye are worried about being rude?"

"That is not all I am concerned about, but, *oui* it is a consideration," she replied. The way Nigel was looking at her—as if her wits had been lost over the side of that ship along with the contents of her stomach, was making her feel very defensive. "It is no small thing to ask your family to shelter someone who has half of France searching for her. And, might I remind you, someone you are not even sure is innocent."

"I shall vouch for you, and that is all they will need to hear."

Silently cursing, she made the fire and spread out their bedding as he tended to the horses. She was pulling some food out of their packs when she realized what he had just said. He would vouch for her. Gisele quickly pushed aside a surge of hope that Nigel now believed in her innocence. That was not exactly what he had said. He could simply mean that he would assure his family that she would not kill him or steal all their valuables and creep away in the night. She had no way of knowing what he had meant, and should cease trying to measure his every word.

After setting their food down on their bedding, she slipped away to relieve herself and wash away the day's dust. She also needed to get away from Nigel for a while, just long enough to compose herself. It would gain her nothing if she demanded to know what he meant by vouching for her. If he did not immediately say that he now believed she had not killed her husband, she would be painfully disappointed yet again, and this time she was afraid he would see the hurt he inflicted clearly displayed upon her face. Now that she knew she loved him, had reluctantly accepted that truth, her emotions were so strong and so close to the surface that she was no longer sure she could hide anything from the man. She was turning her face aside or slipping away for a moment alone more and more.

When she felt strong enough to face him she returned to the camp and sat down beside him. He handed her some bread and cheese, and she sighed with resignation as she ate. The food was filling and good, but she was growing weary of it. She wanted to sit at a table and eat a proper meal. Gisele realized that she could not clearly recall the last time she had done so. Even when she had stayed with one of the few relatives who would shelter her, she had had to remain hidden away, unable to participate in even something as simple as the family meal. She knew she should be grateful that she and Nigel had any food to eat at all, but that gratitude did not ease the longing for a return to the comforts she had been raised with.

"Some food in your belly will help ye recover," Nigel said as he handed her the wineskin.

Gisele took a long drink before handing the wine back to him. "It has already helped. I feel more settled and stronger."

"I wondered, for ye looked somewhat pensive."

She smiled. "I was just feeling sorry for myself. Do not mistake me. You have provided for me very well, but I realized that it has been a very long time since I have sat down at a table for a proper meal."

Nigel grinned and draped his arm around her shoulders, then nodded. "It has been a long time for me, as weel. I understand the longing. Aye, not only to sit up at table, but to have a choice of foods."

"*Oui,* that would be lovely. The game you caught and cooked was most delicious and very welcome," she added hastily.

"But rarely provided. I ken it, and I ken, too, that ye dinnae mean any criticism. My brother's people set a fine table. Ye will find all ye could want, and a lot of it. If naught happens to slow us down, we should be sitting at that table in a week, mayhap less."

Her mouth watered just thinking about it, but then she pushed aside her selfish longings. Nigel had shrugged aside her growing concerns about imposing upon his family, but they had to be discussed. When he had first presented her with the plan it had seemed to be a very good one, but matters were different now. The hunt for her had intensified, and if Vachel was as furious about her escape as she suspected he was it could grow even worse. Only a proclamation of her innocence would stop the hunt, and she could not be sure when or if that would happen. That was a lot of trouble to set upon the threshold of people who did not even know her.

"And seated with us at that table will be a great deal of trouble," she said quietly.

"Ye worry too much about that, lass."

"One of us should. Ye are about to ask a lot of your family. Indeed, ye may be pulling them deep into a fight that is none of their doing and from which they gain nothing."

"Your life isnae nothing," he said in a soft, solemn voice. "Love, they will want to join this fight, and not simply because I ask it of them or because I have sworn upon my honor that I will protect you. They will help you because it is right to do so. It is wrong for the DeVeaux to hunt you like this, to demand your blood for the life of that bastard ye were forced to marry. Any fool can see that, and I dinnae have any fools in my family. Well, not at this moment."

She smiled briefly, fleetingly amused by his last words, but then looked straight at him, making no attempt to hide her deep concern. "You must give them the choice. You must tell them the full truth about why I am being hunted."

"I intend to. It will make no difference. They will see why honor—"

"Non," she interrupted sharply. "Do not tell them of your vow and do not speak of honor, yours or theirs. Do not tell them that you have sworn to protect me. That is to push them toward what we want them to do, and in their hearts they may wish to say *non.* They will feel that if you are bound by honor they are bound just as tightly, for they will not wish to blacken your name."

"They will still say 'aye' to taking ye into their care," he asserted.

"No word of your vow. Do you agree to this?"

"Aye. Ye will see that I speak the truth, however. They willnae act because they wish to save my poor, wee, tattered honor, but because they honestly wish to save you."

Gisele squeaked in surprise when he abruptly pushed her down onto their bed. "And thus ends our discussion?"

Nigel laughed as he began to remove her clothes. "Did ye have anything else to say?"

"Just one thing. If they do decide that I am more trouble than they wish to set upon their shoulders, might I have a proper meal just once before I must leave?"

She laughed along with him, then greedily returned his kiss. It was undoubtedly foolish, but she realized that she felt safe. She also felt hungry for Nigel. The journey had kept her sick for nearly every mile from France to Scotland, and the only touch Nigel had given her was the occasional comforting pat on the back, or to hold her head up while she was ill. Although she was tired, she did not wish to lose another night of savoring the passion they shared.

As she matched him stroke for stroke and kiss for kiss, she silently revealed her love for him. When they were both caught up in the heady grip of desire she had neither the strength nor the will to hide how she felt. Since he was as captivated as she was, Gisele did not fear that he would guess how she felt. She was sure that such a feeling required words to confirm its existence.

Expressing her love through passion, through each caress,

each kiss, also gave her the strength to hide it the rest of the time. It was as if the feeling grew so large at times it threatened to flow out of her, and she feared she would babble it all out in a confused confession to an unwilling Nigel. The very last thing she wished to do was bare her heart to the man and have him graciously hand it back. Within the confines of their love-making, she could feel free to let her heart rule.

Once they had shared their release, the strength of which always astonished her, Gisele let her exhaustion take hold. She curled herself around Nigel, loving the warm feel of his body so close to hers, and closed her eyes. If passion were any indication of how a person felt, then Nigel had to love her too, but she knew that was a fool's hope. Passion did not have to rule a man's heart as it did a woman's. At best, she might become the finest lover he had ever known. As sleep dragged her into its hold, she decided that that was better than nothing. At least she would linger in his mind as a sweet memory. It would be better to be loved in return, but she could find some solace in knowing she would not be forgotten.

Nigel stared down at the small woman sleeping so soundly in his arms. Soon they would be at the gates of Donncoill, and Gisele would be face-to-face with Maldie. It was time he told Gisele about the woman, but he was too much of a coward. It was an awkward tale to tell, and he was embarrassed by it all. He still felt as if he had betrayed his brother Balfour in some way, even though he had never touched Maldie. It did not ease his embarrassment at all knowing that everyone who mattered to him at Donncoill was fully aware of why he had left, including Maldie.

For a little while he had deceived himself by thinking that there was not really that much similarity between the two women. Almost the moment he had stepped upon the shores of Scotland, he had felt that comfortable lie fall to pieces. Gisele and Maldie were both small women, both had black hair and green eyes, and they shared a strikingly similar spirit. Even if he were able to cling to the lie, he would be the only one who would believe it.

Somehow, he was going to have to tell Gisele something between now and the moment they reached the gates of Donncoill or he could find the warm lover he held so close turning very cold. That was a loss he did not want to face. Sadly, telling her could easily bring the same results.

Nigel silently cursed and accepted the fact that he would probably get very little sleep until the dreaded confrontation was over. He had the sick feeling that he was also going to let his cowardice rule and hope for the best. After all, telling her now would bring the same consequences as letting her see for herself. Why deprive himself of a few more nights in her arms?

"What is this?" Gisele asked as she sat down and lightly brushed her hand over the soft mound of delicate white flowers.

"Heather," Nigel answered as he sat down next to her.

"Ah, the thing you and Duncan were so eager to smell."

He smiled and reverently touched the plant. "Aye, 'tis what we said. I think we mean more than that, however. I think we mean the whole land, the smell of Scotland herself. The heather, beautiful though it is when it covers the hills with color, is but a wee part of it all."

She kissed his cheek when he grimaced. "I understand. There is a wildness in the air, a challenge to the people who walk these hills."

Nigel gently pushed her down onto the soft moss-covered ground, amazed and delighted that she understood, that she shared the feeling. They were only a few hours ride from Donncoill, but he had reined in his eagerness to finish the journey and stopped for a rest. Knowing that she could soon be compelled to turn away from him, he ruefully admitted that he had stopped in the hope of making love to her one more time. Her words revealed that she already felt some kinship to the land and that, he knew, was going to make losing her all the harder to bear.

There was one thing he knew he could do, one thing that might stop her from thinking the worst of him. He could tell Gisele that he loved her, could offer marriage. She would still be hurt when she saw Maldie, and would undoubtedly question the veracity of his vow, but those three little words could mean that she would give him a chance to explain. Nigel knew he could not do it, however. He was not sure, his confusion deep and unrelenting. No woman had affected him the way Gisele had, none had stirred his passion as fiercely as she could with just one little smile, and none had kept his mind as interested in her as his body for so long. None except Maldie. He did not want to promise Gisele love and marriage, faithfulness and devotion, then take one look at Maldie and know it was all a lie. If nothing else, he could not hurt Gisele by offering her a heart that was still tightly bound to another woman.

Gisele reached up and smoothed away the frown between his eyes. "For a man who is but a few miles from the beloved home he has not seen in seven long years, you are not looking very happy."

"I think I grow uncertain of my welcome," he replied.

"Because of why you left?" She inwardly tensed, wondering if he would tell her the whole truth about what had driven him to spend so many years away from a land he so clearly loved.

"Aye, that is some of it. There is also the fact that after so long, things will have changed, so will have some of the people. I believe I have changed a little, as weel."

Nigel silently cursed himself for the greatest coward on two legs. There had been a perfect chance to confess all, and he had dodged it as swiftly as he would have dodged a sword stroke. It was a secret, albeit not a very well kept one, that he did not want to have to tell, not unless he was forced to. Nigel prayed Gisele would give him at least one chance to explain himself if the upcoming meeting with his family turned sour.

Deeply disappointed that he had not spoken of the woman

she was sure he had run from, Gisele took a moment to compose herself, lightly trailing kisses over his face so that he could not see the hurt in her eyes. She prayed that he was not going to let her find out some hard truth on her own, through whispered rumors or even with her own eyes. Even if she did not like what he might say, she would prefer to hear the truth from him. There was not much time left for him to do so, however, and wondering just how devastating the secret might be was stealing the beauty of the moment. That was the last thing she wanted to do. She took a deep breath to steady herself, forced herself to smile, and set her mind on easing the uncertainty Nigel was suffering from.

"They will be pleased to see you standing there alive and unmaimed," she said. "If changes have occurred in Donncoill or its people, I suspect they will not be anything you cannot learn about and live with. Beneath it all they will still be the family you knew."

"Aye, ye are right. It has been hard to get news of them or send them word about me, and I began to think I would find myself amongst strangers. Or, that I would feel I was. That is foolishness, perhaps born of being too eager to get home."

"So, shall we return to our horses?"

"Nay, not yet." He slowly began to unlace her gown. 'Tis a fine, sun warmed day, and ye willnae have to be here long to ken what a blessing that is. I thought I might enjoy it a wee bit."

"Ah, so, it is the day you seek to enjoy," she murmured, tilting her head back so that he could have freer access to her throat.

Nigel just laughed and proceeded to make love to her. He had an urge to stop right there, build a shelter, and keep her in it. He would be near enough to his family to see them whenever he wished, but Gisele would never have to lay eyes on Maldie. He knew that was pure madness, and pushed it aside. Even if he could keep Gisele away from his family, it would probably only be for a little while. Someone would say something, or Maldie herself would arrive to see what he was hiding. He could

not avoid the confrontation he dreaded, only pray that it would
not be as bad as he feared.

Gisele frowned as she welcomed Nigel into her body. Her
passion was running hot and wild, but she was not so blinded
by it this time that she did not notice some difference in Nigel's
behavior. There was the smallest hint of desperation in his caresses, in the fierce way he pushed them to desire's heights, as
if he felt this would be the last time they would make love.
Gisele decided she did not want to know why he should think
of such a thing, feared even thinking it herself. She wrapped
her body around his and decided to lose herself completely in
the way he made her feel. If this were to be the last time she
was in his arms, she did not want to dim the pleasure of it by
thinking too much.

Nigel said little when they finally ended their embrace and
began to put their clothes back on. He had murmured a few
flattering words, but Gisele had not been fooled. Usually his
pretty words made her feel wanted, beautiful, and desirable.
This time she felt as if he just spoke practiced words, ones with
no feeling or thought behind them. She felt the sting of shame,
as if she had just been used as he had used the whores in France,
but she struggled to subdue that appalling thought. It was not
easy. Suddenly, there was a distance between them, and it terrified her.

As they remounted and started their journey again she told
herself not to be a fool, that she was seeing dark shadows where
there were none. Nigel was unsure of what he would find at
Donncoill, and his mind was occupied by fears and concerns.
It was no more than that. Her own uncertainties about meeting
his family had just made her uneasy, and she tried to put the
blame for that discomfort on Nigel.

She had almost convinced herself of that when Donncoill
finally loomed into sight. It was an impressive if unfinished
keep. Gisele knew that when the building was done it would
rival many in France. Nigel was not going home to some poor,
small tower like others she had seen in their journey, but to a

strong *demanse* that any man should be proud of. Yet the closer
they got, the slower his pace. She got the distinct feeling that
Nigel would turn and run if he could find any sound reason to
do so. That made no sense to her, and she ached to stop, drag
him from his horse, and demand that he tell her exactly what
was troubling him.

The greeting they got as they rode through the high iron gates
was as hearty a welcome as any man could want. Even that did
not fully lighten Nigel's somber expression. As he helped her
down from her horse she had to bite her tongue to keep from
demanding to know what troubled him so. Gisele did not like
surprises, and she had the growing suspicion that she was about
to suffer a very large and extremely unpleasant one.

A big man who seemed to be all different shades of browns
grabbed Nigel as he stepped inside the door of the keep and
hugged him tightly. That loving greeting was swiftly repeated
by an older man and then a smiling, beautiful youth. If Nigel
had feared that he would not be welcome or that his family
would have become distant, that fear had soundly been put to
rest. When he turned to take her by the hand, however, she got
one clear look into his eyes and felt her blood chill. He was
still uncertain, almost afraid. She suddenly did not want to know
what had put that look in his eyes, and fought the sudden urge
to turn and run from Donncoill. If something made Nigel afraid,
she felt no shame in being terrified by it. She just wished she
knew what it was.

She responded to everyone's polite greeting as she was in-
troduced to Nigel's brothers Balfour and Eric, and the man
James. The way the men were looking at her and then at Nigel
made her nervous. It was as if they all shared some dark secret.

"Nigel," called a sweet voice, and all the men turned to look
at the woman hurrying down the stairs.

Gisele watched as the woman greeted Nigel with a hug and
a kiss on the cheek before turning to her. She could feel everyone staring at her, but did not care. All of her attention was on
the woman Nigel was introducing as his brother Balfour's wife,

Maldie. It was hard not to shudder as she felt her blood turn to ice in her veins.

There was no ignoring the similarities between herself and Maldie. As Gisele noted each one she felt sicker and sicker. Her heart began to clench so tightly in her chest she found each breath painful. She knew this was the woman Nigel had run from, but that was not the reason she felt such agony ripping away at her insides.

Maldie was a little older than she, and very big with child, but that was about all that kept them from looking as if they had emerged from the same womb. Maldie had the same thick, black hair she did, the same deep green eyes, and was almost exactly the same size and height. All this time, while she had been falling in love with the man and wondering if she could ever get him to care about her, while they had been lovers greedily indulging their passion all the way across France and Scotland, Nigel had not even truly seen her. He had used her. Not sure she could win his heart, she had found some comfort in knowing that his passion and his companionship had been hers for a while, that she would at least be a sweet memory. She had been a complete fool. He had not been making love to Gisele DeVeau, but his brother's wife.

Twenty-two

"You should have told me, Nigel," Gisele said quietly, wanting to rage at him but knowing this was not the time nor the place to do so. "It was most unkind of you not to."

"Gisele—" he began.

This was worse than he had imagined. He had not seen her look so stricken since he had watched her try to scrub away Vachel DeVeau's touch. Nigel ached to smooth that look from her face, to put the life back into her eyes, but he feared he had just lost all chance of doing so. And, sadly, he now knew he wanted that chance, that he wanted her and no one else. It had taken just one look at Maldie to know, without doubt, that nothing remained of the feelings he had once had for her. He no longer loved Maldie, and probably had not for a very long time. He loved Gisele, the woman who was now looking at him as if he were the lowest, cruelest man she had ever met. Not telling her about Maldie may have been the biggest and most costly mistake he had ever made.

"Non." She shied away from his touch when he reached for her. "It is too late."

She felt so torn up inside that she was surprised she was not bleeding all over the fresh rushes beneath her feet. The tense, discomforted looks on the faces of Nigel's family helped her to subdue her pain, although she knew it would be a short-lived respite. That amount of hurt would not allow itself to be ignored for too long. Nigel's family did not deserve to be witness to it,

however, nor did she want to bare her soul before them. She
certainly did not want to bare it before Nigel. If there were
going to be any discussion or consequence of Nigel's heartless-
ness, he could suffer them alone. He certainly deserved to. She
needed to go somewhere where she could be alone, to try to
deal with the emotions churning inside of her.

"It is an honor to meet you all," she said, pleased that her
voice sounded calm, if a little strained. "However, if I may
impose upon your kindness, I would really like a room. I need
to wash the dust of travel away and get some rest."

"Of course ye do," said Maldie, stepping forward. After sending Nigel a sharp, angry look that promised severe retribution,
she took Gisele by the arm and urged her toward a plump, aging
woman standing at the foot of the stairs. "Margaret, please take
the Lady Gisele to a room and see that she has all she needs."

Nigel finally pulled free of his shock and indecision, but
when he moved to follow Gisele up the stairs, Maldie firmly
blocked his way. "I need to talk to Gisele."

He briefly considered just moving Maldie out of the way,
then glanced down at her swollen belly. Balfour would not appreciate him handling his wife that way. Nigel also had the
suspicion that she was right to stop him. Gisele would not wish
to hear a word he had to say at the moment, and he was not
quite sure of what he wanted or needed to tell her. She might
enjoy hearing him beg for forgiveness, but it would not be
enough to ease the sense of betrayal she must be feeling.

"Ye needed to talk to her long before this, I am thinking,"
Maldie snapped. Grabbing him by the arm, she pushed him
toward the great hall. "Now, ye will talk to us."

When did Maldie become the laird of Donncoill?" Nigel
asked, glancing at his brothers and James as Maldie herded the
four of them toward the head table in the great hall, pausing
only to order a page to bring them all some food.

James smiled faintly as he sat down across from Nigel. "I
suspect it wasnae long after she first rode through these gates.
We were just a wee bit slow to see that we had lost the power."

He then gave the younger man a stern look. "I think ye havenae accounted yourself well in this, laddie."

Maldie gave out a sharp, derisive noise as she took her seat on Balfour's right. "I think he has behaved like a bastard, and probably a big fool," she said, ignoring the murmurs of protest from Nigel's brothers and James. "But, ere we tear that bone apart, mayhap ye can tell us just who our guest is, and why she has traveled all this way."

After briefly considering running from the room, Nigel took a deep breath and related Gisele's story. He only hesitated a moment before also telling them what he knew about her time with the brutal Michael DeVeaux. These people would never betray her confidences. By the time he was through he had no doubt that they would put all the strength of Donncoill between Gisele and the DeVeaux. Nigel just wished she were there to see their determination for herself.

"And when did ye decide she hadnae killed the mon?" asked James, idly filling his plate with some of the food the page had brought.

Nigel stared at the man, wondering how he could have forgotten James's ability to see straight to the heart. "It took me a wee while. I didnae fault her for killing the bastard, as I could see why she would be driven to do it. Then, when she insisted on learning how to use a sword, there came the moment when I saw clearly that the lass couldnae kill a mon. Oh, she might do it if there was a true threat to her life or mine, as was proven the day I was wounded. But to murder and mutilate a mon when he was drunk nearly senseless? Nay, she could ne'er do that, no matter how much the bastard deserved it. I think it was the kinsmen of some lass he took and probably beat half to death."

"If Gisele's kinsmen prove her innocent, it may mean that those people pay dearly for what was no more than justice," Balfour said.

"Aye," Nigel agreed reluctantly, "but at least they are the true killers. If someone else isnae shown to have done the deed, then an innocent lass will pay for it with her life. In truth, I believe they deserve punishment for saying naught when she was accused, and continuing to do naught while she was running and hiding for a year."

"There is that," agreed Balfour.

"And now, may we talk about the newest crime done to that lass?" demanded Maldie, glaring at Nigel.

"Loving, he has saved that lass's life," Balfour said quietly, gently patting Maldie on the hand.

"I ken it, and for that he should be praised, although I suspect he may not have had the purest of motives at the beginning. All that doesnae matter. I find this hard to say, but we all ken why ye left seven years ago. Now ye return bringing a lass who looks enough like me to be my sister. I truly hope, nay, pray, that ye havenae——" She stuttered to a halt, unable to put the thought into words.

Balfour looked at his brother "Ye havenae used the wee lass that way, have ye, Nigel?"

Nigel grimaced, then almost smiled at the way they all tried so hard not to say exactly what they thought. "Nay, I havenae tried to replace the woman I wanted with that poor girl." He saw Maldie wince, and felt honestly sorry that she was discomforted by the discussion, but at least this once they had to speak the blunt ugly truth.

"Are ye sure, Nigel?" asked Eric, his almost pretty face solemn. "If we can see the likeness, ye cannae say ye didnae."

"Oh, aye, I saw it. Even with her hair cut short, even in lad's clothes which she wore for most of our flight across France, and even with that odd little way she speaks our language. Aye, I saw it verra clearly, and it has troubled me every step of the way. Each time I thought I kenned what I felt for the lass, I found myself doubting it. How could I not?"

"Ye should have told her. E'en if ye had to confess to your own confusion, ye should have told her."

"Lad, we have e'er admired your honesty, and wish we could be as quick to speak the truth as ye are, but sometimes it just isnae that simple."

"Ye are lovers. The lass has kenned a lot of betrayal in the last year or so. By nay telling her, ye have added to that in her mind. She had no word of warning from you, no hint that ye were torn in your feelings, and yet I suspect she kenned ye had left this land because of a woman. And so, she comes here thinking her lover is taking her to a place where she might find safety and peace, and what does she find? His ghosts. The moment she set eyes upon our Maldie, she kenned who ye had left, why ye had left, and quite quickly decided why ye took up with her."

"Eric is right," Maldie said quietly. "Ye let her come to this place with nay a word of explanation, nay a word to give her some feeling that all ye have shared during your time together meant anything to you. Even if she had convinced herself that ye cared in some small way, it was all proven false when she saw me. Nigel, think. The lass must feel something for you, as she allowed ye to become her lover despite all the hurt and betrayal she has suffered. Who kens what she had decided in her mind, but I doubt she ever thought she was just being used as some replacement for the one ye wanted. And I can promise ye, that is what she is thinking right now. She is feeling like the greatest of fools."

" 'Tis clear ye decided that wasnae how it was ere ye got here," said Balfour. "So, why didnae ye tell her that? If ye had, all ye would have to do now is soothe a few doubts."

"I didnae ken it for sure until I was here, until I actually saw Maldie and Gisele together," he answered quietly.

"Jesu," Maldie softly cursed. "Ye waited until ye could compare us?"

"Nay, it wasnae quite that base. It was the only way I could clear away the last of my confusion. I couldnae hurt her by telling her what might well have turned out to be lies." He grimaced in self-disgust. "Instead, I remained silent, and have probably hurt her in a far worse way."

"Do ye want the lass?" asked James.

Nigel smiled crookedly. "Aye, I want the lass."

"Then ye are going to have to woo her."

"James, I dinnae think she will allow me to come within sight of her. 'Twill be verra hard to woo her from a distance."

"She has to stay here. She has nowhere to go, and people are looking for her to fit a noose about her bonny neck. It may not be easy to get her to sit and listen, but that is what ye must do. Now ye must tell her the whole truth, and ye have to show her that ye want her and her alone. Come, lad, ye have ne'er had trouble with the lasses before. If ye put your mind to it, I think ye can win this one. 'Twill take time, but isnae she worth it?"

"Oh, aye, she is. I am just not sure she will think I am worth anything after this."

Gisele sprawled on the bed and stared up at the ceiling, her hands clenched tightly at her side. She had bathed, eaten the food brought to her even though it tasted like sour ashes in her mouth, and donned the crisp, clean, linen nightdress set out on the bed by Margaret. There was nothing left for her to do, nothing left for her to try to distract herself with. She was completely alone with her thoughts, and she desperately wished she was not.

Deciding there was no point in fighting the strong urge to weep, she gave in to it. She turned onto her stomach and sobbed into the soft pillows until there were no more tears left, her eyes empty and stinging. To her dismay, it left her exhausted but not enough so that she fell right to sleep. Nor did it completely dim the pain.

She still found it hard to believe that Nigel had betrayed her. Despite the proof she had seen with her own eyes, there was still one foolish part of her that wanted to believe she was wrong, that there was some good explanation for it. He was the first person, aside from kinsmen, that she had trusted in a very long while. It was very hard to accept that she had been utterly wrong to do so.

He had used her, and she would be an even greater fool if

she did not accept that harsh fact. She looked almost exactly like the woman he loved and could not have. Even if she could swallow her pride and accept that, it would be hard to do so when that woman was such a part of his life. One could not live a lie if the truth were right there to see every day. He would never be able to remove himself completely from the object of his yearning, either, not unless he cut himself completely off from his family. That she knew he would never do.

A soft rap at the door drew her attention, and she quickly sat up and wiped her eyes as the door slowly opened. She was both relieved and disappointed that it was Maldie and not Nigel who cautiously entered. Part of her wanted to never set eyes on Nigel again, but another part of her ached for him to come crawling to her, begging forgiveness and clearly explaining everything. She prayed he had not sent someone else to do the job for him.

"Dinnae look so suspicious, Lady Gisele," Maldie said as she sat down on the edge of the bed. "My husband's idiot of a brother doesnae even ken that I am here."

"I will leave in the morning," Gisele said, a little surprised at her words but realizing that the decision had been made the moment she had seen what a fool she had been.

"Nay, ye cannae leave. Ye have nowhere to go, and ye are in danger. Donncoill may be the last place ye wish to be right now, but 'tis the safest."

"I could return to France," she said, and cursed the reluctance she could hear in her voice.

"And hang. That is no answer to all of this mess, although I think ye may be hurting enough to believe hanging couldnae be any worse. I ken the feeling. I endured it ere Balfour and I had the wit to realize we needed to be together. Well, I realized it first, but women are often much smarter than men in such matters."

"Nigel and I cannot be together."

Maldie reached out and gently clasped Gisele's hand in hers. "I am no threat to ye. I have ne'er loved anyone but Balfour, and ne'er will." She smoothed her other hand over her swollen belly. "We breed our third child and, praise God, we will breed more."

"I do not fear you, m'lady, nor do I place the blame for this on your shoulders. That does not change the fact that you are the woman Nigel loves. That I look like you is the only reason I am even here, the only reason he felt even the basest of emotion for me." Gisele took a deep breath to steady herself, for just saying the words was like twisting a knife in an open wound.

"Aye, Nigel left here because he wanted me and kenned that I would ne'er return his feelings. He feared he would cause trouble for me and Balfour, or that in some way the situation would slowly push him and his brother apart. That is true no longer. I have ne'er been sure it was true, even back then. I am not the woman Nigel loves, not now, and mayhap not for a verra long time."

"Are you certain he did not send you here?" Gisele asked, yanking her hand free. Maldie's words stirred a flicker of hope in her heart, and she wanted nothing to do with that.

"Aye, verra sure. I am the woman ye think he wants. I just felt I should come and speak about this. I may not be the whole problem, and I am certainly not to blame for the pain that fool has caused you, but I am a small part of this mess."

"I am sorry," Gisele muttered, dragging her fingers through her hair. "It was rude to imply that you were lying. Very rude."

"I ken that ye are nay of a mind to listen to this, but heed me for a moment. Take my words into your mind and heart and let them rest there, think on them now and again. What Nigel has done seems cruel beyond words, but I swear to you that the mon isnae a cruel mon. This was done out of ignorance, his own confusion, and cowardice."

"Nigel is no coward." She was astonished at how quickly she leapt to his defense, and was not sure she liked the soft, fleeting smile that crossed Maldie's face.

"When it comes to matters of the heart, every mon can find the hint of cowardice in his soul. Ye easily guessed who I was and what it all meant, that ye may have been no more than the living embodiment of a ghost he tried to cling to. Do ye not think he saw that, too, that mayhap he wondered on it himself? That perhaps he questioned every feeling he had? That it was the last thing he wished to confess to?"

"He should have told me, warned me in some way. He should have at least given me the truth ere he bedded me."

"Ye will get no argument about that. He deserves a good flogging. All I ask is that ye listen and watch for a while. Ye love him, and I willnae believe ye if ye try to deny it. At least see if there is any way ye can forgive this hurt he has inflicted. If ye cannae, weel, that is the end of it. Howbeit, although ye may think ye have been the greatest of fools I think ye will be an even greater one if ye dinnae stay a wee while and see what he does next."

Maldie stood up and, smiling faintly, reached out to lightly ruffle Gisele's curls. " 'Tis much like my son's hair. Rest, Gisele. Get your strength back, weep, curse the mon for the pretty fool that he is, and get all of that anger out of your heart. Ye will need a clear head in the next few days. And think on this," she added as she paused in the doorway, "sometimes a fool holds onto a belief for so long he cannae see that it is no longer the truth. 'Tis nay longer a belief or a dream, just a habit."

Maldie smiled to herself as she slipped out into the hall and quietly shut the door behind her. Then she squeaked in surprise when a deep, familiar voice said, "Ye have been interfering, havenae ye, sweeting?"

"Well, aye, a wee bit," she said, as Balfour pulled her away from the door.

"This is Nigel's problem."

"I ken it, and I also ken that he is the only one who can truly mend it. Howbeit, I am a small part of this. I am also the only woman she can speak to aside from the maids. I just felt I needed to say something. She loves him."

"Are ye sure?"

"Oh, aye, verra sure. Nigel has deeply wounded her, but he hasnae killed her feelings for him. If he is wise and she is able to forgive, I think they will be all right."

Gisele cursed and flopped back down onto the bed. Forgive, Maldie had said. That was not going to be easy. Nigel had lied to her, perhaps not in words, but in his heart. He knew her better than anyone. She had told him some of her darkest secrets, ones she had not even had the courage to tell her family. He had to have guessed how seeing Maldie would affect her, yet he had done nothing to soften the blow. That was not going to be easy to forgive.

Maldie was right, though. She did love him, still loved him, even though he had hurt her more than anyone had in a very long time. Michael had hurt her pride and her body, humiliated her, and made her afraid. Her family had betrayed her and made her feel alone, unwanted. Nigel had torn the heart right out of her. Yet, there, right beside all of the pain she was suffering, lingered love. Gisele was not sure that was wise. How many times did she have to be struck down before she decided loving him gave her more pain than happiness?

And what about pride, she thought with a hint of anger. Was she expected to swallow that for the sake of love? She was the one who had been wronged. She was also not the one who was confused about what she did or did not feel, or for whom. It seemed unfair that she should now be expected to show a readiness to forgive and listen.

But she would, she admitted with a sigh. At least for a little while. Maldie was right. She would be a fool if she did not at least linger at Donncoill long enough to listen. There was always the small chance that he would say all she needed to hear, that he would find the words to soothe the pain he had inflicted, and her love for him made her want to take that chance. Gisele prayed that she would be able to forgive him enough so that she did not think every word out of his mouth was a lie.

* * *

Nigel stared at the door to Gisele's bedchamber. He already missed her, and that feeling was sharpened by the fear that he would never hold her in his arms again. Uncertainty gnawed at him. He was willing to bare his soul, but would she be willing to listen?

"I dinnae think it would be wise to see her tonight," Eric said as he grasped Nigel by the arm and tugged him down the hall to the room they would share.

"Nay, probably not. Yet, I fear that if I wait her anger will harden."

"Then ye shall have to think of all the right words to soften it."

"I ken that ye all believe I can talk any woman into softening toward me, but Gisele isnae just any woman."

"Nay, I could see that e'en though my meeting with her was verra brief, and not verra pleasant."

Once in the room he would share with Eric for a while, Nigel sprawled on the bed. "Well, this woman may ne'er give me a chance to say what I need to say. And, considering how poorly she has been treated by others in the last year, even if she does agree to listen to me she may not be willing to believe a word I say."

"Then ye will have to keep saying it until she does," Eric said, his voice muffled as he tugged off his jupon.

"Repeating myself will add the appropriate ring of truth, will it?"

"It might," Eric replied, ignoring Nigel's sarcasm.

"I eagerly await the day ye find yourself in love with a lass."

Eric smiled faintly as he slipped beneath the covers. "With ye and Balfour as my examples, I pray I have the sense to learn from your many mistakes." He laughed when Nigel lightly swatted him on the arm.

"Ye may be the cleverest lad that has e'er lived behind these walls, but believe me when I tell ye a mon's wits can turn to mud when a lass touches his heart." Nigel stood up and began to remove his clothes. "I should have kenned better, but I didnae. Despite all of my experience, I stepped wrong in every way possible."

"Ye must not worry so," Eric murmured as Nigel slid into bed. " 'Tis nay over yet."

"Ye didnae see the look in her eyes, laddie, not the way I did. I have seen it but once before, and it chilled me then. I was able to pull her out of the dark mood she had fallen into, but that time I wasnae the one who had caused it. This time her pain is all of my doing. Who is there to pull her out of it now?"

"We will, and ye will. Ye love her, and I have the feeling that, if she doesnae love ye now, she is verra close to doing so. Just speak from your heart."

Nigel sighed as he stared up at the ceiling above the bed. Eric made it all sound so easy, but he could not share the boy's confidence. He would tell Gisele the truth and he would certainly be speaking from the heart, but he would not blame her one little bit if she spat upon both and walked away.

Twenty-three

It was hard, but Gisele bit back a smile as she watched Nigel approach her where she sat near the kitchen gardens. For two weeks he had wooed her, and she had let him. The morning after she had been so devastated he had forced her to sit still and told her everything, from how he had come to believe himself in love with Maldie to why he had left Donncoill despite his family's protestations. He had readily confessed his doubts about why he wanted her, even why he had been so adamant about helping her. He had also apologized for not telling her all of this sooner. She found that she could actually understand how he could remain uncertain until he had finally seen Maldie again for the first time in seven long years.

She had forced herself to remain aloof, however, for the first week. She had not wanted to allow her need to believe him lead her astray or make her give him her trust, only to have it abused again. He was so earnest in his wooing, so sweet and attentive, that she had begun to weaken. Surely a man could not work so hard to win her if he did not care about her?

That hint of uncertainty was the only shadow on her happiness. Nigel wooed her, spoke of how he admired her in many ways, but he never spoke of love. The few tender kisses he had stolen told her that the passion they shared was still strong, but that was no longer enough. The hurt she had suffered when she had thought he had just used her showed her that she could not simply be his lover and hope to remain a sweet, pleasant memory in his mind. She needed more. She needed love, marriage, children, and all the rest. She did not want to be just a memory. She wanted to be his life.

"I see ye have come out to enjoy the sun," Nigel said as he sat down next to her on a low stone bench.

"I quickly learned that you were right. This land is not blessed with many sun-filled days, and one should take full advantage of them when they do arrive."

He put his arm around her and gently kissed her cheek, before touching the cloth she held in her hands. "Needlework?"

"You need not sound so surprised. Are not all ladies taught how to ply a needle?"

"Aye, and no need to bristle. I meant no offense. I guess I too quickly grew accustomed to seeing ye with a sword in your wee hands."

She smiled and nodded. "I rather miss our lessons."

"There is no reason why they cannae continue."

"Not yet," she murmured. "I believe I should be here a little longer before I completely shock your people."

Nigel smiled, but said nothing. He ached to speak of marriage, but knew it was too soon. She had only just begun to soften to him. It was difficult to hold back, however. He wanted more than a few chaste kisses. He wanted her back in his bed. He also wanted to know that she would not be leaving it again.

There was one other reason to hesitate. The day after he arrived he had sent word to her family with one of his fastest men. Nigel was sure that Gisele would be more open to the idea of marriage if she knew she did not have a death sentence hanging over her head any more. He had asked for word on how close they were to proving her innocence, as well as permission to make her his wife. The first he was very interested in. The second he did not care about, except that it might please Gisele. If she would have him, he would marry her whether her family approved or not.

For as long as he could, Nigel sat with Gisele, holding her small hand in his and stealing the occasional gentle kiss, before he excused himself with the claim that he had work to do. His whole body ached from wanting her, but he did not dare to reveal that hunger. Gisele needed to see that he wanted her for more than the passion they could share. Nigel cursed as he walked to the well, drew up a bucket of cold water, and poured it over his head. He had not thought that wooing Gisele would be so difficult. As he shook the water from his hair he heard someone laugh, and turned to see his brother Balfour standing behind him.

"Finding the wooing a wee bit hard to bear, are ye?" Balfour asked, grinning widely.

"I am nay doing this for your amusement," Nigel drawled, leaning against the stone side of the well.

"I ken it, but it serves that purpose well enough. Your wooing appears to be going smoothly, though."

"Aye, smoothly enough. Gisele is nay longer looking at me as if she wished I would fall into some deep pit, preferably one that led straight to hell. I am just nay sure how far she and I have come in this last fortnight."

"How far did ye wish to have come by now?"

"Far enough so that I didnae have to be here soaking my head to cool the fever in my blood."

Balfour laughed, draped his arm around Nigel's shoulders, and started to walk them back to the keep. "Mayhap 'tis time to speak of more than how fine the weather is, or how bonny she looks."

Nigel nodded. "It may be, but I was hoping to see a wee bit more softness from her, some clear hint that my love words would be welcomed." He held up his hand when Balfour began to speak. "I ken what ye are about to say. I must speak first and hope for the best. I ken it. I am but a coward. I will let that rule me for nay longer than a day or two more. And then, cowardice be cursed to hell, I will speak."

Gisele smiled sweetly at young Eric, but the moment he left her alone in the garden she felt her whole body slump with weariness. Pretense was exhausting, she mused. She was trying so hard to remain pleasant and appear untroubled when her mind was so crowded with unanswered questions and doubts that her head was beginning to throb.

Nigel had suddenly become more intense in his wooing, his kisses less chaste and his words more heavily imbued with meaning. It was as if he had abruptly decided that he had coddled her enough, or given her long enough to fully forgive him. It was such a strong change from the day before, however, from the pretty flatteries and gentle wooing, that she felt somewhat unsettled. The fact that his family had all stopped to talk to her, their hints easy to read, showed her that it was probably not vanity that told her Nigel was about to declare himself, to speak of marriage. She was not sure if he would also speak of love, and that uncertainty stung, but she could not shake the strong feeling that she was going to be asked to make a very big decision very soon.

She buried her face in her hands and cursed. Everything seemed to be going her way. After watching Nigel and Maldie she was sure that he no longer loved the woman, no more than any brother loves a sister. He had wooed her very prettily for a fortnight, had even thoroughly explained himself. Even if he did not express love, Gisele knew she would marry him if he asked her to. Foolish though it might be, she loved him enough to marry him and hope that she could win his heart over time. She knew she would never be able to resist taking that gamble.

There was, however, one thing she had allowed herself to forget—the DeVeaux. In all this time there had been no word from her family. The hunt for her was obviously still on. Now that she had come to know the Murrays, had enjoyed their kindness, she knew she could not be responsible for bringing trouble to their gates. If any one of them were hurt or killed because she had led her enemies to their door, had used them to hide behind, she would never forgive herself.

She had been selfish, she decided, reveling in comfort, good food, and kindness without a thought to the consequences for

the ones offering them to her. Gisele wondered if she had also
allowed herself to be lulled by the Murrays' belief in her innocence. She suspected that now even Nigel believed, although, he
had said nothing, to her utter annoyance. It did not mean that
anyone else believed in her yet, however, and she had to face that
cold fact. There was little chance that the Murrays' belief in her
innocence would be enough to turn back the DeVeaux, either.

There was no doubt in her mind about what she had to do
now. She had to leave, had to go and take all of her troubles
with her. It was also her responsibility to prove her innocence.
She had left that in the hands of others for far too long. Gisele
sighed and shook her head. She had left everything in the hands
of others, from her safety to the food that she ate. It was time
to show some backbone and stop expecting the rest of the world
to help her. If nothing else, she thought with a sad smile, she
would have the advantage of surprise on her side. No one would
expect her to go back to France and confront her accusers.

The ease with which she slipped out of Donncoill at dusk
amazed Gisele. It also made her feel a little guilty, for she knew
she was taking advantage of the Murrays' trust and friendship.
Her only consolation was the knowledge that what she was doing was for their own safety. She nudged her pony along the
trail she and Nigel had followed into Donncoill two weeks before and forced herself not to look back, fearing that she could
easily weaken in her resolve.

Night had fully fallen by the time she reached a small village.
Gisele suspected it would be safer to camp outside of the village, but she was a coward. She had slept alone in the wood a
time or two while traveling alone in France, but only when there
had been no other choice, and she had hated every minute of
it. *And now a thief,* she thought with a wince of shame as she
handed the frowning innkeeper money for a room for the night.
She hoped Nigel would forgive her for lightening his purse
when she paid him back in full, as she had every intention of

doing. Even if she did not survive this journey home, she would make certain that her family was clearly instructed to settle all of her debts.

Once alone in her room, she stripped to her chemise and sprawled on top of the tiny bed. She felt trapped, afraid, and unhappy, despite knowing that she was doing the only thing she could. The Murrays considered it a matter of honor to keep her safe and help her, but that did not make it right or fair for her to use that to her own advantage. She was ashamed that she had already done so for so long.

Gisele closed her eyes. She knew sleep would be a long time in coming, but she intended to do her best to clear her mind and get as much rest as she possibly could. Rest would be needed for the days ahead, needed to maintain the strength she required to keep going. It was certainly going to be needed to force herself to get back on a ship and sail to France. There was too much that could make her turn back, such as her deep fear of being alone, of facing the DeVeaux, even of getting herself thoroughly and completely lost. There was also Nigel. He had been close to giving her some part of what she craved, a lifetime together, and at least the hope of winning his love. She prayed that he would not come after her, for she knew he could easily convince her to return to him and Donncoill, and that would be wrong.

"Where is Gisele?" Nigel asked Maldie as he strode into the great hall and stopped before her and Balfour where they sat at the head table.

"I havenae seen her for many hours," Maldie replied, then looked at Balfour, who shrugged and shook his head. "In truth, I was a wee bit surprised when she didnae come join us for this meal. I had thought of sending Margaret to her chambers to see if she was unwell."

"Gisele isnae in her chambers, either. I have already looked there." Nigel signaled to a page and sent the boy out to the stable, then sat at the table and idly picked at the food spread out before him.

"Do ye think she has fled Donncoill?" Balfour asked after several moments of tense silence.

"I dinnae ken," Nigel replied. " 'Tis the only possibility I have yet to consider. She isnae any place within this keep that I can see, and why would she hide from me? From any of us?" When the breathless page returned and reported that Gisele's horse was gone, Nigel pounded his fist on the table and cursed. "She has run away."

"But, why?"

"I dinnae ken, do I?" Nigel snapped, but then took a slow, deep breath to calm himself. " 'Tis clear that she told her plans to no one, or I would be aware of them by now, so I can but guess at the reasons for her leaving. I have a few sound ones."

"Ye dinnae think her enemies somehow reached her here, do ye?"

"Nay," Nigel replied without hesitation. "Gisele would ne'er have gone with them peacefully, and I have seen no sign that there has been any sort of struggle anywhere within the keep. And someone would have seen something, assuming that any stranger could have gotten inside these walls unseen, anyway, which I greatly doubt."

Balfour nodded. "Nor could they have then left here with an unwilling lass. Do ye go after her?"

"Oh, aye, but it must wait until the dawn. I cannae track her in the dark."

"Nigel, this makes no sense to me," Maldie said. "She was safe here. Why would she ride away alone? Surely she has not forgotten that she has enemies who wish to kill her?"

"Nay." Nigel shook his head. "In truth, I would wager that those enemies are exactly why she has left. The lass has e'er wavered between accepting help and feeling it was wrong or cowardly to pull others into the danger surrounding her."

"Oh, aye, I understand." When both men stared at her as if she had lost her wits, Maldie just shrugged. "In her place, I believe my mind would have traveled the same path. This is her trouble, nay ours. If that trouble then puts ones ye care about into danger then ye leave and take that danger as far away from them as ye can."

"Mayhap," Nigel reluctantly agreed. "But if the foolish lass had waited a day longer, or spoken to me of her fears, I could have stopped this." He held up a paper he had clutched in his hands. "There is no danger now. She is pardoned. The real killers of her husband have been found and, sadly, punished. 'Tis all over."

"Then ye had best hurry and find her. She may be safe from the DeVeaux now, but it isnae safe for a lass to be riding about all alone."

"I ken it. I will find her, and I may well chain her to a wall here until I can talk some sense into her bonny little head."

The hours until dawn crawled by for Nigel. He tried to sleep but found it impossible. Instead he paced his room and cursed the sun for being too slow to rise. Despite his efforts not to, he thought of every danger that could befall Gisele out there alone in a country she did not know. He even recalled her tendency to get lost, and feared he could lose a lot of time trailing her all over the countryside.

Dawn's light had barely begun to grace the sky when he was striding to the stables, a sleepy-eyed Eric trailing behind him, asking, "Are ye sure ye dinnae want me to come along?"

"Aye, laddie," Nigel answered as he saddled his horse. "Go back to bed."

"It may help to have two pairs of eyes looking for the lass's trail."

"Nay, for her horse leaves a distinctive marking upon the ground. I had meant to get the beast reshod for fear others would recognize her trail as easily as I could, but I ne'er got the chance. I am heartily glad of that now."

"And, ye wish to be alone with her when ye find her," Eric said carefully, watching his brother closely as the man led his horse out of the stable.

"Aye." He mounted and smiled down at Eric. "There is a lot I must tell that foolish lass, and I think I would rather do that alone."

"Will ye go to the port where ye came in and wait for her there?"

"I would if I could trust the lass to find her way back there, but she has an inclination to get lost. Dinnae fret o'er me, lad. I will find her and I will bring her back, if I dinnae throttle her for worrying me half to death."

He waved farewell to his laughing brother as he rode out of Donncoill's gates, but his confidence quickly wavered. Gisele had already been gone for hours, tempting danger. Even if he found her safe and alive, he might find that he was wrong about why she left Donncoill. She might have run away from him. It was not a thought he found very comforting as he began to follow her clear trail.

Gisele grimaced as she dismounted and looked at her horse's hoof. She was barely an hour's ride from the village where she had spent a restless night when the horse had begun to favor its right front hoof. To her relief it was merely a pebble caught in his shoe, but she decided to walk for a while to see if the animal had suffered any bruising or serious injury. It was clear, however, that she would not cover very many miles today, and that both disappointed and worried her.

Now that she had decided what must be done she was eager to get it over with, despite her fears. She also did not want to linger in Scotland for any longer than it took to get to a port. That would give Nigel a better chance of finding her and trying to stop her. She had to be free of the DeVeaux before she could even consider a life with the man, but she was sure he would not understand that.

A soft noise behind her drew her out of her thoughts, and she looked around. Although she saw nothing, her insides tightened with fear. Something was out there, lurking in the shadows of the trees. She glanced at her horse, saw that it still limped slightly, and cursed. Even if she mounted quickly and spurred the animal to a gallop, she would not get very far before she had to stop again. She could also harm the animal beyond repair.

The sharp sound of a twig snapping sent a shiver of fear down her spine. She put her hand on her sword, thanking God that, she had retained the wit to bring the weapon despite her upset and confusion as she had left Donncoill. Since there was no hope of escaping whatever danger trailed her, Gisele quickly tethered her horse. If she survived whatever or whomever crept her way, she did not want to look around afterward and find that her horse had been frightened away.

Out of the shadows emerged two filthy, poorly dressed men, and Gisele swiftly drew her sword. They grinned widely, and she felt anger begin to push its way through her fear. Men were so arrogant. She might not equal them in size and strength, but she was suddenly eager to show them that their derision of her skill was seriously misplaced.

"If you have followed me from the village thinking to enrich your paltry selves, I should turn back now," she said, pleased with the hard, cold tone of her voice. "I have naught of any worth."

"Ye arenae a Scot," muttered the shorter of the two men.

"A clever thief," she drawled. "I am all atremble."

The way both men narrowed their eyes beneath the shaggy tendrils of their filthy hair told Gisele that insulting them might not be wise, but she shrugged aside that doubt. They had come here to rob her, perhaps even to rape and kill her. She did not think sweetness and flattery would change their minds. Deriding them helped her to remain calm, and gave her some small sense of satisfaction.

"Ye may not have the coin we seek, although I am thinking your purse isnae empty, but there be one or two other wee things we can help ourselves to," said the shorter man.

"Aye," agreed his tall, skinny companion. "Like your horse,

that fine bauble dangling on your neck, and your wee bonny self, eh, Malcolm?"

"Ye have the right of it, Andrew," Malcolm agreed, and he edged closer to Gisele.

"Come any closer, you filthy bastards, and I will ensure that you do not have anything left to take me with," she threatened, and was momentarily pleased to see them both take a step back.

"Ye ought to be more kindly, lass," said Malcolm. "It could make this a wee bit easier on ye. Aye, we may e'en leave ye alive."

"Your kindness overwhelms me." She set herself into her fighting stance and watched both men frown. "Are you prepared to pay for such small gains with one or both of your meager lives?"

They hesitated yet again, and Gisele knew it was because her stance told them she might not be as unskilled as they had first thought. She prayed that they were both craven cowards. If they were, it might take only one small bloodletting for them to decide she was not the easy prey they had thought she was and flee.

Malcolm struck first. and Gisele easily deflected his crude sword thrust. He was no fighter, wielding his weapon more like an axe or a stick, but she told herself not to get too confident. Andrew stood by, agape with surprise and uncertainty. She prayed that would continue, for she could not fight two men at once. After just a few moments, Malcolm stepped back, sweating and softly cursing.

"I believe you may now understand that this will be no easy work," she said, using the respite to recoup the strength she had used.

"Aye, Malcolm," muttered Andrew. "I dinnae see that she has anything worth dying for."

"The lass cannae hold firm long enough to kill me, fool," snapped Malcolm who then glared at his companion. " 'Twould go a lot faster if ye stepped in to give me a hand."

Andrew frowned and rubbed a dirty hand over his weak chin.

"Weel, I am nay sure I have the stomach for fighting with a wee lass."

Gisele allowed herself a brief inner sigh of relief. Here was a weakness she might take advantage of. Although Andrew was no more than a lowly thief, he obviously had some vague sense of what was right, some line he would not cross. She just had to hope that Malcolm, the obvious leader of the pair, could not talk the man into crossing that line.

"Ye would rather stand by and watch me slaughtered?" Malcolm yelled.

"Weel, nay, but ye just said that she couldnae kill you." Andrew took a cautious step back when Malcolm faced him, sword in hand. "I dinnae think it will help matters if ye start hacking away at me."

"We can get good money for that horse," Malcolm said in a softer, cajoling voice.

"I think he be lame."

"Nay. We watched her take the pebble out. 'Tis but a wee tenderness that will pass. That bauble she wears is worth a fine purseful, as weel. And, my friend, how long has it been since ye had any lass as fine as this one, eh?"

"Aye, there is that."

This was not going well, Gisele decided, her brief flicker of hope swiftly dying. Andrew was slowly allowing avarice to win out over what few morals he had. She struggled against letting her growing fear cloud her mind. If they both confronted her she had no chance, but she would not just give up her life. They would be forced to pay dearly for accosting her. They would also be forced to kill her, she decided with an oddly calming sense of resignation. She would do all in her power not to become a victim of rape, and if that meant dying by one of their swords, then she would die.

"Come, lad, give us a hand. Together we can knock the sword from her hands and then all will be ours—the horse, the necklace, and the lass. We can have us a fine time."

"Sorry, lass," Andrew said as he stood next to Malcolm, his sword in his hand. "A mon has to eat, ye ken."

"I did not realize that rape put food on the table," she said.

"Nay, it doesnae," said Malcolm, "but it can make a mon enjoy the meal more. Now, if ye were a clever lass ye would put that wee sword down and let us be about our business. Ye will suffer less that way."

"And I think the lass is clever enough to ken that ye are the greatest of liars," drawled a cold, deep voice from behind the two men.

Twenty-four

Gisele stared at Nigel with the same look of complete surprise that contorted the two thieves' faces. How did the man keep finding her? Although his arrival was heartily welcomed at this precise moment, she knew that would be short-lived. He was going to be asking her a lot of questions, and she knew he would not like her answers. Standing firm against Nigel might prove to be harder than standing against Malcolm and Andrew.

She shook free of her shock and watched the two thieves. For one brief moment they faced Nigel squarely, then Malcolm began to slink away, edging toward the trees. A minute later Andrew realized that his companion had every intention of deserting him, and quickly followed. Nigel made one swift lunge at the two men, who immediately turned tail and disappeared into the surrounding trees. It annoyed Gisele that Nigel could inspire such fear while all she seemed to inspire was amusement and annoyance.

The moment the men were gone Gisele sheathed her sword and heard Nigel do the same. She took a deep breath to strengthen herself and looked at him, then inwardly winced. He did not look happy with her.

"I think we will return to the village now," Nigel said as he grabbed the reins of her horse before she could and then watched the animal take a few hesitant steps. "Ye have done well, havenae ye? But one night alone and ye have nearly got yourself raped and killed, and ye have crippled this poor beast."

"He is not crippled," she snapped, following behind Nigel as they walked to where he had tethered his mount. "He had a pebble in his hoof, and is but a little tender. It will heal."

Nigel gave her a look that made Gisele decide it might be best to remain quiet for a while. He lifted her up onto his saddle, hooked her horse's reins over the pommel, and then mounted in front of her. She ached to tell him that he was being arrogant and had no right to order her around, but the confrontation with the robbers had left her doubting her own judgment. Nasty and spiteful though his words had been, there was some truth in them. She had been on her own for only a little while and had already found herself in serious difficulty. Maybe she had been mad to think she could get all the way back to France on her own.

All the way back to the village she struggled to think of ways to defend her decision to leave. Her confidence had been badly shaken, however, and she was no longer sure her reasons were sound. Had she really been running to France to clear her name, or had she been running from Nigel and the feelings she had for him? Gisele inwardly cursed when she discovered that she had no answer for that question.

The innkeeper gave her a strange look when Nigel ordered the same room she had left but a few hours before. The man probably thought she was Nigel's errant wife, and Gisele opened her mouth to try to explain, then quickly closed it. It was all too complicated to explain, and she would probably just leave the man thinking she was mad.

The moment they entered the room she pulled free of Nigel's grip on her arm and sat on the edge of the bed. He leaned against the thick, roughly cut post at the foot of the bed and stared at her. It took all of Gisele's willpower to not squirm guiltily beneath his gaze like some scolded child. She had nothing to feel guilty about, she told herself firmly.

"And just where did ye think ye were going?" he finally asked, struggling to control his anger.

When he had first come upon her in the wood he had nearly

charged in, sword swinging. He had been that furious and concerned. It had not taken him long to see that she faced two cowards who might be willing to test themselves against a small lass, but would never stand to fight a fully armed knight. Although the fear he had felt for her safety had eased, the anger it had bred was still churning inside of him. Gisele did not completely deserve that, and he knew visiting it upon her would also seriously hinder any sensible discussion.

"I was returning to France," she replied, mildly fascinated by the way the anger slowly left his expression.

"Ah, ye are weary of life, are ye? Suicide being such a great sin, I suppose it makes some sense to just walk back into the grasp of those ye ken will gladly kill you."

He might be conquering his anger, she mused, but he clearly had no intention of dulling the sharp edge of his tongue. "I intended to go home and clear my name. I decided that I had left that duty in the hands of others for far too long. Hiding behind others was not working, so I felt it was past time to try confrontation."

"Did ye really convince yourself that the DeVeaux could be talked to as if they were reasoning people?"

She scowled at him. The man had a true skill for finding the one real weakness in a plan. "They are not the only ones I could plead my case to."

"Weel, now there is no need to plead it to anyone," he said and thrust a piece of paper at her.

Gisele had to read the letter three times before she was able to believe in the words written there. "I am free?"

"Verra free, and the DeVeaux have been warned to leave ye and your kinsmen alone or suffer unnamed consequences. That threat came from the king himself. 'Tis clear that your family wielded almost as much power as the DeVeaux, once they decided to believe in you and seek to prove your innocence."

"But they seemed so afraid of that family and its wealth and power."

"Outrage over your treatment must have conquered that fear."

"I feel so grateful, so elated, yet this freedom comes at a great cost to others. Two men have been hanged."

"They were the true killers, lass," he said gently. "Your husband deserved his death, but that doesnae mean the way he was killed was right or lawful. And, those two men were content to sit quietly and let a wee lass take the blame. In a way, they were willing to kill ye, as weel. 'Twas honorable of them to avenge the rape and beating of a kinswoman, but that honor was tarnished when they let an innocent woman take the blame."

"I know. 'Tis just a shame that they had to die, that there was apparently no other recourse but murder to gain the justice they and their poor kinswoman so deserved."

"So now there is no need for ye to go to France and martyr yourself. Ye may return to Donncoill with me."

He watched her closely as he spoke, taking careful note of her sudden agitation. She would not meet his gaze, and absently plucked at the old, thinning blanket covering the tiny bed. Getting her to return to Donncoill with him was not going to be as easy as he had hoped it would be.

"Since I am free, there is no longer a need for your protection. You have fulfilled your vow. Your honor is unstained." Gisele did not want Nigel clinging to her out of some misplaced sense of duty.

Nigel moved to sit next to her, ignoring the way she tensed slightly as he pulled her into his arms. "Honor has naught to do with why I ask ye to return to Donncoill with me."

"I do not need a place to live. I am not without funds, and I have a small property I may reside upon."

"Nor do I ask ye to return with me out of some misguided sense of duty."

She softly cursed, but did not resist him as he gently pushed her down onto the bed, neatly tugging her around until she was sprawled beneath him. He too quickly guessed her every doubt and concern, yet somehow managed not to tell her what she wished, and needed, to hear. The feel of his long body on top of hers, however, was making it difficult to think. It had been too long since she had tasted the passion they could share. It was easy to let wanting push aside all interest in talk.

"I will not become your mistress," she said even as she tilted her head back so that he could more easily cover her throat with warm, tantalizing kisses.

"I wasnae asking it of ye."

Before she could muster the wit to ask him just what he did intend, he kissed her. The hunger in his kiss brought her own rushing to the fore, unwilling to be ignored or brushed aside. She wrapped her arms around him and fully returned his kiss. Gisele knew she was giving him a silent but clear agreement to set aside all talk for a little while, to once again revel in the heat of their passion, but decided that it did not matter. As she had ridden away from Donncoill one sharp regret she had suffered from was that she had not made love with Nigel one last time. If she still had to walk away from him at the end of this day, at least she would not suffer from that regret.

They had been apart for too long for the reunion of their bodies to be a lingering pleasure or a gentle one. Gisele tugged off his clothes as swiftly as he tugged off hers. They both shuddered when their bodies finally touched flesh to flesh. She found that she could not get enough of the feel or the taste of him, touching and kissing every inch of his strong body. Nigel returned her every kiss and caress with the same fevered urgency until they both shook from the strength of their need for each other.

She cried out with eager welcome when Nigel finally joined their bodies. Wrapping her limbs around him, she greedily met every thrust of his body. The way their voices blended as they found release as one only enhanced the pleasure rushing through her body. Gisele held him close as he collapsed in her arms, and fought to cling to the mind-clouding delight they had just enjoyed. She did not want to think, but as her breathing slowed and her heartbeat returned to its normal pace, she knew she could not lie there drunk with passion and just ignore the world.

Nigel reluctantly eased the intimacy of their embrace. He glanced at Gisele's small hand as she moved it absently over his chest, then looked at her face. Her gaze was fixed with stubborn firmness on the movement of her hand. Although it was tempting to just make love until they both fell into an exhausted sleep, he knew that now was not the time for that. Neither of them might wish to talk, but they had to. He gently grasped her chin in his hand and turned her face up to his. It was another moment longer before she allowed her gaze to meet his.

"Mayhap I have wooed ye too gently," he said, "and that has led to naught but confusion."

She inwardly tensed, wary of what he might say, but calmly replied, "You showed a true skill for the art of wooing."

"Thank ye, but I clearly wasnae skilled enough to make ye stay with me, was I?"

"I was going to France to clear my name, no more. As I have said, it came to me that I was asking others to face a danger I myself was too cowardly to face."

"And ye are certain ye werenae running from what my wooing would lead to?"

"I was not sure where that might end," she said quietly, briefly looking away from his intent gaze. He did not need to know all of the doubts she had suffered from.

"Where all wooing is meant to end—with marriage. Ye left ere I could ask ye to be my wife."

Her heart skipped so hard it was almost painful, but she found herself not to let false hope and the lingering sweet memory of the passion they had just shared cloud her wits. "Why?"

"Why?" He frowned at her in confusion. "Why what?"

"Why were you going to ask me to be your wife?"

"Lass, ye are supposed to say 'aye' or 'nay,' not 'why'."

"I need to know why before I can say 'aye' or 'nay'. Nigel, until you got the word from France that I was innocent, you still thought me capable of butchering a man."

"Nay." He grimaced when she eyed him with a hint of suspicion. "Do ye recall the time I was teaching you how to use a sword, that first time that ye disarmed me and I said that was when ye must strike the death blow?" Gisele slowly nodded. "The way ye looked was enough to tell me that ye hadnae killed your husband. Aye, if ye were in a fight for your life or in a fight for mine, ye could kill, as ye showed me the day I was wounded. But, nay, not coldly and brutally as was done to your husband."

"You might have told me when you had this revelation."

"I am sorry, lass. I meant to, but there were a few other things I needed to think on at the time."

Gisele smiled and lightly caressed his cheek. "I know. Soothing my hurt feelings was of small importance, and I realize I should have been satisfied that you thought me worthy of your protection and help." She cocked one eyebrow and drawled, "And you have still not answered my question."

"What we have just shared wasnae answer enough?" When she just frowned, he added, "I asked your family for their blessing, and they have given it. Ye must ken by now that my family would eagerly welcome ye into the clan."

Nigel was not sure why he was so reluctant to say the words he knew she wanted to hear. He was, he realized, a complete coward. After the hurt he had inflicted upon her by not telling her all about Maldie, he knew he owed Gisele the full truth now. No one deserved the baring of his soul more than Gisele did, but he could not seem to force the words past his lips. He needed some hint from her that his words of love would be welcomed and returned.

Gisele wondered if shaking Nigel vigorously would make the words she sought fall out of his mouth. She was beginning to think that he loved her, or was very close to doing so. His almost embarrassed reluctance to speak of anything but family approval and passion was her strongest hint. Nigel had a true skill with words, could easily convince her that she would be a fool to refuse his proposal, yet never speak of love. He seemed unable to muster that skill at the moment.

That left her with two choices. She could either accept his proposal, allow him to think that talk of passion and family approval was enough for her, or she could hold out until he was forced to say more. She did not have the patience for the latter and the first, she mused, could easily lead to dissatisfaction and unhappiness. There was one way to pull the words from him, and that was to make the confession first. It was a gamble. She could be wrong in thinking that his feelings for her were deeper than passion, and it would hurt to speak of love and get no vow in return. Gisele inwardly shrugged. The rest of her life was at stake. It was worth the risk.

"Nigel, I am honored that you would ask me to be your wife. It is certainly pleasing to know that my family as well as your own will approve of the match. I do not believe I need to say that I enjoy the passion we share, and would be more than willing to continue indulging in that pleasure. But, I fear all of that is not enough."

"I no longer love Maldie. Ye ken that, dinnae ye?"

"I saw that within days after arriving at Donncoill, and it would certainly make a marriage between us go along much more smoothly," she drawled and smiled faintly, then touched her fingers to his lips when he began to speak. "I must finish this ere I lose the courage to do so. I need more than what you have talked of. I need your heart, Nigel, for you hold mine."

She watched him carefully, almost afraid to breathe. He looked stunned, but she was not sure if that were a good or a bad thing. When he pulled her into his arms and held her almost too tightly she began to feel a little more secure. There was certainly a lot of emotion revealed in his touch.

"When did ye decide that ye loved me?" he demanded, starting to trace her face with small kisses.

Gisele had to smile. His reaction was all she could have hoped for, except that he still refused to say what she needed to hear. Forcing herself to be patient, she threaded her fingers through his hair and briefly touched a kiss to his mouth.

"I think it may have been when you were wounded. I feel as

if it has been there for a long time. Recall that time I ran away and was captured by Vachel?" He nodded. "I ran away from you, from what I suddenly realized I felt for you. There was enough trouble on my plate. I foolishly thought that I could run from that new one, that I could run from what was in my heart."

"Nay, 'tis hard to do. One cannae deceive it, either. It kens the truth no matter what your poor fevered brain thinks. I thought myself in love with Maldie for so long that I mistrusted every feeling I had for you."

Gisele forced herself not to tense with the anticipation she felt. She also swallowed the urge to just demand that he tell her what he felt. He needed a little more time. She did decide, however, that she would not give him too much more. The way he said so much but never enough could easily drive her mad.

"I understand that, Nigel. I was hurt, but I did come to realize that you truly meant me no harm. You were but confused. Maldie was a dream you had clung to for seven long years. Such dreams are hard to discard."

"More a nightmare at times. No one likes to believe he has given his heart away uselessly. I should have said something to you, though. That was wrong. Mayhap if I had confessed to my confusion it could have been unraveled sooner. I knew the moment I looked at Maldie that she was no longer the woman who held my heart in her small hands. More important, I kenned that I wasnae trying to hold onto her ghost, either. Aye, ye look like her, but ye arenae her. Ye arenae taking her place in my heart. Ye have made your own. I was a fool nay to see that."

"I have a place in your heart, do I?" she asked softly.

"Ye fill it, lass. Ye are in every corner of it."

He laughed quietly when she hugged him tightly. It was going to be all right. They had both found what they needed. Nigel could barely believe his good fortune.

"I have been a fool and a coward, lass," he murmured against her throat. "I am surprised that ye have had the patience to keep me in your heart."

"At times you did seem to be worth it," she said, and laughed when he gave her a gentle nudge.

He raised himself up on his elbows and cupped her face in his hands. "Well, ye are truly stuck with me now, my bonny French rose. I love ye, and I cannae find the words to tell ye how wondrous it feels to ken that ye love me, too."

She eagerly returned his tender kiss, then held him close, moving her foot up and down his strong leg. "There are years ahead of us for you to learn the words." She grinned when she felt him chuckle against her breast, then frowned slightly when he picked up her amulet and kissed it. "Why did you do that?"

"Well, ye said it was from your grandmother, that she said it would bring ye good fortune."

Gisele smiled and idly stroked the medallion. "And it has. I am free and, more important, I am loved."

"Oh, aye, and I think it will take me all of our lifetime to show ye just how much ye are loved. I but thanked your grandmother as I believe I, too, have benefitted from the luck in that bauble."

"Mayhap, but not as much as I have."

He lightly straddled her and slowly grinned. "Are ye meaning to argue this matter?"

"I believe I am."

"Then prepare to be argued with most vigorously, lass. If we mean to determine which of us is the most fortunate or which of us loves the other more, it could take a verra long time."

"With a lot of persuasion, I hope."

"A lot of sweet, exhausting persuasion," he agreed as he brushed a kiss over her lips. "And I dinnae mean to stop persuading ye until we are both naught but dust."

Even as she started to return his kiss, Gisele lightly touched the medallion resting against her breasts. *Thank you, Nana,* she thought, then gave herself over to the passion she knew would be hers forever.

Please turn the page
for an exciting sneak preview
of Hannah Howell's newest
Zebra historical romance
HIGHLAND PROMISE
coming in August 1999

Scotland, 1444

Bethia Drummond watched the two sweating men throw the rock-strewn dirt on top of her sister's body and held her tiny nephew James a little closer. Orphaned before his first birthday by the greed of his own kinsmen, he was going to need a lot of love and, much more important, a lot of protection. She swallowed her tears and tossed a few sprigs of white heather onto her sister's grave. Her heart found it hard to believe that her womb-sister Sorcha was gone forever, but her mind knew that Sorcha now lay entwined forever with her love, her husband Robert, beneath the deepening dirt. Put there, she thought with a rising fury, by the avarice of Robert's family.

She stared across the slowly filling grave at Robert's uncle William and his two sons, Iain and Angus. They were Drummonds only by name, never by blood, William having taken the name when he married Robert's aunt Mary. The barren Mary had willingly taken William's two small sons as her own, but none of her kindness and love had penetrated their thick, evil hides. The woman had, without doubt, clasped a whole nest of adders to her bosom and paid dearly for her charity. The woman's death barely a year past had been a slow and agonizing, and very suspicious, one. Now two more obstacles to the lands and wealth of Dunncraig were gone, and she held the last. William and his two hulking sons would not get James. Bethia

swore on her sister's grave that she would see all three men
dead first, and that they would be made to pay for all of their
crimes.

When William and his sons approached her, Bethia tensed.
She resisted the urge to turn and run, taking the happily gurgling
James far away from the three dark men. It would be neither
safe nor wise to let them know that she was suspicious of them.

"Ye need not fear for the laddie's care," William said in his
rough voice as he lightly ruffled the little boy's bright red curls.
"We will care weel for the wee bairn."

Bethia wanted to scrub the man's touch off the boy, but forced
herself to smile. "My sister asked me to care for her child. 'Tis
why I came here."

"Ye are a verra young lass. 'Tis sure that ye dinnae wish to
waste your life caring for another woman's child. Ye should be
away making a few wee bairns of your own."

"Caring for the bairn of my womb-sister could ne'er be a
waste, sir."

"Mayhap this isnae a good time to discuss this." William
forced his thin-lipped mouth into a parody of a sympathetic
smile and patted her on the shoulder. "Ye are still wrapped too
tightly in your grief for your poor sister. We will talk of this
later."

"As ye wish."

It was hard not to yank herself away from his chilling touch,
but Bethia forced herself to smile at the three men again. She
then turned and walked back to the keep with a hard-won calm.
Bethia wanted to scream out her suspicions, wanted to un-
sheathe her dagger and plunge it deep into William's black heart,
but she knew that would gain her nothing except one brief,
pleasant taste of revenge. The man's sons would quickly and
bloodily avenge him, killing both her and James. In truth, she
would probably accomplish no more than giving them a ready
explanation for the boy's death, as she could not be sure she
could even kill William.

Defeating William and his sons and making them pay for

their crimes required care and planning. She needed to subdue the emotions twisting her insides into a painful knot. Bethia knew that she would also need some help, and she could not count on finding any amongst the cowed people of Dunncraig. William had a tight grip on all who lived at the keep, one Robert had not seen or had been too often away at court or fighting in France to break. Robert's naivete or neglect had cost him and Sorcha their lives. Bethia had no intention of allowing James to join them in their cold grave.

"Your father was all that was brave and honorable," Bethia told little James as she entered the small, dark room they shared, "but he should have watched his home fires much more carefully, laddie."

She settled the yawning child in his cradle and sat on the edge of her small bed to watch him. Sorcha's brilliant green eyes blessed his sweet little face, and his hair was only a little brighter than his mother's. The envy Bethia had sometimes suffered over her sister's often acclaimed beauty now seemed petty and sad. She might have a duller brown hair and the curse of mismatched eyes, as well as a far less womanly figure than her sister, but she was still alive. Sorcha's highly praised beauty and charm had always seemed such a blessing, but it had not saved her.

And, she was stronger, Bethia decided as she watched the fair James fall asleep. Sorcha had been like a candle, admired for its light and warmth, for the beauty of its color-rich flame, but also easily snuffed out and left cold, lifeless. She had always been more wary than Sorcha, more able to see the evil in people. It had surprised her when Sorcha had sent word asking her to come and help with James, for Dunncraig was filled with women eager and able to help care for their laird's son and heir. Bethia now wondered if some hint of suspicion or fear had finally crept into her sister's loving, trusting heart.

She sighed and vigorously wiped away a tear. If it had, it had come too late. It did, however, explain Sorcha's odd choice of words in her missive. She had asked her sister to come and

watch over James. Not nurse him, play with him, visit him, or
aid his mother, but to *watch over* him. And that was exactly
what she intended to do.

Every breath she took, every whisper of her skirts over the
rush-covered floors, made Bethia's heart skip painfully as she
crept along the shadowed halls of Dunncraig. She knew how to
be quiet, yet that skill appeared to be failing her miserably. No
outcry came, however, as she made her way through the keep
and out into the bailey. It had taken her three torturous days to
find a way out of Dunncraig, one she could possibly get to
unseen, and it felt as if it was taking her almost that long to get
to it. And every step of the way she was terrified that James,
so sweetly oblivious to the danger he was in, would make some
sound that would give them away.

For each minute of those three days she had wavered between
doubting her suspicions and searching for a way to flee unseen.
The death of James's little puppy had brutally ended all of her
doubts about her suspicions. Bethia doubted she would ever
know why—after blissfully eating and drinking everything
brought to her and James the first day after the funeral—she
had suddenly felt compelled to test the food on the second day.
When the puppy had died after tasting the food, she had wept
out of guilt for using the poor, trusting animal in such a way
and out of a strange mixture of fury and fear because all of her
suspicions had been so gruesomely proven right. The fact that
she had not been able to give the little animal a burial worthy
of his sacrifice only added to her anger. She now knew that the
slow, painful deaths of Sorcha and Robert had been caused by
poison, and not by some unnamed, wasting sickness as was
claimed.

Finally, she reached the spot she had been seeking, a small
break in the wall behind the reeking stables. Robert had been
unaware of the deadly enemies within his keep, and of the crumbling state of his keep, as well. If he had seen how poorly the

place was kept, he never would have left William in control of the accounts. Bethia was not sure what William and his sons were doing with the money from the lands and tenants, but they were certainly not maintaining the keep they were so willing to kill for.

As she squeezed herself and James through the opening a few pieces of the crumbling wall clattered noisily to the ground. She held herself still within the opening, holding her breath as she waited for the outcry. It surprised her a little when none came. Such a noise should have caused one of the men at arms to at least glance her way. As she cautiously slipped out into the night and hurried toward the woods at the far end of the surrounding fields, she felt a little more confident about her chances of escape with every step she took. The men guarding Dunncraig were obviously as lax in their duties as William was in keeping Dunncraig strong.

It was not until she entered the frightening yet welcome shadows of the forest that Bethia dared to breath a sigh of relief. She knew it would not be long before a pursuit was begun, but she had taken the first step toward freedom and safety, and she allowed a touch of hope to enter her heart. A horse would have been a great help but she had not dared steal one, not even dared retrieve the sweet little mare she had ridden in on. She would have never gotten the animal out through her tiny bolthole. Bethia silently promised the little mare that she would not leave her in that rotting stable any longer than necessary. Without a horse, however, she was going to have to do a lot of walking to put any distance at all between herself and James and their enemies.

James shifted in the blanket sling resting against her chest, and she idly rubbed his back as she started to walk. "Be at ease, my bonny wee laddie." She took one last look at Dunncraig, wishing she could have bid farewell to Sorcha, but promising that she would return. "I will see that those swine who feed out of your father's trough will soon choke on their ill-gotten meal. And may God heartily curse all men who seek to fill their pockets with the riches of others," she whispered as she marched deeper into the wood.

"Are ye sure ye ought to go and face these people?" Balfour Murray asked his young foster brother Eric as he sat down at the head table in the great hall of Donncoill and began to fill his plate with food.

Eric smiled at Balfour, then winked at his brother's wife, Maldie, who just rolled her eyes and began to eat. "We have tried every other means to gain my birthright, but everything we do is either contested or ignored. This game has been played out for thirteen long years. I grow heartily weary of it."

"I still cannae see how confronting the fools will change anything."

"It may not, but 'tis the only thing we havenae tried."

"There is still the king to turn to."

"We have tried that, too, although mayhap nay as ardently as we might have. Howbeit, I think our liege would prefer nay to take a side in all of this. The Beaton lairds may have been swine, and still are, but they have ne'er angered or offended the king. The MacMillans, my mother's clan, are also on amiable terms with the king, considered loyal and able fighters. I believe I may be the proof they cannae deny. I carry the Beaton mark upon my back, and many have said that I carry the look of my mother and her kin. Mayhap 'tis time the Beatons and MacMillans see that proof with their own eyes."

"Do ye think the Beatons will heed the truth e'en if ye bear your back and force them to see the mark there?" asked Maldie.

"Nay, mayhap not, but it cannae hurt to try," Eric replied. "I have heard nay ill about the MacMillans. They may but heed the lies told by the Beatons too closely. Mayhap I can finally make them see the truth."

"Ye must take someone with you," insisted Balfour. " 'Tis a pity Nigel went to France."

"Gisele has now born him three bonny sons. 'Twas past time they were shown to their kinsmen in France."

"Aye, I ken it. If ye can but wait a while until my work is done I can come with you, or Nigel may have returned."

"This is my fight, Balfour, and mine alone."

It took Eric the rest of the evening and most of the next day to convince Balfour that this was something he had to do alone. Neither of them feared any real threat from the Beatons or the MacMillans, for they and their quarrel were all too well-known to the king. Any harm coming to Eric on the lands of either family would bring a swift and harsh response, and both families knew it. There were other dangers in traveling alone, however, and Balfour did not hesitate to list them.

He was still listing them three days later when Eric was leading his packed horse out of the stables. "A mon to watch your back wouldnae be a bad thing," he said, frowning as Eric just smiled and mounted his black gelding.

"Nay, it wouldnae," agreed Eric, pausing to tie his long, thick, reddish gold hair back with a wide strip of blackened leather. "Howbeit, ye have more need of able-bodied men then I do. I can care for myself, Balfour. I dinnae go to battle, and I think I can fight off a thief or two or e'en outrun them. Cease mothering me," he added gently.

Balfour grinned. "Go on your way then, but if ye meet with more trouble than ye can deal with, pause at an inn and send back here for a mon or two. Or return, and we will set off in more force when the work in the fields is done."

"Agreed. I will send word of how I fare."

" 'Tis best that ye do, for if we havenae heard from ye in what we feel is too long a time, we will come hunting for you. Go with God," Balfour added as Eric rode through the gates.

Eric waved, then continued on. He was torn many ways about what he was doing. What he sought was indeed his birthright, yet it galled him to have to go and beg for it. Balfour had gifted him with a small peel tower and some land to the west. At times he felt inclined to cease trying to get what was not willingly being offered, to just go and make a life at the peel tower. Then his sense of what was right and fair rose in his breast, and he went back to struggling to gain his birthright.

There was also the often ignored fact that he was not a Murray by blood. The ties were as strong, but legally the Murrays owed him nothing, did not have to provide for him in any manner. But they did. They called him brother, and they meant it. That made the refusal of the Beatons and the MacMillans to accept him as kin all the more infuriating. He had a right to all that had been his mother's and his father's. In his heart he knew he could never be anything but a Murray, but he intended to retrieve all that had been stolen from him by the lies of the Beatons. If his blood kinsmen wanted to fight over it, then fight he would. For thirteen years they had clung to the diplomatic, gentle way. Now was the time for confrontation.

It took him only a few hours to reach the gates of the Beaton's keep. Although he was not surprised when they refused him entry, he was disappointed. His father's cousin had slipped onto the lands within days after his father's death, and clearly intended to stay. Sir Graham Beaton was as cruel and clever as his father had been, and—if only for the sake of the long suffering people who lived in and around the keep—Eric would like to see the man unseated from his stolen lands. It was clear that that was going to take a fight.

As he rode away, fighting to ignore the insults flung from the walls, he decided to continue on to the MacMillans. If he could win his battle there, he would have more men, more power, and more money to fight the Beaton usurper. Eric suspected that Sir Graham knew the truth, and thought that by refusing to heed any of the calls to surrender the stolen lands he could hold onto his riches. An alliance through blood with the more favored MacMillans just might be enough to force the man to face the truth, to concur with what he fought to deny and decry as all lies. Eric became even more determined to win the favor of his mother's kinsmen. It now meant more than the legal winning of his birthright. It could easily mean the final ousting of a long line of despicable Beaton lairds.

"Maman?"

Bethia swallowed a sudden welling of tears as she held the ornate silver *quaich* up to James's mouth and let him sip the water it held. The small, shallow drinking cup, its two handles beautifully carved with an old Celtic design, had been her sister's wedding cup. Their father had spent a great deal on it, and searched long and hard for the best craftsman to make it. To hear Sorcha's child ask for her as he drank from that treasured memento made her heart clench with a sorrow she had not had time to deal with.

"I fear I must be your *maman* now, laddie," she whispered as she ruffled his silken curls and gave him a small piece of bread to chew on. "I ken that I am nay as good as the one those bastards stole away from you, but I shall do the best I can."

A small voice in her mind murmured that she would at least keep him alive, something his mother had almost failed to do, then cursed the disloyal thought. In the two days she had been creeping through the wood, inching her way toward home and safety, she had found herself suffering more and more unkind thoughts about her sister and her husband. She cursed their weakness, silently derided them for their blindness, and wondered how such a sweet boy could have had such fools for parents. Each time she thought such things she then felt overwhelmed with guilt.

"I need time to sit and look into my heart," she said to the boy, and idly chewed on a piece of bread. "I am so angry, and 'tis odd but most times I am angry at your poor parents. They did naught but get murdered, which isnae their fault, not truly. Aye, they could have been more alert, more cautious, mayhap looked at those around them instead of at each other all of the time, but those arenae faults."

"Maman?"

"Nay, laddie, no *maman*." She kissed his forehead. She's gone. 'Tis just me and ye now. Mayhap that is why I am so angry. Sorcha should still be here. She was young and hale, nay ready for a cold grave. I fear I can think of too many things she and her bonny husband could have done to save themselves, and then I become angry that neither of them did any of those things. There is only one mon I should curse—William. Aye, and his two brutish sons. That is where I must direct all of my anger, eh?"

"Baba."

"Baba? What is a baba?" She smiled, then sighed. "We dinnae ken much about each other do we, James? I dinnae think that fleeing men who wish to kill you will give us much time to do so, either. Mayhap when we get to my home, to Dunnbea, we may take time to learn of each other, and your *grandmére* will be most eager to help. Aye, and your *grandpére*. Ye willnae be alone, sweet James, though none of us can replace those ye have had stolen from ye. There will be love and caring aplenty, and mayhap that will ease the loss ye have suffered. 'Tis a blessing ye are still such a young bairn, for the loss and pain may nay be so deep or painful."

Bethia knew she was fortunate in one thing. James was a very even-tempered child who did little fussing or crying. He had his mother's sweet nature, Sorcha's ever flowing happiness with life and the world around her. It served her well as they ran for their lives, but she was determined that Sorcha's son would learn the value of a little wariness and caution.

She was just preparing to pack up their things and begin her long walk again when she heard a soft noise. Cursing herself for not watching more closely, she drew her dagger and stood in front of the child. Two men slipped out of the shadows of the surrounding trees. She frowned slightly, for they did not look like William's men.

"Ye willnae take the bairn," she said firmly.

"We dinnae want the bairn," the taller of the two men said,

briefly glancing at her dagger and then the silver cup James still held in his tiny hands.

"Ye are naught but base thieves."

"Weel, 'tis certain we arenae what ye were expecting, but we arenae base thieves. We are verra good ones, and it looks as if luck has smiled upon us."

Bethia knew she ought to just let them take what they wanted, that fighting them would only endanger her and James. What they wanted to steal, however, was all she had left of Sorcha. Her mind told her to pick up the baby and run, but her heart, still aching with grief, was determined that these men would never touch Sorcha's things.

"Ye willnae take what is mine without a fight, sirs," she said coldly, praying that they were abject cowards.

"Now, lassie, are those things really worth your life or the bairn's?"

"Nay, but the question should be, are they worth yours?"

Two

The sound of voices pulled Eric from his thoughts. He tensed in his saddle and listened more carefully, finally determining the direction they came from. He had decided it was best to take the less traveled routes to his mother's family to avoid any trouble, yet it appeared that he was about to ride into some.

Cautiously, he edged his mount toward the voices. He briefly considered dismounting and approaching on foot, but decided to remain mounted. If there was trouble ahead and it was more than he could deal with, he wanted to be able to get out of its reach as fast as possible.

When he first saw the people through the trees he had to resist the urge to rub his eyes in disbelief. A tiny, slender, chest-nut-haired woman stood facing two sword-wielding men with only a small dagger. Eric stared at the bairn behind her for a full moment before he believed it was there.

"Now, lassie, are those things really worth your life or the bairn's?" Eric heard the taller of the two men say.

And then the little woman replied, "Nay, but the question should be, are they worth yours?"

Brave, he thought. *Foolish, but brave.* It was enough to make the two thieves hesitate, and Eric decided that gave him the perfect opportunity to help the woman. As the two men assumed a fighting stance, Eric boldly rode into the small clearing. He had to smile at the way all three people gaped at him as if he were some apparition formed by the mists of the forest.

"I think the lady wishes to keep her things, sirs," he drawled as he drew his sword. "If ye wish to keep your brutish heads upon your cowardly shoulders, I suggest ye run—now—verra fast and verra far."

The men hesitated barely a heartbeat before stumbling back into the wood. Eric watched their flight until he could no longer see them, and then turned to look at the woman. She still stared at him as if he were a ghost, and he took full advantage of her open-mouthed confusion to look her over carefully.

His brother's wives were small, delicately built women, but he suspected this one would look small even next to them. Her hair was thick and long, hanging in soft waves to her small yet shapely hips. It was a rich, deep chestnut color, the sunlight that broke through the cover of the trees decorating it with glimpses of red. Her face was small, vaguely heart-shaped, with the hint of a stubborn chin, a small straight nose, and an incitingly full mouth. What grabbed and held his attention, however, was her eyes. Wide, thickly lashed, and set beneath delicately arched brows, they did not match. The left one was a rich, clear green, and the right was a brilliant blue.

After swiftly examining her form from her small but tempting breasts to her tiny waist, he glanced at the baby behind her. The little boy had strikingly red curls and green eyes. Eric suddenly found himself keenly interested in whether or not the child was hers and where the father was. He looked back at the woman and smiled as she began to shake free of her shock.

Bethia was stunned when the tall, lean knight had ridden in and sent the robbers racing for their meager lives. It took her a long time to shake aside her astonishment. She knew he was studying her, and found herself carefully studying him back.

He was a beautiful man, she mused, and knew there was no other word to describe him. His long, reddish gold hair fell below his broad shoulders, so thick that even tying it back could not fully contain it or hide it. His face was one of the most perfect she had ever seen, with a smooth, high forehead, high, wide cheekbones, a long, handsomely unbroken nose, a strong

chin, and a mouth that even she, in all of her innocence, recognized as dangerously sensuous. Deep, rich blue eyes were
framed by surprisingly long, brown lashes and set perfectly beneath faintly arced, light brown brows.

His face was not all that was beautiful, either. His body, attired handsomely in a crisp white shirt and a plaid she did not
recognize, was tall, lean and muscular. Broad shoulders, a trim
waist and hips, and long, well shaped, muscular legs were
enough to make any maid's heart beat faster. It was not surprising that she had thought he was a vision. Men like him simply
did not ride out of the trees and save one's life.

That started her wondering what he was doing here, at this
spot and at this opportune time. She held her dagger at the ready
as her suspicions began to grow. Just because he was a pleasure
for her eye did not mean he was a good man. He could be
working for William. She might not have been rescued after all,
simply changed one danger for another.

"Who are ye, sir?" she demanded. "I dinnae recognize your
plaid, or your clan badge."

"Such a sweet thank ye for my aid," he murmured.

Bethia refused to let his soft reprimand embarrass her. There
was too much at stake to be over concerned with courtesies. "I
am nay sure I have been rescued yet."

Eric bowed slightly in the saddle. "I am Sir Eric Murray of
Donncoill."

"I dinnae recognize the name or the place, so ye must be
verra far afield, sir."

"I seek out my mother's family. And what are ye doing in
the depths of the forest with naught but a bairn and a dagger?"

"A fair question, I suppose."

"Verra fair."

She eased her wary stance only a little, trying not to let his
deep, attractive voice lull her suspicions. "I am taking my
nephew to my family."

The word nephew made Eric a little happier than he thought
it should. "With no one to aid or guard you?"

Bethia tensed again as he sheathed his sword and slowly dismounted. There was nothing threatening in his movement, but she could not trust anyone. James's life was at stake, and that was something far too valuable to gamble with.

"There was no one I felt I could trust with his life." She backed up, planting herself firmly between James and him as he took a small step toward her. "I think ye may understand that, at this moment, that also includes you, sir."

"Ye dinnae recognize my name or my clan, lass. I cannae believe ye dinnae ken exactly who your enemies are, and 'tis clear that I dinnae number among them."

"Not yet."

He smiled faintly. "I have told ye who I am, but ye havenae returned the kindness."

Bethia wished the man would cease smiling at her. That beautiful smile threatened to steal away her wits, soften her wariness, and make her ready to believe he was her savior. His deep voice was almost like a caress, making her feel unforgivably rude for not trusting him immediately. He might not be one of William's men, but she began to think he could be dangerous in many another way.

"I am Bethia Drummond, and this is my nephew, James Drummond, laird of Dunncraig."

"Dunncraig?"

"Ye ken the place?"

"Only that it is but one of the many I must pass to get where I am going."

"Weel, depending upon which way ye ride, ye may have already passed it."

"I ride to the MacMillans of Bealachan."

Bethia knew the family well, but that only eased her wariness a little. He might not be going to them as a friend. "Why?"

"They are my mother's kinsmen."

"Yet ye speak as if this is the first time ye travel there."

"It is, but the reasons for that make for a long, sometimes

dark tale, and I cannae say I feel inclined to relate it whilst a dagger is held to my throat."

Even as she did so Bethia knew it was a mistake, but she glanced down at her dagger to see where it was pointed. It angered her, even frightened her, but did not surprise her when his long fingers wrapped around her wrist and he easily snatched the dagger from her hand. She waited tensely for his next move, and frowned a little when he simply released her and turned to smile at a happily gurgling James.

" 'Tis wondrous to see such unconcern. 'Tis the blessing of being a bairn." Eric glanced at her as she edged around until she stood next to the boy. "Children can trust so easily."

" 'Tis because they are still innocent." She quickly pulled James up into her arms, and glared at Eric over the child's curls.

He straightened up and stepped closer to her, pleased when she did not step away. It showed him that, despite her angry wariness, she might yet come to trust him. The way she spoke of trusting no one with the child's life told him that she was in danger, or certainly thought she was. Eric was determined to help her, and he strongly suspected it had a lot to do with beautiful mismatched eyes and full mouth he already ached to taste.

"Which is why they require others to watch o'er them," he murmured.

"That is what I am doing," she snapped.

"And ye think ye need no help in that?"

The man stood so close it made her head swim. She was too much aware of how only James's tiny body separated the man from her. Her gaze was filled with his beauty. Worse, he had lowered his voice, the rich seductiveness of it making her heart beat so fast and loud she could not think over the pounding of it. The man seemed to affect her much like a too large tankard of hearty wine.

"Mayhap I could use a wee bit," she grudgingly agreed, "but that doesnae mean it must be you."

"Oh, but I think it must." He reached out to ruffle the child's curls, inwardly smiling when his fingers brushed Bethia's stubborn little chin and she jerked her head back as if his touch had burned her. "Where are ye headed?"

"To Dunnbea," she replied without hesitation, then cursed herself for her lack of guile.

"Which is another of the places I must pass as I ride to meet my kinsmen."

"Aye."

"The MacMillans of Bealachan arenae feuding with the Drummonds of Dunnbea, are they?"

"Nay. They have long been allies."

"Then we ride the same path."

"I go by a verra twisted route. It may slow your pace."

"Nay, for I, too, go by a verra twisted, hidden route. As ye can see, I ride alone. I seek to avoid trouble during my travel."

She almost smiled. "Then I should leave me far behind, kind sir, for there is a great deal of trouble following me about."

Bethia was not sure why she was being so elusive, so reluctant to accept his aid. It was true that she did not know the Murrays of Donncoill, but she suspected that was because there was not much to hear, at least not much that was a bad. Tales of evil done by men traveled far and wide, but if they behaved themselves only their most heroic deeds were spoken of. The MacMillans were his kinsmen, and they were close, longstanding allies of her own family. He was going in the same direction she was. He had just saved her from what could have been a deadly confrontation, and although he had taken her dagger he had made no threatening move toward her or James. Good sense demanded that she ask his protection.

"Come, lass, put aside your pride and accept an honest offer of help."

" 'Tis nay just pride that makes me hesitate, sir."

"Have I not just shown ye that I mean no harm?"

"Aye, but 'tis nay just myself I must consider in any and all decisions I make."

"I would ne'er hurt a bairn."

There was a taut note in his lovely voice, and Bethia almost

smiled. She had insulted him. That eased a great many of her
suspicions and doubts. Although she still felt uneasy, she began
to think it was not because she did not trust him to help her,
but that he was dangerously attractive. She had never been as
unsettled by a man as she was by him. That danger would be
her own to fight or succumb to, however, and she had to think
only of James now.

"Then, sir knight, I ask ye, upon your honor, to get me and
the bairn safely to Dunnbea," she finally said, and inwardly shivered with a delight that almost frightened her when he smiled at
her.

"A promise easily made, m'lady."

"Easily made, mayhap, but ye may find it nay so easy to
fulfill."

"I am nay without skill with the sword I carry."

"I am sure, but there may be many a mon trying to stop me
and this lad from reaching my family. Sir, ye have just stepped
into the midst of a deadly fight. On one side, at this moment,
is just me and this bairn. On the other is a black-hearted mon
named William and his two grasping sons, Iain and Angus, and
all the men they can force or pay to chase us down."

"Why?"

"Because William seeks to steal what is rightfully this child's.
He has already set his wife in her grave, then murdered my
sister and her husband. The day before I left he tried to murder
me and the bairn with poison. I believe that is his choice of
weapon. The mon seeks to hold Dunncraig, to claim through
marriage and death what was ne'er his."

Eric kept his expression calm, but inside he was heartily cursing. He bore little similarity to the men Bethia was fleeing, but
instinct told him that she would not like his reasons for traveling
to the MacMillans. He decided to wait to tell her that truth. She
barely trusted him now, and he wanted to prove himself a little
more before he told her something that might well smother that
newly born trust.

"Ye have found yourself a mon with some knowledge of such

flights. My brother and his lady fled across France, running from men who wished to hang her for a murder she did not commit. Mayhap I can finally put to use some of the tales he told me."

"Why is your brother nay traveling with you to meet your mother's kinsmen?"

"Because his mother isnae mine." He almost laughed at the confused frown that crossed her pretty face, swiftly followed by a look of intense curiosity. "Another long tale. Best we save such things for later. 'Tis a long journey yet ahead of us."

"I ken it. And, I suppose we had best get started."

She hesitated when he held his arms out for the boy. Then, her heart pounding with unease, she placed James in his arms. It was the first time James had been out of her grasp since his mother had died and she fought the urge to snatch him back. If she were going to trust the man with their lives, though, she certainly ought to be able to trust him to hold the boy for a few moments.

Eric watched as she collected up her things, pausing to smooth her hands over the little silver cup before putting it in her bag. "I think the mon asked a good question, lass," he said quietly. "Were those things really worth risking your life and the bairn's?"

"Nay," she answered easily as she stood up. "At least that was what my mind yelled, but I fear that at that moment my heart spoke even louder. The cup was my sister's wedding cup. She was my womb-sister, and she has been dead barely a week. I couldnae let that mon take it or any of the other things I managed to cling to and slip out of Dunncraig. It was foolish. I ken it."

"Aye, but eminently understandable." He took her by the arm and led her over to his horse. "Your grief is too new."

"I am nay sure it will e'er grow old," she whispered.

"Aye, no two people can be closer than those who have shared a womb. But life has a way of dulling the sharp edge of such loss. Ye ne'er forget, but ye learn to accept." He handed her James and attached her small bag to his saddle as she settled the little boy in the blanket sling she wore. "And, she left ye the best of herself."

"Aye, true enough," she said, as she briefly combed her fingers through James curls. She frowned at the horse. "Are we all to ride him, then?"

"Aye," Eric replied as he lifted her up onto the saddle.

"The weight of a big mon and two others may be more than he can bear." Bethia frowned at him when he laughed as he mounted behind her. "What amuses you?"

"Ye calling me a big mon."

"Weel, ye are."

"Mayhap to a wee lass like you, aye, but trust me in this, lass, I am nay so big."

"And I am nay that wee," she grumbled then inwardly cursed when she heard him chuckle.

"Ye were the second born, werenae ye?" he asked as he nudged the horse into a slow amble.

"Aye, and, aye, I was verra small and sickly, but I grew bigger and stronger."

"Oh, aye, a veritable mountain of a woman."

"Ye make jest of me."

"Mayhap, but meaning no unkindness. Believe me, little Bethia, when ye see me next to another mon, ye will ken that I understand exactly how ye feel. 'Tisnae easy to be the runt."

"I am nay a runt," she snapped, then pressed her lips together when he just chuckled.

Bethia knew that was exactly what she was, but she did not like to hear it said. Neither did she believe Sir Eric ever felt small. He certainly did not feel small to her as he wrapped his long arms around her and took up the reins. She felt completely enfolded in his long body. In fact, she felt smaller and more uncertain than she had in a very long time.

Slowly, she became aware of the fact that he was nuzzling her hair. She tensed and tried to pull away from him, but his arms allowed her little room to move. Although she did not fear for her life or James, she no longer felt very safe.

"Sir, what are ye doing?" she demanded, and inwardly grimaced over the soft unsteadiness of her voice.

"Smelling your hair," he replied.

Her eyes widened, for she had not expected such blunt honesty. "Well, ye may cease such play this verra moment."

"Kind of ye to give me leave to cease, but I am nay sure I am of a mind to."

Eric knew he was acting outrageously, but he felt an urge to see how far he could push her. He wanted her, faster and more fiercely than he had ever wanted a woman, and he was curious to see if there was any response in her, no matter how small. Bethia fascinated him and made him hungry, and he wanted her to suffer likewise.

"Weel, ye can try to put your mind to it now."

"If I must."

"Aye, ye must."

"I but flatter ye, lass."

"Weel, I have more important things to think about than some mon's flatteries. I think I shall have to make ye give me another promise."

"Oh, aye? And what would that be?"

"That ye will treat me with the respect due a lady of my birth."

"Oh, aye, that I can do."

Bethia tried to turn her head to look at him, but could not get a clear view of his expression. She had a feeling that she should have worded her request more carefully, that the man had not promised what she had wanted him to. She stared ahead of them and tried not to feel anything as he held her in his arms.

It was going to be a struggle to ignore his allure, she realized. Something deep inside of her responded hotly and immediately to his touch, his smile, even his voice, and she suspected it was a very heedless part of her. Sir Eric Murray might have arrived just in time to save her, and might well keep his promise to get her and James safely to Dunnbea, but Bethia began to think that was all he had promised, and would. She could not change her mind now, she thought as she looked down at a dozing James, but she began to think she had just traded a deadly danger for a far more subtle one.

ABOUT THE AUTHOR

Hannah Howell is an award-winning author who lives with her family in Georgetown, MA. She is the author of seven Zebra historical romances: *Only for You, My Valiant Knight, Unconquered, Wild Roses, A Taste of Fire, Highland Destiny,* and *Highland Honor,* as well as a novella in *Scottish Magic.* Hannah is currently working on her next Zebra historical romance, the third title in her medieval trilogy focusing on three brothers. *Highland Promise,* Eric's story, will be published in July, 1999. Hannah loves hearing from readers, and you may write to her c/o Zebra Books. Please include a self-addressed stamped envelope if you wish a response.